As you read this splendid story you get a sense of the dedication of each of these citizen soldiers, these men of the mountains, to their God, wives, families, land, and their burgeoning dream of a new nation. It was a fragile dream, but one growing ever stronger; a dream of freedom, self-determination, and the right to govern oneself in matters of faith, family, fortune, and self-government.

The reliance on the citizen soldier has been critical to our nation's preservation of liberty and freedom. It was no different 232 years ago. My heart swelled with pride as I experienced their struggles while reading this splendid story and participating in the brotherhood with those brave militiamen.

—Robert Askelson
Chief Petty Officer, USNR, Ret.

OVER
the
MOUNTAINS
To
FREEDOM

OVER *the* MOUNTAINS *to* FREEDOM

LEWIS T. RICH

CREATION HOUSE
A STRANG COMPANY

OVER THE MOUNTAINS TO FREEDOM by Lewis Terry Rich
Published by Creation House
A Strang Company
600 Rinehart Road
Lake Mary, Florida 32746
www.creationhouse.com

Unless otherwise noted, all Scripture quotations are the author's
paraphrase of the Revised Standard Version of the Bible. Copyright © 1946,
1952, 1971 by the Division of Christian Education of the National Council
of the Churches of Christ in the USA. Used by permission.

Design Director: Bill Johnson
Cover design by Amanda Potter

Library of Congress Control Number: 2008939239
International Standard Book Number: 978-1-59979-549-2

First Edition

08 09 10 11 12 — 987654321
Printed in the United States of America

Contents

Introduction

THIS BOOK IS a fictional novel about people as well as about events as they might have occurred during the American Revolution. People like the characters portrayed in this book earned the freedoms enjoyed by succeeding generations of Americans. The book fictitiously but realistically tells a story about part of the American Revolution from the perspective of a participant, Major Jonathan Tipton of North Carolina.

The American Revolution was a true civil war, featuring neighbor against neighbor, and in some cases relative against relative. Both the Tory side and the Patriot side included rich and poor people among their constituents.

The lands of today's western North Carolina, and the mountains of what is now northeastern Tennessee but was then part of North Carolina, had been settled mostly by Scots-Irish and German Protestants. These people generally tended to favor independence from Britain. In the eastern and coastal portion of North Carolina, however, many of the settlers had originally come from among the English and Highland Scots. Due to their longstanding business relationships with Britain, these easterners tended to be loyal to the crown. Those loyal to Britain were called "Tories" or "loyalists." The colonists who favored independence were called "rebels" by the British and by the Tories, but called themselves "Patriots" or "Americans."

Although some Native American Indians fought with the Patriots, the British gained support from larger numbers of Native American Indians by using various enticements. One such promise was that should the British win, white settlement would be restricted to the lands east of the

Appalachian Mountains. Given the history up to that point in time, it is highly unlikely that the British would have honored that promise had they prevailed. The British did, however, provide muskets, powder, and shot to the Indians in return for the Indians' commitment to attack and harass the Patriots.

Likewise, many Black Americans were promised their freedom if they would serve with the British. Black Americans also served with valor on the Patriot side, including some who were already free and some who gained their freedom in return for serving, as mentioned briefly in this book.

Many people today do not realize just how fierce the Cherokee Indians were as warriors, and how persistently they fought to hold on to their homeland. Their pride and resistance is reflected to at least a small extent in this book. White settlers considered the Chickamauga band of Cherokee Indians hostile. In actuality, the Chickamauga Cherokees were among those Indians who were most devoted to protecting their land and preserving their own freedom. It was simply a matter of perspective.

This work includes generally accepted dates and public information about military and historical events that are found in multiple reference works, United States government sources, and at various historic sites. Unless by coincidence, none of the words "spoken" by characters in this novel are actual quotes by any real person of the same name as the character. Naturally, the book also includes fictitious events that enhance the reading experience.

There is a truthful saying that "Freedom is not free." This is not only true today, but was a powerful truth to those who struggled and endured to prevail in the American Revolution.

Chapter 1

The Colonel and the Major

THE RIDER WAS sitting comfortably in the saddle as he navigated down the narrow mountain trail on a cool, yet unseasonably mild morning in early February 1777. Jonathan Tipton was one of an eight-man party traveling eastward from their mountain cabins. Jonathan had just left his home in the mountains of North Carolina on a journey that would change his life forever.

Jonathan was genuinely happy to be traveling with his close friend, Colonel John Carter. The colonel had recommended Tipton to the governor for appointment as an officer in the militia. The primary purpose of this trip was to obtain a letter of appointment from Governor Richard Caswell.

Colonel Carter had elected to have six other men accompany them. He had purposefully selected five young men who were among the brightest and most able members of the district militia. They were all neighbors within a twenty-mile area, and the five were privates in the militia. The sixth man was William Parker, who was also a Patriot sympathizer, but had not yet joined the militia. Parker operated the only mercantile store in the Washington District, except that Isaac Shelby conducted extensive trading at his property to the north, and Colonel Carter himself did quite a bit of trading, as well. The colonel obtained goods through his family's mercantile firm in Virginia and supplied many of the goods that Parker sold and traded in his store.

It had been only fifteen minutes since the men left the home of Private John Taylor, which was the easternmost of the men's homes. Even so, they had sent a lead rider about one hundred yards ahead of the remainder of the party. The lead rider acted as an advance set of eyes for the group. They knew from experience that a single rider, rather than a group, is more likely to spot others at a distance than to be seen first.

Suddenly, all the members of the party saw the lead rider, Joseph Griffin, dismounted and stopped, holding the reins of his horse. Griffin was standing to the right of the trail near a large tree. They stopped immediately. At Private Griffin's hand signal, they dismounted and walked with their horses to the point where Griffin had stopped. Griffin said softly, "Look." He pointed toward a hill on the far side of a lightly forested valley.

Jonathan saw what Griffin had spotted. Less than a mile away he counted a party of eleven Indians on horseback. At this point the men were still within six miles of the closest of their homes just left behind. Inasmuch as they were at a somewhat higher elevation than the Indians, and because the Indians were traveling diagonally away from them they were certain the Indians had not spotted them. "Let's go to Half Knob," directed Colonel Carter. He pointed to the crest of a small adjoining mountain. The knob was a prominence on the southeast face of the mountain. From that point they would be able to observe the direction in which the Indians were traveling. The men mounted and proceeded quietly, at a moderate pace. As they moved, they could see the Indians intermittently through the trees.

Within twenty minutes they reached the knob. As they approached the end of the tree line near the knob, Colonel Carter was now in the lead. He dismounted. He did not have to say anything, as all the men knew they wanted to remain inconspicuous. They all dismounted accordingly. "We'll watch them for ten more minutes," said Colonel Carter. "If they are going south, we will continue as planned. If they turn westward at the bend in the creek and head upstream toward our homes, we will have to backtrack and be sure they don't go to Taylor's or Nelson's homes."

They observed as the Indians crossed the creek and continued southward. Now satisfied that the Indians were heading in a direction away from their homes, the men resumed their eastward trek.

"They did not appear to be a war party," Jonathan said, directing his comment to Colonel Carter. "And there were no British or Tories with them." No reply was necessary, and none was given.

Not a man among them had any regret regarding the inconvenience of having delayed their trip by well over an hour to be sure these Indians were not a threat to their families and homes.

The current journey would take Jonathan Tipton from his home in the mountains to Hillsborough. Jonathan and his wife had moved from Virginia to the frontier of western North Carolina four years ago. He had never been to the part of the state wherein Hillsborough lay. He recalled hearing of Hillsborough's location as being roughly the north central part of the state.

The Washington District where Jonathan lived had not yet been admitted as a county at that time. To date it had been officially recognized as a large, ill-defined district on North Carolina's mountainous western frontier. Its status as a county was pending with the legislature. All eight of the men in the party with Jonathan Tipton lived in the far northwestern part of the mountainous region of North Carolina. They all resided within a few miles of the Watauga Settlement, where William Parker's mercantile store was located.

Born in Virginia in 1750, Jonathan Tipton was now twenty-seven years old. He was formally schooled during his childhood in Virginia. His literacy had served him well. During the past year, Colonel Carter had been placing Jonathan in charge of militia patrols against the Indians. The colonel knew that the written messages delivered to him by riders dispatched by Jonathan were consistently clear and concise. Better yet, they reflected sound judgment and thorough assessment of situations. Literacy was definitely in Jonathan's favor at the present time. Colonel Carter had advised him the day before they departed that Governor Caswell was insistent that any officer he appoints must be able to read and write.

Colonel Carter was certain that Jonathan Tipton would be a good militia officer. Jonathan was a man who spoke with clarity and conviction. He made frequent eye contact with a person to whom he talked or listened. Jonathan's actions in the militia and as a neighbor and friend over the last four years proved to Colonel Carter that Jonathan was both honest and reliable.

Each man was riding his own horse; four additional horses were being led by the party. Two of these horses belonged to Colonel Carter and two belonged to William Parker. Colonel Carter's horses were lightly loaded with food and supplies. The horses belonging to William Parker were loaded with deerskins to be traded in Hillsborough. Parker would trade the skins for wool blankets, coffee, musket balls, and gunpowder for his mercantile store. He also hoped to trade his two horses for some additional merchandise he needed for his store, specifically two new long rifles and two pistols.

His store was the only such store in the Watauga Settlement and the surrounding Washington County district. Coming from a family mercantile background in Maryland, William Parker was fully aware of the concept of supply and demand. He knew that the planned trades would work to his advantage if they enabled him to keep firearms in stock at his store in the mountains.

Colonel Carter had kindly offered William Parker the use of his two extra horses to transport Parker's newly acquired goods on the return trip, if necessary.

"Mr. Parker," John Taylor inquired, "how many merchants' stores are there in Hillsborough?"

"Two, as of the last report I had. Both are general mercantile stores, and I hear they are fairly well stocked despite the war," William Parker replied.

Jonathan had heard most of the men comment that they planned to make some sort of purchase or trade while at Hillsborough. He now knew that there were two mercantile stores there. He also knew it was the place where Governor Caswell was temporarily residing, and where the legislature would next meet, having most recently met in Halifax. The legislature had, of necessity, changed venues repeatedly from New Bern to Halifax, and now to Hillsborough, in order to prevent the British and Tories from attacking or capturing the legislators and the governor.

Colonel Carter remarked to Jonathan, intending for all to hear his words, "As we discussed yesterday, it will take about six or seven days to get to Hillsborough. We will plan to remain there only one to two days and will then return."

"Right, sir, it is best not to be away from home any longer than we have to." Jonathan Tipton always called his friend "sir" or "Colonel" in the presence of other soldiers.

After a moment of silence, Jonathan's thoughts wandered to his wife and the five young children he had left at home. The children had each been born only about one year apart. Johnny, the youngest, was only eleven months old. William and Samuel had been born in Virginia, and were now five and four years of age, respectively. Mary was three and Hannah was two. Jonathan and Frances had been married in Virginia when he was twenty years old and she was only fifteen.

In the absence of conversation on the trail at the moment, Jonathan continued thinking about home. Frances was an energetic and cheerful wife. Jonathan's love for her was the centerpiece of happiness in his life. His sons William and Samuel were by then able to help with many of the chores. At five years of age, William was quite capable of gathering and chopping firewood.

Riding eastward, Jonathan thought about the safety of his wife and children while he was gone. The presence of local militia patrols would hopefully stave off any Indian raids. Captain John Sevier was in charge of the militia while Colonel Carter was away. Sevier, in Jonathan's opinion, was both capable and reliable. Jonathan did not, however, care for some of the seemingly arrogant and self-serving comments he had heard Captain Sevier make. Sevier, it seemed, was always trying to impress Colonel Carter. He was glad that Colonel Carter had never placed him under Captain Sevier for any patrol or scouting mission.

Jonathan reminded himself about the Indians being so strong in numbers that they were always a threat. He and Frances had a standing rule that one pistol and one rifle would remain loaded and at the ready on the wall racks near the fireplace. She was very capable with either gun, and William at age five was already able to load and fire the rifle. At the first sign of any Indian near their home, Frances was to fire one shot in the air toward the woods just to the north of the home of their neighbors, Tom and Mary Callahan. Then, she and the children would yell loudly in the direction of the Callahan's home before getting the children inside the house and bolting both the front and back doors. If they saw a large party of Indians, and if time allowed, Frances and William would open the pens and scatter their cows and horses into the woods so the Indians might not find and steal all of them.

Tom Callahan, their neighbor and friend, was both brave and reliable. He and his wife, Mary, had three teenage sons, along with their two young daughters. Callahan has agreed that if there was Indian trouble while Jonathan was away, he and one of his sons would come to the aid of Frances and the children, leaving his other two sons and wife to protect their own home. Tom would go immediately to Jonathan's home and depending on the circumstances would either help defend Jonathan's family and home, or would take Jonathan's family to Tom's own home and make a united defense there. Similar neighborly understandings were quite common among the families on the frontier. The thought crossed Jonathan's mind that, later during this trip, he might start a discussion with Colonel Carter and the other riders regarding any suggestions they could come up with to improve the safety of their backcountry families and homes.

Jonathan recalled that when he had been in Virginia and was making the decision to move his family to the North Carolina frontier, nobody had provided any clue regarding how fierce the Cherokee Indians in that area were as warriors, nor how determined they were to protect the land they considered their own from invasion by white settlers.

During the previous summer, the settlers around Jonathan's home had chosen the name "Fort Caswell" for their new fort. Almost immediately, because the fort was at the Watauga settlement, people started calling it "the fort at Watauga" and then "Fort Watauga." *Now,* Jonathan thought to himself, *it is almost always called Fort Watauga.*

Last July, in 1776, the Indians began raiding and killing settlers throughout the Watauga area. Most of the settlers and their families were forced to take refuge in the fort. Then, for two weeks in late July to early August, more than three hundred Indians laid siege to Fort Caswell. Jonathan and his family had been entrapped in the fort with the other settlers. Then a relief force of other frontiersmen arrived and broke the siege.

Jonathan remembered leaving the fort with his family to return to his home. He recalled how happy he and Frances had been to get back home and find that the Indians had not burned their home. He also remembered the extensive time and effort he and his neighbors had put into rounding up the livestock that they had scattered into the woods so the Indians might not find them. He thought of the large party of fifty or sixty Indians near their homes, which had prevented Jonathan and his closest neighbors from herding their cows to the fort. Indeed, they had been fortunate, he decided, to make it safely to the fort with their horses and their own lives.

Jonathan's thoughts drifted from one topic to another. He thought about how he was looking forward to meeting Governor Caswell. He remembered when last spring he had heard about the Americans' overwhelming victory at Moore's Creek Bridge. The American forces had been led by then-Colonel Richard Caswell, who was then promoted to general and was subsequently selected by the legislature as governor.

As he rode, Jonathan contemplated the news that had reached the mountains about the war. Several battles with war parties of Indians led by British officers had occurred in July and August around Seneca and other places in northwest South Carolina. These battles were not extremely distant from home, and they had been occurring with increasing frequency.

Then, month before last, discouraging word had reached the mountains that New York had fallen to the British, and that thousands of American soldiers had been taken prisoner. Jonathan tried to dismiss from his mind the thought that this defeat might be the beginning of the end for the revolution.

The route that Colonel Carter chose would take them through the settlement at Salisbury, North Carolina, which was a key center of Patriot support. According to the Colonel, troops under General Rutherford kept supplies in and around Salisbury. It was a place far enough away from British strongholds to be relatively safe. Several barns and other outbuildings in the Salisbury area reportedly contained supplies of gunpowder and musket shot. One stable, the Colonel says, also contained as of a couple of months ago a reserve supply of eighty brand-new muskets belonging to Rutherford's army.

One young man from the Watauga area, Thomas Howard, had approached Colonel Carter several months ago. Thomas Howard was nineteen years old, the oldest of seven children. He had asked the colonel about serving full-time for the American cause. The colonel, knowing there was no full-time militia activity in the mountains in and around the Washington district, had recommended that Howard join up with General Rutherford's army in Salisbury. Those forces were known to see some action several times each month against British, Tories, Indians, or some combination thereof. Rutherford's men frequently rode southward into South Carolina or eastward within North Carolina to confront the enemy. Howard had taken a note of recommendation from Colonel Carter, and had headed out alone to find General Rutherford's army. A report had reached the Watauga area just weeks ago that Howard had in fact been serving with Patriot forces in Salisbury. The colonel was aware of the news and intended to inquire about Howard when they reached Salisbury.

The eight riders arrived at Salisbury in mid-morning. Having been received with welcome by a local captain named McGahee, Colonel Carter inquired of him: "A lad by the name of Howard joined General Rutherford's ranks here a couple of months ago, Captain. Would you happen to know his whereabouts?"

"Yes sir, Colonel. It happens that Howard has been assigned to me," the captain replied, scarcely hiding his pleasure. "Howard is a fine young soldier," Captain McGahee continued. "General Rutherford and most of his officers and men are in South Carolina right now, but we have a company of men here with me to protect this place and our supplies. Private Howard is doing some work over at the Miller's farm right now. The Millers are putting him up in one of their outbuildings while he is there."

"I'd like to see him," the colonel said.

"I'll take you to him. It is only about two miles from here."

The party, now nine strong, rode to the Miller's farm. As they passed the main cabin, Captain McGahee greeted Mr. and Mrs. Miller. The men continued onward toward the barn.

Thomas Howard was working in the barn when he first saw the riders about half a mile away. Not yet being able to discern who they were, he followed standing orders. He closed the barn door, grabbed his rifle, and concealed his presence until he could identify the riders as friend or foe. Observing the riders as they approached the Miller's cabin, he first recognized Captain McGahee. Thomas was filled with excitement when he first recognized Colonel Carter and then Privates Smith Ferrell, Joseph Griffin, and Benjamin Webb. These were people from home! Howard partly opened the barn door and stepped outside, rifle in hand. He then stood at attention.

"They've taught you well," Colonel Carter said to Thomas Howard.

"Yes, sir."

"Well, fall out and welcome the home boys. They'll all be glad to see you." The riders dismounted. Greetings and introductions were then warmly exchanged.

Jonathan Tipton had seen Thomas Howard several times, but did not really know him. Private Griffin, though, had said that Howard was his best friend.

"What are you working on in the barn?" Joseph Griffin inquired.

"Cartridges," Howard replied. Then he turned his head toward Captain McGahee. "Captain, can I show them?"

Captain McGahee replied in a joking tone of voice, "Of course. They are on our side, you know."

"You won't believe it," Thomas Howard said as he fully opened the barn door, revealing the contents of the barn. Jonathan immediately saw a workbench made of split logs supported by stumps at each end. On the table were dozens and dozens of freshly wadded cartridges. A third stump beside the table was obviously used as a work seat. Beside that stump was an open barrel of gunpowder. The remainder of the contents impressed even Colonel Carter and Jonathan Tipton.

"I have been pre-wadding musket cartridges for the army. Here on the left is our powder," Howard said, pointing to at least two dozen tightly sealed barrels. Then pointing to his right, he said, "Over here are our cartridges. I have wadded them all this week." Private Howard pointed to three barrels and about fifty deerskin pouches that were full of pre-wadded cartridges. The cartridges were for use by certain companies of General Rutledge's troops that used muskets. The majority of his men used long rifles. "Behind me are our lead balls," he said, extending his hand aft. There were eight barrels and twenty large boxes of lead balls. "We have four sizes of balls. Some are for muskets, and two sizes are just for different sizes of long rifles."

"Wow," said Joseph Griffin, unable to contain his astonishment. "You've got enough powder and balls to kill the whole British army." Of course, Griffin's assessment was inaccurate, but he and the other young privates were truly amazed.

Colonel Carter, barely concealing his own degree of surprise, turned toward Jonathan Tipton. "Jonathan, this is a very good thing for our cause."

Captain McGahee interrupted. "And, Colonel, it is only one of four such arsenals that General Rutherford has here in this area. That is why he keeps at least a whole company of men here at any given time. Private Howard is not just wadding cartridges. He is guarding this whole supply. If he or the Miller family gets an alert to me, my men will be mustered and on the way within twenty minutes. The Tories are not going to get any of this without a real fight."

Thomas Howard spoke up. "That's not all I do, though." He did not want his friends from home to think of him as just a wadder and guard. "I have been on three patrols with Captain McGahee. One of them was with General Rutherford's whole army. We went down almost all the way to the fort at Ninety-Six in South Carolina. We found a company of

British cavalry and Tories, but they got away. The other times we fought against Tories."

The men all understood. To some extent they may have even envied Howard. He was here fighting the war against British and Tories. At this point, the others, Colonel Carter and Jonathan Tipton included, had fought only against Indians. The Indians were truly fierce and ruthless fighters, but they all understood by now that it was the British and Tories that must be defeated.

The party of eight men remained in Salisbury for only about two hours. After traveling eastward from the mountains to Salisbury, the party then left that place. One day later they were heading northeast toward Hillsborough. Colonel Carter had traveled to Hillsborough twice before, although by slightly different routes, guided by a friend. He estimated they were within a day and a half from Hillsborough.

As the party was coming around a bend on a narrow trail in a lightly forested area, the lead rider, Benjamin Webb, turned around abruptly and galloped the short sixty yards back to the rest of the party. "There are lots of riders coming. I don't know who, but they are right there," he said, pointing to the spot only one hundred yards away where about sixteen men who had spotted him were now rapidly approaching with weapons drawn. There was nothing to do but to draw their own weapons and defend themselves.

The riders were not uniformed. "At least they are not British regulars," Jonathan thought. A loud voice boomed from one of the oncoming riders as they slowed and spread across the trail in a semicircle: "Who are you, you lousy Tories?"

The two groups were now separated by only sixty feet. On both sides rifles were leveled and ready to fire. Were the strangers actually Patriots, or were they Tories pretending to be Patriots to gain an advantage? Colonel Carter was the only one of his party who was wearing a uniform. Seeing that the loud voice came from a man wearing on his shoulder what appeared to be the epaulet of a captain, Colonel Carter replied, "I am American Colonel John Carter. We are headed to Hillsborough to meet with Governor Caswell." Carter knew that if he had guessed wrong he and his men would likely be killed, wounded, or taken prisoner. The response was immediate.

"Captain Caleb Rogers, Orange County mounted militia, at your service, Colonel."

What a welcome reply! They were among friends. Colonel Carter's uniform and his bold verbal demeanor had quickly convinced the Orange County militiamen of their true identity and purpose.

Captain Rogers addressed Colonel Carter again. "Colonel, we are out looking for Tories. They have been very active hereabouts, and just last week Tories burned the home of Private McAdam." He pointed briefly toward Private McAdam. "If you wish we will be glad to escort you to Hillsborough."

"Your generosity is truly appreciated," Colonel Carter replied, "but if you will just give us the best directions to Hillsborough, including where to ford the Haw River, that will be helpful enough."

"Just head straight east," said Captain Rogers, pointing in the appropriate direction, "and in about an hour you will come to a wagon trail. Take a right, southward. Follow the wagon wheel ruts, and in a few miles you will reach the ford on the Haw River. Go straight across and keep following the wagon road. You may want to camp just the other side of the river. Keep following the wagon road and you can be in Hillsborough by tomorrow afternoon."

The encounter with Caleb Rogers and his men, which had begun as a potentially deadly mistaken identity confrontation, had instead turned out to be helpful. It also imparted to Colonel Carter, Jonathan Tipton, and their party a very favorable impression of the dedication of the local Patriots to the American cause.

In mid-afternoon on February ninth, they arrived in Hillsborough. The wind was from the northeast, and the weather had turned very cold. Hillsborough was smaller than Jonathan had anticipated. Other than the outlying farms, there were only about sixteen homes in the town.

As arranged by the governor, Colonel Carter was lodged with a local family in the Hillsborough area. Jonathan and the other six men took shelter in a small log cabin that had been abandoned a week earlier by a Tory family. The cabin was beyond a small open field just a half mile east of Hillsborough. No furnishings remained, but the fireplace and chimney were intact. Gathering some firewood and starting a fire, the men prepared to settle into the cabin. They would reside there that night and the next night only. All were glad that it had not been so cold prior to this point in their trip.

Like each of the men, Jonathan had an overcoat and a rolled blanket. Just as they had done on the outdoor part of the journey, the men slept wearing their overcoats and with their blankets wrapped around them.

The fire had provided some warmth, but now, well after sunset, it was dying down. Jonathan could feel the cold draft that seemed to seep through every small crack between the logs.

He must get some sleep, for the next day he and Colonel Carter were scheduled to meet with Governor Caswell.

Shortly after sunrise, Jonathan met Colonel Carter at the house where he was being lodged. The colonel, as expected, was ready and waiting. The meeting room that the governor was using for a temporary office was close by, so they walked the short distance to that destination.

"Jonathan, this is what the whole trip is about. I believe all will go well."

"I hope so." As was typical of Jonathan, his response was brief and to the point.

The sentry outside the governor's door recognized them from the day before. "Sir, wait here for me to announce your presence." The meeting room was a building with only a single room, so guests had to wait outside. The wait was frigid on this February morning.

Within a few seconds, the sentry returned.

"Colonel Carter, Governor Caswell wants to meet privately with you, sir."

Several minutes after Colonel Carter entered, the door was opened from the inside. Governor Caswell appeared at the door. "Mr. Tipton, please do come in from the cold."

Jonathan entered the meeting room. Colonel Carter was seated at one of four chairs at a small wooden table on the left side of the room, adjacent to a small fireplace. Jonathan observed that the remainder of the meeting room contained six long benches that would accommodate perhaps ten people on each bench. The building was obviously not intended to be a seat of government, but was simply a single small town meeting room.

"Please take a seat," the governor said as he gestured at one of the four chairs. Jonathan sat down. The governor remained standing.

Governor Caswell picked up one of the many pieces of paper that were on the table. He wasted no time. "Major Tipton, first of all it pleases me to present this written letter of appointment to you as a major in the Washington District militia. It is well deserved, and I have no doubt that you will serve our cause well. I have also signed a second rendition of the letter that will remain within the files of the state legislature."

Before Jonathan could reply, Caswell continued, "Secondly, it is my pleasure to give you these two shoulder epaulets. Although we do not presently have any uniforms in supply, you can have the epaulets sewn to your coat."

"Thank you, Governor. I am honored to serve the state of North Carolina." Jonathan accepted the epaulets. He could not think of anything else to say. No harm was caused by his brevity, as Governor Caswell instigated a friendly conversation, completely removing formality and putting Jonathan and Colonel Carter at ease.

"Colonel Carter has told me that he and you have your hands full of Indian trouble in the mountain settlements."

"There has been plenty of trouble. The Indians burn settlers' homes and kill the men, and usually kill the women and children, too. Sometimes they have taken women and children to be their slaves." Jonathan continued, "We do the best we can with militia patrols, and have fair success at protecting the settlers, their homes, and crops. On two occasions our patrols have spotted British officers riding with Indian war parties."

Governor Caswell looked first at Jonathan and then at Colonel Carter. "You must do your utmost to keep the Indians at bay on the frontier. If you do not, the British and Tories will certainly complement their forces in the central and eastern parts of the Carolinas with large numbers of Indians. You certainly received news of the attack last September when more than one thousand Indians attacked South Carolina's General

Williamson and his men on the Coweecho River. The militiamen were in a narrow valley. The Indians came out of both sides of the forest late in the afternoon, about sunset. There were so many Indians coming from the darkness that General Williamson's men called it the battle of the black hole. You know how close that place just this side of the mountains is to where you live on the other side."

"It is only about three days by foot," Colonel Carter replied. "We did hear about that battle. After General Williamson's men survived the attack, we feared the Indians would attack the Watauga area again, like they did last July. If there had been a thousand Indians instead of the three hundred that laid siege to Fort Watauga in July, Jonathan and I, as well as our families and neighbors, would likely be dead."

"General Williamson discovered another thing that I want to tell you about," announced Governor Caswell. "His men captured a British officer and some Indians, and learned that the British have been recruiting Indians with the promise that the British will not allow any white settlement west of the mountains if the Indians fight with them.

"The last of what I have to tell you today," Governor Caswell continued, "is that the problem with the British and Tories is far worse than that with the Indians. The British control much of the coastal area of North Carolina and South Carolina. Their fleet can supply them at will, and they could land an army just about anywhere on the coast at any time. The saving grace is that we still control Charlestown, and continue to trade with France and receive goods and military stores from them. On the other hand, in the northern states, General Washington's main American army was driven out of New York, all the way to Pennsylvania. The British control Philadelphia, and the American army is out in the countryside, not too distant from Philadelphia. The one bit of good news we received week before last is that Washington's army made a surprise attack in a snowstorm on the morning after Christmas, capturing a thousand Hessian troops under Colonel Rall. Washington's men also captured more than a thousand muskets and bayonets, and great stores of powder, blankets, and some artillery pieces."

"That is a victory of some significance," replied Colonel Carter, trying to project optimism.

Jonathan remained silent, absorbing the news provided by Governor Caswell.

"Any victory at all is important if we are to gain independence from the king and his absurd taxation and regulation. When you look at how things are going here in the southern colonies—pardon me, I mean states—the British and Tories are strong along the coast. Here in this part of North Carolina, though, General Rutherford's forces are controlling the Tories for the most part. In South Carolina, you have Governor Rutledge, General Williamson, and Colonels Marion and Sumter controlling some portions of the state. Fortunately, in Georgia we still control Savannah, as well."

The governor paused, and then continued, "The British have the greatest fleet in the world and the greatest army in the world. What we must have is determination and the wisdom to choose when and where to fight them. I like the tactics of attacking and disappearing that are used by Colonel Marion. South Carolina's Governor Rutledge calls him "the Swamp Fox" because he strikes the British and then disappears into the swamps or forest. Nevertheless, we must beat the British on the battlefield on a grander scale to actually defeat them." Then, abruptly, but not rudely, he asserted, "Gentlemen, I know you are anxious to get back to your families, so you may be excused."

"Governor, it has been good to see you again," said the colonel.

"It is an honor to know you," said Jonathan.

As Jonathan Tipton and Colonel Carter departed from the meeting room, Jonathan thought about the fact that he was not at all surprised at the warm welcome he had received from Governor Caswell. After all, Jonathan's father and grandfather had known the Caswell family well in Maryland, before Richard Caswell had moved to North Carolina and before Jonathan's father had moved to Virginia. That must certainly have helped in the governor's decision to approve Jonathan's commission.

Gathering the remainder of their party, Colonel Carter, Major Jonathan Tipton, and their men headed west, toward home.

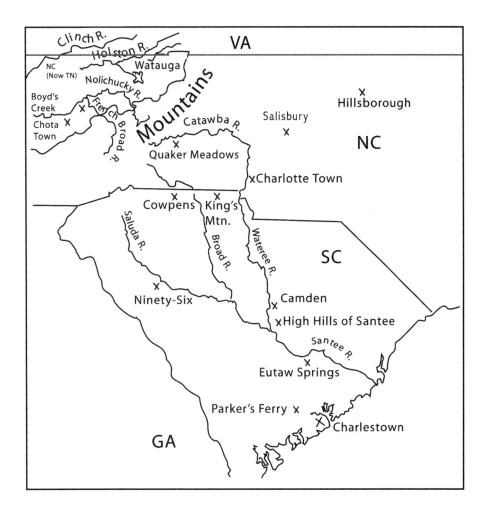

Chapter 2

Skirmish at Salisbury

COLONEL CARTER BROADCASTED for all to hear as they rode along, "Major Tipton, you will be in charge of Captain Trimble's company of militia and Lieutenant Gibson's men. As you know, they all live to the south and east of the Watauga Settlement. I will continue to have Captain Sevier, Captain Robertson, and Captain Anderson report to me with their companies. The fine militiamen riding with us today—Ferrell, Griffin, Nelson, Taylor, and Webb—all reside in your district, and will be under your command. That is one of the reasons they were selected for this trip. When we get home they will help spread the word of your command. I will advise Captain Trimble and Lieutenant Gibson personally."

"Thank you, Colonel. These men and the others under Captain Trimble and Lieutenant Gibson are the men you have had me patrolling with all along, anyway. It should continue to work out well." Jonathan paused. "Sergeant Bragg has patrolled with us up to now, but his cabin borders rather closely toward the western side of the area you mentioned. Will the sergeant be with my command as well?"

"Absolutely."

Jonathan was relieved. He considered Sergeant David Bragg to be just as valuable as Captain Trimble or Lieutenant Gibson. Bragg, who reported to Captain Trimble, was an excellent scout. He was a large, powerful man who, depending on the situation, took or recommended bold actions based on his sound judgment.

Colonel Carter noticed smiles on the faces of Griffin and Taylor. He knew that they were happy with the formal selection of Major Tipton as their leader.

On the homeward bound journey, the men traveled at a slightly faster pace than when they had headed eastward to Hillsborough. The quickened pace was somewhat inspired by the desire to get home. It was also facilitated by the fact that they were familiar with the route. The men also wanted to minimize their exposure to the frigid February weather they were encountering along the route.

The party proceeded with vigilance and due diligence, posting a lead rider and dispensing two riders to trail the main party by about fifty paces.

One morning as they rode, Jonathan recalled when, back in Virginia as a youngster about thirteen years of age, he and his brother Joshua played a game in the woods. When they were hunting, or just exploring, they would always try to see first and not be seen or heard first by any human or large animal they might encounter. For hunting, it meant success or failure in bringing meat to the table. In the case of humans, they most frequently encountered friendly white settlers, and they almost always saw and heard the other party first.

One day he and his brother knew they were getting good. Both of the brothers had large feet for their ages, and were perceived as adult hunters by anyone who saw their footprints. In mid-morning, while hunting, they spied a party of Indians walking up a trail several hundred yards behind them. It had rained early in the morning, so there were no tracks on the trail but those of Jonathan and Joshua. They were at the summit of a hill at a place where the Indians had not seen them. Continuing down the middle of the trail, the brothers left their footprints clearly visible, until, at one point, Jonathan jumped hard off the trail onto a large flat rock, telling Joshua to follow into his exact footsteps and then do the same. Thus, their footprints disappeared from the trail. The boys followed a patch of rocks down to a creek, then waded about twenty yards upstream and scrambled up a wooded hill from which they could observe the Indians on the trail. They could also easily escape toward home from that point if discovered. Their hope, if their ploy was successful, was to startle the Indians with the disappearance of their tracks and to observe the reaction of the Indians.

As expected by the brothers, the Indians had seen their footprints on the trail. When the lead Indian got to the point where their footprints disappeared, he suddenly stopped, made a hand signal for the other four Indians to stop, and looked around quickly in every direction, fearing an ambush. It was just what the boys had hoped for. The Indians, being good trackers, figured out in seconds what had happened, and ventured warily onto the rocks in search of the two persons who may be lying in ambush. Reaching the creek, the Indians properly assumed the two individuals had just gone to the creek to avoid being tracked. The Indians realized they were not in danger, and then proceeded down the trail. Nevertheless, Jonathan and his brother had succeeded twice at their game. First, they saw the Indians before being seen, and secondly, they had alarmed the Indians with a clever exit from the trail.

Jonathan's daydreaming was suddenly interrupted by a sharp barrage of ten to twelve gunshots, straight ahead in the direction they were traveling. Colonel Carter's small group of men had just come into view of the Miller's farm near Salisbury. This was the place where they had met with Private Howard and Captain McGahee just a few days ago. Jonathan was alarmed when he saw that at least twenty redcoat British soldiers had surrounded the Miller's cabin and were firing toward the cabin. He saw and heard the return fire from two rifles inside the cabin. Only seconds later, Jonathan saw one British soldier fall to the ground, apparently hit from behind by a third shooter somewhere out in the field. Adrenalin pumped through every blood vessel in his body.

Colonel Carter quickly assessed the situation. The redcoats were firing on the Millers inside their cabin. The British must have been tipped off that patriot supplies were being kept on the Miller's farm, but they did not realize that the location of the supplies was at the barn.

"That's Howard out in the field behind the British!" exclaimed Joseph Griffin. "He's all by himself!" About the same time, one of the British soldiers spotted Colonel Carter's mounted party and shouted an alarm to his fellow redcoats.

"Let's go," said Colonel Carter, leading the riders at a gallop toward the barn. They headed directly toward Thomas Howard's position near the barn. Upon reaching his position, the men quickly dismounted, dispersed into a line, and commenced firing at the British. Jonathan took careful aim at a British soldier who had turned away from the cabin and was now taking aim toward the newly arrived Patriots. Squeezing the trigger gently, Jonathan fired. The redcoat soldier fell. Jonathan knew that the soldier was wounded. He thought his shot had struck the man in the chest, and that he was probably dying. Two more redcoats fell in that first volley of deadly accurate shots from the frontiersmen. Although still outnumbering the Patriots, the remaining British soldiers abruptly mounted their horses and fled southward, undoubtedly toward one of their strongholds in South Carolina.

As soon as the British fled, James Miller and his wife, Margaret, emerged from their cabin, each with a rifle in hand. Colonel Carter, Major Tipton, and their party had fortuitously arrived just at the right time. Otherwise, the British would certainly have killed the Millers and Private Howard, and would have discovered and stolen or destroyed the Patriot's essential military supplies. As the British soldiers disappeared from sight, Mr. and Mrs. Miller joined Colonel Carter and his men, along with Thomas Howard, just outside their cabin.

Looking at Colonel Carter, James Miller exclaimed, "They said they were going to burn us out!"

"They would have done it, too!" Thomas Howard chimed in.

Right at that moment, the whole group saw about twenty riders approaching at a gallop. Thomas Howard immediately recognized the riders as Captain John McGahee and his Patriots.

"It's OK," Howard stated in a relieved tone of voice. "It is Captain McGahee and his company."

The skirmish had been a close call. Despite their most urgent response upon hearing shots fired at a distance, Captain McGahee's men would have likely been several minutes too late to have saved the Millers, Howard, and the arsenal. This incident registered firmly in Jonathan Tipton's mind. He added it to memories of fights against Indians in which some combination of timing, luck, preparedness, or bold action had swayed the outcome of the conflict.

After exchanging formalities with Captain McGahee and his men and accepting their sincere thanks, Major Tipton, Colonel John Carter, and their men continued their westward trek. They were anxious to get home.

From Salisbury, the men traveled toward the northwest, in the direction of the mountains and the Watauga area. On the second day out of Salisbury, they traveled until well after sunset. Then they camped by the Yadkin River. Having reached the higher foothills of the mountains, the men thought they might be able to reach home as soon as two days later.

Jonathan wrapped his blanket around his head and upper body, reclining at the trunk of a large tree as he tried to sleep. The ground was frozen. The freezing temperature of the February night penetrated his blanket and clothing. Unable to fall asleep quickly, he thought about the war. He remembered when, in 1774, news had reached the Watauga area that the British had completely closed the port of Boston as punishment for the colonists' resistance to taxes and other acts imposed by the British Parliament. By closing the port, British ships and troops had forcibly shut down the livelihood of most of Boston's residents. At that time, those events had seemed distant to Jonathan. It had seemed to him that those events were likely to be temporary in nature, and would be resolved with no major change of life in the colonies. He also remembered that things had not in fact improved. Instead, the oppression by the British Parliament had worsened, enforced by the invading British army and navy.

Jonathan also recalled his brother's visit from Virginia in late 1775. His oldest brother, John Tipton, had told him that the prevailing sentiment among leading citizens in Virginia was that an attack by the British on one colony was an attack on all the colonies. Of course, there were some Tories who said they would always be loyal to the king. His brother had also advised him that a Continental Congress from all the colonies had met and created an American Continental Army.

The colonies, his brother had told him, had agreed to fight to protect one another. Since the visit from his brother, the colonies had declared themselves to be free and independent states, and had constituted the United States of America. Now, in February 1777, Jonathan thought of the British inciting the Indians to attack the settlers. He thought about the large British armies that had invaded the states. Jonathan remembered the various books he read in his youth about great European wars of the past. He wondered how the large battles in the northern colonies were being fought, how the officers decided what strategies to use, and how violent the fighting was. The persistent thought that came to mind over and over was, "Is it possible that the states can really defeat the British and win their independence?" Despite the frigid weather, Jonathan finally fell asleep.

The men were all awake at daybreak. It was too cold to sleep, and, although tired, they were ready to head home. At first light, they were mounted and on the trail. After one more night on the trail, the party reached home before dark on the following day. First, William Nelson and John Taylor had separated from the main party in order to take the shortest route to their homes. Then, one by one, others had done the same. For the last half-mile before parting to go their separate ways, only Colonel John Carter and Major Jonathan Tipton remained.

"Well, we certainly traveled rapidly on the return trip," mused Colonel Carter.

"Everyone was anxious to get home. I am, too." Jonathan's reply was simple and straight to the point.

"There's Elijah Bates's cabin. Let's stop by just for a couple of minutes and see what the news is here at home." Colonel Carter made it a point to emphasize the brevity of the planned stop. At this point, Jonathan's cabin was only about two miles to the north, and Colonel Carter's home was about two miles to the northwest. Neither wanted much delay in getting home.

As they rode slowly up a side trail to the Bates's cabin, Jonathan could see the small plume of smoke rising from the chimney. Elijah Bates worked his small farm, and was a private in the area militia. He was an intelligent and gregarious young man. Elijah's small farm and one-room cabin were typical of those of area settlers. Some, like Jonathan, who had been in the area longer had added second rooms to their cabins. Jonathan knew that Elijah went into the Watauga settlement at least once every week, and would surely know what news existed.

As they approached the cabin, Elijah Bates opened the door and stepped outside, rifle in hand. Elijah waved, as they were now close enough that he could recognize them. "Hello there," he shouted. Elizabeth, his wife, joined him, standing by his side.

Before Jonathan or Colonel Carter said anything at all, Elijah Bates blurted out, "Sir, there has been bad Indian trouble! About eight miles north of Watauga, not too far from Captain Sevier's cabin, John McVay and his wife were killed and scalped. John's brother, Ben, who lives right next to him, was shot in the shoulder, too."

"When was that?" The colonel wanted to know more.

"Day before yesterday," Elijah replied. "I went into Watauga yesterday and found out about it. The McVay cabins are only two or three miles west of Captain Sevier's cabin. The captain was assembling militia for a regular patrol and heard the shooting. They rode straight toward the sound of the shots. There were about forty Indians, led by Chief Dragging Canoe. They stole all the McVays's horses, and killed their four cows. Ben and his wife, Sally, and their two daughters were shooting from inside their cabin with two rifles and a pistol. They saw what happened at his brother's cabin. They saw the Indians drag John's wife out into the open and kill her and scalp her. Captain Sevier had fifteen men with him.

27

When the Indians spied them coming, all the Indians fled and got away. If Captain Sevier had not come, Ben and his family would certainly have been killed and scalped like his brother and his wife were."

"Thanks, Elijah. We have been away to see the governor in Hillsborough, and we have to get home. Oh! I almost forgot to tell you. You have been on patrols under Jonathan's command before. Now he is officially Major Tipton, appointed by Governor Caswell himself."

"That is good, very good! Congratulations, Jonathan, I mean Major Tipton."

"Elijah, you can still just call me Jonathan when we aren't around the men. We are still friends first and soldiers second. Since Colonel Carter is here, I do appreciate you calling me major, though. Nobody else has done that yet, except for the men who were with us in Hillsborough."

Colonel Carter abruptly mounted his horse, and Jonathan followed suit.

"We've got to go," said the colonel, tipping his hat to Elizabeth. "The best to both of you."

Several minutes after leaving the Bates's cabin, Jonathan and Colonel Carter separated. The colonel continued westward toward his home, and Jonathan headed north. It was just two more miles to home and family.

Chapter 3

Trouble on the Frontier

THE SHADOWS OF late afternoon were long, and the wintry breeze was frigid. Over the next small rise on the trail were Jonathan's home and family—the essence of his life. Seeing a faint plume of smoke over the rise, Jonathan knew that it was smoke from the fireplace of his own home.

As Jonathan approached within fifty paces of his cabin, the front door swung open. Five-year-old William and four-year-old Samuel came running out the door, followed shortly by three-year-old Mary. Immediately dismounting to exhilarated shouts of "father, father, father," Jonathan quickly found himself hugged around the left leg by William and around the right leg by Samuel. Mary jumped to his waist, and Jonathan lifted her to his chest with his free arm, continuing to lead the horse with his other hand. Making his way with pleasant difficulty, Jonathan saw the smile of his wife, Frances. She was holding eleven-month-old Johnny in her arms, and tiny two-year-old Hannah was standing beside her, just outside the cabin door.

Directing William to take the reins of his horse, Jonathan set Mary down, picked up Hannah in his left arm, and embraced Frances with his right arm, simultaneously kissing infant Johnny on the cheek. Amidst this warm reunion, the bitter coldness of the weather had seemingly disappeared.

Stepping inside the cabin, Jonathan's wife gently placed Hannah in the arms of older brother Samuel. Then she and Jonathan fully embraced each other, kissing gently on the lips.

"Oh, Jonathan, I am so glad you are home!"

"Frances, I love you so dearly," Jonathan responded.

Having taken the horse to the barn, William came in from the cold. With the entire family now together, Jonathan proclaimed clearly, "Children, your father is now a major in the American militia." Frances looked him in the eyes, smiled happily, and hugged him again.

William, the oldest, having listened to adults talk about the militia and the war, exclaimed, "Father is a major!"

Later that evening, the children had all fallen asleep. An occasional crackle accompanied the gentle sound of the split logs burning in the fireplace as Jonathan said the bedtime prayers for himself and Frances. Jonathan and Frances quietly made love for the first time in just over two weeks. It seemed much longer to Jonathan after traveling such a long distance over a period of seemingly endless days. Jonathan's journey to Hillsborough had been a success. Nevertheless, lying in bed with Frances, the thought that he frequently stated to his children ran through his head. That thought was, "Home is the best place."

The Tipton home was a two-room cabin constructed of pine logs. The roof was made of split pine logs. The front room had been built when Jonathan and Frances arrived in 1773. It measured nineteen feet wide and fifteen feet deep. The back room, completed in late 1775, was almost identical to the first room in size. Each room had a fireplace. The only windows consisted of four removable wooden blocks in each room. Each wooden block was about one foot wide and six inches high; and each could be used as a gun port in lieu of a window in the event of an Indian attack. The cabin was located on the gentle slope of a hillside in a shallow valley. As the terrain leveled only 150 paces down the gentle slope from the Tipton cabin, the soil was fertile. Just another thirty paces farther was Deep Creek, which flowed along the edge of the valley closest to the Tipton home.

The family's barn was directly behind the cabin. About the size of the cabin, the barn had also been built in two increments. The barn contained an open doorway large enough for a horse to be led through from one section to the other. A lean-to overhead roof with side rails had been added down the entire length of one side of the barn. The barn could be a crowded place in the coldest parts of winter, when livestock, horses, and chickens were all inside to be protected from the weather. During most of the year, Jonathan allowed his hogs to roam free in the forest, where they generally ranged in the lowlands, down near the creek. In late autumn, he rounded up as many of the hogs as possible and kept them in the lean-to, or inside the barn when necessary. Some of the hogs were slaughtered during the winter to provide pork and bacon for essential meals. In early spring the remaining hogs were herded into the forest to forage on their own.

Three days after Jonathan returned home, a rider approached the Tipton Cabin. "Father, Sergeant Bragg is coming," shouted William.

Sergeant Bragg dismounted. He did not salute, inasmuch as such formalities were rare in the backcountry. "Hello, Major."

"Welcome, David. It's good to see you."

"Colonel Carter asked me to invite you to a meeting of officers tomorrow at noon at Fort Watauga. He said the meeting will be related to all the Indian trouble we have been having."

"Thanks. I will be there. Can you stay and visit?"

"No. I have to go to Captain Trimble's and Lieutenant Gibson's places to deliver the same message. Then I have lots of things that need to be done this evening at home."

"I understand," replied Jonathan. Sergeant Bragg mounted and rode away in the direction of Captain Trimble's cabin.

"I'll be back before dark." It was after completing necessary chores the next morning when Jonathan bid Frances and the children good-bye. He rode to Fort Watauga to meet with Colonel Carter and the other officers of Washington County.

Although the area surrounding the Watauga settlement was at that time in 1777 still a district, people already called it Washington County. During the prior year, the settlers had named it after George Washington, who was general of the American Continental Army. The settlers had sent John Sevier and two other residents to solicit the North Carolina legislature to add the county to the state. The legislature had recognized the area as a district, but had not yet approved its status as a county.

All the officers were present by midday. Colonel John Carter was present, of course, and in charge of the meeting. Major Tipton was present with the officers who reported to him: Captain Trimble and Lieutenant Gibson. Captain John Sevier was in attendance with the officers who reported to him: Captain Charles Robertson and Lieutenant Valentine Sevier. It did not seem out of place to anyone that Captain Robertson reported to Captain Sevier, who was of equal rank, as Sevier had held the rank more than a year earlier than Robertson, and because Colonel Carter had always had Robertson and his company under Captain Sevier's overall command.

Colonel Carter opened the meeting. "I have called this meeting for the purpose of arranging improved patrols to protect ourselves from the recent increase in Indian attacks. Before we go any further, however, Captain Sevier has some news."

John Sevier addressed the group. His tone of voice ranged from sullen to angry in nature as he spoke. "There has been more Indian trouble up near Ripple Creek since John McVay and his wife were killed last week. It's really bad. Just yesterday, Sergeant Armstrong—I believe most of you knew Isaac—was killed by Indians. He was hunting with his son, Ephraim, when six or seven Indians attacked them. Ephraim fired a shot and then ran through the woods and escaped. Isaac was first shot with a musket ball. The Indians are getting more and more muskets from the British. When we went there to find Isaac, we saw that he had been stabbed over and over again in the gut, and had been scalped. Isaac was buried last night at his farm. For their own safety, because their cabin is fairly remote, Isaac's wife, Mary, and their children are moving into the old shed at Samuel Riggs's farm. Michael Hider and some of my men are helping them move their livestock and belongings today."

"This atrocity and all the others like it are the precise reason for our meeting today," said Colonel Carter. "We must devise a better plan to protect ourselves. Let's get on with it."

After extensive discussion, Colonel Carter directed the establishment of two separate patrol regions. He ordered that daily patrols be conducted in each region, with one region commanded by Major Tipton and the other region commanded by Captain Sevier. The routes and variances in daily patrols were to be determined at the discretion of Major Tipton and Captain Sevier so as to best protect the settlers of the area, and so as to be unpredictable to any Indian scouts. Recognizing the extent to which men must work hard at home to maintain their livelihood, the colonel gave Major Tipton and Captain Sevier great flexibility regarding the size of their patrols, so long as the patrols were in their judgment adequate to provide a deterrent to Indian violence. He directed them that the daily patrols should consist routinely of ten to twenty men. Colonel Carter insisted that this was reasonable because at that time Major Tipton's two companies included seventy-four men and Captain Sevier's two companies included seventy-eight men.

The area along both banks of the south fork of the Holston River, both banks of the north fork of the Holston River, and the area between those forks southward to the confluence of the Holston's south fork and the Watauga River were to be patrolled under the command of Captain John Sevier. At his discretion, Captain Sevier would occasionally patrol as far west as the Clinch River in order to scout Indian activities.

The area along both banks of the Watauga River from four miles west of Fort Watauga to the eastern headwaters of the Watauga, both banks of the Nolichucky River, and the area between the Watauga and Nolichucky Rivers was to be patrolled under the command of Major Jonathan Tipton. At his discretion, Major Tipton would occasionally patrol as far south as the French Broad River in order to scout Indian activities.

As directed by Colonel Carter, Jonathan Tipton met with his officers and Sergeant Bragg and set up militia patrols for Major Tipton's area according to the following schedule:

- Monday/Tuesday – Captain Trimble with 15 to 20 men

- Wednesday/Thursday – Lieutenant Gibson with 15 to 20 men

- Friday/Saturday – Sergeant Bragg with 15 to 20 men

- Sunday – Major Tipton with 12 men

Although Sergeant Bragg was not present, Jonathan knew that Bragg would accept the responsibility of leading patrols. Jonathan also knew that David Bragg was at least equally competent to any officer in the district to lead any patrol.

It was difficult to get men for Sunday militia patrols. Jonathan assumed the officer role himself, and estimated that he could identify at least twelve men to ride with him on most Sundays.

There was no church or minister in the area yet. However, a devoted Christian settler named Ebeneezer Tarpley did conduct religious services at Fort Watauga on the first Sunday of each month. Jonathan figured that he would occasionally swap patrol days with one of his officers, so that Jonathan, Frances, and the children could attend services.

From that point forward, Major Tipton's men were constantly in service, taking their turns on patrols and protecting the settlers as they cultivated their land and attended to their livestock and homes. Additionally, the men were sometimes summoned for special scouting parties, venturing further out into Indian territory. Due to various causes, patrols that were intended to include fifteen to twenty men often included only ten or eleven men.

Life on the frontier was difficult. There was much work to do at home for every man in the area. Illnesses in their families and necessary work or difficulties with their crops sometimes caused men to miss patrols. Nevertheless, a patrol of some number of men was accomplished nearly every single day.

On two separate occasions in the summer of 1777, scouting parties spied large war parties of more than two hundred Indians heading toward the Watauga area from the southwest. Chief Dragging Canoe was the leader of both of these threatening forces. In both cases riders were sent to warn settlers throughout the area. Many families chose to seek refuge in Fort Watauga, leaving their homes overnight.

In both instances Colonel Carter summoned all four companies of militia that were at his disposal. He left the reliable and well-respected Captain Charles Robertson with about half of a company of men at the fort, along with older men and teenage boys, in order to protect the fort. The other three and one-half companies, about 110 men, rode directly toward the approaching Indians. In both cases, the Indians, observing such a force of well-armed men approaching, retreated from the area.

Each time, Colonel Carter decided not to pursue the Indians. Some of the younger men strongly verbalized their support of pursuing the Indians. Colonel Carter, however, exercised wisdom in his decision-making. He knew from experiences in 1775 and 1776 that a larger force was both prudent and necessary for a successful venture against a large party of Indians. He knew that the Indians, if pursued, would likely be reinforced as they went deeper into the territory that they controlled. The colonel's judgment was that he would have no part in being vastly outnumbered and possibly ambushed. Nevertheless, the direct show of force by the mounted militia had the desired effect, because no major Indian invasion of Washington County occurred in the year 1777.

One morning in October 1777, Landon Carter, the oldest son of Colonel Carter, rode to the home of Jonathan Tipton. As he saw Jonathan walking toward him in front of the Tipton cabin, Landon dismounted.

"Major Tipton, my father told me to ride over here and ask you to come visit him this afternoon. He says he has some news to share with you, but did not tell me what it was."

Landon Carter was a very bright young man. He was well educated, having been schooled at Liberty Hall in Virginia before the Carters had migrated to their present home near Fort Watauga. At his current age of seventeen, Landon had already served repeatedly on militia patrols for over a year.

"It is good to see you, Landon. Does the colonel want me to come right away, or is the matter not urgent?"

"I don't think it is urgent, sir. He just wants you to come sometime today. He said he will be available all day, whenever you want to come."

"Landon, please tell the colonel that I will be there in early afternoon."

"Yes, sir," Landon replied in a pleasant tone of voice. He mounted his horse and rode away.

Jonathan did make the short trip to see Colonel Carter, and following the visit he headed home. While riding home he thought about the news he had received in the discussion with Colonel Carter. Jonathan felt a need to share the news and his feelings about it with his wife.

"Frances, Colonel Carter received a dispatch from the governor today. It was a letter from Governor Caswell appointing John Sevier lieutenant colonel of Washington County. That makes him, instead of me, second in command to Colonel Carter. Colonel Carter told me this news today. He said that Sevier had been a captain in Virginia before he moved here."

Jonathan continued, "Colonel Carter learned that about ten weeks ago, Sevier sent his son on horseback to deliver a letter to Governor Henry in Virginia. Governor Henry, a friend of Sevier's family, knows that the former royal governor had appointed Sevier as a captain in the militia of that colony some years ago before he moved here. Sevier's letter requested Governor Henry to write our Governor Caswell in North Carolina and request him to appoint Sevier as colonel in Washington County. Three weeks ago, Colonel Carter received a dispatch from Governor Caswell requesting his opinion, because Colonel Carter is already the colonel for this county. Colonel Carter sent a rider with his reply to the governor that he supported commissioning John Sevier to a higher post than captain, but not as a full colonel, because the county is not of sufficient population at this time to justify such appointment as would result in two colonels. Colonel Carter expected that John Sevier would be appointed as a major, and was quite surprised when he read the letter of appointment as lieutenant colonel."

"Are you terribly upset?" Frances was obviously concerned about her husband's reaction.

"I am. I was furious at first. Then, Colonel Carter explained to me that Governor Caswell's letter described the fact that he considered Sevier's service as a captain in Virginia as well as his so-called hero status from the Indians' attack on Fort Watauga last year. I still don't like it, but Colonel Carter has to support it, so I will just have to live with it." Jonathan's anger surfaced. "Sevier is brave beyond doubt, but he is also selfish."

Frances replied, "It will be all right."

"I don't care. I have been a major in this county for eight months and here comes a captain who used to serve in Virginia and he gets appointed above me. I should be the lieutenant colonel and John Sevier should be the major."

In October of 1777, a district election was held to elect two representatives to attend the November 1777 session of the North Carolina Legislature. The legislature was expected to decide whether or not to approve the creation of Washington County. Colonel John Carter ran unopposed for one of the delegate positions. John Sevier was elected as the other delegate by an overwhelming majority. The only person who ran against him was Ebeneezer Tarpley, who garnered only a handful of votes.

At its November 1777 session the general assembly of North Carolina approved the creation of Washington County. The legislature established a tremendously large county by assigning it the boundaries on the east from the Virginia/North Carolina line in the mountains to the North Carolina/South Carolina line in the mountains and extending due west all the way to the Mississippi River. Some of the men in Washington County had explored westward for up to two weeks and had never reached the Mississippi River. Thus, upon learning of the boundaries the people of the area knew their county was large but wondered just how large it was. They did realize, however, that everything west of their current area of residence was, for all practical purposes, Indian territory. A proclamation of the State Assembly could not change that.

Returning from an uneventful patrol in early December 1777, Jonathan decided to stop by Colonel Carter's home, both to report the absence of any threat to the immediate southwest, and simply to visit as a friend. Landon, the colonel's oldest son, met Jonathan in front of the home and offered to take Jonathan's horse to the stable for shelter during his visit.

Although he planned only a brief visit, Jonathan accepted, as it was a very cold day.

Then, Susan, the wife of Colonel Carter, invited him in and motioned for him to sit near the fireplace. "John will be with you in just a moment."

John Carter entered the room. With a big smile, he extended his hand to shake Jonathan's.

"Welcome, Jonathan. How was your ride today?"

"Very good. There is no sign of Indians within a half day's ride to the southwest, and the settlers just to the south of here have neither experienced nor heard of any Indian trouble for the last ten days."

"Good. I have some good news to share with you, too. A letter arrived from General Rutherford yesterday. He wrote about a big victory by the Patriot army under General Gates and General Lincoln over the British under General Burgoyne at a place called Saratoga. It was in the state of New York. The battle happened in October, the month before last. The Patriots had a huge army of fifteen thousand men and defeated a large British army, killing more than one thousand British soldiers and capturing six thousand."

"Did he say how many men we lost?"

"No, but the letter implies that it was a significant victory. If our army captured six thousand British troops, we must have won quite an overwhelming victory. He also wrote that the British still control New York and Philadelphia, and that the fighting up north is fierce. Battles occur frequently, and the British appear to be winning two to our every one. Nonetheless, I believe that the victory at Saratoga proves that we have some chance to win the overall war in the end."

For the next few months after that visit with Colonel Carter, life was tolerable in the area of Washington County surrounding the Watauga settlement. Conducting the militia patrols had been and remained an inconvenient necessity. Even by early August of 1778, however, there had been no significant trouble with Indians. There had been the occasional theft of horses by Indians, usually from settlers in the most remote locations, and word had reached the area of increased hostile activities by the Indians in South Carolina. Things in the Watauga area were quiet.

Jonathan Tipton thought that the near absence of Indian activity made things seem far too quiet.

Late one afternoon in August of 1778, Jonathan had just finished disemboweling and cleaning a deer that would provide his family with good meat for more than one meal. He sat down on a large stone by the creek near his cabin, and thought about news that had been received about the war. He recalled that in about April he had heard about the February 1778 treaty of alliance with France. That seemed to bode well for the Patriots' cause. France was a major world power. Both the army and the navy of France were nearly the equals of their British counterparts. Then, just a week ago, on the first of August, Colonel Carter had received a letter telling of a huge battle having occurred on June 28, 1778, at Monmouth Courthouse in New Jersey, involving the armies of General Washington and General Henry Clinton. Both sides claimed victory. If both sides claimed victory, he thought, at least the Patriots were holding their own on the battlefield against the British. The letter had also said there was lots of fighting continuing in New Jersey and Pennsylvania. Jonathan summarized his thoughts in his own mind. He thought about how good it was to be home. Either the militia patrols were effective, or the Indians were thoroughly occupied as allies with the British in South Carolina to the extent that they had not been attacking the Watauga area settlers.

The next thought that entered Jonathan's mind was that perhaps he should join the fighting in the northern states. After all, it appeared that was where the outcome would be settled. He then rationalized that he could not leave his home and family to do so, especially when it was difficult enough to live on the frontier. He also remembered when he and Colonel Carter had met with Governor Caswell a year and a half ago. The governor had told them how important it was for them to keep the Indians under control on the frontier. Jonathan needed to remain in the mountains and continue with what he was doing.

"Father, Father!" It was his son, William, running down the slope toward the creek, interrupting Jonathan's contemplations. "Mother said she needs you. Two large stones fell from the chimney into the fire. She wants you to be sure the house does not catch fire!"

"OK, let's go," said Jonathan. He hoisted the deer onto one shoulder and walked briskly up the slope to the cabin. Young William, now six years old, struggled to keep up with his father.

Entering the front door of the cabin, Jonathan found Frances calmly pouring a bowl of water over the last flames of the fire that had been burning in the fireplace. Ashes had been scattered over a wide area of the floor surrounding the fireplace when the stones had fallen from the chimney. Frances had decided to put out the cooking fire. She had also used a metal poker to pull the two stones from the fireplace. It never ceased to amaze Jonathan how calm she was in unexpected situations. It seemed to him that she could handle almost anything well.

"Jonathan, I will have to cook in the fireplace in the other room this evening. By morning the chimney will have cooled down, and perhaps you can repair it."

"I will look at the chimney from the outside right now. Based on the size of those stones, I believe they are from the outer side." Jonathan's guess was correct. The stones had fallen from the outer side of the chimney, and he made the repair the following day.

During autumn of 1778, signs of possible trouble with the Indians became more frequent. First, in late October, a militia patrol under Sergeant Bragg had spotted two Indians spying on settlers along the Nolichucky River. Then, on consecutive days, patrols under Captain Trimble and Lieutenant Gibson had seen Indians in parties of two, as well. During the same week, similar reports were made by the militia patrols along the north fork of the Holston River. Lieutenant Colonel Sevier and Lieutenant Robertson led those patrols. In each case the Indians had avoided being captured or killed.

As word spread of these sightings of Indians, the settlers became concerned, and increased their vigilance accordingly. There was an increased sense of importance on every militia patrol, as well.

Because of the escalation in Indian activity, Colonel John Carter invited Lieutenant Colonel John Sevier and Major Jonathan Tipton to meet at his home at noon on October 30, 1778. When they met, Colonel Carter opened the meeting by summarizing the reports from the militia patrols. "In recent days your patrols have reported seeing Indians in settled areas on a daily basis. We must conclude that there is some reason for this increased activity by the Indians. Perhaps they are spying in preparation for small raids on settlers, or perhaps they are planning a larger attack. I would like your thoughts and ideas regarding this."

Nodding his head at John Sevier, Colonel Carter said, "John, what is your opinion?"

"I think the Indians are planning to attack us. I recommend that we assemble the strongest force possible for an expedition and attack the Indians first, before they attack us. We need to go into Indian territory and attack their villages, as well as any war parties that come out to resist us. We will need to request men from Colonel Campbell in Virginia, along with his own participation, of course. By doing this we can muster at least two hundred and fifty men for the expedition, still leaving at least eighty to one hundred men to defend the settlers here at home. By attacking the Indians and making a display of force, we will discourage the Indians from ever attacking our settlements. We will save homes from being burned and women and children from being killed or captured."

"When do you suggest that we mount the expedition?" Colonel Carter had carefully listened to Sevier's aggressive recommendation.

"We can march in about two weeks, if Colonel Campbell will cooperate with us. I believe he will do it. I can send a rider tomorrow morning, and we should have his answer in about five days."

Turning toward Major Tipton, Colonel Carter inquired, "Jonathan, what do you recommend?"

"Colonel, I suggest that we send four scouting parties of two men each into Indian territory to spy on the Indians. The four parties can head in different directions. They can observe the known Indian villages and can scout for any large assembly of Indians or any large Indian war parties. Then, depending on the reports from the four scouting parties, we can meet again and decide what action to take. If a large assembly of Indians or a large war party is found we can take aggressive action such as Lieutenant Colonel Sevier has suggested."

Colonel John Carter looked right at Jonathan Tipton as he spoke. "You don't think the Indians are going to attack, do you?"

"They may not be planning to attack any time soon," replied Jonathan. "They may be spying on us just to judge how many settlers are here now, since so many new people have come here in the last year. With winter fast approaching, I don't think they will attack now. They may be more likely to attack in late winter or early in the spring, hoping to discourage a new wave of settlers. If we send out four scouting parties to spy on them, we will likely learn more about what we can expect from the Indians right now."

John Sevier spoke up. "Colonel Carter, we need to attack the Indians first, before they attack us."

Colonel John Carter remained silent momentarily, as the three men remained seated at a table in the front room of the Carter home. He knew that he had opposing recommendations from two men, both of whom he held in high esteem. He respected both John Sevier and Jonathan Tipton, and valued their opinions. He wanted to make a decision, and he wanted to make it now.

Colonel Carter stood to speak. "I want each of you to select men for scouting parties."

Looking at John Sevier, he said, "John, direct your two scouting parties of two men each to cover as much Indian territory to the west and northwest as they can cover in ten days. Use your judgment to direct them more specifically to areas where you know Indian villages are located or where Indians might assemble."

Then, turning his head toward Jonathan, Colonel Carter continued, "Jonathan, direct your parties likewise, except to the south and southwest."

"I want both of you to send word to me tomorrow regarding who you are sending in each party. The scouting parties must depart on the morning after tomorrow. As soon as they return, I want you to report to me what they observed."

John Sevier's face turned beet red. Colonel Carter had chosen to use

Jonathan's approach. Sevier was fuming internally, but he respected Colonel John Carter, and did not say anything except "Yes sir." John Sevier stood, politely shook hands with both Jonathan and Colonel Carter, and walked out the door.

The scouts departed two days later, during the first week of November. Three of the scouting parties returned on the tenth day and the last party returned on the eleventh day. All reported seeing no war parties, and that the Indian villages upon which they had spied appeared to be the normal small villages. Colonel Carter decided not to mount any expedition, but instead to continue with the militia patrol scheme that was already in place.

Hearing a knock on the door of his cabin, Jonathan looked out the peep notch. Seeing a familiar face, he opened the front door.

"The British have invaded Georgia and captured Savannah." The man who had come to Major Tipton's home was Smith Ferrell. It was now January 1779. It had been almost two years since Smith Ferrell had accompanied Jonathan on the trip to Hillsborough. "Thousands of British soldiers took over Savannah two days before New Year's Eve. Colonel Carter got the word by a dispatch today. He said you should know. They say there were more than thirty British ships in Savannah harbor."

"Has the Colonel asked me to come to any meeting about this?"

"No sir, he just wanted you to be aware of it. I am supposed to go to Colonel Sevier's home next."

"Thanks Smith. Go ahead. It is always good to see you, even though the news you brought is certainly disturbing."

Mounting his horse, Smith Ferrell left at a slow trot up the trail in the direction that led toward John Sevier's home. Jonathan knew that Savannah was far distant from the mountain settlements. Nevertheless, it was alarming indeed that a large British force was now in the south. The terrible war of the north would likely be paralleled closer to home.

Springtime came, and through mid-April there had been no attack by the Indians. Jonathan Tipton met his regular Sunday patrol group at Elijah Bates's cabin, as arranged. The Bates's cabin was a fairly central location for the men who usually rode the Sunday patrol. One difference on this particular day was that recently-appointed-Lieutenant John Talley was a participant. After that day's patrol, Major Jonathan Tipton would no longer have to take a turn in leading any of the daily patrols. Leading the patrols would be covered among Captain Trimble, Lieutenant Gibson, Lieutenant Talley, and Sergeant Bragg.

Meeting shortly after daybreak, Jonathan's patrol numbered twelve men. The plan for the day was to cover part of the western area between the Watauga and Nolichucky rivers. The route was planned for three hours to the southwest, one hour generally to the north, and then about three hours generally eastward back to a separation point about a mile west of the Bates's cabin. Jonathan planned to take Lieutenant Talley with him and stop by Colonel Carter's home after the patrol. He would advise Colonel Carter of the results of the patrol, and would reconfirm to the colonel that Lieutenant Talley would be handling the Sunday patrols from that point forward.

The first two and one-half hours of the patrol were routine. They passed near and observed the homes of seven families. The men were vigilant, but there was no sign of trouble.

"Smoke!" Elijah Bates said one word loudly.

Looking straight ahead, near the intended extreme southwest point for this particular patrol, Jonathan saw a column of smoke above the trees.

The nature of the smoke was foreboding. Some of the men had seen smoke like this before. It was not smoke from a chimney and not from a campfire. It was the smoke of a burning building, and it was located right where a young couple had just finished building their cabin.

"That is Paul McLean's cabin!" exclaimed Lieutenant Talley.

Jonathan led his men at a fair gallop towards the smoke, slowing briefly and cautiously when coming in direct view of the cabin so as to avoid any possible ambush.

The bodies of Paul McLean, Clara McLean, and their infant daughter were a gruesome sight to behold. Their cabin was burning beyond hope of salvage and appeared to have been burning for at least twenty minutes or possibly longer.

Studying the tracks of the Indians, the men found that the Indians had been on horseback. The tracks led to the southwest, into Indian territory, and not directly toward another cabin or a settlement. Based on the tracks, it appeared that the attack had been made by no more than nine or ten Indians. Some of the men knew that Paul McLean had owned four good horses. The horses were gone, stolen by the Indians. The Indians had been gone long enough that it was not likely they could be caught if they were heading directly into Indian territory. On the other hand, if they stopped to attack another cabin, it might be possible to catch up with them.

Acting quickly, Jonathan Tipton altered the planned route and led the patrol southward for twenty minutes to the cabin of George Hart, as he and his family might be in danger. Arriving there, the men found that George and Ann Hart were safe, and had not been attacked. Jonathan told them of the murder of the McLean family, who were their nearest neighbors. He also advised them that if it were discovered that numerous bands of Indians are marauding, a patrol would be sent to escort them and other area settlers to the safety of Fort Watauga. He assured them that even if the attack on the McLeans appeared to be a single attack, they could count on more frequent patrols in the area. Lastly, he suggested to George Hart that George should gather some of the neighbors from the surrounding area and conduct a brief service at the McLean property within the next couple of days. Jonathan told George Hart that he was detaching some men to bury the McLeans today. They would be buried about forty paces to the north of the ruins of the burned cabin, Jonathan told him. Having no time to waste, Jonathan mounted and quickly led the men away.

Major Tipton's patrol headed west in order to reach the cabins of several settlers out toward Limestone Creek who might also be threatened. Jonathan detached Lieutenant Talley with three men to return to the McLean property and bury the victims of the Indian attack. He instructed John Talley to rejoin the patrol as quickly as possible in the area of the three cabins to the west.

Upon leaving the Hart cabin, Jonathan instructed Elijah Bates to leave the patrol.

"Elijah, I want you to ride immediately to Captain Trimble's home and then to Sergeant Bragg's cabin. Tell them to assemble their combined patrols into a larger unit of at least thirty men under Captain Trimble for tomorrow. Tell them I said to ride to this same area tomorrow. Then go to Colonel Carter's home and report what has happened today and what I have ordered for tomorrow's patrol. Also, advise Colonel Carter that I will come to his home before noon tomorrow to discuss the matter. Darn, that's too much to remember. Let me write a note for you to take to Colonel Carter." Realizing that there was too much verbal information for Elijah Bates to remember, Jonathan took a couple of minutes to write a note for him to deliver. "Just remember to tell Captain Trimble and Sergeant Bragg what happened today. Tell them to combine their patrols tomorrow and ride to this same area. Then give this note to Colonel Carter."

The settlers at the three cabins to the west had not been attacked. Having discovered no additional Indian hostilities throughout the day, Jonathan arrived home well after dark.

On the following day, at noon, Jonathan met with Colonel Carter. The two decided that, pending reports from Captain Trimble's patrol, no additional actions were necessary at that time.

Later that day, Jonathan was relieved when Captain Trimble arrived at his home just before sunset and reported no additional trouble or sign of Indian activity. Jonathan directed Captain Trimble to go to Colonel Carter's house and advise the colonel of his findings. Jonathan knew that Captain Trimble would be out late, and would then have to get up early again the next day for another patrol. Jonathan also knew that in the absence of additional Indian hostilities, Captain Trimble would be able to spend the rest of the week at home, attending to activities necessary to sustain his family and maintain his property. The fairness in the design of the schedule of the militia patrols was in providing protection for all, while giving the militiamen adequate time to provide for themselves and their families.

In July 1779, Colonel Carter advised Jonathan of news he received in a letter from General Rutherford. A large British force of twelve hundred men had defeated nine hundred Patriots under General Benjamin Lincoln in a battle at Stono Ferry, near Charlestown, on June 20. General Lincoln and his troops still controlled Charlestown, however. It was also mentioned in the letter that lots of battles and skirmishes were occurring all up and down the coast of South Carolina and Georgia. Colonel Carter provided his opinion. "Jonathan, the British are operating with Savannah as their base of supply. They are getting more and more aggressive along the coast. I would not be surprised if they tried to take Charlestown soon."

Indian hostilities in Washington County were scattered throughout the remainder of 1779. It seemed that the British were influencing the Indians to a greater extent in South Carolina, where skirmishes, raids, and battles all flourished.

News trickled in about events in the war. Colonel Carter was often the first one to receive the news. In March 1780, he learned that Private Howard, who was from Washington County but who had been serving under General Rutherford, had been taken prisoner by the British in January 1780 in a battle called "Buford's Massacre."

An important item of very bad news was received in May 1780. Charlestown had fallen to the British on May 12, 1780. British General Henry Clinton with about ten thousand troops laid siege to the town, captured it, and took General Lincoln and more than five thousand soldiers prisoner. All of the significant ports in the South were now under British control.

In June 1780, Jonathan Tipton sent Sergeant David Bragg and Private Moses McKay into Indian territory to spy on the Indians. Colonel Carter had insisted that periodical scouting missions like this should be done. Jonathan supported this concept wholeheartedly, and ordered this particular mission on his own initiative. On this occasion, Sergeant Bragg reported back to Jonathan with surprising results. Only a five-day ride to the southwest, Bragg and McKay had come upon a large assembly of Indians, most of them warriors, with only a few women and children in the camp. David Bragg estimated that at least three hundred warriors were present. Beyond that, four red-coated British soldiers were in camp.

They had a wagon loaded with boxes of the size that would hold muskets, along with other containers that likely held powder and shot.

"We must go to Colonel Carter's home right away," said Jonathan.

Major Tipton and Sergeant Bragg advised Colonel Carter regarding the Indians, and the colonel made plans to attack the Indians.

Colonel Carter evaluated his ability to form an attack force. Due to continuing settlement in the county, he now had six companies of militia totaling just more than 250 men at his disposal. The colonel had recommended appointments and promotions of officers to lead the growing force. Recently approved appointments of officers had included: Charles Robertson from captain to major; Edward Anderson, captain; Robert Sevier, captain; James Gibson from lieutenant to captain; Landon Carter, captain; and William Newcombe, ensign. Three companies of militia were assigned to Lieutenant Colonel Sevier. Major Tipton had two companies. One company, commanded by Captain Landon Carter, usually reported directly to Colonel Carter, but was sometimes assigned to either Lieutenant Colonel Sevier or to Major Tipton, as Colonel Carter deemed suitable.

Colonel Carter decided to take all six companies on the expedition to attack the Cherokees. The force would consist of about 230 men. Twenty men, including several from each company, would remain behind to garrison Fort Watauga if necessary. In that case, they would be supported in the fort by older men, along with women and teenage boys in defending the fort.

On the second Monday of July in 1780, the militia force assembled at Sycamore Shoals. They proceeded toward the southwest in two columns, one led by Colonel Carter and the other by Lieutenant Colonel Sevier. They would travel on parallel routes and would meet at the small fort at Limestone Creek, near George Gillespie's home. From there they would head directly toward the large assembly of Indians that Sergeant Bragg had discovered.

As they left Sycamore Shoals, Colonel Carter explained part of his logic to Jonathan. "There is little to no chance of surprising the Cherokees with such a large force as we have. Since their numbers appear to be slightly larger than ours, I hope they will stand and fight, rather than retreating. We, like the Indians, have good scouts all about us, and will not be surprised or ambushed, either."

It just happened that Dragging Canoe and six other chiefs had left their encampment the day before with three hundred warriors, heading to the northeast. The militia and the Indians were heading directly toward each other. They were on a collision course.

Dragging Canoe planned to kill as many settlers as possible, burn their cabins, take their horses, kill their livestock, and drive the settlers out of the whole area south and west of Fort Watauga. He did not plan to attack the fort, but wanted to send a message that lasting settlement to the south and west would not be possible.

Late that afternoon, the two columns of militia rendezvoused on George Gillespie's property, beside the very small fort at that place. The Gillespie home was located far southwest of the area generally populated by white settlers. Several months before, word had reached Jonathan from some of the militia scouts that Gillespie and his closest neighbor often hunted deep into Indian lands and that he knew much about the terrain, the creeks, and where rivers could be forded.

Arriving at the rendezvous point, Jonathan Tipton heard a comment from one of his men. "George Gillespie must be crazy to try to live way out here in Indian country."

Jonathan smiled as the thought passed through his mind that Gillespie may not be crazy, but he was definitely brave.

About that time, a broad-shouldered man walked toward Jonathan.

"I'm George Gillespie, and I would be honored to join your company for the attack."

"Welcome, Mr. Gillespie. I am Major Jonathan Tipton, and we can surely use a man such as yourself. We are heading toward the Chero-kees tomorrow morning. I assume you know this territory well. Is that correct?"

"I probably know it better than any other white man."

"This is Sergeant David Bragg. Please talk with him for a while now about the lay of the land, and join up with him at daybreak as a scout ahead of our column."

"You can count on it, Major."

The full militia force was saddled and riding just after daybreak, about ten minutes behind Bragg, Gillespie, and the other scouts.

By mid-afternoon, both the Indian scouts and the militia scouts had detected the presence of their opponents. The Indians had been traveling to the northeast and the militia had traveled two days to the southwest. Both parties stopped briefly, just three miles apart.

Colonel Carter called a meeting of officers and the scouts who had observed the Cherokees. The report was that of about three hundred Indians, only about one hundred of them were mounted. The others were traveling by foot. The Indians were following along a gap that had been the intended path of the militia. If both sides continued, they would collide in the gap. No one among the officers and scouts expected a simple face-to-face clash, however. If the Indians did not retreat, they would certainly try some sort of strategy to gain an advantage.

"I think the Indians will retreat," said Colonel Carter.

John Sevier spoke up. "We have learned from the scouts that these Indians are mostly from the Chickamauga bands of Cherokees. They will fight. Chief Dragging Canoe is probably leading them. They are crafty, but they will fight."

This time, Major Tipton agreed with Lieutenant Colonel Sevier. Jonathan suggested, "Let's strike them now. They are only three miles ahead. We can hit them with about two hours of daylight remaining. Otherwise, they will have overnight to escape or devise plans that we might not like."

"Major Tipton is right," Sevier said. "We are all mounted. We can get to them now and take away most of their choices." It was never difficult to persuade John Sevier to support a plan to attack.

"Let's do it, but let's do it intelligently," responded Colonel Carter. "We will keep the force together. We will not go charging off helter-skelter chasing small groups of Indians and become divided. Not a company will leave the main body without your specific permission, and that can be only after you have gotten permission from me. Make sure all your officers know that."

The Indians had been planning, too. Chief Dragging Canoe guessed right. The white men would come right at them, and would do it immediately.

The militia rode in eight side-by-side columns, separated by about six feet between columns. The valley was lightly forested, with very little undergrowth, and provided no barrier to the columns. Scouts were posted in every direction. A thirty-man lead party was up front, and a twenty-man rear guard trailed the main body by two hundred feet. They crossed a shallow, rocky creek and headed into the gap toward the Cherokees.

Suddenly, a party of about forty mounted Indians rode directly toward the lead party of militia. At a distance of about two hundred feet, the mounted Indians fired one round of shots and turned around and retreated rapidly back toward a more heavily wooded part of the gap. The reason for Colonel Carter's orders became obvious. Nobody chased the mounted Indians. It was clear that they wanted to be chased. If chasing them, the militia would not be in good order, and the Indians would get the ambush opportunity that Dragging Canoe had tried to set up.

Then, at Colonel John Carter's order, the militia broadened their line, still unified but now covering most of the width of the narrow gap. Major Tipton led the left and Lieutenant Colonel John Sevier led the right. Colonel Carter was at the center. The lead party slowed and merged into the main line, and then dropped behind to strengthen the rear guard. Particular care was given to strength in numbers on each flank of the main body, as the officers expected the Indians to attack heavily on the flanks. They continued forward at a deliberate pace.

The battle began in earnest with fierce firing on the right flank, both by militia with rifles and Indians with muskets, a few rifles, and bows and arrows. Then, about eighty to one hundred mounted Indians attacked the front of the main body of militia. Just afterward, a barrage of fire erupted on the left flank.

The superior firepower of the militia quickly dominated the front, and the Indians who had dismounted took to their horses and retreated after about ten minutes. On both flanks, however, Indians on foot had used the forest and the downhill advantage toward the gap to create fierce, hand-to-hand fighting. The militia dismounted and fought as foot soldiers. It was fortunate for the militia that their leaders had the foresight to anticipate the need for strength on the flanks. At first, both militia flanks collapsed toward the center. Then, both flanks held their ground. Next, the Indians, suffering heavy losses, scrambled uphill and disappeared into the lengthening afternoon shadows of the forest.

When the Indians began to retreat, although the battle was ongoing, Colonel Carter sent for Jonathan Tipton and John Sevier to meet with him immediately. It was obvious, as the fighting waned, that the militia had won. Darkness was approaching, and Colonel Carter wanted to determine the next action. He addressed Lieutenant Colonel Sevier and Major Tipton quickly. "There is about an hour of daylight left. It would not be wise to pursue them after dark. We should care for our wounded and find out if any of our men are missing. We need to make a count of the number of casualties, see how many Indian prisoners we have taken, and then return to the open field on the other side of the flat creek that we crossed. It will provide a position that is secure from any surprise counterattack by the Indians. Do you both concur, or do you have other suggestions?"

"You are right, Colonel. I am in full agreement," responded Lieutenant Colonel Sevier.

"Good plan. I also concur," chimed in Major Tipton.

An officers' meeting was convened that evening when the militia had established camp north of the creek. Captain Trimble reported that several of his men who had fought against the Indians in 1775 and 1776 recognized Dragging Canoe as one of the mounted Indians who attacked the front of the militia line. This confirmed John Sevier's earlier supposition that Dragging Canoe was the leader. After listening to suggestions from his officers, Colonel Carter decided to send scouts out in the morning in various directions to ensure the Indians had not actually remained in the area. The consensus of the officers was that if the Indians had gone, the militia under Colonel Carter should settle for the victory and not pursue the Chickamaugas further into Indian lands.

After the meeting disbanded, Colonel Carter requested Lieutenant Colonel Sevier and Major Tipton to remain. "I am going to write Governor Caswell, Colonel Campbell, and General Rutherford about this battle. What should I call it?"

"Well," replied Sevier, "it took place just a little way past the shallow, flat creek. Nobody seems to know a name for that little creek; not even George Gillespie knows. Why don't you call it the Battle of Flat Creek?"

"I'll do just that. Heaven knows that the governor can use a little good news from the mountains after getting all the bad news he has received from the coast."

The following casualty report was included in Colonel Carter's three letters:

BATTLE OF FLAT CREEK		
	Washington County Militia	**Indians**
Killed	2	22
Wounded	17 (2 seriously)	at least 30
Missing	None	captured 2
		Found only 22 bodies but the Indians carried off some dead.

It was confirmed by scouts the next day that the Indians had, in fact, left the area and headed west, further into Indian lands. Thus, the victorious militia force made the return ride to their settlements and homes. One of the two seriously wounded men had suffered a gut wound, and died two days after the battle. Nevertheless, the resounding victory raised hopes that the Indians would be reluctant to make raids on the settlers.

In late July, Jonathan heard about two battles that had taken place on the same day at Brattonsville, South Carolina, and Williamson's

Plantation, South Carolina. The battles at both locations occurred on July 12, 1780; and both places were located in the northwest part of South Carolina, not far from the mountains of North Carolina. The Patriots had won one of the battles, and the British and Tories had won one.

On the second Sunday of September, Jonathan, Frances, and their children arrived about half an hour early for church service, which had by then become a weekly event. The churchyard was abuzz with groups of men talking about something that seemed important. Recognizing John Sevier and Michael Hider standing in one group, Jonathan made his way there. The news was about General Gates' defeat at Camden, South Carolina. A huge battle had taken place on August 16. There were thousands of troops in both armies. General Gates' American army of more than three thousand men had been completely routed by the British under General Cornwallis. Governor Caswell had taken a post as a general under Gates for the battle, but Caswell's brigade was beaten soundly. Some of the continental soldiers and militia had stayed and fought to the death, but most had been killed, captured, or had fled. General Gates himself had fled on horseback so fast that he was said to have traveled faster than a hawk can fly, covering sixty miles in one day in running away from the British. In the days after the battle, General Gates' army consisted of less than one thousand men. Additionally, the British had captured all of the American artillery pieces. The bad news about this battle went on and on. General Rutherford had been captured by the British. The British and Tories were in almost full control of South Carolina and appeared to be headed for total domination of the South.

Beginning on the same day as the news of Gates's defeat and continuing steadily throughout the second and third weeks of September, sixty families of refugees, totaling more than 250 people, arrived at Sycamore Shoals. They had fled from the area of North Carolina east of the mountains, seeking refuge from British and Tory forces that had burned their homes, killed their livestock, and destroyed their crops. A few arrived with horses and wagons, but most walked, carrying what few possessions they could manage.

Colonel John Carter became seriously ill in early September. He was not only unable to lead the militia, but was so incapacitated that he was not even able to get out of bed. Because of Colonel Carter's illness, Lieutenant Colonel Sevier was made acting commander of Washington County militia forces.

On the twenty-first of September in 1780, Major Tipton paid a visit to the very ill Colonel Carter at his home. While Jonathan was there, a rider arrived with a letter for the colonel. The letter was from Colonel Isaac Shelby, who had taken his regiment to aid the Patriots in South Carolina. Colonel Carter asked Jonathan to read the letter aloud to him. The letter read:

Dear Colonel Carter,

This letter is to advise you of some unfortunate news, as well as some dastardly practices that the British and Tories have used. On the recent eighteen[th] day of September of this year a Patriot force under my colleague and friend, Colonel Elijah Clarke, was defeated in their attack on the British force at McKay's trading post in the north part of Georgia. A dozen of Colonel Clarke's men were captured when a British relief column attacked them from the rear. Two of these prisoners were promptly hanged, without any proper cause, of course. Even worse, the other ten were turned over to the Indians who were fighting with the British to be slaves for the Indians. One of these men escaped the next day and reported to Colonel Clarke that the Indians had killed and scalped three of the prisoner slaves who refused to walk fast enough for the Indians' liking while carrying heavy loads of goods, as ordered by the Indians.

As last known, these Indians were heading north by west toward the Indian country in the mountains. Our British, Tory, and Indian enemies are ruthless and treacherous. We must remain united in our efforts to defeat them.

I am presently camped near Musgrove's Mill in South Carolina. It is my pleasure to advise you that on August 18 my men soundly *defeated a considerable force of Tories and British regulars. They were posted at Musgrove's Mill, but we drew them out into an ambush.*

I remain your faithful friend,
Isaac Shelby, Colonel
18ᵗʰ of September 1780

Jonathan knew that Musgrove's Mill was west of the fort at Ninety Six, in the northwest part of South Carolina, not very distant from the mountains. The war had intensified in the South during 1780, and it was getting closer and closer to the mountains and Jonathan's home on the frontier.

Jonathan Tipton often thought about the war. He thought about the struggle for independence from the British crown. He wondered what the result would be if the Americans won. Would there actually be one nation, or would the actual outcome be thirteen individual, state nations? Jonathan remembered when, as a child in Virginia, he had heard a conversation between his uncle and his grandfather. His uncle had made some comment about resisting the king's taxation. Jonathan recalled his grandfather's response: "Such talk is blasphemous! Opposing the king's law is treason." Those had been the words of Jonathan's own grandfather. Jonathan thought about how different things were now. He certainly opposed "the king's law," far from the position of his own grandfather. *Things do change with time*, he thought.

Jonathan Tipton attended a meeting of all the militia officers of the county on September 22, 1780. "Colonel" John Sevier had called the meeting. Everyone called him colonel by then, even though he was actually still a lieutenant colonel. Jonathan did not find much resentment in that, however. He had become accustomed to the fact that Sevier outranked him. After all, Jonathan thought, Sevier was now acting as the full colonel for the county, due to the illness of Colonel Carter.

Arriving at Fort Watauga for the meeting, Major Tipton was surprised at the presence of Colonel Isaac Shelby. Shelby was the commander of the Sullivan County militia. Sullivan County had been formed just the year before from a part of northern Washington County and a part of Virginia that had been surveyed and found to be within North Carolina's boundary.

Colonel John Sevier opened the meeting. "I thank Colonel Shelby for being here today. We have a new challenge. British Major Ferguson has an army of more than a thousand men, mostly Tories, along with some British troops, just on the other side of the mountains. He sent a written message that Colonel Shelby received. Colonel Shelby held up the piece of paper on which the message was written for all to see. Colonel Shelby read the message to his officers in Sullivan County last week, and I am asking him to read it to you now. I know some of you have heard rumors about this. We are going to give you the actual facts." Turning toward Isaac Shelby, Sevier continued. "Colonel Shelby, please proceed."

"Major Ferguson has requested each and every one of us to sign an oath of loyalty to the British crown." A smattering of mumbling and groans was heard. "Our friend Colonel Charles McDowell from Burke County came here this week with 160 men and their homeless families. Ferguson's army of Tories and redcoats have burned their farms and stolen their livestock and would have killed every man among them had they not sought refuge here. They have come here asking us for help. They have felt firsthand the force of the message I am about to read you from Major Ferguson."

Colonel Shelby then continued. "Major Ferguson's message was delivered to me by one of my men who had been taken prisoner and was paroled for the purpose of delivering this message. That man is Samuel Phillips. He is standing here beside me. Phillips fought bravely against Ferguson's army before being wounded and captured, and I am glad to have him back safely."

Cheers rose from the group of militia officers.

Shelby continued, "Ferguson and his army have advanced to Gilbert Town, just on the other side of the mountains. The message is addressed to 'the militia officers of the western waters.' That is us. By 'the western waters' he means our rivers that flow westward and southwesterly from the mountains. The following are Major Ferguson's words to us: 'If you do not discontinue all your opposition to British authority and sign oaths of loyalty to His majesty, the king, I will bring my army over the mountains, hang your leaders, and destroy your homes, crops, and livestock with fire and force of arms.' The message is signed by Major Patrick Ferguson."

Angry voices among the officers revealed their discontent.

Chapter 4

Over the Mountains

At their recent meeting on Friday, September 22, Colonels Shelby and Sevier, along with Major Tipton and the other officers, had unanimously agreed to gather as many men as they could, and go over the mountains to strike Ferguson's army, to prevent him from carrying out his threats against them. A gathering of all available forces would be held at Sycamore Shoals on the Watauga River on the afternoon of Monday, September 25. They would march on the following morning. The men were to use horses to the extent possible, but men on foot were not to be excluded. The officers ensured the word was spread about Ferguson's threat and the necessity to assemble as many able men as possible on the twenty-fifth.

Colonel John Carter, having been ill since early September, would not be able to make the journey over the mountains. In fact, he had not even been able to attend the officers meeting on September 22, and Lieutenant Colonel Sevier had acted in Colonel Carter's place. On the twenty-fourth of September, Jonathan rode to Colonel Carter's home and requested that he not be placed under the command of Lieutenant Colonel John Sevier. Colonel Carter understood that Jonathan had always reported directly to Colonel Carter himself, and that despite the difference in rank of major to lieutenant colonel, Tipton had regularly been assigned patrols and command responsibilities equal to those of Sevier. John Carter also knew that if things had been different politically Jonathan Tipton would be equal in rank or superior in rank to John Sevier. He knew it would be a testy situation to have Tipton directly under Sevier's command. Because of his understanding, Colonel Carter agreed to Jonathan's request. He provided a letter for Jonathan to present to Colonel William Campbell, requesting that Jonathan's two companies be placed under Colonel Campbell's command. Colonel Carter also sent his son, Captain Landon Carter, bearing a note to John Sevier, advising him that Major Tipton's companies would operate independently until under the command of Colonel William Campbell, at which time any decisions would be at Colonel Campbell's discretion. Jonathan was highly satisfied with this. He had dreaded the thought of being under the supervision of John Sevier. At least he was clear for the over-mountain campaign, as he would be with Colonel Campbell. Jonathan expected that upon returning home, he and Sevier would return to normal militia service under Colonel Carter's command.

During the day on Monday, September 25, the forces of Lieutenant Colonel John Sevier, Colonel Isaac Shelby, and Colonel William Campbell assembled at Sycamore Shoals. On the afternoon of the twenty-fifth, the unexpected arrival of two hundred mounted troops under Colonel Arthur Campbell from Virginia boosted everyone's spirits. Colonel Arthur Campbell himself had to leave with ten of his men to return home to protect his home area from Indians, but the mountain men had gained 190 men, now totaling just over one thousand. In addition, the officers learned that Colonel William Campbell had sent a message to Colonel Cleveland of Wilkes County, North Carolina, requesting him to meet them at a place on the east side of the mountains on September 30, or as close to that day as possible, with all the troops he could raise.

All but 210 of the 1,000 men who assembled at Sycamore Shoals were mounted. Heartened by the sizeable force that had been assembled, Colonel McDowell and his 160 men went ahead that afternoon and departed over the mountains ahead of the main force. Their early departure was designed to get over the mountains to hasten the march of Colonel Cleveland and the men from Wilkes and Surry Counties, as well as to gain intelligence regarding Ferguson's movements.

Late in the afternoon, the men from all the regiments were summoned to assemble by the river at the shoals. Lieutenant Colonel John Sevier addressed the men. He described Ferguson's threat to invade the mountains to the assembled men, saying, "British Major Patrick Ferguson has already burned the homes and destroyed the crops of Colonel McDowell and his men. Colonel McDowell's men and their families have come to our side of the mountains seeking refuge and help. Major Ferguson has now sent us the threat that he will bring his army over the mountains and destroy our homes and crops and kill our livestock. You can be certain that he also intends to kill many of us."

Colonel Sevier, an inspirational speaker, continued, "Both Colonel Carter and I have met with the governor and with the legislature. Do you know what the British say about us living here, on the western side of the mountains? They have proclaimed that this is Indian land and we have no right to live here because of the British treaties with the Indians. The British insist that this area will be cleared of white settlers and returned to the Indians. If the British and Tories win the war, we will lose our land and our homes. We will have to move east to somewhere that the British say we can live. If you don't want the British telling you where you are allowed to live, we must defeat Ferguson's army. We must help our fellow Patriots on the eastern side of the mountains, those like John Pruett and Silas Sharp and their families, whose homes were burned by Ferguson's Tories and who have been driven over the mountains to take refuge with us. We have met here and have formed our own army. Tomorrow morning we shall march over the mountains and strike Ferguson before he is ready. We will drive him away from our doorsteps and from the lands of Colonel McDowell and his men."

At sunset on September 25, an officers' meeting was held at Sycamore Shoals. Colonel Carter attended although he was seriously ill. He arrived at the meeting by wagon, as he was unable to ride a horse. Just prior to the meeting, at the request of Colonel Carter, Jonathan Tipton was placed under Colonel William Campbell's command. This action followed Major Tipton's ardent plea to Colonel Carter that he not be placed under the direct command of his nemesis, Lieutenant Colonel John Sevier. After the officers meeting, Jonathan engaged in a friendly conversation with Captain Moses Shelby, the younger brother of Colonel Isaac Shelby. Jonathan was surprised when Moses advised him, "Both my brother and your Colonel Sevier have spent most of their personal wealth to provide supplies, powder, and shot for the expedition over the mountains." Jonathan thought about his feelings toward John Sevier. Despite personal misgivings, he had to admit to himself that John Sevier was indeed one of the most committed Patriots who could possibly exist.

Following the officers' meeting, Jonathan returned home for the night of September 25, knowing it would be the last night at his home for a matter of perhaps two weeks, or possibly even longer. He had allowed all of his men who lived close by and wished to return home for the night to do so, rather than remaining at the encampment at Sycamore Shoals, with the understanding that they would all return by daybreak. He would rise early in the morning to be with his men at daybreak, in order to depart with the army on the over-mountain campaign. Tom Callahan, his neighbor, was to come by Jonathan's cabin, and they would leave before daybreak for the short, twenty-minute ride to Sycamore Shoals.

Before sunrise on Tuesday, September 26, Jonathan embraced Frances warmly, as they were both huggers more so than kissers, and said simply, "Good-bye."

"I love you," she replied.

"Do not worry." Jonathan then turned to Tom Callahan. "Let's go." Jonathan mounted his horse, and he, Tom, and young Thomas Callahan, Jr., now eighteen years of age, rode toward Sycamore Shoals.

As Frances watched Jonathan ride away in the dim pre-dawn light, she knew that he had considered all the known facts and circumstances, and had decided he must act. She had known in her heart that it would not be possible to persuade him not to go, and she had not even tried to do so.

Right at daybreak, Major Jonathan Tipton arrived at the riverside location where his men were assembling. Upon arriving, Jonathan was greeted by a young man that he immediately recognized.

"Major Tipton, I have been assigned to your command," said James Sevier, none other than the son of Lieutenant Colonel John Sevier.

"By the authority of what officer?"

"By Colonel Carter, and also with the consent of my father." The young man's tone of voice was respectful.

Jonathan thought quickly. "Very well. See Captain Trimble. Tell him I have assigned you to his company under the lead of Lieutenant Talley. Then, take a place with the other men."

Jonathan retraced his thoughts. The thought immediately passed his mind that Lieutenant Colonel John Sevier had arranged placement of his son in Major Tipton's unit as reprisal for Jonathan having been removed from Lieutenant Colonel Sevier's command and being assigned to Colonel Campbell. Jonathan thought that young James was placed there by his father to spy on him and to report everything that went on in Jonathan's command, especially anything that might be construed as negative. Jonathan decided to place young James Sevier under William Trimble, who was his best Captain. Within Captain Trimble's company, James could also be under the close supervision of Lieutenant Talley. Yes, this would work.

Jonathan observed the mass of men and horses. This would be by far the largest force with which he had been involved.

The Reverend Samuel Doak had already delivered a strong and well-conceived prayer for the large assembly of militiamen. About fifteen minutes after the prayer, twenty more men from the southern settlements arrived. Upon hearing about the prayer they had missed, they asked Reverend Doak to say another prayer for them. He obliged. Inasmuch as this prayer was conducted right next to the location of Jonathan Tipton and his men, they knelt along with the latecomers. After all, thought Jonathan, at a time like this an extra prayer could do no harm.

About an hour after daybreak, Reverend Doak addressed the smaller group of men consisting of the twenty latecomers, Major Tipton's two companies of men, and several other men who gathered around. In a prayer that was very brief compared to the one delivered earlier to the main force, Reverend Doak said to the men, "You will be marching over the mountains and through forests and through farmlands to confront a dreadful enemy. The enemy has burned the homes and destroyed the crops of our friends. They have killed many of our fellow countrymen. Now they are threatening to bestow the same evil actions upon us. I beseech the Lord Almighty in His divine judgment to bless this army and provide these men with protection. I pray that He will enable us to defeat the evil enemy by the almighty power of God." He repeated emphatically, "By the almighty power of God! Amen."

Jonathan heard quite a few of the men repeat, "By the almighty power of God!" Then, he said aloud to nobody in particular, "By the almighty power of God."

On that morning the army departed from Sycamore Shoals. The over-mountain militiamen made good progress on the march. Traveling lightly, the typical man had only his rifle, powder, shot balls, a blanket, a cup, and a small pouch of provisions. The pouch of provisions in most cases consisted primarily of parched corn meal mixed with maple sugar, which made for easy and tasteful eating. There was not a single wagon to slow their progress. A few of the men strapped skillets to the load on their horses, and shared the skillets with others at times to heat their parched corn meals, to warm water, or to cook any meat they might kill and cut during their journey. The men made a march of something more than twenty miles on that day before stopping to camp for the night.

For the next several days, the small army continued in a southeasterly direction toward the North Carolina settlements. Thinking about home as he rode, Jonathan felt a persistent concern about the safety of his wife, his children, and their neighbors while so many of the men were away. The Indians were a true danger, and they far outnumbered the settlers even when all the men were at home. At least Colonel Carter was there. Even though he was very ill, he would know what actions to order to best defend the families of the men who were away. Thankfully, Major Robertson, who was very capable, had agreed to stay home, as well. The defensive force remaining at home under Colonel Carter and Major Robertson in Washington County was quite limited. It consisted of about forty men of the regular militia, including two whose wives were about to give birth, plus forty-five relatively old men who could not handle the physical rigors of the over-mountain campaign but could fight ably to defend their families, and quite a few youngsters aged thirteen to seventeen, who could also help defend the area.

As the men made their way slowly downhill on a rather wide part of a trail down the bald face of a small mountain, Captain James Gibson rode to the side of Major Tipton. Gibson inquired, "Jonathan, there are two Negroes with Colonel Campbell's Virginians. Did he bring his servants along?"

"No, James, those two men are slaves owned by Lieutenant Gilbert Locke, of Colonel Campbell's Virginia regiment. I met Locke yesterday. He said he offered the two black men their freedom if they would come along and fight against the Tories. He knows they are good shots, as they have provided many meals for his family. He knows they will fight because they helped him fight a band of Cherokees that attacked his farm. Locke is an amazing man. He owns several hundred acres of land, and is going to give each of them their own land and let them live there as free men. What astonishes me most is that he taught both of those Negroes to read."

"The slaves can read?"

"Yes," replied Jonathan, "the lieutenant said he taught them to read so they can read the Bible, and soon they are going to become free men, as well. Yesterday, I was with Lieutenant Colonel Sevier when one of them brought a message that Lieutenant Locke had sent him to deliver at the direction of Colonel Campbell. The Negro read the message from a piece of paper on which it was written. He had not memorized the message, but I saw him actually read it. I know there are some free Negroes in Maryland, but not many at all in Virginia. Because of what Mr. Locke told me, I think those two will be good soldiers on our side."

On Saturday, September 30, the over-mountain men reached Quaker Meadows, the home of both Colonel McDowell and Major McDowell. There they met up with Colonel Cleveland and Major Winston with 350 men, the additional strength in numbers bolstering the spirits and confidence of the militiamen. The force now numbered more than 1,350 men.

On Sunday, the army marched past Pilot Mountain and set camp at the gap between two small mountains. Colonel Charles McDowell was designated in a meeting with the other colonels to leave and seek out General Gates to request a commanding general for the army. The colonels had determined that Colonel McDowell should request that either General Morgan or General Rutherford be assigned to command their forces, and should be dispatched with all urgency. It was recognized that it would take Colonel McDowell several days to find and reach Gates' headquarters, and at least several more days for any appointed general to reach them. Major Joseph McDowell would take command of the regiment from Burke and Rutherford County until the return of Colonel McDowell.

Following the meeting of the colonels, Colonel Campbell advised Jonathan that another important decision had been reached. Principally because of the insistence of Isaac Shelby and John Sevier, the colonels had determined to hotly pursue Ferguson's army, and not to await the possible arrival of a general. Lieutenant Colonel Sevier, acting in charge of the Washington County regiment, was accepted by the other colonels as their equal in rank.

Because of miserably heavy, wind-driven rain on the second day of October, they remained camped at the gap, only about eighteen miles north of Gilbert Town. Just before sunset, the rain subsided. Some of Jonathan's men, having covered some relatively dry branches at the onset of the rain in the morning, were the first to get a campfire started. Then, using flaming branches from the first fire, they got a second fire started. Four men from Captain Colvill's Virginia company approached the Washington County men who surrounded the first campfire. One of the Virginians carried a large jug of some sort of homemade wine. "If you will share your fire with us, we will share our spirits with you," said the

Virginian. Tipton's men readily accepted the offer. The jug was passed around from man to man. Some drank straight from the jug, and others poured wine into their own cups. For quite a while that evening, the men sat and stood around the fire, reminiscing about their home lives and families, telling tales of fights with Indians, and having a generally good time.

On the following day, they made only a short march and encamped alongside a small creek. On Wednesday they reached the vicinity of Gilbert Town, and learned that Ferguson's army had retreated southward from that place. Jonathan and his men were still grouped with the Virginians under Colonel William Campbell. Colonel Campbell had been elected in a meeting of all the colonels to be in overall command until a general arrived. Jonathan knew that Colonel Sevier had objected to the continued assignment of Jonathan's men from Washington County, North Carolina, to report directly to Colonel Campbell. Colonel Campbell had reminded Lieutenant Colonel Sevier of Colonel Carter's request, and that Colonel Carter was the ranking officer of Washington County even though he had remained behind.

Because of experience in battles with the Indians, Jonathan was confident. He felt the confidence of the other officers and his own men that they would succeed. Some of them had fought battles in small groups of two or three men against two or three Indians. On the other extreme many of them had fought as members of forces of several hundred men against hundreds of Indians. Nevertheless, he could not help thinking that the large enemy force under Ferguson was composed of white men, many of whom had similar background and skills, and they would be well armed. One matter of concern was that according to Colonel McDowell and his men, most of Ferguson's men had bayonets.

On Thursday afternoon, intelligence was received that Ferguson had learned of their approach and that was why he had left Gilbert Town. Upon setting camp, an officers' meeting was held in the evening. The Patriot leaders summarized the makeup of their forces:

Colonel William Campbell, Virginia	390 men
Colonel Isaac Shelby, Sullivan County, NC	240 men
Colonel John Sevier, Washington County, NC	240 men
Major Joseph McDowell Burke & Rutherford Counties, NC	160 men
Colonel Benjamin Cleveland and Major Joseph Winston, Wilkes & Surry Counties, NC	350 men
Total	1,380 men

It was decided that they would select all men who had good horses to immediately pursue and overtake Ferguson. The men on foot or with weak horses would be under the command of Major Herndon and Captain William Neil of North Carolina, who were instructed to follow after the horsemen as fast as possible.

The decision to make haste in the pursuit of Ferguson's army seemed to Jonathan to be the correct approach. Many of the men were restless, having ridden and camped for well over a week, enduring the discomforts of weather and skimpy rations. They were anxious to find Ferguson's army, get the fighting done, and get back home.

Shortly after daybreak on October 6, 1780, Major Jonathan Tipton's two companies rode southward with the mounted force. Inasmuch as they had left 480 men behind because they were on foot or their horses were weak, the mounted militiamen pursuing Ferguson's army numbered nine hundred. They rode toward a place called the Cowpens, believing that Ferguson had headed in that direction. After traveling a short distance, they reached a cornfield and halted. The men pulled ears of corn, cut raw corn from the cobs to eat or ate it right from the cobs, and fed some of it to their horses.

During the break at the cornfield, Jonathan observed the colonels huddling in a brief meeting. Following the meeting, Colonel Campbell approached Major Tipton and said, "Major Tipton, I need to speak with you. Will you walk over this way with me?" He extended his hand in a direction that would be conducive to a private conversation.

"Jonathan, I have placed you under the command of Colonel Sevier. He has mentioned to me several times in recent days that his regiment needs additional strength, and that the logical thing to do is to place you and your men under his command. Colonel Sevier has been most persistent about this. I have decided that he is right. I have advised him that you will be second in command of his forces because that is what I believe Colonel Carter would want. When Colonel Carter first advised me that Lieutenant Colonel Sevier would be acting in his place and asked for you to report directly to me, he spoke highly of you. My decision is final. You need to get your men and move to the far end of the cornfield where Colonel Sevier's regiment is resting. In about ten minutes, when we resume the march, you will march with Colonel Sevier and the rest of the Washington County regiment."

Jonathan knew that Colonel Campbell's decision was the right one. After all, the men from Washington County should by all reasonable logic be serving together. He did not particularly like John Sevier on a personal basis. He still resented everyone calling Lieutenant Colonel Sevier "Colonel" and the fact that Lieutenant Colonel Sevier was acting as a full colonel on an equal footing with the other real colonels. He still thought things should be different. From Jonathan's perspective, if merit and not personal contacts and politics had determined their fates, Jonathan himself and not John Sevier would be the lieutenant colonel, and thus the present acting colonel. Nevertheless, Major Tipton knew that the strange mutual respect that he and Sevier shared for each other as reliable, courageous leaders would enable them to work together successfully.

Jonathan hastily gathered Captain Trimble, Captain Gibson, and Lieutenant Talley. "Tell your men we are leaving Colonel Campbell's regiment. We are going back to the Washington County regiment with Colonel Sevier and the rest of our neighbors and friends. Get the men mounted immediately. We have about five minutes to join the regiment." Most of the men knew or had learned during the march about the unusual peaceful animosity between Major Tipton and Colonel Sevier, and knew that was why Colonel Carter had ordered them to march with Colonel

Campbell's Virginia regiment. Jonathan knew the men would be happy to be reunited with the men from their home county.

Upon reaching the place called Cowpens in late afternoon, they met up with Colonel James Williams of South Carolina, with 340 men; and Colonel Hambright and Major Chronicle of Lincoln County, with 60 men. These officers and their men, all mounted, were also pursuing Major Ferguson's army. This increased the size of the Patriot force to about 1,300 men. Even more importantly, meeting and combining forces with such a large command that had the same objective bolstered the spirit and confidence of both the militia soldiers and the officers. At that point, Colonel Campbell learned from Colonel Hambright and Major Chronicle that Ferguson was located in a position about 25 to 30 miles toward the east from Cowpens.

Because of the urgency of catching up with Ferguson and his army, they began their march eastward about eight o'clock in the evening on Friday, October 6, and continued overnight into the morning of October 7. It rained heavily and steadily beginning early Saturday morning, and the rain continued until almost noon. The men did their utmost to keep their guns dry, wrapping them with whatever they could, including blankets, hunting shirts, and even their own coats, subjecting themselves to the rain and wind.

Just before noon, the wind shifted and the rain stopped, replaced by sunshine and a cool, dry breeze. About the same time, the column learned from a local man that Ferguson and his forces were only eight miles ahead. Shortly thereafter, scouts captured two Tories. Threatened with death, the two Tories confirmed that Ferguson was about eight miles ahead, on top of King's Mountain. Word passed quickly among the men. They were anxious to deal with and destroy Ferguson and the army of Tories.

Upon learning that Ferguson was located on King's Mountain, Major Chronicle advised Colonel Campbell that he and Captain Mattocks had hunted in the area a few months ago, and had even camped on top of King's Mountain and knew the area exceedingly well. Using this knowledge, the mounted force headed on a route that would take them eastward until they hit the road that ran in a southeast direction from North Carolina into South Carolina. Major Chronicle knew that was the best way to approach King's Mountain.

A brief halt was made and the officers met briefly, establishing a plan of attack. Then they returned to their men and shared the plan. It consisted of surrounding Ferguson's army. Based on Major Chronicle's knowledge of the hill, it was not a large mountain, but more of a big, rocky hill, and their force could surround it adequately for an attack. Colonel Campbell would lead a column to the right of the mountain; and Colonel Sevier would lead his and McDowell's regiments past Campbell's Virginians on the south side of the hill. Colonel Shelby would lead his men to the left and cover the northwestern part of the hill; and Colonel Cleveland would continue further to the east beyond Shelby's position to the left to complete coverage of the north and northeast faces of the hill. Colonel Campbell's and Sevier's columns would cover the south and southeast areas of the hill, except that Major Winston's battalion would thrust rapidly ahead of the main column on a more southerly course to secure an early arrival near the east end of the hill. Major Winston's thrust would help to ensure encirclement, and would thwart any attempt by Ferguson to retreat to the east. Colonel Sevier's men, along with Major McDowell's men, would assault the mountain in the area between Colonel Campbell's forces and Major Winston's battalion. Once all the forces were in place, Colonel Campbell would order his men to shout loud Indian war whoops and begin firing. Then, the general attack would commence with all men advancing upward to defeat the surrounded enemy.

As they returned to their men, Lieutenant Colonel Sevier addressed Major Tipton, Major McDowell, and Major Walton. "If anything happens to me, Major Tipton will take my place and be in charge of my forces. Be sure your officers and men know this." All the majors acknowledged the order.

"Fight like heroes, for that is just what you will be," Jonathan urged his men. "And remember that the power of almighty God is with you."

About that time, Colonel Campbell rode up. He looked directly at Jonathan's men, turning his head to scan each and every man, and said,

"If any of you want to avoid this fight and go home, do so now. Do not go into battle and then run. Don't give up ground to the Tories. We know that most of them have bayonets. If you must give up any ground, then rally and take it back. If any of you want to leave, go now." Not a man moved. "Good. I will stay here and fight them every minute of every day for as many days as it takes. I know you will be with me. Victory, freedom, and living or dying is what this is all about!" Colonel Campbell then rode at a fast pace toward another group of men toward the front of the column. Jonathan saw him stop there, and knew he was giving them the same speech, the same opportunity to leave now if they did not want to fight.

When they reached a point about three miles from the mountain early in the afternoon, orders were given and passed back through the column that no talking or shouting of commands would be allowed, in order that the force might approach as close as possible before being discovered.

Colonel Sevier's regiment was assigned with providing the advance scouts in front of the army. Major Tipton's command provided three of the eighteen advance scouts. Less than one mile from the mountain, Sergeant David Bragg and Private William Nelson surprised three of Ferguson's pickets and captured them without firing a shot. Upon threat of being shot, the three pickets confirmed that Ferguson and his army were still on the mountain. David Bragg had Nelson and one of the other scouts escort the captured Tory pickets back to the fast-approaching main body of troops. Bragg maintained his position, advancing only a short distance to a point where the mountain was in sight. He and the other scouts took positions in the woods, awaiting the imminent arrival of the rest of the army. When William Nelson arrived back at the main column, he advised Major Tipton and Captain Trimble, "Major, we found out something that might be interesting. We scared the captured Tories so bad that they told us about the appearance of Colonel Ferguson. They called him a colonel and not a major, but it is the same man, their leader. He is left handed, and always carries his sword in his left hand. He does not wear a regular British redcoat. He wears some sort of light-colored, checked hunting jacket."

Jonathan turned his head toward Captain Trimble. "Captain, spread the word among all our men about Colonel Ferguson's left-handed sword-carrying and him wearing a light-colored, checked jacket instead of a red coat. If it turns out to be true, one of our men might pick him off. I will advise Colonel Sevier."

The army of Patriot militiamen proceeded. Because of the trees along their route they could not see King's Mountain, but they knew it was close by.

Chapter 5

King's Mountain

SHORTLY AFTER TWO o'clock in the afternoon on October 7, 1780, Colonel Campbell gave the order, and Major Winston led his small force, riding at a fast pace, on the wide route they would take to block the far end of the mountain. If Ferguson decided to retreat, Winston's men would fight a delaying action that would enable the main body of the over-mountain army to catch up and attack Ferguson's army.

The main column arrived from the west at a location shielded by trees from direct view of the mountain. Here they halted, dismounted, and tied off their horses. They were less than two-thirds of a mile from the mountain and had not been discovered. Fourteen men were ordered to remain with the horses. Except for the officers, the men proceeded forward on foot.

Unlike some of the other officers, Jonathan Tipton elected not to remain on horseback, but to travel by foot with his men. Jonathan had

Private Benjamin Webb lead his horse alongside. That way, if he needed the mobility provided by a horse, it was available.

Jonathan summoned Elijah Bates to join Benjamin Webb at his side. "I want both of you to remain near me at all times during the battle in case I need to use either of you as a messenger."

They emerged from the woods and continued to the mountain. Just moments after they started to proceed along the right side of the mountain, Jonathan heard a volley of shots on the other side of the mountain. *The shots must be coming from the Tories,* he thought. *They are firing at Cleveland's men. Or are they firing at Shelby's men?* Immediately following the shots, the roll of drums resounded from the top of the mountain. He could see figures rushing to fill the defensive positions along the summit of the mountain, some of the figures clad in red, some in white, and some in buckskin. Jonathan thought quickly that this mountain was more like a fairly large hill that was somewhat rocky in places.

The next four minutes until reaching the assigned position on the south side of King's Mountain seemed like an hour, as scattered shots were fired by the Tories atop the mountain. None of Jonathan's men were killed or wounded by the scattered firing. Jonathan was thankful, as he knew that some of the Tories were excellent marksmen, even at the present range. He could see the red coats of the Provincials and the simple attire of the other Tories along the ridge of the mountain. He knew from meetings with the other officers that the Tories, especially the five or six companies of Provincials, were all well-drilled in bayonet charges. Such charges were among the worst fears of the militia.

Reaching the designated position, Major Tipton deployed his men in a rough line along the base of the mountain, behind the cover of rocks and trees. The rest of John Sevier's men were to his right, with Major McDowell's men yet further on the right; and Colonel Campbell's Virginians were on Tipton's left. The still irregular shots from the Tories became more frequent. At this point, Jonathan grabbed the attention of the two men nearest him, Elijah Bates and Benjamin Webb, who had just tied Jonathan's horse to a nearby tree. "Elijah, Benjamin, kneel down here for a second. I've just got to say a quick prayer." All three men knelt.

"Lord, be with us in this battle, just as you have been in our battles with the Indians. If it be thy will, please keep us safe and lead us to victory. Amen." The men took their positions, ready to advance and fire.

At that exact time, Jonathan saw a company of the mountain men on horseback charging uphill ahead of him. He knew that it was Major Lewis of Virginia attacking a Provincial strongpoint at a key position on the mountain, as had been planned. Major Lewis's attack followed a gradual grade that had been described by Major McDowell, but Lewis and his men were exposed to a furious fire from the Tories. Nevertheless, the attack succeeded and the redcoats retreated from the strongpoint. Then, according to plan, Major Lewis and his men retreated to dismount and join the attack on foot. Four horses fell during the attack, struck by balls fired by the Tories. Only one of those four horses arose and made it back down the hill. At least one rider remained down. Having seen the rider struck by a bullet, falling uncontrollably from his mount, Jonathan believed the downed rider was dead. A fleeting thought came to him that this was the first death he had observed that day, but how many more would he yet see?

Then, from the opposite side of the mountain, a barrage of gunfire erupted. *It must be Shelby's men and the Tories,* thought Jonathan.

At almost the same time, Campbell's Virginians opened fire immediately to his left. Almost all of the Virginians yelled Indian war whoops as they began to advance uphill. Although it was obvious from the sounds that the attack had already started on the opposite side of the mountain, the Virginians' use of war whoops was the signal for the overall attack to begin.

As Jonathan advanced slowly uphill with his men, he saw John Sevier to his right. Sevier, now dismounted, bravely strode forward, not with a sword in hand, but a rifle instead, encouraging all his men to advance. Jonathan and his men, along with all of Lieutenant Colonel Sevier's and Major McDowell's men, unleashed a deafening barrage of shots. Return fire from the Tories resounded from the ridge above. Then, as both sides reloaded and continued firing, the mountain men advanced uphill, seeking the shelter of rocks and trees about two hundred feet forward of their prior position. The smoke and smell of gunfire mixed with the noise of the fierce battle. This attack was not a suicidal, standing rush forward, but was instead a determined advance from one somewhat protected position and then forward to another.

The sounds of gunfire and men shouting were all-encompassing as the frontiersmen steadily made progress up the mountain, taking advantage of the natural cover provided by rocks and trees. Jonathan thought it was remarkable that the crest of the mountain had little cover, and yet had been chosen by Ferguson as a defensive position.

While reloading, Jonathan observed young Tom Callahan about fifteen feet to his left at this point in the battle. Callahan noticed rifle or musket fire coming from behind a large, roughly triangular rock some sixty yards in front of his position. He took aim and fired there when the Tory peeked up to fire a shot of his own. A minute or so later, the Tory peeked up to fire again, and Tom fired a second time. Jonathan could not tell for sure if Callahan hit the Tory, but the firing from behind that rock ceased.

The battle increased in fury. Young Private Martin McGahey knelt just to Jonathan's right, reloading his rifle as rapidly as humanly possible. McGahey thrust the ramrod down the barrel and suddenly keeled over sideways, blood spurting from his neck, having been mortally wounded by a musket ball. Benjamin Webb crawled quickly to the aid of McGahey, and pressed a wadded bandana against his neck. Then, seeing immediately that there was no hope of saving McGahey, Private Webb resumed firing at the Tories. Amidst the smoke and noise, Jonathan could see red-coated Provincials reinforcing the already strong Tory position in front of his own position and in front of Campbell's Virginians.

The Tories and Provincials fired a volley in unison. Suddenly the enemy advanced along a broad front with fixed bayonets. Coming downhill in front of Campbell's Virginians and the left third of Sevier's regiment was a wall of red-coated Provincials and plain clothed Tories, almost all of them brandishing bayonets. Major Tipton's two companies on the left end of Sevier's line and Major Walton's companies in the left part of the line were facing a full frontal bayonet attack. The Tories advanced despite a veritable shower of fire poured into them. Much of the terrain was not favorable for an effective bayonet attack. There were large rocks and trees around which the bayonet-wielding Tories had to maneuver. As the Tories bunched up going around rocks and trees, the excellent marksmanship of the mountain men took a heavy toll on them.

When the Tories reached the line of Colonel Campbell's and Sevier's men, Major Tipton's two companies stood firm, reloading and firing repeatedly. At several points men engaged in hand-to-hand combat with rifles, hatchets, and long knives against muskets and bayonets. The two companies under Major Walton, just to Tipton's right, gave way and retreated before the intimidating mass of bayonets. Despite the urging of Major Walton to hold their ground, his men scrambled a distance of over four hundred feet downhill. On the left, however, Jonathan Tipton's companies under Captains Trimble and Gibson continued to stand firm, their tenacious fire forcing the Tory bayonet advance to a halt along their front. The thinned line of bayonets was not nearly as terrifying as the massed bayonet line had originally appeared to the mountain men. A few of the bayonet-wielding Tories reached Tipton's line to create hand-to-hand fighting, but enough of the Patriots reloaded quickly enough to pour another round of deadly fire into the Tory ranks.

As Jonathan reloaded, he saw Private John Price about twenty feet to his left. One of the Tories reached that place as Price was reloading and made a forceful thrust at Price with his bayonet. At the same moment that the bayonet penetrated into his abdomen, John Price pulled his trigger, firing a shot point blank into the left shoulder of the attacker. The Tory reeled backward momentarily, and then made a second thrust of his musket using his right arm, fatally driving the bayonet into the chest of John Price. The Tory, bleeding profusely from his left shoulder, turned around and made his way uphill, keeping as low to the ground as possible due to the furious hail of shots, as he retreated toward the top of the hill.

Just to his right rear side, Jonathan saw Captain Jesse Beene, of Major Walton's troops, trying to reload as he retreated. Beene stumbled and fell, dropping his rifle. Quickly getting to his feet to retrieve his rifle, he grabbed it by the barrel. Finding himself facing the business end of a Tory bayonet, he swung his rifle at the Tory, knocking the Tory's rifle out of his grasp. A second swing of the rifle smashed into the Tory's left knee, but shattered Captain Beene's rifle, separating the barrel from the stock. Both men drew their long knives and were in hand-to-hand combat in a standing position. Suddenly, the Tory reeled as a ball passed through his temple, killing him instantly. Almost simultaneously, Captain Beene fell awkwardly to the ground as a ball shattered his left knee. Beene, though writhing in pain, regained his composure as the Tories charged downhill past his position in pursuit of the rest of Major Walton's troops. Beene crawled about five feet and picked up the musket, powder, and pouch of balls that had belonged to the dead Tory. Unable to walk, he positioned himself behind a rock, reloaded the rifle, and began firing at the Tories. Captain Beene was in an isolated position, as the rest of Major Walton's men had retreated, and the Tories had passed Beene and were now downhill behind his position. Suddenly, without an order being given, Private Adam Sherrill of Captain Gibson's company bravely ran forty yards to Captain Beene's position and assisted him to the position held by Major Tipton's companies.

The Tories were now right upon Major Tipton's men, all along their front. Something struck the stock of Jonathan's rifle and almost knocked it out of his hands. *It must have been a ball*, he thought. At least it hit his rifle and not his body. He glanced quickly at the partly splintered stock and then speedily raised the rifle to his shoulder. He fired at a Tory who was now only fifteen feet away, charging directly at him with bayonet ready. The ball struck the Tory in his right arm, causing him to drop his musket and fall down right in front of Jonathan. Jonathan Tipton quickly grabbed his long knife and thrust it into the Tory's chest.

The enemy along the front of Major Tipton's two companies of men began to retreat uphill toward their original defenses. Major Tipton's men took careful aim at the retreating Tories and fired, striking several of the enemy and ensuring that the retreat continued. Then, with Captain Trimble's company holding the front, Major Tipton had Captain Gibson's company form at a right angle to the front line and fire downhill at the flank and rear of the Tories who were confronting Major Walton's men. Gibson's company reloaded and continued to fire into the Tory line, many of the Tories falling. When Walton's men had fallen back, they and the rest of Colonel Sevier's men had taken cover among rocks near the base of the mountain and had resumed firing at the Tories, as well. Their flight was not in pure fear. It was intended to avoid direct contact with the bayonet charge, but also to give them time to reload. The Tories, now taking fire from their front and their right flank, began to retreat uphill, but not directly back uphill, as they sought to avoid the heavy fire coming from Tipton's men.

Lieutenant Colonel Sevier alertly perceived that the Tory bayonet charge was being torn apart by Tipton's well-directed fire from their flank. John Sevier courageously rallied Major Walton's men, halting them behind cover at the base of the mountain where they began to reload, resume firing, and eventually pursue the Tories back up the mountain. These men would fight. They would not run. Tipton's stand and flanking attack enabled the rest of Sevier's troops to rally. Now Sevier took to the front of his men and led a counter charge up the mountain. The Tories retreated to their original line along the crest of the hill, took cover, and resumed firing; but the mountain men were close upon them.

The rest of Sevier's regiment reached the point where Tipton's men held firm. Then, Tipton's men joined the advance, now attacking uphill.

To the left, Colonel Campbell's larger force of Virginians had initially held their ground beside Jonathan's two companies, and had then fallen back slowly. The Virginians were now pushing back up the hill against the Tories.

The Tories and redcoated Provincials on the left had massed again in front of the Virginians and were commencing a second bayonet charge, but this time just in front of the Virginians, and not in front of Tipton's men. All of a sudden Jonathan could see Campbell's Virginians falling back again, retreating from the bayonet-wielding Provincials and Tories.

The Tories, advancing downhill, were soon to the back left and downhill from Jonathan's men. Jonathan sprinted fifteen yards to his left to Captain Trimble, whose men had halted their own advance and were firing from behind trees and large rocks. "William, get as many of your men as you can to turn around and fire into the back of the Tories on the left! They are forcing the Virginians downhill." The two officers both ran from man to man in Trimble's company, directing them to form a line along the left flank, and soon they delivered fire into the Tories' flank. Seven Tories fell. Then, another volley, and four or five more fell. Some of the Tories, seeing nobody standing in close proximity either on their right or their left, began scrambling back up the hillside. Then, the entire enemy line began a rapid but orderly retreat. Colonel Campbell's Virginians had first taken cover, and now they rallied and pursued the fleeing foe.

Tipton's men turned back toward the crest, catching up with the rest of Sevier's men, taking cover, firing, and moving further uphill. Jonathan could see John Sevier ahead, right at the front of his men, leading with bravery and gallantry. Lieutenant Colonel Sevier was the first of his regiment to reach the crest of the hill.

The Tories who were retreating uphill in front of Campbell's Virginians did not stop at their original line of defense, but fled toward the northeast, along the ridge line, toward the Tories' main encampment at the northeast end of the mountain. Jonathan was close enough to the ridge now to see Tories fleeing in the same direction from the other side of the ridge. He knew that Colonel Shelby's men were forcing those Tories to retreat. In this area at least, the battle was being won. Jonathan and his men continued to surge forward, as did the rest of John Sevier's men and Colonel William Campbell's men. Then, Colonel Shelby's men joined them from the other side of the mountain in driving the Tories toward the northeast end of the mountain. Still, the thunder of hundreds of rifles and muskets continued. The sound of shouts by men of both sides combined with smoke and gunfire in a din of fast-paced pandemonium.

When the enemy reached the place where their wagons and tents were located, they stopped and began reloading and firing, trying desperately to hold their ground. The Tories had lost control of most of the battleground, and were now limited to the northeast end of the mountain. An incessant roar of shots continued from both sides. Within a few minutes, the onslaught of the Patriots forced the Tories from that position.

Jonathan and his men advanced more rapidly now, along with the massed Patriot forces, forcing the Tories and Provincials into further retreat. Ferguson's forces were now being forced into a smaller and smaller defensive position. With the ebb and flow of battle, accompanied by smoke and confusion, the Patriot forces were not positioned in any manner similar to their original configuration of surrounding the mountain. Instead, they filled any gaps in the attacking force and approached from whatever position they found advantageous. In many cases, men who had been in the same unit were separated and intermingled with men from other commands, but they were all an integral part of the effective attack.

About forty yards to his right, Jonathan saw five mounted redcoats riding briskly downhill, trying to make an escape through the lines. Despite the smoke, he could tell that several of the riders were officers. They had not proceeded far downhill before two of the men fell from their horses, having been hit by a barrage of fire from the Patriots. One horse fell, and the redcoat who had been riding it began running back uphill toward the Tory lines, but he fell to one or more shots, as well. Two officers succeeded in making the ride back uphill to the Tory lines. One of the men who had been shot and had fallen was being dragged around by his horse, as his foot was caught in a stirrup. The horse was dragging the officer directly toward Jonathan's position, and Private John Taylor was able to stop and secure the horse. As Jonathan walked over to the horse, he watched John Taylor free the officer's foot from the stirrup. He could now see that the officer who had been dragged was dead, riddled with shots. Jonathan also saw the unique coat that had been described by the Tories captured earlier in the day. The dead officer was none other than Major Patrick Ferguson. Loud cheers went up from Jonathan's men, and then from all of Sevier's men who were nearby.

Cheers did little to delay their further attack on the Tories, however. The Tories, who were now bunched up in a small mass and completely surrounded, were desperately delivering defensive firing as quickly as they could reload. More and more Tories fell wounded and dead, however, due to the avalanche of fire directed at them from all directions by the surrounding Americans. The distance between the Americans and the Tories was now only forty yards. Jonathan saw a white handkerchief appear briefly atop the bayonet of one redcoat, but it was immediately knocked down by a British officer. Captain Gibson, who was firing from behind a large rock right next to Jonathan, said loudly, "Major, we've got them. They can either surrender or we will kill them all." The firing continued full bore on both sides. Then, two white handkerchiefs, three, and then four white handkerchiefs became visible among the Tories through the smoke of the battle.

Some of the Patriot militiamen, not knowing that the white flag was a symbol of surrender, continued firing. Jonathan yelled, "Stop firing. Stop firing." He saw Lieutenant Talley put his hand on top of John Taylor's rifle just as Taylor was taking aim, halting Taylor from firing another shot.

The firing diminished somewhat as the number of white handkerchiefs and cloths increased to ten or eleven. Some of the Tories shouted, "Quarters, quarters, quarters," the term for surrendering to receive no further hostility, but a few Tories were still firing, and all of the Tories were still holding their guns, refusing to throw them down.

Sergeant David Bragg and Private Adam Sherrill, along with Smith Ferrell began to yell, "Drop your rifles if you want to surrender." Jonathan sensed the mistrust of his men toward the Tories.

At least a dozen of Major McDowell's men were now intermingled with Major Tipton's men, and several of them continued firing. Jonathan shouted again, "Stop firing," to which several of McDowell's men responded by yelling, "Give them Buford's quarter," referring to the British massacre of defenseless Patriots after their surrender several months earlier at a place called Waxhaws.

Striding over to one of these men, Jonathan placed his hand on the man's shoulder as he leveled his rifle to aim, and said, "We will not massacre them. We will take them prisoner." Upon that action, the men in the immediate proximity stopped firing, and held their loaded rifles at the level, aimed at the Tories, as many of the Tories had still not dropped their muskets or rifles. Firing dwindled on both sides, and within another two minutes ceased. Amid the smoke and the groans of the wounded, voices of Patriot officers and men continued to call out, demanding the Tories to throw down their rifles. Being totally surrounded and in a hopeless situation, the Tories finally complied. All the shooting had stopped.

Colonel Shelby rode his horse to the front of the line of Tories and shouted, "Sit down. All of you sit down right where you are." When they complied, Shelby shouted, "Officers only, stand and march to the south end." He pointed with his pistol toward the south. The officers stood and walked as directed, forming a group separate from the other Tories.

As soon as the officers had been separated, the mass of Tories other than officers were ordered to stand and walk about 150 feet to the southeast, and then sit down again. They were thus separated from their guns, which had been laid down at the place where they had first been captured and ordered to sit down. As the disarmed Tories were seated, Captain James Gibson shouted at the top of his voice, "Three hurrahs for freedom!" Then, in amazing unison, the refrain came from the victorious Americans, "Hurrah, hurrah, hurrah!" reverberating on the mountain and through the woods.

When the battle was over, Jonathan took notice of the wagons circled on the northeast end of the top of the mountain. He also noticed the tents of the Tory encampment, some now torn down, but all spaced neatly in the area where the wagons were located. He thought it strange from what he had read and heard about war that with so many wagons and so much baggage the Tories did not have a single artillery piece. It was also fortunate for the Patriots, as even three or four field pieces might have turned the tide of the battle.

About twenty minutes after the prisoners had been secured, Jonathan saw Lieutenant Colonel John Sevier approaching on foot. He carried two swords, with scabbards, that had been taken from royalist officers. "Jonathan, you will have more use for this than our prisoners will," said Sevier, handing him a sword and scabbard. Jonathan thought about this action by Sevier. *Sevier must think he is being magnanimous. No, he actually appreciates what my men did in the battle today. He might even appreciate me.*

"Thanks, Colonel," Jonathan replied. With so many soldiers around, he addressed Sevier by his commonly called rank, rather than by his first name, as he would have done in private, and rather than by his actual rank of lieutenant colonel.

Now that the battle was over, Tom Callahan walked back to the triangular rock to see if in fact he had killed the Tory at that site. To his horror, Tom discovered his dead cousin, Jake Callahan from Burke County, who had chosen to side with the Tories. A bullet had passed through the right side of his forehead. Tom was saddened to the point that he cried, tears dripping from both eyes, running down his cheeks. Not even his own father, who was also serving in Major Tipton's command, could console him throughout the remainder of the afternoon and that night.

The battle had lasted just over an hour, but the groans of the wounded continued into the darkness of night, and throughout the night. A British surgeon who had been captured among the Tories worked frantically to attend to the wounded. There were far too many wounded men on both sides to be cared for by one doctor. At first, he was directed by Patriot officers to the location of men to whom they wanted him to attend. Then, after about an hour, the doctor was directed to a level spot of ground beside a creek, and captured Tories were forced to carry the wounded to that site.

The Patriots, having secured the prisoners before darkness fell, camped on the battleground that night. Guards were set in two-hour shifts over the prisoners. Sentries were posted outside the perimeter of the encampment, as well, in order to detect any approach of British or Tory forces that might be attempting to reach Ferguson's army and attack the Patriots.

The groans of the wounded and dying men made the scene distressing. Some men who were not on guard took care of the Patriots who were wounded as best they could. The British doctor was continually enrolled in that care, as well, and tended to wounded men of both sides, though he was made to give priority to the injured among the Americans. Many of the wounded prisoners cried repeatedly during the night for water.

Some few of the guards obliged, but many prisoners went without water for long periods of time.

Captain William Trimble approached Major Tipton. Trimble said, "I have been down by the creek where the surgeon is working, and learned that Colonel Williams of South Carolina had been gravely wounded. He received one musket ball high between the shoulders and another low in the groin. They don't think he is going to remain alive."

At the end of the battle, Jonathan was as physically exhausted as his men were. They had not rested because of marching overnight in pursuit of Ferguson's army on the night before the battle. They had little or nothing to eat overnight and all day on the day of the battle. The furious battle had sapped them of energy.

Colonel Campbell ordered Captain Colvill of his Virginia regiment to oversee a count of killed and wounded on both sides. Captain Colvill in turn assigned Lieutenant Locke and several of his men to count the dead and wounded Americans and asked his friend Captain James Elliott and his company to count the dead and wounded among the British and Tories. Colonel Campbell ordered Lieutenant Samuel Newell to get a count of the prisoners.

At sunset, Jonathan was standing with Colonels Campbell, Sevier, and Shelby, just outside a captured tent that had been Major Ferguson's head-quarters. Colonel Campbell was now using it as his own headquarters. Lieutenant Newell approached and looked at Colonel Campbell. "Sir, we counted 729 prisoners. That includes nineteen officers and very many wounded prisoners. Some of them are badly wounded and are likely to die soon."

Then, in the dim remnants of light from the setting sun, Lieutenant Locke, Captain Colvill, and Captain Elliott approached. Captain Colvill spoke, "Colonel Campbell, we have a pretty accurate account of our own losses, but with all the activity in moving the wounded men down by the creek where the British surgeon is located, we cannot be sure the count is accurate. It is the same with the British and Tories, and I fear that many of the wounded on both sides may die. Our count for now is that our side has lost twenty-five dead so far, with sixty-five more wounded. We are making a written list of the names of the dead, sir. Major Chronicle, Captain Mattocks, Captain Robert Sevier, and Major William Edmondson have passed away. Colonel Williams is very badly wounded. We will be able to complete the list in the morning, sir, and the number of dead may increase even after that."

"I am most regretful about our losses," responded Colonel Campbell. "How about the Tories and British?"

"Captain Elliott and his men had a very difficult time with their count, with bodies being on all parts of the mountain, and with the wounded being moved." Reading from a small piece of paper, Captain Colvill continued. "The Tories and British have at least 190 killed. Nine of them were officers. Their wounded are about 160 to 175. When daybreak comes, we can get a better count."

Major Tipton and his men were part of the guard and sentry force from eight o'clock to ten o'clock that evening. Immediately after the guard was relieved at ten o'clock, Jonathan settled down with his small blanket on the ground inside one of the captured enemy tents and got some badly needed sleep.

On Sunday, the morning after the battle, the victorious but still weary Patriot militiamen set about burying the dead as quickly as possible. Colonels Campbell and Shelby were very insistent that it was important to get underway on the march toward the home counties of most of the men of the American forces. Their present position at King's Mountain was between the large army of British General Cornwallis at Charlotte Town and the British fort and garrison at Ninety-Six, in South Carolina.

Except for Major Ferguson, who was buried in a separate grave, most of the Tories and British were buried in two shallow mass graves. One grave was for the red-coated British Provincials, who were Tories that had been trained and uniformed as British soldiers, and one grave was for the non-uniformed Tories. Some of the Tory dead were buried quickly in shallow individual graves at the sites where they had fallen, and were only lightly covered by dirt and leaves.

Captain Andrew Colvill and his men had been working feverishly since sunrise to make accurate counts of the dead and wounded. Jonathan

Tipton and Colonel Sevier were meeting with Colonel Campbell and ten other officers in preparation for departure when Captain Colvill arrived and handed Colonel Campbell a written summary of the counts of those killed, wounded, and taken prisoner. Captain Colvill had written part of the report in all capital letters and part in lowercase letters.

- COUNT OF LOSSES AND PRISONERS AS BEST ASCERTAINED ON THE MORNING OF 8 OCTOBER, 1780

- AMERICANS KILLED: 26, including 9 officers

- AMERICANS WOUNDED: 64, including 7 officers

- TORIES AND BRITISH KILLED: 206, including 10 officers

- TORIES AND BRITISH WOUNDED: 169, badly enough wounded to be unable to march

- TORIES AND BRITISH PRISONERS: 722, including 19 officers, but only 553 prisoners are able to march.

- TOTAL ENEMY LOSSES THAT WE CAN COUNT: 928

Captain Colvill had not signed the note, inasmuch as he viewed it informally, just as Colonel Campbell did. It was quite simply the best that could be accomplished under given circumstances and under the pressure to march within an hour.

Colonel Campbell read the summary aloud for the benefit of the other officers who were present. As soon as Colonel Campbell finished reading the note, Captain Colvill spoke, "Sir, I am informed that despite the efforts of the guards some prisoners were able to sneak away in the darkness last night and escape. I do not know how many, nor can we determine which regiment was on guard when they escaped. I can only give you the count we have made this morning."

"Captain Colvill, your diligence and that of your men in this unpleasant task is genuinely appreciated," said Colonel Campbell.

"Colonel Sevier, Colonel Campbell," interrupted Major Jesse Walton as he arrived, "We have made the required accounting for captured guns and supplies. We have seventeen baggage wagons. We will use some of them to carry our wounded men who cannot walk or ride their horses, as Colonel Sevier suggested. We captured 1,110 rifles and muskets and ninety-six pistols. Sir, my men found it interesting when counting the rifles, muskets, and pistols that almost all of them were fully loaded and primed. But there were ninety-six brand new muskets in crates on one of the baggage wagons that have never been used at all. The Tories and British had very little in the way of food, and the little they had we ate last night. They have been foraging just like we have. There were two crates of red uniform coats. We burned the coats in a campfire last night. The good thing is that we did get nine small barrels of powder and several thousand musket balls. That's about it, sir."

Colonel Shelby inquired, "How many horses did we capture?"

"Oh, I forgot," replied Major Walton. "We captured 120 horses, mostly in good condition."

Perhaps, thought Jonathan, the mistrust his men had demonstrated toward the Tories was justified. Almost all the Tory muskets and rifles had been loaded at the time of the surrender. If, near the end, the Patriots had dropped their guard and had become inattentive while the Tories were surrounded, the battle may have been resumed in favor of the Tories. It was good to have kept aim on them until they dropped their guns.

Within half an hour after daybreak, women and children from nearby Tory families had begun to arrive. About a dozen of the wounded prisoners that were left behind on the battlefield were considered able enough to help in attending to other wounded prisoners, although they had their own foot or leg wounds that prevented them from walking any long distance. The sentiment among the Patriots was to leave the wounded Tories and let them and their sympathizers take care of themselves. That is just what was done. Thus, 553 prisoners were forced to march under guard with the American force the next morning, and the wounded Tories were left behind.

On the day after the battle, the army marched about fifteen to sixteen miles, with the prisoners under guard, to a large deserted plantation that had been owned by a Tory. The day's long march had been intended to put some distance between the Patriots and General Cornwallis, in case all or part of his British army might be approaching King's Mountain and decide to pursue them. At the plantation they met up with the footmen that had been left behind two days earlier. These men who had been left behind were not nearly as tired or hungry as the men who had been in the battle. The footmen aided greatly in guarding the prisoners. The army camped there for the night, where there was a sweet potato patch so large that it supplied every man in the militia. Sweet potatoes were even given to most of the prisoners.

Jonathan thought about the great victory they had achieved. He enjoyed the genuine satisfaction and high spirits of his tired men. The men realized that they had killed or captured almost the entire army that had been led by Patrick Ferguson, along with all their weapons and supplies. The threat of Ferguson's army coming over the mountains and destroying their homes and crops and killing their livestock had been completely removed.

Just after sunset, an officers' meeting was convened, consisting of all officers of the rank of major and higher. The attending officers were present and had been talking in small groups for several minutes when Colonel Campbell urged, "Let's get this meeting going."

Colonel Shelby spoke up. "We need to devise a plan to determine whether or not the British, either Cornwallis's whole army or a mounted force under Colonel Tarleton, are pursuing us. Has anyone given this any thought?"

Jonathan Tipton had been thinking about just this subject, and replied immediately. "I recommend that tomorrow morning at daybreak we send four two-man parties of scouts to our rear and to the east, riding toward each of the possible directions by which General Cornwallis or Colonel

Tarleton might pursue our army. We will handpick our best scouts. The scouts will be told to ride until late afternoon, covering as great a distance as possible, unless they detect a pursuing force before then. Meanwhile, we can march just a short distance tomorrow. The local people who are friendly to our cause say that a large creek is only three miles to the northwest. The locals say there are still cattle on two of the Tory farms nearby that can provide at least some meat for the men. We can cross the creek in the morning and halt on the other side in the best defensive position we can find. By marching such a short distance, our men will be able to get some much-needed rest. Equally importantly, the short march will allow all of the scouts to return and reach our new camp before midnight tomorrow night with news regarding whether or not the British are pursuing us, and if so the approximate size of the British force." Jonathan continued, "With that knowledge, colonels Campbell, Sevier, Shelby, and Cleveland will be able to determine whether we should remain and fight the British force, or whether we should evade them."

Major Tipton knew that he had spoken quickly, without giving the colonels who were present any opportunity to reply to Colonel Shelby's inquiry. He was somewhat surprised when John Sevier stood and said, "I favor that recommendation. Major Tipton has a sound plan." Colonels Shelby and Cleveland then spoke in support of the plan. Colonels Lacey and Hill, who had lesser roles because of their smaller numbers of men and several majors from the various militia units likewise indicated their consent.

Next, Colonel Campbell addressed the subject of guarding the prisoners. "I have discussed with Colonels Shelby, Sevier, Lacey, and Cleveland just how we should handle guarding the prisoners. We will assign groups of two hundred men to take turns guarding the prisoners during the day, as well as in two-hour shifts during the night. That way, all of our men will be able to get some sleep. Five different two hundred-man groups of guards will be assigned, one group from each of the principal commanders—Colonel Campbell, Colonel Shelby, Colonel Sevier, and Colonel Cleveland—and a fifth group composed from the ranks of Colonel Lacey and Majors Winston and McDowell. Are there any questions?"

"Not a question, just a statement to clear things up," said Colonel Cleveland. "During the day while we are marching, we will use our normal advance scouts, and an assigned two hundred-man group will be dedicated to guarding the prisoners. During the night, 150 men will guard the prisoners, and the remaining fifty men will be the sentries posted surrounding our camp, as usual."

Then, the officers considered recommendations they had received from their men regarding paroling ninety-two Tory prisoners who were either relatives of some of the Patriot soldiers, or were known to them as neighbors and believed to be honorable if they signed for parole conditions. The officers approved, and all ninety-two Tories were offered paroles under the condition that they would never again raise arms against Patriot forces nor commit any theft or hostile act against Patriot sympathizers. A stock of high quality writing paper that had been captured as part of the British baggage proved useful for the purpose of the written paroles. All ninety-two were paroled, and were released within three hours. They walked away unarmed into the darkness to return home. The paroling of these men, along with the escape of sixteen prisoners earlier in the day, reduced the number of prisoners to 445.

On Monday, they made a short march as planned, moving the prisoners almost three miles to the creek, which turned out to be almost thirty feet wide and one to two feet deep. They forded it and camped on the opposite bank of the creek. Sentries were posted in greater numbers than usual, some mounted and at a greater distance than usual from the encampment.

Late in the afternoon, Jonathan Tipton sat on a large rock beside the slowly flowing creek. He was just far enough away from the main body of the army that he could experience the relative silence and tranquility of the place. The occasional cry of a hawk circling overhead reminded him of home. He found it hard to believe that there was war, killing, and destruction in this very land. When at home on the far side of the mountains, Jonathan and the militia had to patrol and react because of threats from Indians. On this side of the mountains the militia had to patrol because of danger from the British and Tories. Jonathan thought that after the great Patriot victory at King's Mountain the Tories would no longer be such a big threat to the American sympathizers in the counties on this side of the mountains. The militia in Burke, Rutherford, Wilkes, Surry, and Lincoln Counties should fare well in protecting their homes, families, crops, and livestock from the Tories. Nevertheless, the large British army under General Cornwallis was still in North Carolina, in Charlotte Town the last anyone had known. Jonathan thought that the Tory army under Ferguson had been beaten so badly that perhaps even the British might hold some fear of the great army of men that had come over the mountains. On the frontier on the other side of the mountains, where Jonathan and his men resided, the Indians would remain a serious threat.

Jonathan thought about young James Sevier, having been placed in Jonathan's command before coming over the mountains. James had certainly not found anything significantly negative to report back to his father. To the contrary, James had not only played a key part in the actions that saved his father's command from possible disaster during the battle, but he had also developed a positive camaraderie with Lieutenant Talley and with Captain Trimble and their men, some of whom he had already known, of course. Jonathan smiled. He and young James had also become acquainted. They liked each other and they shared mutual respect. Young James did not seem to have the same self-aggrandizing traits that Jonathan thought his father sometimes displayed.

By eleven o'clock that night, all of the scouts that had been dispatched to determine if the British were pursuing them had returned. There were no British or Tory forces in pursuit, or if there were they were not in close proximity.

On Tuesday, the third day after the battle, they made a long march, taking the prisoners twenty miles to the north, halting and camping in a wooded area. During the day, several attempts at escape were made by small groups of prisoners. Four were shot, all wounded and not able to continue on the march. These four were left at the spot to fend for themselves as best they could. Two were considered so badly wounded that they were likely to die. At least a dozen others were recaptured, but with the Patriots not wanting to slow the march, attempts to recapture the remaining escapees were quickly abandoned. At the evening count of prisoners it was discovered that eighty-four prisoners had escaped during the day's long march. Three hundred and sixty-one prisoners remained in custody and under guard.

On that evening, a meeting of officers of all ranks was convened. A discussion was held regarding crimes committed by the worst of the Tories. Since Cornwallis' victory at Camden in South Carolina in August, both the Tories and the British under Colonel Tarleton had committed horrendous acts against Patriot men and their families. Some of the worst Tory offenders were now prisoners of Colonel Campbell's force. Colonel Cleveland had recommended to Colonel Campbell earlier in the day that the specific Tories who were known by men from Wilkes, Surry, and Burke Counties to be criminals should be tried and executed. In the months preceding the battle at King's Mountain, some of the Americans had arrived home from militia service to find their homes burned, and their family members had recognized the Tories who committed the atrocities. The wives and children of several of Colonel Cleveland's men had even been killed.

Major Joseph McDowell spoke about the severity of the matter. "When the large Tory force invaded Burke County, many of my men were engaged with me in fighting them, while without our knowledge another band of Tories was raiding the homes of some of my men. We arrived back in the area of their homes. Fifteen homes had been burned by the Tories, led by Captain Smith, who is now our prisoner. Captain Smith knew that Private Willis Baty was serving with my company, and inquired of Baty's wife where he was at the time. She would not tell them, for she in fact had no way of knowing where he was. He then threatened to shoot Baty's fourteen-year-old son if neither the wife nor the son would provide Baty's location. When we arrived an hour later, we saw the young boy's body. They had shot him in the head. I believe we must try and execute the Tories who are evidenced to have committed such crimes."

Colonel Shelby stated in a loud and firm manner, "I recommend that we identify witnesses and prepare to try these pitiful excuses for human beings. We have witnesses who can prove that among the worst of the murdering Tories are Captain Leonard and Captain Watkins. Their misdeeds are as evil as or worse than those of Captain Smith. I believe we can be prepared to try the Tory criminals within two or three days from now."

John Sevier spoke up, saying, "As you are all aware, because the British are not pursuing us, Colonel Campbell has released my regiment to separate from the main force tomorrow and return home over the mountains. We are needed to combat Indian hostilities there. A messenger from home arrived today to advise me that last week the Indians burned the homes of two of my men and killed their wives and children. If any trials of prisoners are held at a time later than tomorrow morning, we will not be present. However, that should not make any difference, as none of my men are witnesses to any of the crimes and horrific deeds that took place on this side of the mountains."

Colonel Campbell declared, "Colonel Sevier's regiment will leave us tomorrow morning, and Colonel Lacey and his South Carolinians are departing tomorrow, as well, to return home."

Colonel Cleveland spoke up, returning to the discussion of atrocities. "The only way we will get the British and Tories to stop their atrocities is to hang the men who have committed them. It will send a message to other Tories, and perhaps even the British will understand."

"Remember that we need to keep some of the officers alive to exchange for some of our officers that the British are holding," said Colonel Campbell. "We will identify the men who should be tried, and we will identify the witnesses and conduct the trials not later than three days from the present."

On Wednesday, the Patriot army marched the prisoners twelve miles and halted in mid-afternoon. Late in the afternoon, Colonel Sevier's regiment left the remaining body of troops and headed toward the northwest to go home. It took four days to traverse the mountains and arrive in Washington County. As the sun set on Sunday, October 15, Jonathan rode his horse down the last half mile of familiar trail leading to his home.

Chapter 6

Defending the Frontier

Jonathan had been home for several days. Simply being with Frances and the children gave him great joy. There was much work to be done, and he applied himself diligently to those tasks. He had already repaired a place on the cabin roof that had been leaking during heavy rains and repaired a section of the wooden fence beside the barn.

The morning sun shone just above the eastern tree line as Jonathan's oldest sons, William and Samuel, walked with him toward the same small field in which they had worked the day before. William, now eight years of age, and Samuel, now seven, had already helped Jonathan for two full days as he cleared two trees and removed the stumps and roots so the family cornfield could be larger for the next season. Addressing the boys in a pleasant, firm tone, Jonathan said, "William, Samuel, we will finish removing the stones from the cleared land before dark today. After we finish, I will let you load and fire two shots each from the pistol."

William replied, "Oh, boy!"

Then, Samuel inquired, "Will we go hunting?"

"No, there will not be enough time for that. We will select targets for your marksmanship, maybe sticks or stones you can shoot at."

Before they passed out of easy earshot of the cabin, Jonathan heard Frances say, "Mary, you must milk the cow this morning, because William and Samuel are helping Father clear the field."

"Yes, ma'am," Mary responded.

It was really good to be home, thought Jonathan, but his thoughts drifted to the serious discussions that had taken place after the prior

Sunday's church meeting of the need to mount a campaign against the Indians, who continued to make scattered raids on the white settlers. Jonathan and the other men had learned from David Bragg that George Gillespie had reported that he expected the Indians to make a major attack on the settlers in the near future. Most of the settlers trusted George Gillespie's judgment and knew that he traded regularly with some of the more friendly Indians. Those Indians knew Gillespie to be a fair and honest man, and also trusted him. At Gillespie's remote location to the southwest, he often possessed the most current and accurate information about the Indians. Jonathan knew that if the proposed campaign came to fruition, it would become necessary to again leave his family.

One morning as Jonathan worked outside his cabin he recognized the single rider who was approaching. It was his neighbor, Tom Callahan.

Jonathan greeted him, "Tom, you look far better today than you did right after the battle." The comment, made in friendly humor, was Jonathan's way of demonstrating his appreciation of Callahan's service.

Displaying his own quick sense of humor, Tom replied, "And you smell better today, Jonathan, for after three weeks on the trail and after the battle I might have mistaken you at twenty paces for a skunk."

They both laughed. Tom was a close neighbor and friend. Jonathan's relationship with him was one of equals. It was not one of an officer to a private that would have been based on their ranks in the militia. After a visit of only a couple of minutes, Tom Callahan mounted and continued on his hunting trip for that day, heading for an area known to harbor a good quantity of wild turkeys.

After the church meeting on the first Sunday of November in 1780, Jonathan stood outside the meeting house, talking with William Trimble, discussing the inadequacy of the meeting house for church services, given the larger population and greater participation in church services, and the resulting need to build a separate church building. Jonathan happened to notice as John Sevier left one of the several groups of people who were indulging in social conversation. Sevier moved directly toward Tipton and Trimble.

Sevier moved his head and eyes to the left and to the right, as if to see who else might be listening, but spoke loudly enough to clearly indicate he had no intent to keep anyone from hearing what he had to say. "Jonathan, William," he greeted them. "I spoke with Colonel Shelby day before yesterday. He learned that last month, on the third day after we left the army to head home, they tried the worst of the Tories, just as we had expected. Nine of the Tory prisoners were hung. They deserved it. They were the worst of the murdering lot."

"Where did they take the rest of the prisoners?" asked Jonathan.

"Colonel Shelby did not say. The message from Colonel Campbell indicated that some of the British and Tory officers were to be exchanged for American officers held prisoner by Cornwallis, but he did not mention the rest of the prisoners." Sevier continued, "It is a good thing we are all back home. A band of Chickamauga Cherokees burned four more cabins down by the French Broad River yesterday. They captured two women and killed everybody else who was home."

Jonathan inquired, "Who were the settlers?"

"It was all the newcomers down there. They just finished their cabins in the last few months. Two of the men were out hunting. They were the only ones who were not killed or captured. The Indians even killed small children and a baby. The two who were not killed are Jack Scott and Alexander McCorkle. I don't know the names of the others. Scott and McCorkle want to ride with us against the Indians and see if we can rescue their wives. If not, they just want to kill Indians." Sevier looked Jonathan Tipton squarely in the eyes. "Jonathan, we have to resume the daily patrols. You know that the patrols stopped when we departed to fight Ferguson's army, and we haven't resumed them."

"My men can start patrolling our area by day after tomorrow. I need the rest of today and tomorrow to contact the officers and men and get ready." The thought passed fleetingly through Jonathan's mind about how reluctant he was to accept the authority of Lieutenant Colonel Sevier, but he simultaneously recognized that, with Colonel Carter suffering from an undeniably serious and lingering illness, he had no real choice in the matter.

"OK," said Sevier. "We will do the same for the other areas. I am worried, though, that the number of Indians involved in these attacks is large. Last week George Gillespie saw a party of at least fifty Indians near his place. That was two days before the four cabins were attacked down south in your area, and that was not the only party of Indians that was seen that day. Two parties of Indians, with thirty to forty Indians in each party, were seen off the North Fork of the Holston, but they saw the hunters who spotted them and did not attack. They probably expected our patrols to be active when they were spotted, and thought the hunters were our scouts. Jonathan, I want you to send a rider to let me know any time one of your patrols observes any large party of Indians, or if you have any fight or skirmish with them."

During the next several weeks in November of 1780, the daily militia patrols were relatively uneventful, except for the frequent sighting of small numbers of Indians. About eight to ten times each week, settlers or the men on patrol would spy pairs of Indians in various areas of the frontier, but the Indians always retreated, disappearing into the forest. Jonathan came to the same conclusion that John Sevier reached—that the Indians were spying in preparation for some large or widespread attack.

On Thursday, November 30, Jonathan heard some good news when he paid a visit to his seriously ill friend, Colonel John Carter, who was by then bedridden most of the time.

Colonel Carter's handshake, once firm and powerful, was now feeble and weak. "Jonathan, I received a letter from General Sumter from South Carolina. He wrote it last week, and a rider brought it to me day before yesterday. Our side has won two battles. General Sumter's force of three hundred men won a battle at Fishdam Ford on the Broad River in the northwest part of South Carolina, just the other side of the mountains. They beat a force of more than two hundred troops under British Major Wemyss on November 9. They captured Major Wemyss and some of his men. The other victory was also won by General Sumter's men. He defeated Colonel Tarleton's force in a battle at Blackstock's plantation in the northwest hill country of South Carolina on the twentieth of this month. General Sumter, however, was wounded with a musket ball through the shoulder. Tarleton was trying to drive Sumter's force away from the British fort at the place called Ninety-Six. There was lots of fighting all around the fort at Ninety-Six from day to day and week to week all of this month, at least through the twentieth. I know that General Sumter could use our help, but we have our hands full with the Indians."

"You are right," replied Jonathan. "It looks like we will be mounting a campaign against the Indians soon. Do you still favor such a campaign?"

"Yes, and, as you know, I have no choice but to let John Sevier run the militia for the county right now. This ailment has made me very weak, and on some days my pain is so severe that I cannot even get out of bed. I know he is not your favorite person, but you must cooperate with him."

Without waiting for a response from Jonathan, Colonel Carter continued, "I sent Landon over to Lieutenant Colonel Sevier's home yesterday to advise him of the victories that General Sumter wrote me about. When Landon got back he reminded me of the all-officers' meeting that will be held after the church meeting this Sunday. I will not be able to go, but Landon will be there. Sevier wants to assemble our men and depart on a campaign against the Indians late next week. The exact date is to be determined at the meeting. He wants to attack and burn all the Indian towns within a fifteen to twenty day march from here, and I suspect that is exactly what we should do, as well. Sevier has already asked Colonel Shelby and Colonel Campbell to have the men from their counties come along. I think we must have additional men from at least one of them in order to succeed. Darn, I wish I could go, but I am barely able to sit up for a little while and talk with you, much less ride and fight."

Jonathan spoke up. "You are right, of course, about my view toward John Sevier. I will cooperate with him, though. It has to be that way for us to succeed against the Indians." After a little more discussion between the two, Jonathan went home.

During the following week, in mid-afternoon on Tuesday, December 5, Sergeant David Bragg rode up to Jonathan Tipton's home. Jonathan greeted him as he dismounted. Wasting no time, Bragg said, "Jonathan, two traders stopped by my place about noon today, on their way to the

Watauga settlement. They said that they learned from some friendly Indians that Chief Dragging Canoe, Bear Cloud, and some other chiefs have assembled a large number of Indians at Chota Town. The traders have heard that Dragging Canoe and Bear Cloud are going to make a big attack on settlements throughout the whole area."

"Who were the traders?"

"One was Jack Tillman. The other was the one they call Smoky Copeland, because he always smells like smoke from a campfire. They are getting out of Indian lands for a while. Copeland says this is going to be the biggest Indian attack ever. He says they have over five hundred warriors and they're going to try their darned best to drive all the white settlers back to the other side of the mountains. I know Copeland, and he is not often wrong."

"I know Smoky Copeland, too," said Jonathan. "We ran into him more than once when we were going after Indians in the past. Well, since we've already planned to assemble day after tomorrow to go after them, it looks like it's going to be at just the right time. I'm going to ride over to Colonel Carter's place. He will probably want to send Landon to tell Lieutenant Colonel Sevier about this news. I'll see you day after tomorrow."

David Bragg rode off toward his home, and within minutes Jonathan was off to give the news to Colonel Carter and his son, Captain Landon Carter.

Two days later, the men assembled at the flats on Lick Creek, as had been planned. By gathering there, the militia placed themselves in a position to protect the settlements from any Indian advance from the southwest, from the direction of Chota Town. They were south of all but a few of the cabins of white settlers. The force that was assembled, all from Washington County, numbered only 170 men. Two companies of militia remained behind in the settlements under the command of Major Robertson, along with the usual older men and boys, to defend against any surprise Indian attack, should the Indians evade the main force of militiamen. Colonel Sevier had insisted on marching immediately, rather than waiting on possible reinforcements. It seemed that the requested assistance from Colonel Shelby in Sullivan County and from Colonel

Arthur Campbell in Virginia was not forthcoming, with one reason or excuse after another given for delays. Sevier had been attempting to gather a force large enough to make a massive assault deep into Indian lands, killing as many as possible, burning their towns, and driving them far away from the white settlements in a convincing manner. He wanted to fight the Indians in their own territory, not within the area of white settlements. Now, it appeared that the men from Washington County would have to do it by themselves.

Having camped near the confluence of the Nolichucky River and the French Broad River, the backcountry militiamen headed generally southwestward the next day, following along the French Broad River. Their destination was Chota Town, an expected journey of about two to three more days depending on the weather, how hard they rode, and whether or not the Indians harassed them along the way. The militia leaders and most of the men knew that in addition to being the last reported position of the large assembly of Indians, Chota Town was the overall spiritual and political capital of all of the Cherokees. It was also one place the Indians might fight to defend, rather than simply using their typical hit-and-run tactics.

That day, the militia force proceeded in three roughly parallel columns, separated by about forty to sixty feet, depending on the terrain at any given point. Lieutenant Colonel Sevier was at the head of the center column with seventy-five men. Major Jesse Walton, with forty-five men, led the right column; and Major Jonathan Tipton, with fifty men, was on the left. Suddenly, Jonathan saw David Bragg, who had been one of the forward scouts, riding quickly back from his advance position. Jonathan held up his hand to halt his column. At almost the same moment, both John Sevier and Major Walton did likewise. All three columns came to a halt without a word being spoken. Jonathan rode toward Sevier's position at the head of the center column, where he met up with David Bragg, Lieutenant Colonel Sevier, and Major Walton. Bragg, a clever and experienced scout, stated in an excited tone, "We have spied Indians lying in wait to ambush us in the tall grass near the ford. Taylor climbed a tall tree and gave them a good look. There cannot be more than a hundred of them. They probably think they can ambush us and then retreat really fast across the river at the ford to get away. Colonel, if we attack them hard we can get most of them. They will not expect a fast attack."

John Sevier's response was decisive. "Jesse, take your men wide to the right and try to block any escape to the north. You will hear our firing before you get to their north, but hold your attack until you get to a blocking position. Then push in so we get them from two directions. Jonathan, bring your men with me in the main attack along the river. Let's do it now!"

Jonathan, along with John Sevier and the main column of Washington County militiamen rode quickly toward the Indian position, dismounting at the location described by David Bragg as being just short of the Indian position. Even as the men dismounted and quickly hobbled their horses, they received fire from the Indians. The Indians, being on foot and in their concealed positions, had not expected the rapid approach. As soon as the militiamen commenced firing, some of the Indians began to run toward the river, and the well-directed rifle shots of the militia struck down quite a few Indians. Then the remaining Indians began to flee toward the river. They had chosen the site of their intended ambush well, as it was near a ford in the river. Most of the Indians were able to flee safely across the river. Surprisingly, instead of taking cover behind rocks and trees on the other side, where they would be ready to fire at any man who dared to follow and enter into the open to cross the shallow water, the Indians continued into the woods. This unusual tactic drew immediate suspicion from Jonathan, who was by now standing with John Sevier and Jesse Walton. Major Walton spoke up promptly with his opinion, the same as the one Jonathan held, saying to John Sevier, "Colonel, they probably want us to pursue them across the river. All the warriors that Dragging Canoe and Bear Cloud have may be over there in the woods waiting to ambush us."

"You are right," said Sevier. Major Walton, post a strong guard at the ford. Major Tipton, post sentries along the river behind us." Looking at Captain James Pearce, Sevier said, "James, post sentries further west, along the river." Then, pointing at two nearby trees, he directed Jonathan and Major Walton, "Both of you get your captains and lieutenants and meet with me over at those two oak trees in five minutes."

The officers suddenly became silent, as two of the militiamen approached, one with blood covering the sleeves of his shirt, tears running down his face, and carrying the bloody scalp of an Indian. "That's for what the savages did to my children," said the man. He then threw the bloody piece of skin and hair onto the ground.

"It's Jack Scott," said Major Tipton for the benefit of all who were present. "He is riding with my men. The Indians took his wife away and killed his children last month while he was out hunting. The youngest was just a baby. They scalped his baby, too." Jack Scott just stood there, crying.

Private Allen McClintock, who had approached beside Jack Scott, said, "Scott came across a wounded Chickamauga who had been shot in the chest. Scott stabbed the savage over and over, and scalped him, too. Then he just started crying and walked over here."

McClintock then put his hand on Jack Scott's shoulder, consoling him, nudged Scott to turn around, and walked with him toward the other men in their company.

As soon as all the officers had gathered as requested, Lieutenant Colonel Sevier said, "First of all, tell your men not to take any Indian warriors as prisoners. Just kill them, like Jack Scott did, if necessary, but don't scalp them. If we get a chance, we can take a few Indian women and children prisoners and try to exchange them for the captured white women. That's probably a long shot, though. More to the point, it is obvious that the Chickamauga Indians we fought today were not the main party of Indians that the traders told us about. Nobody recognized their chief, and some of us have seen Dragging Canoe and Bear Cloud close-up when we met with them at the land treaty meetings several years ago and can identify them on sight. I don't think there were more than seventy of them who fled across the river. Lieutenant Russell, did you get the count of Indians killed and our own wounded?"

"Yes, sir. In just about ten minutes of battle we killed sixteen Indians. None captured. As you already know, we had no men killed. We had only one man wounded. John Beane, in Captain Trimble's company, was shot in the forearm. It is not a serious wound. The Indians thought they were going to surprise us and then just run over the creek. They never suspected we would detect them and attack so fast and from two directions!"

Captain Trimble spoke up, saying, "Beane has been bandaged around the arm and will be fine. He will be able to continue on the campaign."

"Good," said Sevier. "That little hill beyond the woods across the river looks like a good position. From there you might be able to observe the approach or movement of any Indians."

Jonathan said, "I have been on that hill twice before with my patrols. We can send some men right away to scout the hill. If the hill is not occupied by Indians, we can cross the river today and stay on the little hill tonight. It's a good defensive position with wide open views. We will be safe from surprise attack there. We will also have the ford at our back, should we need to retreat. We can post hidden sentries near the ford to warn us in case any Indians try to approach us from the rear."

Sevier replied decisively, "Major Tipton, go ahead and send the scouts to the hill. If it is clear, we will stay on the hill longer than one night. You all know that every day we send riders back to our settlements, and riders from previous days are arriving back in camp on their return trips from home with updated messages and news. We will send two riders today, instead of one. Both riders will continue past the Watauga settlement. One will go to Colonel Shelby, and the other will continue beyond to Colonel Arthur Campbell. They will carry my most urgent request for reinforcements. I will write messages telling both of the colonels that we will wait here for six days for reinforcements before proceeding. If we don't get reinforcements, we will be the ones doing the hit and run raids, not the Indians. Without reinforcements, we will need to avoid fighting the main force of Indians if they really number over five hundred, like the traders said. We will use the six days for scouting. If we have to do this without reinforcements, we will move rapidly by horseback to attack and destroy as many of their smaller towns as we can, and kill as many Indians as we can. We can still serve a purpose. They've got to learn that it is a bad idea to continue raiding our settlements."

By the morning of Friday, December 15, the small force from Washington County had been camped on the small hill near the French Broad River for seven days, waiting for reinforcements under Colonel Arthur Campbell. The Virginians were finally en route, reported to be within three days' march. The men under Sevier, Tipton, and Walton were tired of waiting, although they had been constantly on the alert for possible attack by Indians and had fought several small skirmishes with Indians. By mid-afternoon, hunters began to return to camp, unfortunately with less than ample game killed for food. Skimpy rations were by that time contributing to restlessness among the men. About two o'clock, Captain Moses Guest, with thirty men, was sent to scout southward and determine if any large body of Indians might be close by.

Right at sunset, Lieutenant Colonel Sevier, Major Tipton, and Captain Pearce were sitting on a tree that had been downed by lightning and provided a comfortable place to sit and talk. Captain Guest and his men rode in hurriedly. Guest dismounted and hastily approached Lieutenant Colonel Sevier.

"Colonel, the Indians are only three miles south of here!" exclaimed Captain Guest. "They are along Boyd's Creek. They weren't there when our scouts went there yesterday! We rode into an opening and were upon them too quickly to remain unobserved. When they saw us they fired a couple of shots, but did not hit anyone, and a couple of my men fired back before we made a quick retreat. My scouting party numbered thirty, and there were hundreds of Indians. They were camped all over the hillside near Boyd's Creek and all along both sides of the creek."

"How many were there?"

"We did not get a fair count, Colonel, but there must have been at least three hundred or more. We only saw about thirty or forty horses, so most of the Indians are on foot. My men are pretty sure that some of them are the same Indians that attacked us last week."

"Major Tipton," said Colonel Sevier, "get with Major Walton and ensure that you all double the guard tonight in case the Indians try a night attack. We will attack them in the morning. We cannot wait three more days for reinforcements and let these Indians get away. They are

likely to withdraw as soon as their scouts tell them that we have reinforcements coming."

Early in the morning on December 16, the militia force advanced,
again in three columns but further apart, with several hundred yards
separating the columns. They knew that the Indian scouts would spy
the main column coming, and the Indians would not be surprised. The
smaller left and right columns, however, were concealed in the trees,
and might not be observed. The center column had moved out first, the
left and right columns having separated a short distance into the woods
before the first ray of sun, under the cover of darkness. Even as the full
force of winter approached, the woods provided substantial concealment,
being thick in some spots and having pine trees and other evergreens in
other places. The first snow had melted several days before, and for the
most part the ground was dry, although some low lying areas were soggy.
Lieutenant Colonel Sevier's orders were that as soon as the center column
encountered the Indians, Major Walton's column would attack from the
right, on the Indians' left flank; and Major Tipton's column would attack
from the left, on the Indians' right flank.

About half an hour after the three columns had set out from the
prior night's camp, Jonathan heard the brisk fire of many guns to his
right, and knew that the center force had engaged the Indians. He urged
his men to make way as fast as possible through the muddy, swampy
terrain they had encountered on the left route. When the intensity of
gunfire increased further, Jonathan knew that Major Walton's column
was attacking the Indians' on their far flank. Major Tipton, struggling
through a wet, swampy area that was thick with undergrowth, could
not attack immediately, but he could hear the heavy firing as the militiamen and Indians blazed away at each other. Jonathan urged his men
to move fast, and the men in turn urged their horses, but the mud and
thick undergrowth would not allow sufficient swiftness in their progress.
Jonathan knew he must attack quickly on the Indians' right flank. Given
the best efforts of men and horses, he was finally able to attack about six
minutes after the firing had broken out in the center. Just as Tipton's men
attacked, the Indians retreated hastily to their right rear, toward an even

more heavily swampy area, where horses could not tread and the Indians could not be readily pursued.

Sevier's men, in the center of the fight, had dismounted to fight from covered positions. As the Indians fled rapidly to a position immediately in front of Major Tipton's men, Sevier's men lost contact with the Indians. Since Jonathan's own men were mounted as they emerged from the swamp, Major Tipton ordered a mounted attack. Quickly, his men were riding up to the edge of the swamp into which the Indians were retreating. Private Jeremiah Jack rode fast and caught up with one Indian. Having already fired his rifle, he held the rifle by the barrel, and swung it at the Indian's head. The Indian deflected the blow with his own gun. About that time, an accurate shot from the rifle of Adam Sherrill struck the Indian beside his right ear, knocking him to the ground. In a moment, Jeremiah Jack was off his horse and thrust his long knife into the Indian's chest, leaving no doubt regarding his fate. After firing a final round of shots at the last of the fleeing Indians, the men found the enemy out of sight in the swamp, and ceased firing. Shortly, the men of the other two columns reached the edge of the swamp. They all knew it would be futile to pursue the Indians into the swamp on foot, especially as badly as the militiamen were outnumbered.

Lieutenant Colonel Sevier had mounted, and rode up to Jonathan's position on the edge of the swamp. Sevier was furious. He lambasted Major Tipton right in front of everyone who was present, shouting at Jonathan, "You did not attack their right flank. You let them get away. We had them. I've got half a mind to remove you from command."

Jonathan, not willing to accept such a misdirected attack on his character, replied sternly and in an uncharacteristically insolent manner, "You've got half a mind all right! Neither my men nor I are at fault. You were on dry ground. We were making our way through a swamp. The snow that melted made the swamp muddier than rain would have in the summer. If you want to have a race right now, let's go back a half mile. You take the route through the swamp, and I'll take the route you took; and I'll beat you to this point by ten minutes. My men attacked from that mushy swamp as fast as anyone could have. When we got to where the

Indians were retreating, my men gave a fine account of themselves. We killed darned near as many Indians in five minutes as you and Walton did in ten." Jonathan paused, but he had not come close to cooling down. Blood had begun to seep through Jonathan's coat, on his left arm, just below the shoulder. Blood had also trickled down the inside of his sleeve, and was dripping from his left thumb. "If I did not attack, how did some Indian shoot me in the arm?"

"Just shut your mouth, Tipton," said John Sevier.

"I'll not shut up unless you apologize, John, because I don't deserve any blame at all, and neither do my men. These are the same men that made you the hero at King's Mountain. Today, with just 170 men you have routed Dragging Canoe and at least six hundred Indians. Nobody wants to get rid of Dragging Canoe worse than I do."

Major Jesse Walton, having arrived at the scene and observing the verbal conflict, astutely intervened, saying, "Jonathan, you're bleeding too badly to be arguing with the colonel, or with anyone else for that matter." Walton turned his head to one of the nearby men who was observing the spectacle. "McCorkle, see if you can help the major with his wound and get the bleeding stopped."

Jonathan's wound was not serious. The musket ball had penetrated the upper part of his left arm just inside the skin, and exited the skin two inches behind the entry wound. Although there was quite a bit of blood, it was a simple flesh wound. With a cloth wrapped around the arm, the bleeding stopped during the night. He was fortunate that it was not a disabling injury at all, and he would be able to continue with the campaign.

He may have insulted Lieutenant Colonel Sevier right in front of other men, but Jonathan had been right about one thing. The officers and men all agreed that they had faced a surprisingly large number of Indians. About seven hundred was their general estimate. As it turned out, the massed force of Indians had assembled along the path of the center column of militia, not far from Boyd's Creek, on the morning of the sixteenth. To a man, the militia officers agreed in their belief that the Indians would have attacked the militia that day, had the militia force not attacked first. They had killed twenty-eight Indians and the rest retreated, some of them wounded. In Sevier's force, nobody was killed, and only Major Tipton and eleven other men received wounds. They had won. If the Indians had stayed and fought, however, things might have been very different. Apparently, the Indians had not realized just how badly they outnumbered the militia force that day. Jonathan thought the Indians had probably known the size of Sevier's force, but also knew about the reinforcements, and assumed that since the militiamen attacked, the reinforcements had already arrived, sooner than the Indians expected. The Indians were normally highly proficient at scouting. Now they would certainly figure out just how small Sevier's force was. It would not pay to pursue them.

Just after the battle, word arrived with an advance party of six men sent by Colonel Campbell that he and his force of 380 Virginians would reach Sevier's position in two days. Lieutenant Colonel Sevier sent word back to Campbell, advising him of the battle with a large force of about seven hundred Indians, and letting Colonel Campbell know that he would wait for his arrival before pursuing the Indians. John Sevier met with his majors. They agreed that even the good defensive position of their previous encampment on the hill would not be sufficient to survive an attack by such a large number of Indians as they had faced that day. They determined that they should retreat several miles to the opposite side of the ford on the French Broad River to wait for reinforcements. They retreated across the ford, and there they camped on the sixteenth and seventeenth of December.

Chapter 7

The Chota Town Campaign

THE SPIRITS OF men and officers alike were bolstered when, just before noon on December 18, they were joined by Colonel Arthur Campbell of Virginia and his 380 men, and Major Joseph Martin of Sullivan County, North Carolina, with ninety men. Colonel Arthur Campbell assumed overall command, as he possessed seniority over Lieutenant Colonel Sevier.

"Colonel Campbell, you and your men are a most welcome sight," said John Sevier, extending his hand as he greeted the Virginian when he dismounted. On the frontier, the handshake, and not the salute, was still the norm for the militia. After a warm handshake with Sevier, Colonel Campbell extended his hand to Jonathan, shook his hand, and followed suit with Major Walton.

Sevier then turned and extended his hand to the right, saying, "Major Martin, the arrival of you and your men is a warm surprise. We welcome you kindly."

"Thank you, Colonel Sevier," replied Martin. "Colonel Shelby sends you his warmest regards, as well as his regrets that he cannot join you. Colonel Shelby sent me with ninety of our best men. He believes in your campaign, but remained behind of necessity to protect the settlements."

"I understand," offered Lieutenant Colonel Sevier.

"He wanted me to be clear on one point, Colonel Sevier, with both you and Colonel Campbell. I have already advised Colonel Campbell. Colonel Shelby has almost two hundred men at home, and he understands that you and Colonel Campbell have left much smaller numbers at home in your counties. Inasmuch as Colonel Shelby is in Sullivan County, between your home counties, he is in the center of the settlements west of the mountains, north of your county and south of Colonel Campbell's Virginia settlements. Colonel Shelby intends to cooperate with the commanders you left at home to fend off any large Indian attack at any place along the frontier. He wanted me to be sure to advise you of this."

Looking at John Sevier, Colonel Arthur Campbell said, "I sent a rider home to tell William he can count on Colonel Shelby if need be. You may want to do the same." Arthur Campbell was referring to his brother, Colonel William Campbell. He knew that Sevier and his brother had become friends while serving together on the campaign that resulted in the great victory at King's Mountain.

"I will send word, indeed. We send a rider home every day, and a rider returns from home almost every day with news or no news, as the case may be."

"John, we are doing the same thing," said Arthur Campbell. "It helps the men a lot to know that things are okay back home."

"It's going to help my men a lot when they are told that Colonel Shelby and his two hundred men are ready to help Major Robertson protect their families and homes," was John Sevier's positive reply. Then he turned and said, "Jonathan, Jesse—be sure your men are all told about this."

It was typical, thought Jonathan, that John Sevier had not even mentioned the presence at home of Colonel John Carter. As usual, Sevier did not mention even the existence of Colonel Carter or the status of his serious illness. Lieutenant Colonel Sevier seemed to prefer to be considered the principal officer of the county. At times Jonathan had heard Sevier answer politely, but briefly, when asked about the condition of Colonel Carter, but that was the extent of his courtesy in that regard.

The necessary force was finally in place. All the men had horses. The officers believed that the militia army, now totaling 640 men, was strong enough for a decisive campaign against the Indians. Scouts returning in the morning, just prior to Colonel Campbell's arrival, had confirmed that the large party of more than seven hundred Indians, most of whom had been at the battle at Boyd's Creek, were now encamped at Chota Town.

Jonathan felt a sense of power within the militia army. He realized that he had not felt that way since the King's Mountain campaign. This time, however, he perceived that the confidence was even greater. Most of the men had been at King's Mountain. If they could defeat an army of a thousand well-armed British and Tories, they could certainly defeat any force the Indians might be able to throw at them. He knew, though, that facing the Indians was actually quite difficult now that almost all the warriors had good muskets, either obtained in trade or supplied by the British. It was not like several years ago, when the Indians had only a combination of bows and arrows and some old muskets.

On the following day the men rode before daybreak, continuing until early in the afternoon. Colonel Campbell ordered a halt, and called a meeting of all officers. He started the meeting in typical style, getting right to the point. "Colonel Sevier and I have devised a plan to attack Chota Town. We will have scouts go forward immediately and identify a route that we can use for a night march toward Chota Town. Some scouts will be left along the route, and we will have the lead scout return before midnight. We will march immediately upon his return. We'll head out quietly and start out due west before turning toward the south on the route the scouts will identify. If we march overnight and the weather remains good, we can get there some time during the day tomorrow, before the Indians expect us. They will no doubt spy us coming, but we will be so near that they will not have time to prepare any ambush for us. We intend to ride hard on the town, defeat the Indians, and burn the town. Have your men rest here. Post the regular sentries and have your men get as much sleep as they can during the hours before we march."

Major Tipton spoke up, stating, "Colonel Campbell, I recommend we use David Bragg as the lead scout. He's as good as there is. He knows the lay of the land around Chota Town, and he knows this whole area better than most white men."

Colonel Campbell looked at Sevier, expecting him to answer in some fashion.

"I agree," said John Sevier. "Sergeant Bragg is the best man for the job. If you recall, I mentioned to you that I spoke with Bragg before we came up with this plan. If you agree, Colonel, we will give David Bragg six of our best scouts, and will ask you to provide him with six of your best."

"Very well," replied Arthur Campbell.

The scouts set out within fifteen minutes.

About eleven o'clock that night, December 19, David Bragg arrived back at the temporary encampment. The officers were ready for his return, and the men were ready to mount and get underway. As Bragg dismounted, Jonathan recalled that the sergeant had taken two horses, so he would have one that would not have been carrying a load and would thus be fresher for his return trip. Even so, Bragg's horse was visibly winded and sweating even on the cold, wintry night.

"What's the news, David?" asked John Sevier.

"I went to a point only about five miles short of Chota Town. From there, both I and one of Colonel Campbell's scouts know the way well. I left scouts in pairs at six places along the way. If they spy any large party of Indians moving at night, they will alert us. I don't think the Indians will be moving about tonight, though."

"Let's get going, but have your men move out quietly." said Colonel Campbell.

"With all due respect, Colonel Campbell," said Major Tipton, "the Indians know we are here, where we are right now. I suggest we leave a company of men here with a few of their own sentries, keeping all the fires going, so any Indian scouts will think we are still here. They can throw some logs on the fires before dawn and head out before first sunlight to catch up with the rest of us later in the day."

"If we do that, we will be short a company of men when we reach Chota Town," retorted Lieutenant Colonel Sevier.

Colonel Campbell said in a matter-of-fact tone of voice, "It's a good idea. We will do it. It might be just the thing that makes our plan work." Then, turning to Captain Crabtree, one of his Virginians, he said, "Leave one of your companies here to tend the fires and catch up with us tomorrow."

They rode through the night. As dawn broke on the morning of Wednesday, December 20, the militiamen were only five miles from Chota Town. By mid-morning they began to receive sporadic gunshots from Indians who were firing from concealed positions. The pace of the march quickened. As they approached the town, there was more cleared land, and less opportunity for the Indians to fire from concealed positions. Before noon the lead riders were within eyesight of Chota Town. It appeared that nothing blocked the way between the militiamen and the town. Suddenly, less than a mile from the town, musket fire erupted from the last tree line along the right side of the column. The sheer volume of firing revealed that this was the main Indian force. Acting decisively, Colonel Campbell issued a series of orders. "Lieutenant Locke, Captain Russell, Captain Crabtree—take six companies of our Virginians to the right, dismount, and engage the Indians. Major Martin, keep your men mounted, and be ready to support the Virginians if the Indians attack in force. Keep your eyes on the rear, too. Colonel Sevier, take your men toward the town, wheel right, and attack the Indians from their right flank."

As suddenly as the Indians had begun firing, they stopped and began to flee up the hill behind the trees. Their escape was successful, as the Indians had chosen their ground carefully, and their escape route could not be readily followed on horseback.

As the Indian warriors fled, Allen McClintock tapped Major Tipton on the shoulder, extended his hand toward Chota Town, and said, "Major, look. The Chickamauga women and children are trying to escape."

Jonathan saw in the distance a large number of women and children fleeing the town on foot.

"You're right," he said to Mcclintock. Then, rushing quickly to talk with John Sevier, Jonathan pointed at the fleeing Indian women and children, and said, "John, let's go see if the white women who were captured are with them."

"OK. Get your men mounted. The warriors have retreated in the opposite direction. They were just trying to distract us so their women and children could escape."

Sevier then shouted, "Captain Carter, go tell Colonel Campbell we are heading for the town. Get back fast! Major Walton, get all your men mounted. Let's ride."

Within two minutes all of Lieutenant Colonel Sevier's men were riding hard to cover the last few hundred yards toward Chota Town. As the militiamen caught up with the fleeing Indians less than half a mile beyond the town, the Indian women and children scattered in every possible direction, trying to avoid capture. Most of them did escape, but the militiamen captured eighteen women and thirteen children.

Directing an order to Captain James Pearce, John Sevier said, "Take them back to the town and keep them under guard."

Then, Colonel Campbell joined Lieutenant Colonel Sevier, Major Tipton, and several other officers near the south edge of Chota Town. He issued an order directed to all those present, "Burn the town. We are going to camp here tonight, but none of our men will stay in those filthy places." He was referring to the forty to fifty small Indian homes in the town. Jonathan had seen Cherokee cabins before, each a small log building with no windows and with a large hole in the roof to allow the smoke from the fire to escape.

The men set forth with great alacrity and burned the cabins in the town, first tearing down parts of many of the cabins and stacking the wood for use in campfires. The one larger council house that the Indians used for ceremonies and meetings was also burned.

"Major, there's something you've got to see," said Adam Sherrill. He led Jonathan to the side of a small hill adjacent to the town, where a rough door of woven branches and sticks had been removed, revealing a hollow place in the hill. The hollow was a small natural cave, about four feet high at the entrance, but fully six feet high, eight feet wide, and about twenty feet deep into the hillside. It was filled with baskets of corn, apparently the Indian town's full supply for the winter.

"Adam, get Isaac Taylor and Jeremiah Jack to help you. See how much of the corn is good to use, and carry some of it down. We can use it to feed ourselves and our horses. If there is any left when we leave that we cannot carry with us, we will pile it on the campfires and burn it."

Jack Scott and Alexander McCorkle had quickly discovered that their wives had not been found among the Indian women and children who had been captured. Then, at their own risk, they rode all about the countryside into which the Chickamauga women and children had fled, searching in vain for their wives. Jonathan was not about to try to stop the two men. Instead, he sent ten men to help them and to provide for their safety, less they be attacked by Indians. During their search, Scott, McCorkle, and the others accompanying them discovered that the nearby Cherokee town of Tanasi, about one mile from Chota Town, had been abandoned by the Indians.

As the last rays of the day's sunlight faded over the hill to the west, Jack Scott and Alexander McCorkle returned to the militia camp at Chota Town. Their hopes for that day were vanquished. Their wives had not been found, and if they remained alive they were still being held captive by the Indians.

Colonel Campbell called an officers meeting shortly after dark. "Let's decide what to do with the Indian women and children that are our prisoners. Colonel Sevier, do you have anything in mind?"

"Yes. We can send them tomorrow under guard to a fort in the southern part of our settlements and hold them to exchange for white women and children that the Indians have captured, should the opportunity arise. I think we should hold them at the old fort near George Gillespie's place."

"Okay, can you have some of your men take the captured Indians there?" asked Colonel Campbell.

"Yes. They will depart tomorrow. I'll send twenty men. I will have a full company of men accompany them until they cross the French Broad River. Once that far and still heading north, they will be safe enough under the twenty-man guard, and the company of men will return here at once."

"Good." Then, turning toward Captain Crabtree, Colonel Campbell inquired, "I understand that we had nobody in our own force killed today. Did you get a count of how many Indians we killed?"

"There was only one dead warrior that we could find, but according to reports from the men, there were some that were wounded but escaped, maybe a dozen or more. Among our own men, only two were wounded. Both are minor, and the men will be able to continue the campaign."

"That is good, indeed," said Colonel Campbell. "We will use Chota Town as a base for the next week to ten days, depending on how long it takes. We will burn Tanasi Town and need to attack and destroy Chilhowee and all of the Tellico Towns. We are also going to send a force southward to destroy Hiwassee Old Town and Tuskegee. Maybe the Indians will move westward and not rebuild here. Otherwise, maybe they will at least get the message not to attack our settlements because we have the power to completely destroy all of theirs. This place where we are, Chota Town, is said to be the capital of the whole Cherokee nation, including the Chickamaugas and the other tribes. The Cherokees from hundreds of miles have held all their most important meetings here for many years. Using Chota Town as our own base is part of sending the message of power. This campaign might succeed in driving even Chief Dragging Canoe and Bear Cloud to the west."

John Sevier spoke next, saying, "All of you officers, be sure to talk with your men about this. They know that we plan to destroy some Indian towns, but be sure they know we intend to destroy so many of their towns that it may drive them to the west, so they will not attack our settlements anymore. Don't take any warriors captive. Kill them. If women and children resist, kill them too, just like they do to our women and children."

"Colonel Sevier," replied Major Martin, "some of my men just cannot bring themselves to slaughter unarmed women and children, even Indians."

"If the women and children flee, and your men cannot bring themselves to kill them, then it is OK to let them go," conceded Sevier. "Just be sure to take any weapons and property they may have, so they will be more likely to flee further west. If any of your men can speak a little of the Indian language, tell them to go far west and never come back. The Cherokees tend to listen to what their women have to say."

Colonel Campbell resumed talking. "No one has reported seeing either Chief Dragging Canoe or Bear Cloud today, but we know they are the principal leaders of the Indians we fought today. Since they gave up Chota Town with such little resistance, I don't believe they will make any major attack against us, but watch out for their usual attacks in which they ambush and disappear; and use your scouts well to avoid such ambushes. We will do the attacking. We will do the destroying this time."

On the morning of Thursday, December 21, the militia camp was a beehive of activity. A large force of 270 men under Colonel Campbell was preparing to depart toward the south to attack and destroy the Tellico Towns. Major Jonathan Tipton, with a sizeable force of 250 men, including some of Campbell's Virginians, prepared to attack Chilhowee and two smaller towns to the east. A party of twenty men under Sergeant John Robertson was the first to depart, taking the captured Indian women and children northward. A company of forty men under Major Walton and Captain Samuel Handly escorted them. Major Walton, Captain Handly, and their forty men were to return to Chota Town as soon as Sergeant Robertson's men and the prisoners reached the French Broad River. Lieutenant Colonel Sevier had elected to take sixty men to burn the nearby abandoned town of Tanasi, and then to return to Chota Town. He would remain at Chota Town, ready to provide reinforcements to any of the other groups if needed. Upon Major Walton's return, Sevier's manpower at Chota Town would increase to one hundred men, and his segment of the overall force would return to full strength when Major Tipton returned.

Just after Major Walton's men had left, along with Sergeant John Robertson's men and the captive Indian women and children, one of the regular riders returning from home rode into camp, and approached John Sevier. Lieutenant Colonel Sevier opened and read a letter that had been delivered by the rider. Several officers, including Colonel Campbell and Majors Tipton and Martin, were standing with Sevier at the moment. They waited as he read silently. Then, John Sevier said, "Two pieces of news have been sent by Colonel Shelby. Both are quite good. The Continental Congress passed a formal resolution last month, on November 13, 1780, commending all the officers and men who defeated Ferguson's army at King's Mountain in October. He has enclosed a copy of the resolution for me. The other news is almost as good. Colonel Shelby informs me that General Nathanael Greene has come south, and has taken command from General Gates of all the American forces in the southern states." Handing the documents to Colonel Arthur Campbell, he said, "Colonel Campbell, you may want to read this yourself. Your brother is prominently mentioned in the King's Mountain resolution."

Fifteen minutes later, the mounted militiamen under Colonel Campbell departed to the south toward Tellico Town, and Major Tipton's force left camp heading eastward. Jonathan's force included his own companies under Captain Trimble and Captain Landon Carter, as well as some of Colonel Campbell's Virginians under Lieutenant William Russell and Ensign John Baker.

Considering their recent verbal confrontation at Boyd's Creek, Jonathan was surprised that John Sevier had given him the command of such a relatively large force, and for such a significant objective. He figured it might be a combination of several things. First, despite their differences, Sevier knew that Jonathan was his most capable subordinate commander. Second, by sending Major Walton on the shorter mission to escort captives and return to camp, Lieutenant Colonel Sevier would ensure that he would be working more closely with Major Walton than with Jonathan, for at least a few days. Lastly, if one of the detached groups were attacked, Sevier could lead his men to their support, potentially saving the day and enhancing his hero status. No matter the reason, Jonathan liked having the independent command.

Riding toward Chilhowee, Jonathan said in a matter-of-fact tone to Captain Carter, "Landon, we really need to get Dragging Canoe and Bear Cloud. Of all the Indian chiefs, they are the ones who keep things stirred up. It seems that it is always their Chickamauga warriors that are burning homes, capturing and killing our women and children, and stealing our horses. If we can kill Dragging Canoe and Bear Cloud, our settlements may finally be peaceful places to live."

Proceeding judiciously and carefully to avoid ambush, Major Jonathan Tipton led his 250-man detachment toward the target towns. Chilhowee was a large Indian village less than two days away on horseback. The two remaining towns were smaller, and were both within one day's additional ride beyond Chilhowee. Jonathan's orders were to attack and destroy the towns, and return and rejoin the main force at Chota Town by December 27 if at all possible.

Travel on Thursday had been uneventful. By mid-morning on Friday the twenty-second of December, Jonathan's militia force approached within an hour of Chilhowee, on a part of the trail that was in thick woods. Two scouts on the right had been proceeding on foot due to the steep, rocky terrain along that side of the trail. Both returned hurriedly, running toward the main column. "Indians, they're coming down the hill," shouted the first scout, Smith Ferrell.

"Get ready fast!" yelled Allen McClintock, the other scout.

Suddenly, the air was filled with an unsettling combination of Indian war whoops and gunshots.

Jonathan ordered at the top of his lungs, "Dismount, secure your horses." No sooner than the order was issued, many of the militiamen began returning fire at the Indians.

Indian warriors seemed to appear from behind every tree and every large rock, and they ran downhill, directly toward the militiamen. Soon, fierce hand-to-hand fighting erupted near the front of the column, as a handful of Indians reached that position. The militiamen reacted quickly. Exercising their superb marksmanship, they laid down a deluge of fire into the attacking warriors. After about seven or eight minutes, the Chickamauga warriors retreated up the hill. Inasmuch as the terrain was not suitable for pursuit on horseback, Jonathan elected not to follow the Indians. Setting a strong guard, he had captains Carter and Trimble make a quick assessment of the militia's own casualties. They also had militiamen ensure that all the fallen Indians were actually dead, and count the number of Chickamauga dead. None of the men had seen any Indian chief among the attackers. Isaac Taylor was certain, however, that one of the warriors involved in the hand-to-hand fighting at the front of the column was Little Owl, the brother of Dragging Canoe.

Jonathan's militiamen had met and defeated a party of about two hundred Indians. In the battle, nine militiamen had been wounded, only one seriously, with a gash in his head and a musket ball in his shoulder. They had killed seventeen Indians, and wounded some who got away.

"Major Tipton, shall we send to Colonel Sevier for help?" asked Captain Landon Carter.

"No. We have beaten them. We will continue to Chilhowee and burn it today. Let's get out of this part of the trail. Get your men mounted."

Continuing to Chilhowee and arriving there less than an hour later, they found the town deserted. Giving directions to Captain Trimble and Captain Carter, Jonathan said, "Burn it. Then we will camp here tonight. The Indians selected a good defensive location for this town, even though they chose not to defend it."

On the following morning, Major Tipton's force headed toward the two smaller towns. About noon, Captain Trimble advised Jonathan, "One of our scouts reported that the Indians have not abandoned the two small towns further up the river. They are still there, women, children, and some warriors. They must have thought we would not continue beyond Chilhowee. The first town has about thirty-five Indian cabins and lots of Indians; but the second one only has fifteen cabins, and only a few Indians are there."

Jonathan inquired to Captain Trimble, "How long will it take us to reach the first town?"

"Less than an hour."

"Is the land clear, or do the Indians have cover for an ambush?"

"It's clear enough. No chance of an ambush. The scouts are sure."

"There's no time to waste. Let's ride hard and attack before they flee."

Major Tipton's force attacked the first town, killing five warriors and capturing thirty-seven women and children. Most of the warriors were away from the town, likely with Dragging Canoe or Bear Cloud, wherever they were. The militiamen also captured twenty pigs and two healthy horses belonging to the Indians.

"Release all the women and children," Jonathan ordered. He had never been in favor of killing women and children. Jonathan knew that an adequate number of Indian women and children had already been sent back under guard for possible exchange for white captives. There was no need to hold these women and children as prisoners, and he was certainly not going to kill them.

Scouts returned from the smaller village, reporting that the Indians had fled from it when they heard the sounds of the attack on the larger village. The scouts had gone ahead and burned the smaller village.

Jonathan, looking at Captain Trimble, said, "Take your company of men to that small town right now, and look for the Indians' supply of corn. No corn was found here at this place, and they must have a winter supply of corn somewhere. Find it, take what you can, and destroy all that we cannot use. Go while you still have enough daylight to search, and get back here by dark."

Later that afternoon, the militiamen set camp and slaughtered and roasted the pigs, eating some and packing some cooked meat for the next day's use.

On December 24, the militiamen began retracing their route back toward Chota Town. Then, while continuing the trek on Christmas Day, Jonathan reminisced about home. He shared the emotions of his men, wishing they could be home with their families. On the day after Christmas, they arrived at Chota Town, reuniting with the men under Lieutenant Colonel Sevier.

Jonathan and his men waited along with the rest of John Sevier's force for the return of Colonel Campbell and his men. Jonathan learned that after Major Walton returned from escorting Sergeant Robertson and the captive Indian women and children to the French Broad River, he had led an attack on two small Indian Towns. Major Walton had found both Citico Town and another smaller town abandoned, and had burned both towns. The men at the headquarters at Chota Town also knew from messengers that Colonel Campbell's attacks had been successful in destroying a couple of Indian towns, but details were sparse.

Early in the afternoon on December 29, the large force of men under Colonel Campbell arrived back at the base at Chota Town. They had ridden to the Tellico Towns, found them abandoned, and burned them. Jonathan learned from the Virginians returning from Tellico Town that Captain James Elliott of Colonel Campbell's regiment was killed at Tellico by a single hidden Indian who fired a well-aimed shot and hit him in the chest. The Indian had escaped. The Virginians had also found Hiwassee Old Town abandoned by the Indians, and burned it. They had then returned immediately to Chota Town.

When the militia army was fully reassembled at Chota Town on December 29, Colonels Campbell and Sevier called a meeting of all officers. They knew how badly the men wanted to return home, but also knew that the hostile Indians had not been fully subdued. Scouts had reported that Dragging Canoe had reassembled most of his Chickamauga warriors, along with those of some of the other chiefs, at an Indian town along the bank of the Hiwassee River. Colonel Campbell, with support of almost all the officers, decided to pursue the Indians as far southward to the Hiwassee River, and either catch and destroy them or destroy any Indian towns along the Hiwassee. Then, they would continue the pursuit of the Indians a maximum of not more than seven days beyond Hiwassee, and would then return home.

With a definite end to the mission in sight, the men were content, and they were ready to proceed. By mid-afternoon on the twenty-ninth, the small army started the mounted march toward the town at Hiwassee. Jonathan tugged at the collar of his coat, tightening it as best he could to fend off the cold wind.

Even before the army got to Hiwassee Town, scouts reported that the Indians had moved further south, toward the Indian town of Tuskegee. When the army reached Hiwasssee Town, it had been abandoned. The militiamen burned the town and quickly resumed pursuit of the Indians. For the next several days, the Chickamaugas managed to stay just ahead of the militiamen.

On the sixth of January, scouts reported that about one hundred Indians from the west had joined up with Chief Dragging Canoe's force. Dragging Canoe had led the militia army deep into Indian lands, but the leaders of the force of more than six hundred men under Colonel Arthur Campbell believed they were very close to being in position to deal a devastating blow to the Indians. Colonel Campbell and Lieutenant Colonel Sevier convinced their officers and men to continue pursuing the Indians for three more days.

Finally, just before noon on January 9, 1781, the militia force caught up with a large number of Indians at Tuskegee. Scouts estimated the number of Indians to be somewhat more than three hundred warriors, with only a very few Indian women and children present.

Receiving the reports from the scouts, Colonel Campbell said to his senior officers, "This is not the whole Indian force that Dragging Canoe had with him last week. They must be planning to draw us into an attack, and then attack us from behind with another large force."

John Sevier spoke up firmly, saying, "Colonel, we have received reports from our best scouts. Scouts have reported back from all directions just at the right time. They all say there is not any other sizeable party of Indians anywhere within a two-days' ride from this place. We must attack, and we have to attack them right now!"

Major Jonathan Tipton agreed wholeheartedly with Sevier. This was likely the best opportunity they would get to destroy a large number of the Chickamauga warriors. Jonathan felt he had to speak up.

"Colonel Campbell," he said, "with all due respect, this is what the whole campaign is about. We have to attack this large group of Indians."

"You are both right," replied Colonel Campbell. "Let's do it."

The plan evolved within minutes. Colonel Sevier's troops quickly circled wide and confronted the Indians along one front. Major Martin's men from Sullivan County crossed the river to block any attempt by the Indians to escape across the river. Colonel Campbell's force approached for an attack along a right angle to Lieutenant Colonel Sevier's attack. The result, if successful, would be a triangle of death for the Chickamauga warriors.

All of the men dismounted. Leaving a strong guard with their horses, they proceeded on foot. The fact that the militiamen were mounted had enabled them to overtake and surround the Indians. The Indians obviously knew now that they would have to fight. This large gathering of warriors was likely looking to fight, anyway, thought Jonathan.

Looking the situation over, Jonathan thought that this might be the decisive battle the frontiersmen had long been seeking. The thought passed his mind that they may even kill Dragging Canoe or Bear Cloud if one or both were there with the group. Despite the apprehension of danger and bloodshed, he desperately wanted a decisive victory that would drive the Indians away from the frontier settlements.

As Jonathan walked to the attack of the Indian town along with the rest of Lieutenant Colonel Sevier's regiment, he could see warriors scurrying about. Some of the Indians fired early, without effect, while the militiamen held their fire. When in range, the men took what cover was available, or just knelt down and fired, pouring a hail of fire into the enemy. Jonathan saw two Indians fall in the first round of fire. He then observed puffs of smoke on the other side of the river, where Major Martin's men were making their presence known, cutting off the river as an escape route. Chickamauga warriors were firing their muskets and rifles, along with a few arrows, as well. Their war whoops pierced the air. Colonel Campbell's troops were adding to the hail of fire and the roar of sound and the thickening haze of smoke. Suddenly, all of the Chickamauga warriors charged in unison toward a narrow point along the far side of the line of Colonel Campbell's men. For a couple of minutes, the Indians and Campbell's militiamen became intermingled in hand to hand fighting. The men under Major Tipton and Lieutenant Colonel Sevier had to stop firing, but began advancing rapidly toward the position of the fighting in an attempt to join the fight. Because all of the several hundred warriors attacked a narrow section of Colonel Campbell's line, a great majority of the Indians were able to break through the line and escape.

The militiamen pursued the fleeing Indians briefly, killing several. Then, the Chickamauga warriors seemed to disappear, having dissipated every which direction into the forest and mountains. The Indians would undoubtedly reassemble somewhere, in some number of days, but the militiamen did not know where, of course. Jonathan marveled to himself at the uncanny ability of the Indian warriors to escape, even when they had been surrounded. Their mass attack into a single point in the line of Colonel Campbell's men had not only been brave; it had been brilliant. It was probably the only way they could have avoided almost certain annihilation.

Immediately after the battle, when the horses were being brought forward, Captain Landon Carter took his and Jonathan's horses from the guard, and walked them to Jonathan's location. "Major Tipton," said Landon Carter, "Lieutenant William Russell of Colonel Campbell's regiment saw Chief Bear Cloud. He saw Robert Baker and Bear Cloud fend off each other's tomahawk blows as the Indians broke through the line. Bear Cloud got away."

"Did anyone see Dragging Canoe?" asked Jonathan.

"Not that any of us know about so far."

"We beat them bad," said Captain Carter. "We killed lots of Indians."

Jonathan said, "I don't think we lost a single man killed in our whole regiment."

"We didn't, but Colonel Campbell had three men killed and quite a few men wounded," said John Sevier, arriving and overhearing the conversation. "We didn't have a single man dead or badly wounded in our regiment, but Colonel Campbell had many wounded where the Indians made their charge."

Thomas Gist, running, came to their position and said, "Colonel Sevier, we've caught some Indians, about twenty women and small children. Lieutenant Russell sent me to tell you. They were hiding in the woods."

"Go back to Lieutenant Russell and tell him to bring them to the town and keep them under guard. We ought to kill them, to send a message, since that is what they do to our wives and children," said Sevier.

Hearing Sevier's comment, Jonathan knew right away that John Sevier would not actually give an order to kill women and children prisoners. Sevier was just expressing strong emotion.

By that time, Colonel Campbell had arrived at their location, and said,

"We will keep the Indian women and children prisoners overnight. We are going to let them go when we leave this place, though. I don't approve of killing women and children, even Indians. Beyond that, it is a burden to guard them, and we have already sent enough captured Indians back to the settlements to use for exchanges if we ever get the chance."

"Colonel Sevier, Colonel Campbell," interrupted Landon Carter, "my men report a count of thirty-seven Indians killed today."

"We had them trapped. We should have killed all of them," said John Sevier.

Colonel Campbell scowled. He was irritated by Sevier's comment, thinking that Sevier was blaming Campbell's men for the Indians' escape. After a brief moment of silence, Campbell replied, "We had a great victory here today. The Indians made a brave charge and got away the only way they could. I want all officers to meet by the Indians' big house in ten minutes. We'll wait until after the meeting to burn the town."

Shortly afterward, Lieutenant William Russell and his men arrived, bringing the captured Chickamauga women and children back to the town. Jonathan could see the fear in the eyes of the women. He thought their fear was justifiable, for many if not most of the white men who were present wanted to kill them.

Having become acquainted with Lieutenant Russell, Jonathan commented to him as he passed by, "William, I'm glad you and your men did not slaughter them on the spot. That's what some would have done, but I have never favored killing unarmed women and children."

"Well," replied Russell, "they weren't exactly unarmed. Three or four of the women had knives and one had a tomahawk, but they gave up easily for fear their children would be killed. I don't want to kill them, either. Did you get the word that we saw two of the big chiefs?"

"Your man told Colonel Campbell that you saw Bear Cloud, but everyone agreed that nobody saw Dragging Canoe."

"That's not who I'm talking about, Major. While Robert Baker was fighting Chief Bear Cloud, I almost got a shot off at old Chief Oconostota. He was until not long ago the main war chief of all the Cherokee tribes everywhere."

"How do you know it was him?"

"I was at the land negotiations a few years back, and he was there. Today, he was surrounded by warriors like bees on a nest. There was no way to get a clear shot at him. Heck, I was lucky to be standing at all. My men got pretty bloodied up by the Indians today."

Jonathan thought briefly and said, "They say he is about seventy years of age. It's really strange that he would be in a battle."

"It was him, definitely," said Lieutenant Russell.

Jonathan responded politely, "I don't doubt you in any way. You need to tell Colonel Campbell."

As William Russell walked away to find Colonel Campbell, Jonathan thought about the presence of the old war chief. Chief Oconostota must have been among the large assembly of warriors at Chota Town. Then, when the Indians split up upon the battle at Chota Town, the old chief had obviously rejoined the party led by Chief Bear Cloud, which ultimately retreated to Tuskegee Town. It dawned upon Jonathan at that moment that since Chief Bear Cloud had retreated so deeply into Indian lands, the Indians had obviously given up on any thought of a united offensive against the white settlements. Nevertheless, Chief Dragging Canoe had not been with Chief Bear Cloud that day. Dragging Canoe was considered by many to be the most dangerous of all the Indian chiefs, and he could have regrouped somewhere else with a force of up to four hundred warriors from the remainder of those who split up at Chota Town.

All the militia officers assembled for a meeting late in the afternoon. Colonel Campbell and John Sevier had been talking together privately at a spot about forty paces from where the officers assembled. When all the other officers were present they joined the assembly.

Colonel Campbell did the talking, saying, "Over the last few weeks we have killed one hundred and ten Indians. We have burned more than a dozen of their towns. We destroyed the Indians' supplies of corn. We have killed their pigs and cattle and captured six horses. Seven of our men were killed, and more than a few are wounded. We captured thirty-one Indian women and children and sent them back to be held prisoner and used for possible exchange if we get the chance. We have forced the

Chickamauga warriors far away from our settlements for the present time. We have shown them that it is not a good idea to ally themselves with the British against our settlements, for we are too powerful. Both Colonel Sevier and I know how badly you and your men all want to be with your families. We all missed being home with our wives and children at Christmas time. We will head home." Then, he looked at John Sevier and said, "Colonel Sevier, gather your men, and I'll gather mine along with those of Major Martin. We will tell them what I have just shared with the officers. We'll tell them that tomorrow morning we will head home. As we travel, we will be scouting for any Indians we may be able to find along the way, and if we find any, we will attack them. Otherwise, we are going to head directly to our settlements and homes."

On the morning of January 10, the army of militiamen headed toward home. The long campaign was deemed a success, and thankfully it was finally coming to an end. Jonathan sensed the high spirits of the men, knowing that in a matter of days they would be home with their families. Jonathan's own warm spirits were tempered only by the full force of the cold winter wind.

After days of travel in bitter cold weather with a biting headwind prevailing most of the time, the morning sun rose brightly, accompanied by minimal wind and less frigidity. Jonathan was finally home!

The four children ran gleefully toward the approaching rider. "Father! Father! Father!" they screamed. Not far behind them was Frances, bearing a radiant smile. Dismounting, Jonathan hugged the children. As he and Frances met, the two hugged warmly and followed with a gentle kiss. Jonathan looked into her sparkling green eyes, and then glanced briefly at her lovely dark hair.

"Tell us about the battles, father," requested Samuel. "Did you kill any Indians?"

Jonathan grinned, winked at Frances, and said, "The first thing I will tell you is something you have all heard before. It is that home is the best place in the entire world."

"But tell us about the Indians," said William.

"Father, you were gone too long," chimed in four-year-old Hannah. "I'm so glad you're home."

"Well, I am truly glad to be home, and we did kill lots of Indians. We drove them far away into the Indian hunting lands. We did hurry home. Last night, none of the men could sleep, and we were close enough that we knew the land well, so we rode all night long except when we rested our horses. That is how I got here right now, in the middle of the day."

Frances knew that she should take control of the moment, and said, "Let's all go inside. Father can tell you about his journey while he sits and rests, for I believe he is far too excited about being at home to sleep, no matter how tired he is. Mary and Hannah, with both of you helping, we will have dinner ready within an hour."

As the reunited family took the last few steps together toward the two-room cabin, Jonathan noticed for the first time just how dramatically the weather had changed. Yesterday had been frigid and overcast. The new day was sunny, and was unseasonably warm for the third week of January. It was totally befitting, by the grace of God, thought Jonathan, for a homecoming.

Chapter 8

The New Colonel
and More Conflict

THE GROUNDS OF the church were abuzz with excited conversation just prior to services on the last Sunday in January of 1781. Word had been received of a great patriot victory at Cowpens on the seventeenth of January by a force under General Morgan, with Colonel Pickens' troops and Lieutenant Colonel William Washington's cavalry playing significant roles. Cowpens was relatively close to home, just on the other side of the mountains, only thirty miles from the site of the victory three months before at King's Mountain. At Cowpens, the Americans had defeated Tarleton's British Legion in a battle in which each side had well more than a thousand men. The news was that the British had lost more than nine hundred men, including more than one hundred killed and more than eight hundred captured and wounded. Only Lieutenant Colonel Tarleton and about two hundred of his men escaped. The Americans had lost only twelve men and less than one hundred were wounded. It was another overwhelming victory for the Patriots.

At home later that day, Jonathan said to Frances, "During the return trip from Chota Town last month, the officers and men talked quite a bit about our need to remain home with our families. We determined that we would keep the militia at home indefinitely unless some unexpected threat arises from the Indians or the British. Now, with the news of General Morgan's victory at Cowpens, it looks like we may be able to remain home for quite some time."

"What a blessing. The children and I need you," Frances replied.

As the sun set gently beyond the hills, Jonathan sat at the head of the small table in the center of the front room of the cabin. The five children sat on benches along the sides of the table. Frances sat nearer the fire in the simple wooden rocking chair. A single candle burned at Jonathan's end of the table.

"Tonight," said Jonathan, "I am going to read a short passage from the Holy Bible. It is one you have not heard before. Tomorrow night, I will work with you three, William, Samuel, and Mary, on your own reading; and your mother will continue with Hannah and Johnny on counting numbers." Both Frances and Jonathan believed strongly that their children should be taught to read and write. Inasmuch as Jonathan had received six years of formal education, compared to only two years for Frances, the two of them had decided quite some time before that she would teach them to count and would teach them the alphabet. Jonathan would school them in reading, writing, adding, subtracting, and simple multiplication and division.

"Now, here is tonight's Bible passage. It is part of the thirty-seventh Psalm. It tells about how God will treat good people and how He will treat their evil, wicked enemies." Jonathan began reading from the only book he owned. Although Jonathan preferred to use the correct biblical wording, he sometimes took the liberty to modify some words so that the meaning was easier for the children to understand. Additionally, he sometimes interjected brief interpretations to help them under- stand. "Worry not yourself because of the wicked; be not envious of wrongdoers, for they will soon fade like the grass." Jonathan continued through the twentieth verse, concluding, "But the wicked perish; the enemies of the Lord are like the glory of the pastures, they vanish; like smoke they vanish away. So sayeth the Lord."

Two hours later that Sunday night, as Jonathan and Frances were retiring, the children were asleep. Only embers remained from the evening fire. Jonathan said to Frances, "We have beaten the British and Tories at King's Mountain. We have burned many of the Indian towns and have driven the Indians deep into their hunting lands. Now, General Morgan has beaten a British army at Cowpens, on the other side of the mountains. I do believe we are safer now than at any time since we moved here eight years ago."

One morning during the second week of February, Jonathan was out chopping firewood with his son William, who was now almost nine years old. Both were using long handle axes. He was proud of the strength and productivity of his son for his age, and the stack of wood in his son's pile after twenty minutes was almost two-thirds of the size of Jonathan's work.

A surprising event interrupted their work. None other than Colonel John Carter, riding alone, was approaching via the hillside trail to their cabin. Colonel Carter had been seriously ill for a very long time, and had been bedridden and had not been able to ride at all. Seeing him there was a big surprise. Colonel Carter was obviously in pain, and was barely able to dismount from his horse. After excusing his son so he could talk privately with the colonel, Jonathan received some surprising news. Colonel Carter spoke briefly with Jonathan to give him the news. Then he departed promptly after the brief, unexpected visit.

Shortly after the colonel departed, Frances Tipton approached her husband as he worked to replace a diagonal support log in the stable section inside the barn. She sensed that something was wrong. "Jonathan," she said, "can you tell me why Colonel Carter visited today?"

Jonathan had a respectful, trusting relationship with his wife. He shared information and opinions with her because he knew that she was intelligent and had good common sense. She would be able to discern what information she should divulge to others and what she must keep to herself. He knew that her judgment was impeccable. On this basis, Jonathan promptly revealed the news and his feelings about it. "Colonel Carter came here to tell me in person that John Sevier has been appointed full colonel for Washington County. Governor Caswell did it week before last, and the dispatch arrived at Colonel Carter's house yesterday."

Jonathan paused momentarily and then continued. "Colonel Carter received the news in a letter from the governor yesterday afternoon. He told Sevier last night and he wanted to tell me personally before I heard it from someone else. Because Colonel Carter has been ill for so long, the governor decided to appoint a second colonel for Washington County. He felt the logical choice was Lieutenant Colonel Sevier. You know it never seemed fair to me several years ago when Sevier was made Lieutenant Colonel from Captain when I had already been Major for eight months."

"Jonathan, you told me you knew this might happen if Colonel Carter was ever promoted to general," Frances reminded him. "So it may be disappointing but it is not really a surprise except that it is happening right now, instead."

"You are right, but what really bothers me is that Colonel Carter admitted to me that he wrote the governor recommending Sevier for the promotion. The other bad thing is that Colonel Carter said he is not going to be involved in the militia any more. He is simply too sick. Sevier is fully and completely in charge."

"I can't help but think about King's Mountain," Jonathan continued. "I had been under Colonel Carter for seven years, and then for a few days I was under Colonel Campbell, but then I was assigned to Sevier's command the night before that battle because he needed two additional companies. It was my companies, my men, who carried the day in Sevier's area of the battle. It was my men and the orders that I gave during the battle that made John Sevier the hero of the great battle at King's Mountain." Jonathan paused momentarily, then continued, "Colonel Carter said that he felt he had no choice but to recommend him, considering everyone far and wide knows of Sevier's fame as the hero of King's Mountain. I don't hate John Sevier, and he is certainly a brave man. It is just that if it had not been for his back-door actions years ago, getting the promotion from captain to lieutenant colonel through political connections, things would have been different. I should be the full colonel and Sevier should be reporting to me. I should not be reporting to him. It all came about because of his darned governor-to-governor influence."

Jonathan's next comment summed up his feelings. "I have always respected John Sevier, but I never have liked him very much."

"I know," said Frances. "On the other hand, think how much Colonel

Carter respects you to come tell you about this in person. He has been so weak and sickly that many fear he will pass from this life."

"It is a compliment, indeed, that he came. I hope he makes his way home all right."

The next few weeks of life on the frontier were routine times of hard work and happiness. Then, in the first week of March a sudden onslaught of nighttime horse thefts by Indians struck the southern part of the over-mountain settlements. Especially hard hit was the area from the Nolichucky River to the Doe River, just south of the Watauga Settlement. The homes of more than forty settlers were raided in just three nights. When settlers heard sounds and attempted to thwart the theft of their horses, they were in each case met with a torrent of gunfire from the Indians. All of the settlers, especially the militia leaders, were quite surprised, as they had believed the Indians had been effectively defeated and driven deep into Indian hunting lands. The numerous occurrences of horse theft in such a short time indicated the nearby presence of a significant number of Indians.

On Tuesday, the sixth of March, Captain Landon Carter came to see Jonathan. "Major Tipton," he said, "Colonel Sevier wants both you and me to meet with him at the fort tomorrow at noon. It's about the Indian trouble."

"Do you know what he has in mind?" asked Jonathan.

"No, sir," Landon replied. Having observed Major Tipton as a close friend of his father over the years, the young captain was very respectful to Jonathan.

I'll come by your father's house, and we'll go together to the fort. How is your father's health?

"It's the worst it has been, Major."

"I shall stop and visit him tomorrow," said Jonathan.

The next day, following a brief visit at the Carter home, Jonathan rode with Captain Landon Carter to the fort at the Watauga settlement. John Sevier was already there, waiting for them. Surprisingly, he was alone.

"Hello, Jonathan," said John Sevier, extending his hand. The two shook hands respectfully, but in such a firm manner that it seemed to Jonathan that the handshake was almost a test of will.

"Hello, John," replied Jonathan.

Sevier then said, "It is good to see you, Landon."

"It's good to see you, too, Colonel."

Colonel Sevier then looked at Major Tipton. "Jonathan, you know about the rash of Indian horse-stealing raids down south, and you know the Indians killed Arthur Clements and his whole family three days ago, and stole his horses, of course. Right?"

"That is correct," Jonathan responded.

"Now I have information that will permit us to cut off the Indian raids at their source. The two traders, Jack Tillman and Smoky Copeland, passed through yesterday and told me that the British are stirring up the Indians again and have given them more muskets and gunpowder on the condition that the Indians will harass us. The British want the Indians to keep us at home so we cannot support the Patriots' efforts against the British to the east of the mountains. The Indians have set up a large camp at a spring at the head of a small creek only about four miles south of the French Broad River. You know the general area, I believe?"

"Yes, of course. We have been there together."

Sevier quickly recaptured control of the conversation, saying, "Jonathan, I want you to take Captain Carter, Captain Jacob Brown, Captain Christopher Taylor, and some men to attack the Indians. We will get some extra men from the southern settlements, too. They will be glad to go, but you may have to take horses for them, since the Indians have been stealing theirs. You will need to leave on the day after tomorrow. The Indians' encampment is far too close. It's only going to get worse if we don't hit them hard and fast."

"How many Indians are there, and are they mostly warriors, or are lots of women and children there, too?" inquired Jonathan.

"We are not certain, but these same traders were right before. They said the Indians are mostly warriors, with at least a few women and children, and they have settled into an encampment at the spring that I mentioned just a few miles south of the French Broad River. You have to attack them and kill them or drive them away again. We've got to remind them that it is the settlers that have the power, and not the British."

In a tone of voice clearly indicating concern, Jonathan said, "John, most of the men have been away from home a lot, first to fight the British and Tories, and then to fight the Indians. You know that we have talked about them having too much work to be done at home to undertake any new mission other than one of true urgency."

Sevier exclaimed, "By God, Tipton, if you will not lead this attack, I will see to it that you lose your commission in the militia! I only picked you to lead it because I have to head east in three days to see the governor, and you are the most experienced officer I have. I'm sure that Major Robertson can assume this task if you will not do it."

"I am not telling you that I won't lead the campaign. I was just about to say that it may be difficult to get enough men on such short notice."

Colonel Sevier's next comments surprised Major Tipton. "I already have the men lined up," Sevier stated. "I have spoken with Captain Brown and Captain Taylor. They can both get full companies of their own men, plus we will have some more men from northern parts of the settlements that did not go on the last campaign. Furthermore, Colonel Shelby will supply us with fifty of his men from Sullivan County. You will have at least 250 men, 250 horses, and plenty of powder and shot."

Jonathan replied, "I may be the last one to know about this mission, but I will do it, and I will do it well." Then, turning his eyes toward Captain Carter, he said, "Landon, we will need to start immediately to get as many men as we can."

Colonel Sevier concluded, "I will have Captains Brown and Taylor meet you here at the fort at noon on Friday. Their full companies and the additional men I told you about from Sullivan County will be here. You have my word on this. Can I count on you?"

"Yes," was Major Tipton's simple reply.

As he departed from the meeting, Jonathan thought to himself that John Sevier had been oversensitive about any Indian trouble near the southern settlements ever since Sevier had moved south two years ago to his new home along the Nolichucky River. *Now,* he thought, *Sevier, having supplanted Colonel Carter in command, may be overreacting simply because the trouble is close to Sevier's own home.*

Before daybreak on Friday, Jonathan hugged Frances as he prepared to leave on the mission against the Indians.

"Jonathan, do be careful," said Frances.

He could sense the worried tone of her voice. "Don't fret. I will be back in two weeks or less this time." With that, he mounted his horse and left.

Only several minutes later, at dawn, Jonathan rode up to within twenty feet of the front door of his neighbor, Tom Callahan. Knowing that Tom would be up and about and would have already accomplished several personal chores at that time of morning, Jonathan yelled loudly, "Are you ready to go?"

When Jonathan and Tom Callahan arrived at the fort, they were greeted by Captain Taylor.

"Good morning, Major Tipton," said Taylor. "Colonel Sevier sent supplies to the fort yesterday afternoon, and he asked me and several of my men to remain here overnight to protect them."

Jonathan looked around. Sure enough, there was as much powder and shot as his men would be able to carry, along with twenty extra horses for any men who did not have horses of their own. Almost immediately, men began to trickle in, at first mostly those in Captain Carter's company. Then, just before nine o'clock in the morning, Captain Taylor's full company rode in, followed shortly by Captain Jacob Brown with about thirty men. Jonathan knew that Brown's company would pick up about twenty more men as they passed through the southern settlements en route to attack the Indians. Next to arrive was Captain James Gibson, of Major Tipton's normal command, with forty-seven men.

About ten o'clock, Captain John Elliott and his company of fifty men from Sullivan County appeared, just as promised. Jonathan's force already numbered 220 men, not counting the twenty or so who would join them to the south. The militiamen were well armed with their own personal long rifles, tomahawks, long knives, and plenty of powder and shot.

Major Tipton and Captain Carter had done their fair share of work in gathering the force, and Colonel Sevier had been good to his word in delivering two companies of men along with fifty of Colonel Shelby's men from Sullivan County. Jonathan thought about one thing he really did like about Colonel Sevier, that John Sevier was a man of his word. He could always be counted on to do what he said he would do.

Jonathan called a brief officers' meeting before the departure of the militia force. He opened the meeting by saying, "The report we have is that there is a large Chickamauga encampment about three days' ride to the south. Those Indians are responsible for all the recent horse thefts and for killing Arthur Clements and his whole family. We are going to find the Indians and attack them. We will kill as many of them as we can, and drive the rest as far away as we can. However, we are not going to make this a month-long campaign just to drive the Indians further away. The men need to get back home to their farms and families just as badly as you do, so we need to strike the Indians hard and fast. Let's get the men home in two weeks or less. Tell this to your men. We're going to strike hard and fast and get this done so we can get home within two weeks. Are there any questions before we ride?"

Captain Elliott from Sullivan County spoke up, saying, "Are we going to send riders home daily and have riders returning regularly from home, as was done in the last campaign?"

"Yes," responded Jonathan, "a single rider will be sent homeward each day, going through the southern settlements, the Watauga settlement, and all the way to Sullivan County. Each day's rider will depart at a different time of day, so that if the Indians are on the lookout they don't know what time of day a rider might be leaving." After a moment of silence, with no further questions, Jonathan continued, "Well, let's ride."

Jonathan was slightly uncomfortable with the fact that his best scout, David Bragg, was not a part of this mission. Bragg, like so many others, simply had too much work to do on his farm. Nevertheless, some good scouts were present. In fact, most of the men were competent scouts in a pinch, and Andrew Caldwell, one of the best of all the scouts in Colonel Shelby's command, had come with Captain Elliott.

As the militia force headed southward, Jonathan Tipton was glad that he was independently in command. He and John Sevier respected each other's abilities, but Jonathan was never content with serving under Sevier. *If this mission was necessary,* thought Jonathan, *at least Colonel Sevier's commitment to visit the governor prevented him from being in the lead. If the information from the traders was accurate, this mission will be for the greater good of all the settlers on the Washington County frontier.*

On Monday, the third day of the trip, the militiamen crossed the French Broad River in early afternoon. The water at the ford chilled both men and horses on what was otherwise a mild, sunny March day. The day before, scouts had confirmed the location of the Indian encampment, just where the traders had indicated. The militiamen were now less than four miles from the Indian camp. Major Tipton, riding with Captain Elliott at the head of the column, saw a lone scout from the front riding hard toward the column. He soon recognized the approaching scout as Benjamin Webb.

"Major Tipton," said Webb, "I've been scouting with Andrew Caldwell. We spied the Indians lined up on a ridge on a little hill to the west, just before you get to their camp. There is nobody at all in their camp. Just like Captain Gibson said last night, the Indians know we are coming, and they are trying to ambush us."

"Can you tell how many there are?" asked Jonathan.

"No, sir."

Suddenly, three shots rang out from the rear of the column, followed by six or seven more in rapid succession. Then, also from the rear, amidst Indian war whoops, Jonathan heard the loud shout of Captain James Gibson, saying, "Dismount and shoot. Dismount and shoot." Then, a fierce exchange of shots erupted from the back of the column.

Mounted Indians had surprised the rear guard of the militia, had ridden right past them on the left, and were in close contact with the back of the main column. Other Indians had continued along the left of the column, shooting from horseback at the militiamen. Never before had Jonathan ever witnessed such a large-scale mounted attack by Indians. Seeing that the Indians were riding past, shooting, rather than engaging in hand-to-hand fighting, Major Tipton and Captain Elliott simultaneously yelled,

"Dismount." They knew instinctively that the men's marksmanship would be far more accurate if they were on foot.

The firing picked up at the front of the column, as Jonathan and Captain Elliott, along with their men, returned fire with their passing enemies. As the last of the mounted Indians passed, the shooting subsided.

Jonathan issued a series of quick commands. "Benjamin," he said to Private Webb, "get Elijah Bates and John Taylor and follow the mounted Indians at a distance. Send Taylor back in ten minutes and let me know where they are heading. We are not going to chase them into an ambush.

Turning toward Lieutenant Talley, Jonathan ordered, "Check with all the captains and inform me of any wounded and killed on our side, and of the Indians."

Then, Jonathan directed, "Lieutenant Newcombe, ride back in the column and have all the captains keep their men dismounted and at the ready for a few minutes. Get all the captains to meet me at the middle of the column right away."

Within five minutes, Jonathan was meeting with the five captains: Elliott, Carter, Brown, Taylor, and Gibson. "We've got three scouts following the Indians. One will report back in a few minutes. We've got to get more scouts out ahead. Have all the scouts that were out when the Indians attacked returned?"

"All of mine are back," said Captain Jacob Brown. Similar responses followed from Captains Taylor, Elliott, and Gibson.

Captain Landon Carter replied, "My scouts were the rear guard. They are all with us, but William Brannum, rest his soul, was killed. Some of my men are sure they saw Chief Bear Cloud leading the Indian charge."

"I saw him myself," said Captain Brown. "It was Bear Cloud with the Indians on horseback for sure."

Wasting no time, Major Tipton immediately resumed issuing directions. "Captain Elliott, send Andrew Caldwell back out, on the right, with at least three men to scout the Indian position on the ridge if they are still there. Have him send a man back with a report as soon as he spots the Indians, and have him send another back whenever he can report further. We'll be heading forward down the valley, and they will find us easily. Landon, put some additional men with your scouts back as the rear guard. Captain Gibson, send three men to catch up with Webb, Bates, and Taylor and help them scout. Tell them to report back anything of use they might see."

Turning toward Captain Brown, Jonathan said, "Jacob, send scouts out to the left front, and have them send reports back, as well." Then, looking at Christopher Taylor, he said, "Captain Taylor, provide the close-in scouts for the front, left, and right of the column, about one hundred yards out. Tell them to remain within shouting distance."

Lieutenant Talley had arrived during the conversation. He had the casualty count, but could tell that it was not the right time to interrupt Major Tipton's intense discussion with the captains. Talley, at last sensing it was time for him to speak up, said, "William Brannum was the only man killed. Two other men of the rear guard were wounded, and two men near the back of the main column were wounded, all with minor wounds. Otherwise, three horses were shot by the Indians and had to be killed."

As Lieutenant Talley spoke, Jonathan thought to himself that it was a good thing that these Chickamauga Indians, who were good marksmen on foot, were not accurate with their shots from horseback.

Talley continued, "Two Indians were killed, and about five others are reported to have been wounded, but escaped on horseback. We've never seen so many Indians attack on horseback. There must have been about 150 of them."

"OK," said Major Tipton. Then, he resumed giving instructions to the captains, saying, "Except for Captain Elliott's men, we are going to ride to the base of the ridge where the Indians are waiting. There, we will dismount and leave Captain Taylor with forty-five men to watch the horses and be our rear guard while we attack the ridge on foot. Meanwhile, Captain Elliott's men will have dismounted a half mile earlier. Their horses will be led forward by Taylor's men, while Captain Elliott and his men sneak up the hill and attack the Indians' flank. Let's get the men mounted and proceed toward the Indian camp. Be ready for anything. We may need to change plans depending on information from our scouts regarding the Indians' location and where the mounted

Indians have gone. Bear Cloud has already pulled one surprise with the attack on horseback. We are going to outfox him if we can, but one way or another we are going to beat him.

The militia force headed forward with Major Tipton, Captain Elliott, and Captain Jacob Brown at the head of the column. The forward scouts soon reported that the Indians were still posted on the ridge, but that the Indians who had made the attack on horseback had dismounted in a forested area on the left side, planning to catch the militiamen in a crossfire.

Then, Jack Dougherty, one of Captain Elliott's scouts, returned, having been sent back by Andrew Caldwell with details regarding the Indians on the ridge. "Captain Elliott, Major Tipton," he said, "there are about 170 to 200 Chickamaugas on the ridge. Andrew said to tell you we can definitely surprise them from their flank and just to their rear if you will send the men."

"Excellent; that's just what we're going to do," replied Captain Elliott.

Major Tipton's orders came immediately. "Captain Elliott, have your men dismount. Take your men uphill on foot. We are just at the right place right now, and still out of sight of the ridge. We'll proceed slowly enough to give you time to get in place. Try to attack as soon as you hear us attack them from their front. If you get there early and feel you need to attack to keep the surprise, go ahead. You'll probably startle them badly from that direction if they still think we're all down in their front." Then, looking at Captain Brown, Major Tipton said, "Jacob, have each of your men lead one of the horses belonging to Captain Elliot's men."

By now, all the captains had gathered at the front of the stopped column. Planning quickly, Jonathan stated, "With the other party of Indians in the woods on the left, we will strengthen our rear guard. Captain Gibson, when we get to the base of the hill where the Indians are located, you will have twenty of your men under Lieutenant Talley remain with Captain Taylor and the horses. Expect heavy action from the Indians in the woods on the left. You, Captain Brown, Captain Carter, and I will lead the rest of your men and all of their men uphill to attack the Indians on the ridge on our right while Captain Elliott hits them from their flank or slightly to their rear. Once we gain the advantage on the Indians on the ridge, I will stay with you and Captain Brown and his men as they join up with Captain Elliott's men." Then, looking Landon Carter squarely in the eyes, Jonathan continued, "At that time, Landon, you will then take your company back downhill to reinforce Lieutenant Talley and Captain Taylor. Be sure your men know that they can expect to be ordered to turn around and go downhill for that attack. Captain Taylor and Lieutenant Talley will be outnumbered until you can make that attack."

Captain Elliott led his men uphill on foot. The rest of the men mounted and rode slowly forward along the trail through the small, lightly wooded valley.

The forward scouts intentionally passed between the Indians in the woods on the left and those on the ridge on the right at the intended ambush site, letting the Indians believe they had not been discovered. The scouts had orders to return to the force upon hearing any shooting, and join Captain Taylor's company.

When the main body of militiamen reached a point about a hundred yards short of where the Indians waited in ambush, Jonathan gave the order to dismount. All the men dismounted and hobbled their horses, tying their front feet together so they could not wander afar. Major Tipton, Captain Brown, Captain Gibson, and Captain Carter led 125 men on foot uphill to attack the Indians on the ridge on the right. Upon seeing the advancing militiamen, the Indians on the ridge commenced firing. Shooting downhill, most of their shots were high, missing their marks. Jonathan and the militiamen spread out and advanced from tree to tree, firing when within effective range. Jonathan saw two Indians fall, struck by accurate shots.

Suddenly, a volley of shots rang from higher on the hill. It was Captain Elliott and his men. Not only had Major Tipton's uphill attack reversed the advantage of surprise on the Indians, but now Elliott's men had completely surprised the Indians on their flank. Within the next minute, Jonathan saw five more Indians fall wounded or killed along the ridge, and then a sixth. Jonathan's men advanced faster, and the Indians along the ridge began to retreat. Jonathan ran over to Captain Carter and shouted, "Landon, take your men downhill now and reinforce Captain

Taylor and Lieutenant Talley on their right. Attack immediately and hit the Indians hard."

Captain Taylor's full company, along with Lieutenant Talley and twenty men from Captain James Gibson's company remained beside the trail with the horses. The bulk of these men deployed in a position to stave off the expected attack from the Indians in the wooded area to the left. Sure enough, the Indians rushed out of the woods in an all-out attack on Taylor's position. The excellent marksmanship of the sixty-five militiamen helped, but soon the attack by about 140 Indians resulted in bitter hand-to-hand combat. There was a real danger that these militiamen would be overcome, and the Indians would take the militiamen's horses, as well.

This was when the brilliance of Major Tipton's plan took effect. Captain Carter's full company of fifty men charged downhill, stopping only when they were fifteen paces from the fighting to pour a salvo of shots into the Indians. Landon Carter aimed at a fierce looking Indian that he thought fit the description of Chief Bear Cloud, and killed him with a shot to the head. Immediately, two warriors picked up the fallen Indian and began to carry the body away. James McCann, who was standing next to Captain Carter, fired, wounding one of the warriors and causing both warriors to fall and drop the body to the ground. Captain Carter and James McCann immediately rushed toward the wounded Indian and the body that they were almost certain was that of Chief Bear Cloud. Both warriors stood their ground beside the lifeless body. Landon Carter pulled his pistol and fired his one shot, striking the healthy warrior in the stomach, but the Indian did not fall. Landon swung at him with a tomahawk, but the Indian skillfully blocked the blow with his own tomahawk. Landon dropped his rifle and took a quick step backward, drawing his long knife. Now holding his knife in his left hand and his tomahawk in his right, he could see blood oozing from the Indian's stomach wound. Nevertheless, the alert eyes and quick movements of the Indian indicated that he remained a formidable foe. Suddenly, Landon inadvertently stepped on the body of Chief Bear Cloud, causing Landon to stumble. The wounded warrior lunged forward and swung a forceful blow with his tomahawk.

Landon barely dodged the blow, and was off balance and defenseless as the Indian drew back his hand to deliver an intended fatal blow. Just at that second a flying blur of humanity came seemingly from nowhere, diving at the Indian with whom Landon was engaged. It was Robert McCann, brother of James McCann. He made a flying tackle of the Indian and stabbed him through the throat, and followed with a final stab into the chest. Meanwhile, James McCann disposed of the other Indian with less difficulty, as the earlier shot had shattered the Indian's leg bone so badly that he could bear weight only on one leg when standing.

The initial volley of shots from Landon Carter's men had killed or wounded more than fifteen Indians in a matter of seconds. Then, without reloading, Captain Carter's entire company rushed into the melee of hand-to-hand fighting at the same time that Captain Carter and James McCann had rushed forward. The situation for the Indians in the valley had gone from one of advantage to one of death and defeat.

"Captain Carter, that is Chief Bear Cloud," said Private Robert McCann, pointing at the dead chief.

"I thought so," said Landon Carter. Then, looking quickly at the battle scene, he could see dozens and dozens of Indians running toward the woods, while his own men and Captain Taylor's men loaded their guns and fired at the fleeing Indians. This part of the battle had been won.

Up on the ridge, the militiamen under Major Tipton, Captain Elliott, and Captain Gibson completely routed the Indians, chasing them off the ridge and pursuing them two hundred yards into the forest before Major Tipton ordered a halt. Because the Indians on the ridge had begun to flee upon being surprised by Captain Elliot's strike on their flank, the fighting on the ridge had not been as ferocious as that down in the valley. The militiamen on the ridge had taken only very light casualties, with one man killed and six wounded; but thirteen Indians had been killed along the ridge. As the men on the ridge halted and regrouped, they listened as the shooting and yelling quieted down in the valley.

"Major Tipton, our men have won the battle down on the trail," commented Captain Elliott. "Otherwise, we would be hearing Indian victory yells."

"You are right," replied Jonathan. "Let's get back down there and reassemble the whole force."

Major Tipton and the militiamen walked slowly downhill, some assisting the wounded men. One of the militiamen from the valley was making his way uphill, directly toward Jonathan. Although the man appeared to be tired, he was walking fast. As the man approached closer Jonathan recognized him. It was Private Robert McCann, who served regularly under Landon Carter.

At a distance of fifteen feet Robert McCann spoke loudly and clearly, stating, "Major Tipton, we've killed Chief Bear Cloud!"

"Are you sure?"

"Yes. Captain Carter killed him, shot him in the head. My brother saw it. We have Bear Cloud's body." Cheers arose from those nearby, followed by shouts spreading the information among all the men who were moving downhill.

James McCann spoke again, directly to Jonathan, and said, "Captain Carter told me to let you know two more things. First, he said that Captain Taylor has lost quite a few men and had some wounded in the fighting in the valley. Second, maybe even worse, it's about the six forward scouts who were supposed to come back as soon as they heard the first shots. They never came back. Nobody has seen them at all."

As Major Tipton arrived in the valley and approached Captains Taylor and Carter, a single rider came in at a gallop. The rider stopped and quickly dismounted. It was Benjamin Webb, one of the forward scouts who had not returned up to that point. Jonathan's first thought was that it was curious that Webb had approached not from the front, but from the rear of their original route. Benjamin Webb excitedly spouted, "Major Tipton, we stole almost all the Indians' horses, sir. I was with two other scouts. We were out front scouting and came across more than a hundred horses being guarded by only four warriors and two Indian boys, so we found the other three forward scouts and attacked the six Indians while the big fighting was going on. We herded the horses around the back side of the hill. We are holding them about a half mile back on the trail. We have 120 Indian horses. Most of them are ones that were stolen from our settlers. Major, we need men there fast, to guard the horses in case the Indians come."

Jonathan and the other officers were astonished. Covering his surprise, Jonathan turned to Captain Gibson and said, "James, get your whole company mounted and go back with Webb to where the horses are. The rest of us will come back there after we take care of the wounded, probably about an hour. We will camp somewhere near there tonight."

Captain Gibson hurriedly assembled his men, and they rode with Private Webb toward the location of the captured horses.

Jonathan ordered Lieutenant William Newcombe to make an account of killed and wounded on both sides. He instructed Newcombe, "William, I want the count to be as accurate as possible—counts of the dead on both sides and an accounting of our wounded—but don't try to get any count of wounded Indians who escaped. The men can never tell just how many they actually wounded."

Jonathan would write two short letters that night, providing information about the battle at Indian Ridge. He would have riders leave the next morning to deliver them. One letter would go to Colonel Shelby in Sullivan County, and would be delivered by one of Captain Elliott's men. The other letter would be for Colonel Sevier, and would be delivered to Major Robertson with instructions for him to open it and read it, and to hold it for presentation to Colonel Sevier upon his return from his visit with the governor. Jonathan knew that Colonel Shelby and Major Robertson would assume the unpleasant task of notifying the families of the men who had died in the battle. Otherwise, the news that Chief Bear Cloud had been killed would certainly be the biggest news on the frontier since the news of the victory at King's Mountain five months earlier.

Before sunset, the militiamen had encamped at a good location about half a mile back on the trail, near where the captured horses had been taken by the scouts who captured them. Gathering the captains and lieutenants, Major Tipton advised them of his next plan. "We will send scouts in eight directions tomorrow morning to locate the Indians and scout their movements. We will wait here for the scouts to return tomorrow night, unless scouts return sooner with certain news about the Indians.

If the Indians are heading into Indian country to the south or southwest, we will take satisfaction in this battle at Indian Ridge and will go home the day after tomorrow. If they are regrouping or heading toward our settlements we will catch up with them and attack them. We will send three sets of scouts toward our settlements to make sure the Indians have not gone behind us. The other five sets of scouts will go into the Indian lands." Jonathan asked if the officers had any questions or suggestions, and found that to a man they were comfortable with his plan. They all hoped, as he did, that the Indians were retreating rapidly into their own territory. All the men wanted to go home.

"Lieutenant Newcombe," said Jonathan, "have you completed the accounting for the battle?"

"Yes, Major. It was undoubtedly a big victory. The bad news is eight men were killed, and we had thirty-four men wounded. Of the wounded, most of them are not badly injured and it looks like none of them is likely to die. Up on the ridge we had two men killed and six wounded. Down in the valley we lost six men and twenty-eight were wounded, mostly in Captain Taylor's company. Here is a list of the men who were killed," said Lieutenant Newcombe, handing a piece of paper to Jonathan.

Major Tipton looked at the list, which read: four men from Captain Taylor's company, James Guest, Ezekiel Burk, William Howard, Calvin Scott; two men from Captain Gibson's company, George Murphy and Hugh Mccoy; one man from Captain Elliott's company, Jacob Talbot; and one man from Captain Carter's company, William Brannum.

Jonathan had Lieutenant Newcombe read the list aloud to the officers. The mood became somber. Voices became silent.

"God rest the souls of these brave men," lamented Major Tipton. Then he said, "Lieutenant, please continue your report. What about the Indians killed?"

After another pause, William Newcombe continued his report. "We counted the bodies of forty-nine Indians that were found, not counting some that the Indians carried away. As we all know, Chief Bear Cloud was killed. That's my report, Major."

Captain Jacob Brown then said, "One of my men scalped Chief Bear Cloud, and I am going to personally present the scalp to Colonel Sevier."

"We are not savages," interjected Jacob Brown, "but this is one scalp that Colonel Sevier will not object to."

Jonathan Tipton recaptured the direction of the discussion, and said, "I will write letters tonight to colonels Sevier and Shelby, advising them of the battle. Right now, I want you to select your scouts. I want to meet with you and all of tomorrow's scouts right here, half an hour from now. I want each captain except for Captain Taylor to provide two pairs of scouts. That will cover the eight directions that need to be scouted. We need to get the scouts' input and decide together the directions they will scout tomorrow. Because Captain Taylor's company suffered so many casualties in the battle today, he will not be required to provide scouts for tomorrow."

Later that night, well after the meeting with the scouts had been completed, Captain Carter approached Major Tipton. The two were among the few men other than the sentries who were not attempting to sleep, as it was past midnight. "Major Tipton," said Landon Carter, "I've talked with some of the officers and quite a few of the men, and none of them can remember any time when so many Indians were killed in one battle, or even in a whole campaign involving two or more battles."

"You and the men may well be right, but I cannot be too happy when we had eight of our own men killed," replied Jonathan.

"The men are in high spirits," said Landon. "They are all talking about having killed forty-nine Indians in one day, really more than that if you could count the ones the Chickamaugas carried away. My father will certainly be proud of you."

"Thank you, Landon. Colonel Carter will be proud of you, too. The problem is that a little while ago I finished writing the letters to Colonels Sevier and Shelby. When I wrote the names of the men who were killed, it made me think of their families and our families, and whether or not it is even worth being out here to settle the frontier. Maybe we should have just stayed in the east where things are civilized."

Landon replied, "But, Major Tipton, the war with the British is even worse in some parts of the east and north than the trouble with the Indians is for us. And you and our men beat the British and Tories at King's Mountain last October."

"Landon, you know that our trouble with the British is far from over. Their armies still control Charlestown, Savannah, and many parts of the south, not to mention the north."

"Yes, my father has told me the same things."

Jonathan said, "Losing eight men will not sit well with Colonel Sevier, especially when four of them were those of Captain Taylor, who has worked so closely with Colonel Sevier."

Landon replied, "But Captain Taylor told me that he favored your plan before the battle, and he favored it after the battle."

"Thank God for that," said Major Tipton. "I hope it helps, because I expect Colonel Sevier to try to crucify me."

"Major, I know that you and he have not seen eye to eye on many things, but I don't see how he can fail to understand that this was a great victory."

"Well, Landon, let's see what happens tomorrow. If the Indians are fleeing fast into their own lands it will shed a positive light on today's battle."

On the following day, the men reveled in their victory. Their principle concern was what news the scouts would bring back at the end of the day. Hunters brought back sufficient game by noon, and the men ate well in the afternoon. Throughout the day the men discussed details of their actions in the great victory, and the officers congratulated Major Tipton repeatedly. Jonathan, however, could not clear his mind of the eight militiamen who had been killed and his thoughts of the children back home who would soon learn they no longer had fathers.

Jonathan wondered to himself if it had been wise to leave Captain Taylor's company along the trail in the valley with only the small reinforcement from Gibson's company under Lieutenant Talley. Should he have left two entire companies there? If he had done so, however, would the lack of the surprise downhill attack have caused the battle to go more toward the Indians' favor? Would even more militiamen have been killed? Then he rationalized that this was the first time he had ever second guessed himself on such a major issue. The victory had been one-sided in favor of the militiamen. If Sevier criticized him at a later date when the two met, Jonathan would stand up for the men and the officers who had won the victory, as well as for himself, just as he had done following Sevier's unjust criticism after the battle at Boyd's Creek last December.

Well after dark, three sets of scouts returned, having seen no sign of Indians. These scouts had scouted back toward the white settlements, and it was not likely that the Indians, having been thoroughly defeated in battle, would be so aggressive as to head that way. Shortly thereafter, another set of scouts returned. Major Tipton and the other officers listened carefully as the scouts reported what everyone was hoping to hear. They had found what appeared to be the entire band of Indians they had faced, now far to the south, and still traveling southward. Only a dozen Indians were mounted, and the rest were on foot.

"Spread the word," Jonathan said to the other officers. "We are heading home at daybreak. One thing first, Captain Brown, since your men live in the southern settlements and know them best, you will take charge of the captured horses and distribute them to all the settlers who lost horses in the recent Indian raids. Since we captured more horses than were recently stolen from the settlers, give extra horses to families who suffered any deaths. Use your own judgment."

Early the next morning, Jonathan led the militia force northward. It was Wednesday, March 14.

On Thursday, as the main body of militia passed through the southern part of the area sparsely settled by white men, Captain Jacob Brown had already detached groups of his company to distribute captured horses to settlers who had sustained losses. Captain Brown, however, had remained with the main body, and was riding alongside Major Tipton. As they crossed a small stream, Jonathan noticed a cabin under construction just a couple of hundred yards upstream. "Jacob," he asked, "do you know who is building that cabin?"

"Yes," replied Jacob Brown, "it's a young man named Howard. I know his father, but his father could not come with us because he was shot in the hip a few weeks ago when the Indians stole his horses and he tried to stop them. The younger Howard has not been here long, and has not yet joined the militia."

"Would his name happen to be Thomas Howard?" asked Jonathan.

"I believe so. Like I said, he's new to the area. I've heard he has served in the war, but he is new to the area and is not a member of my company yet. Do you know him?"

"Yes, I think so. Continue forward with the men. I am going to pay him a brief visit. I'll catch up within half an hour." With that, Jonathan turned upstream.

As he approached the cabin, Jonathan saw two men at work, along with a young woman who was contributing energetically to their efforts.

"Private Howard?" Jonathan called out.

Having instinctively picked up his rifle at the sight of an approaching rider, Thomas Howard relaxed somewhat upon the realization that first, the rider knew his name, and secondly, the rider appeared to be an American officer.

Jonathan recognized the young man.

"I haven't seen you since the skirmish at the Miller's farm at Salisbury," said Jonathan.

A big smile came across Thomas Howard's face. "You're the major who was with Colonel Carter," he said. "That was about four years ago."

"Right, I am Major Jonathan Tipton. And you, Private Howard, did quite a job of fighting the British that day."

Jonathan dismounted and Thomas Howard stepped forward and shook hands with him. "Major Tipton, this is my wife, Sarah, and this is my neighbor, Joshua Hood," he said.

"What brings you here?" asked Jonathan.

"Well, we just arrived two weeks ago, and it's a long story. I got captured by the British and then got released in a prisoner exchange about three months ago. Then I went back to Salisbury and married Sarah. I met her while I was in Captain McGahee's company. Her father and mother live on a farm near the Millers, outside Salisbury. Anyway, my father gave me sixty acres of land here, part of the land he bought two years ago, so that's why Sarah and I are here. My father will be here in a little while to help us with the work on my cabin the best he can, although his hip is injured. At first I thought you might be him, but you were coming from the wrong direction."

Jonathan replied, "I hope you will join Captain Jacob Brown's company of militia. Captain Brown's men are returning home today. They are part of a force of 240 men just getting back from a victory over a large Indian force. I am sure you will hear all the details from your neighbors or your father. I must leave, as my men are heading toward home."

"Yes, sir," Major Tipton. The best to you, sir."

The victorious militiamen arrived home in mid-March. As usual, there was no grand parade. Indeed, there were not even any large settlements through which such a parade could have been made. Instead the men scattered, heading to their individual homes, each by the shortest route. Nevertheless, word of the victory was quickly known almost universally among the settlers. The victory became known as the Battle at Indian Ridge.

A week later, Colonel Sevier returned from his visit with the governor.

The next Sunday, Jonathan saw Major Robertson at church. "Charles," he said, "how did Colonel Sevier react to my letter about the battle when you gave it to him?"

"He read it. He said Captain Gibson had already told him about it, and he set it aside. Then he started talking about a battle in the middle part of North Carolina that the governor told him about. Colonel William Washington's cavalry beat British Colonel Pyle and his troops. Colonel Sevier never mentioned the battle at Indian Ridge again."

Colonel Sevier had routinely sent letters to the governor, other colonels, generals, and even on occasion to Congress to report every victory against the Indians. Major Tipton subsequently learned that in this case John Sevier did not send a written report of the Battle at Indian Ridge to anyone. The only document he generated was a letter to Colonel Shelby thanking him for providing Captain Elliott and the fifty men from Sullivan County, and praising their actions. Jonathan knew that if Colonel Sevier had led the militia victory at the Battle at Indian Ridge, letters would have been dispatched to both General Greene and the governor. The thought passed through Jonathan's mind that if John Sevier had been involved in the battle he would have been especially eager to take credit for the fact that Chief Bear Cloud had been killed.

At home, thinking about the results of the battle, Jonathan said to Frances, "John Sevier may not give me any credit for the victory at Indian Ridge, but he cannot take the satisfaction away from the officers and the men."

"You're right, Jonathan," she replied, "and they will always know who led them in the great battle when Chief Bear Cloud was killed."

News continued to arrive regarding the war. In early April, news was received of a large battle that occurred in mid-March between General Greene's army and British General Cornwallis's army at a place called Guilford Courthouse. Both sides claimed to have won. At the end of the day, the British held the field of battle, but had suffered far greater casualties than the Americans. Then, in May, news arrived that Cornwallis had retreated to Wilmington, along the coast, but that a strong British army under General William Phillips had landed at Yorktown, Virginia.

Furthermore, the traitor and now British General, Benedict Arnold, was at Yorktown with General Phillips.

On Monday, the twenty-fifth of June 1781, a rider came to Major Tipton's cabin. It was Private Thomas Gist, of Captain Brown's company. Jonathan recognized him immediately. Gist rode up slowly and dismounted.

"Welcome, Thomas," said Jonathan. "I haven't seen you since we returned from Indian Ridge."

"It's good to see you, Major. Living down toward the Chucky River, I don't get up here near this part of the Doe River very often. I'm here on a matter of business. Colonel Sevier has requested that you meet with him at his home on the day after tomorrow, at noon."

"Did he say what it is about?" asked Jonathan.

"No, but he is inviting just you, Major Walton, Major Robertson, and Major Valentine Sevier, so it must be important."

"What did you say? Valentine Sevier is a captain, not a major," said Jonathan, expressing both surprise and disbelief.

"No sir," said Gist, "that is one of the things Colonel Sevier took care of in his last visit to see the governor and General Greene. He told me so himself."

After rolling his eyes in an almost involuntary expression of disgust, Jonathan said, "Please report to Colonel Sevier that I will be present at the meeting."

"Yes, Major Tipton. I must go next to see Major Robertson," said Thomas Gist. Wasting no time, he mounted and departed.

Jonathan said to his wife, who had heard the entire conversation between him and Thomas Gist, "Frances, it only took John Sevier three months from the time he was promoted to colonel to get his brother promoted to major."

"Did we need another major for the militia?" she asked. "After all, more and more people have settled the area."

"No, we didn't need another major. It's just John Sevier working his connections with powerful people again. I don't like John, but I respect him because he is a brave and able man. On the other hand, Valentine Sevier definitely does not measure up to his brother, and I think it's absurd for him to hold the rank of major."

"But there's nothing you can do about it, Jonathan," said Frances.

"I know. Other than sharing my opinions about this with you, I will likely not mention them to anyone else except Colonel Carter, when I visit him. He's one man I can confide in and trust. John Carter is a good man even if he is bedridden with illness most of the time, now."

Jonathan arrived at John Sevier's home about twenty minutes before noon on Wednesday, the twenty-seventh of June 1781. Majors Jesse Walton and Valentine Sevier were already present, and Charles Robertson arrived just a few minutes after Jonathan Tipton. Inasmuch as it was a very warm day, John Sevier suggested that they meet under the shade of a large tree near his home. The horses of the visitors were watered and then secured under another tree nearby.

John Sevier addressed the four majors. He said, "Gentlemen, I received a letter from Governor Nash several days ago. He requested that we provide men to support General Greene against the British.

When I last met with the governor, I told him we have plenty of trouble with the Indians, especially with the British stirring them up against us and providing them with guns and powder. The governor also wrote about expecting General Greene to ask us for help. I forgot exactly what he wrote."

Then, pulling the letter from a shirt pocket, Sevier read it aloud, "If you do not provide some support of an immediate nature, I anticipate that General Greene will of necessity make a personal and even more urgent solicitation for your assistance and support. I will genuinely appreciate your response by messenger not later than the sixth day of July, with regard to the number of men and horses you can provide. Such force as you can provide should report to General Greene by the fifteenth day of July at his intended place of encampment at the High Hills of Santee, along the Santee River. Your officers and men should proceed by way of Charlotte Town. The Patriots there will provide you with intelligence regarding General Greene's location in case, because of events of war, his encampment is not at the High Hills of Santee."

Valentine Sevier looked at his brother and commented, "You can tell from the letter that the governor has no idea whether or not General Greene's army will be at that place called the High Hills."

Jesse Walton chimed in, "That part of South Carolina is low country. There are no high hills there."

Colonel John Sevier responded calmly, "The fact is that there are at least a couple of small rises there that they call hills. Another fact is that we are going to provide a company of men week after next, and I need one of you to lead them. I cannot go at this time because I am preparing for meetings with the governor and the legislature. Beside that, I am planning another campaign against the Chickamaugas. I will definitely go to General Greene's aid a few months from now, perhaps in September, or maybe sooner if the general himself makes an urgent request. Meanwhile, right now we need to send about a company of men to General Greene. We will still have enough men remaining to mount an attack on the Indians."

Jonathan thought quickly. If he went to help General Greene he would be in command of the troops who went with him, and would undoubtedly be assigned by Greene to work under the command of one of his subordinate generals or colonels. If he stayed home, however, he would have to participate in the Indian campaign under the direct command of Colonel John Sevier. The latter option was not appealing at all to Jonathan.

Jonathan spoke up and said, "I will go to support General Greene. Captain Gibson and a few of his men will probably be willing to go with me. I believe Captain Carter will go, too, but we will need some volunteers from some of the companies under the rest of you."

Colonel Sevier said, "My son James will go with you, Jonathan. You have your first volunteer."

Upon that comment by John Sevier, majors Walton, Robertson, and Valentine Sevier began to speculate on which of their men might be willing to go to the support of General Greene. The consensus was that at least forty and possibly up to fifty men might be raised.

Decisions had been made. Men from Washington County would go over the mountains again, this time to support the main southern army under General Greene. They would try to raise at least forty to fifty men. Major Jonathan Tipton would lead them, and they would depart on the seventh of July.

Upon the close of the meeting, Jonathan noticed James Sevier working on the repair of his father's barn. Jonathan approached the barn and called out, "James, your father has volunteered you to go with me to the aid of General Greene's army."

"Well, not exactly," responded James. "I volunteered myself. I told my father that if you were going to lead the men going to help General Greene I would be glad to go along."

"You're a most welcome first volunteer," said Jonathan.

After departing from the meeting, while proceeding toward home, Jonathan reflected on what had taken place at the meeting. It dawned on him that John Sevier had hoped that Jonathan would volunteer to go to General Greene's assistance. Sevier had been fully prepared to say that his son, James, would accompany Jonathan. Sevier knew that James and

Jonathan had grown to respect each other when James was assigned to Jonathan's command at King's Mountain. *Darn,* Jonathan thought. John Sevier had been clever, and this time it was a positive thing.

Chapter 9

Contending with the British

I AM GOING TO lead some men to join General Greene's army," Jonathan said to Frances. "We are going to try to get forty to fifty men to go right away. John Sevier is going to stay here with most of the militia to fight the Indians. If all goes well against the Indians, he will bring at least a hundred men to join up with me and my men in support of General Greene."

"Why must it be you?"

"Because I volunteered."

"You volunteered?"

"Yes. I never want to be away from home, but the cause of the revolution is important. Besides, if I don't go to the aid of General Greene, I will still be away from home, but would be with Sevier going against the Indians. I would rather be under one of General Greene's colonels fighting against the British."

"It's just not fair to me and the children for you to go off fighting all the time."

"Frances, you know that we have to defend ourselves against the Indians. Then, with all that's happened, if the British win the war, they will come and hang me, Sevier, and the other officers, or at least put us in prison. I'm going to fight them now, while we still have a chance to win."

Tears appeared in the corners of Frances' eyes. Jonathan hugged her. His mind was made up, and she could not change it.

The men gathered at Fort Watauga early in the morning on July 7, 1781. Leading thirty-eight mounted frontiersmen, Major Tipton headed over the mountains again, this time to join the main American army in the south under General Nathanael Greene. As the journey began, Jonathan thought about how he had been incorrect in his supposition that Captain Landon Carter would accompany him right away to support General Greene. Landon Carter had decided to remain home because of the illness of his father. Colonel John Carter's illness was now critical, and although his family and close friends prayed for his health, they feared he would soon pass away.

Jonathan was highly satisfied with the volunteers who constituted his small force. Captain William Trimble and twenty-eight of the militiamen who regularly served under Major Tipton were present, along with Captain Edward Anderson and eight men who usually served under Majors Walton and Robertson. All of these frontiersmen had experience fighting against the Indians, and most had fought at the great battle at King's Mountain against the Tories and British. Jonathan knew that most of the men in the county had stayed home because of genuine needs, or that they had gone with Colonel Sevier on his new campaign against the Indians. Jonathan knew that he would again miss Sergeant David Bragg, who was the premier scout of the county. On the other hand, he felt that he was fortunate to have Privates Smith Ferrell and Elijah Bates, who had become excellent scouts themselves.

The men traveled steadily, leading four packhorses carrying extra powder and shot. As they crossed over Yellow Mountain, Jonathan reminisced about the previous time he and many of these same men had passed through that same area. That had been on the way to find Ferguson's army, and had led to the battle at King's Mountain. This time, Jonathan traveled with a much smaller group, but was going to join a much larger army. General Greene's army was reported to be over two thousand strong. The British, on the other hand, were reported to have a force of more than three thousand based in Charlestown, and other British and Tory forces were all over the south. There were uncertainties in Major Tipton's mind. Who would be Jonathan's immediate superior officer? What would he be like? Would the battles be large or small? Where would they be fought? His mind wandering as he rode, Jonathan realized that although he had just recently left home, he was already looking forward to the day of his return.

Major Tipton led his men through Burke County, then past Ramsour's Mill and across Tuckasegee Ford on the Catawba River, all in North Carolina. Along the way, people supportive of the rebel cause helped by providing directions and information. Then, crossing into South Carolina at some indefinite point, they reached the town of Camden. Having learned that the British had abandoned their fort at Camden in May, Major Tipton and his men viewed the aftermath of the British occupation as they passed through the town. Jonathan saw the burned out ruins of about a dozen homes and the burned out buildings in the British fort at Camden. Lord Rawdon, the British commander, had ordered the homes of Patriot supporters and most of the buildings of the fort burned when his army evacuated.

All the country from two days' north of Camden to the American encampment at the High Hills of Santee was destitute of provisions. The effects of years of war were evident. There were no crops to be seen. There was no livestock. The poor inhabitants of the area had nothing to spare, and very little indeed in the way of food for themselves. It seemed that the British had devoured or destroyed everything that could possibly be eaten except for wild game that could be killed by the skilled hunters among the mountain men.

Major Tipton and his thirty-eight men finally reached General Greene's camp at the High Hills of Santee on the fourteenth day of July. After a touchy encounter with sentries who initially suspected them of being Tories, Jonathan and his men were warmly accepted and led into camp by a Captain Bacot of one of the South Carolina militia units.

"Your men can settle in next to mine for a while," said Bacot. "I will take you to General Greene's headquarters. Either he or Colonel O'Neal will let you know your assignment. I don't know what regiment he will put you with. The general's tent is about two hundred yards this way." Bacot gestured, pointing in the direction the two men were walking.

"Wait here," said Captain Bacot a minute or so later. "There's General Greene." Bacot nodded toward a man talking with two other officers about sixty feet away.

Several minutes later, Jonathan saw Captain Bacot returning, accompanied by another officer.

"This is Colonel William O'Neal," said Bacot. "He is a kind of right hand man to General Greene."

Although saluting was not practiced back home on the frontier, Jonathan realized that it would be necessary at times here with the regular army. Accordingly, he saluted the colonel.

Returning the salute, O'Neal then shook hands with Major Tipton. "The general will see you now," said Colonel O'Neal. He led Jonathan toward the general. "General Greene, this is Major Jonathan Tipton from Colonel Sevier's regiment of over mountain men."

Jonathan saluted General Greene, who then reciprocated.

"How many men do you have?" asked Greene.

"Thirty-nine, including myself."

"Can I expect more men from Colonel Sevier's regiment?"

"Colonel Sevier wanted to come when he received your message, but he is defending the county against Indians. He has about 250 more men, but even when he comes he will have to leave quite a few men home to discourage the Indians from attacking. The British have armed the Indians with lots of muskets, powder, and shot."

"We could use some of that powder ourselves," said Greene, glancing at Colonel O'Neal to indicate that a supportive comment would be appropriate."

O'Neal pitched in, "Major Tipton, you should know that some of our men have only two or three rounds of powder and shot."

Addressing his response to General Greene, Jonathan replied, "Well, sir, we cannot supply the whole army, but my men brought all the powder and shot we could carry by horseback, and four pack horses with additional powder and shot. I believe we could give three pack horse loads to your army and still have an adequate supply for ourselves."

"That will be most welcomed," said Greene. "I want you to take it to General Marion. His men need powder more desperately than anyone. Do you know when Colonel Sevier will come?"

"No, sir, but I do know that when he comes, he plans to bring as much powder and shot as he can acquire and carry."

General Greene said to Colonel O'Neal, "I am assigning Major Tipton and his men to General Marion. They will need to proceed to Marion's position immediately. Based on the reputation that Sevier's men gained at King's Mountain, I believe Major Tipton and his frontiersmen will fit in well with General Marion's men. Give him an appraisal of our situation and that of the British and Tories. Then assign a detail to take him to catch up with General Sumter."

Facing Major Tipton, Greene said, "Don't have your men settle into camp here. Give your men an hour to rest, and head south with Colonel O'Neal's detail to catch up with General Sumter's brigade. You will travel under General Sumter to reach General Marion. You can travel until just after darkness before camping tonight, and should be able to catch up with General Sumter sometime tomorrow morning."

Colonel O'Neal accompanied Jonathan as he headed back toward his men. "I'm going to have Captain Bacot and six of his men escort you to catch up with General Sumter's brigade. They left yesterday afternoon, but most of his men are on foot. Since your men are mounted, you should overtake them tomorrow, like the general said. You do need to understand, Major Tipton, that not all of General Greene's main army is present here in camp. Both General Sumter's full brigade and General Marion's small brigade are south of here. Marion has about two hundred men. He is near a place called Biggen Church, where the British have a strong force—maybe five hundred men or more. We are not sure."

Colonel O'Neal continued his description of the recent history and status of the army. "Last month General Greene took the main part of the army to Ninety-Six, in the western part of this state, and set a siege on the British fort there. The British colonel named Cruger had five hundred men at Ninety-Six. We were about to take the fort when Lord Rawdon approached with two thousand reinforcements that had arrived from Ireland and had immediately marched all the way from Charlestown to the fort. General Greene had to lift the siege and retreat, as the British and Tories outnumbered our force. General Greene had of necessity left parts of his army in the eastern part of South Carolina to contend with the British forces based in and around Charlestown. When we retreated from Ninety-Six, Lord Rawdon followed us at first, but when we stopped at a favorable place to fight him he retreated to Orangeburgh. That was about the beginning of July. Lord Rawdon posted a strong defensive position at Orangeburgh. About the first week of July, Colonel Cruger evacuated the fort at Ninety-Six and marched down and joined Rawdon at Orangeburgh. By that time, General Greene had brought the main American army here to the High Hills of Santee."

Arriving at the site where his men were resting, Jonathan informed them of the plan to join Sumter and Marion. Jonathan noticed that the arrival of his small group of men had scarcely been noticed except by General Greene, Colonel O'Neal, and Captain Bacot and his men. They had been welcomed in earnest, however, by those people.

Just as Major Tipton's men were departing to join General Marion's force, another arrival garnered great attention and raised the spirits of the entire army. A young officer and about twenty men arrived, herding nearly one hundred hogs and bringing in three wagonloads of flour. These men had skillfully navigated their way from the Hillsborough area, avoiding the British and Tories, to deliver their precious cargo. Cheers reverberated throughout the army for the new arrivals. The army would have adequate food for at least a few days.

As they observed the celebration for the arriving hogs, Major Tipton and his men, along with Captain Bacot and his six-man detail, continued riding slowly through the American camp. They exited to the south. The presence of two thousand men, along with nine field artillery pieces and a dozen supply wagons, had been quite impressive to Jonathan and his men. Jonathan sensed that his men felt more confident now that they had firsthand knowledge of the main American army in the south.

After camping overnight, they caught up with the rear of Sumter's column the following afternoon. After they joined the column, Major Tipton was taken forward and introduced to General Thomas Sumter.

Following introductions, General Sumter asked Major Tipton some of the same questions that General Greene had asked, inquiring about the possible arrival of Colonel Sevier and more men. They rode slowly, their horses at a walk. Jonathan remarked to General Sumter that he had heard General Greene refer to Francis Marion as "General Marion," but that he had more recently heard some soldiers and even some officers refer to Marion as "Colonel Marion." Jonathan inquired of Sumter, "Are there two officers with the last name of Marion, one a general and the other a colonel?"

General Sumter responded, "Believe me, there is only one Francis Marion. He was a lieutenant colonel just last year in 1780 before Governor Rutledge appointed him brigadier general in late December. Then, General Greene took command of all the American army in the South and soon gained half a dozen small, but brilliant victories from Marion and his men. Major General Greene quickly recognized Marion's skills and warmly accepted Marion as a brigadier general in the southern army. I likewise admire General Marion. This will be the first time he has served in a situation in which our brigades are combined. Of course, I will be in overall command, as General Greene has ordered."

Jonathan listened. Just as he was about to thank General Sumter for the clarification, a messenger rode up and stole the general's attention. Major Tipton did not learn the nature of the message, but observed from Sumter's reaction upon reading the note that it was not a matter of much significance.

General Sumter met up with Francis Marion on July 17, 1781, at a place described to Jonathan as being two miles north of a small local church where a strong British force was posted. Sumter promptly introduced Major Tipton to General Marion and released Jonathan and his small group of men to Marion in accordance with General Greene's orders.

The combined force of seven hundred men, including 160 who were mounted, proceeded to march toward the British position. The British and Tory force was commanded by Colonel Coates, who General Marion described as a highly competent officer. Coates had just over six hundred men, including one hundred cavalry.

About a mile short of Biggin Church, a fierce attack on the front of Sumter's column by Coates' cavalry stopped the advance for more than half an hour. Eventually, the lead troops of the column drove back the British cavalry.

Several skirmishes ensued, each resulting in a British retreat. When the Americans approached the church, they saw that it was burning. Intelligence was soon gained from a captured British soldier that Colonel Coates had his men set fire to the church, into which they had loaded their baggage and non-essential supplies. The British had then retreated quickly, without encumbrance of baggage or wagons. They could then travel as fast as the pursuing Americans. The captured soldier said that Colonel Coates thought he was facing the main American army under General Greene. Of course, that belief was far from the truth.

Major Tipton, with General Marion, was following closely behind Lieutenant Colonel Henry Lee's lead troops, when one of Lee's men rode quickly back to them with a report. "General Marion, the British have split into two columns. The main column, about five hundred men counting their cavalry and a rear guard, are retreating toward Quinby Bridge. Another column of about a hundred men on foot have split off and are heading toward the ford upstream from the bridge."

Francis Marion thought for a moment and said, "Major Tipton, since your men are all mounted, take your men and twenty of my mounted men under Captain Milton. Catch up with the one hundred British foot soldiers. Attack them and be sure they don't control the ford."

Jonathan led fifty-nine mounted men toward the ford, and within thirty minutes caught up with the British detachment. In another ten minutes the Patriots had passed around the enemy and cut them off from the ford. Dismounting, the Patriots formed a line across the road, which was little more than a wide trail in a lightly wooded area, to confront the oncoming British. Just as the enemy started to break their column and form a battle line, Major Tipton's expert marksmen unleashed a full volley of fire. More than a dozen of the British fell on the first round. Having taken heavy casualties so quickly, the British formed in somewhat disorganized fashion and fired an ineffective return volley. The Patriots had taken cover low to the ground so that the enemy shots went mostly over their heads. In less than a minute, the second round of American fire downed several more British, including a lieutenant and a sergeant. Immediately, Jonathan saw one small white flag raised in the center of the British line, then two, three, and four white cloths raised on bayonet points of enemy muskets.

Jonathan yelled, "Hold your fire! Hold your fire!" His men ceased firing as ordered. Then Jonathan shouted in the direction of the British, "Lay down your weapons." He heard the shouts of an enemy officer to his men, ordering his troops to lay down their arms. Jonathan sent some mounted troops to the left and some to the right of the enemy, and met the British officer, a captain, to accept his surrender. Taking the enemy as prisoners in good order, Major Tipton and his men marched ninety of the prisoners away from the ford, toward the rear of General Sumter's position. Twelve British soldiers who were too badly wounded to travel were left behind, along with two who suffered relatively minor wounds and could care for the others as best they could.

Meanwhile, as Jonathan later learned, British Colonel Coates stopped his retreat after crossing Quinby Bridge to wait on his rear guard. American Lieutenant Colonel Henry Lee's mounted troops had overwhelmed Coates' rear guard. Two companies of the mounted Patriot militia crossed Quinby Bridge and attacked Coates' main force, initially surprising the British and driving them backward. Coates' men had weakened the bridge, removing some of the planks and loosening others. Their small rear guard had crossed the bridge, as had two companies of Lee's cavalry, but when more Patriots tried to cross, the planking gave way. Two horses and their riders plummeted into the water. The two companies that had attacked had to retreat and hold their ground until other approaching Patriots in General Sumter's force could repair the bridge well enough to cross. Thus, Coates' men had time to post themselves in a favorable defensive position at Shubrick's plantation house, using the house and the nearby outbuildings and fence in their defenses. About the same time, Colonel Coates had learned from his cavalry that he was not facing General Greene's main army, but in fact a force about the same size as his own. He was ready to fight.

When Sumter's force was finally in place, he ordered an attack. Marion's men would attack from the left, and Sumter's larger force would attack from the center and right. General Marion's men had to approach across an open field, and the British fired from covered positions in the house, in a barn, and from behind a fence into their approaching line. Eighteen of Marion's men were killed and fourteen were wounded. One of the men killed was a fine young captain whom Jonathan had just met earlier that day. Sumter's men who attacked the center were able to advance with the cover of the many trees approaching the front of the plantation house. However, the other regiment of Sumter's men on the right, under Colonel Thomas Taylor, had to approach in open ground, much like Marion's men, and took heavy casualties. Eight of Taylor's men were killed, and eleven were wounded. Observing the slaughter, a retreat was ordered by General Sumter.

Retreating only half a mile, the Americans set up camp in a defensive position. They were still strong enough that it would not be wise for Colonel Coates to attack them.

Being close enough to discern the cessation of firing in the area of the principal battle, Jonathan sent Captain Milton to General Sumter to advise him of Major Tipton's situation in possession of ninety British prisoners, along with their arms and ammunition. Captain Milton returned, requesting Jonathan's presence in Sumter's camp for an officers' meeting. Additionally, General Sumter wanted all the captured powder and shot sent immediately to Sumter's location because supplies were so low that some of his men were completely out of ammunition.

Pursuant to General Sumter's request, Major Tipton attended the officers meeting after the battle, on the evening of July 17. Seventeen officers were present, all majors and above in rank. General Sumter presided, but General Marion seemed terribly agitated. Among the officers, they were able to summarize the day's results: the Patriots captured 121 British prisoners, took 160 weapons, and killed an estimated 20 British and wounded 40. By their own counts, there were 31 Americans killed and 51 wounded.

After the casualties and results of the battle had been gathered and summarized, General Sumter spoke first, addressing the entire group of officers. "We have posted ourselves in a strong defensive position for the night. Tomorrow we will withdraw to rejoin General Greene's forces at the High Hills of Santee.

Francis Marion had been standing with his arms folded in front of him. His face was red as if angry. General Marion finally spoke. Addressing General Sumter in the presence of all the officers in attendance, he said, "I told you that we should not attack the position the British took at Shubrick's plantation. I led my men in the attack you directed, moving across an open field into an enemy firing from covered positions. It was pure stupidity, and I'll never do it again. I advised you before today's fighting that we should harass the British with many small attacks. When we hit and fall back and hit them again and fall back again it is very effective. The enemy suffers casualties and fear of attack at any time when we use that strategy. If we had done that some of my best men would still be alive, and more of the enemy would be dead."

Wanting to quiet Marion, General Thomas Sumter interrupted. He stated bluntly, "Thank you for your input, General."

"I'm not finished," said Marion. "We should not retreat tomorrow. We should leave your main force here in this defensible position, daring the British to attack, although I think they will not. While the bulk of the force is here, my men and those of Colonel Lee, along with Major Tipton's mountain men can harass and damage the British very effectively. That is what I recommend, General Sumter."

"I must remind you that General Greene placed me as the senior commander," said Sumter. Then, turning his focus away from Marion and addressing the gathering of officers, Sumter said, "The decision is final. We will depart for the High Hills of Santee tomorrow. The exception is that General Marion and his men, as usual, will retire to one of their camps on the Santee."

Then, addressing Francis Marion directly again, Sumter said, "Of course we are all aware that General Greene has given you the autonomy to mount surprise attacks on the enemy at will. If you want to take on Colonel Coates, go ahead."

General Sumter closed the meeting by stating abruptly, "Officers, you are all dismissed."

Just after the meeting, Colonel Thomas Taylor approached Jonathan. "Major Tipton, General Sumter told me to get you to march your prisoners to the open area right over there, in our camp, where they can be adequately guarded overnight. After you move the prisoners, my men will give you a hand in guarding them. If left where they are, such a large number of prisoners might give your small command trouble, and some of them might possibly escape."

"The help will be most appreciated, Colonel."

Jonathan and his men delivered the British prisoners as directed.

While arrangements were being made for shifts of men to guard the prisoners overnight, Jonathan thought to himself about the officers' meeting. He had been quite surprised at the verbal exchange between Francis Marion and Thomas Sumter, which occurred right in the presence of other officers. Then the thought crossed his mind that it reminded him of his own verbal confrontation with John Sevier just last year, following the battle with the Indians at Boyd's Creek.

On the following morning, as the Patriots prepared to march, Francis Marion approached Jonathan Tipton. General Marion said, "Major Tipton, I want you to take your men and return with General Sumter to the High Hills of Santee. I know that General Greene assigned you to my command for this attack, but I don't know if he wanted you to remain or return, so I'm going to play it safe and send you back. You should know that I will welcome you and your men to serve with me at any time, but I will never serve under General Sumter again."

"Considering what you said last night, I understand," replied Jonathan.

Jonathan and his men traveled with General Sumter's force back to the main American camp at the High Hills of Santee.

One day in camp, Jonathan had some free time. He walked down to the river, sat down, and looked across. The setting was peaceful and did not reflect in any way the war, hunger, and great personal struggle that existed at the time. He thought about the small hills upon which the American camp rested. The terrain in this part of South Carolina was vastly different from what he was accustomed to in the mountains of western North Carolina. The vegetation was different, too. When he thought about living creatures, he singled out the rattlesnakes in South Carolina. There were deer, birds, squirrels, and many other common animals, but nobody liked the rattlesnakes. Jonathan was careful with every step he took in any area of undergrowth or high weeds. Jonathan stood, tossed a stick into the river, watched it drift briefly, and walked back to camp.

There was one soldier by the first name of Solomon in Captain Bacot's company from South Carolina who was a great storyteller. Solomon approached a group of Tipton's men who were sitting around a campfire and introduced himself. "Hello, mountain men. I am Solomon and I am from a place not too far from here in South Carolina." Then, Solomon proceeded to tell them a story about a British soldier who was captured earlier in the war.

The South Carolina soldiers all swore the story was true. As Solomon told it, "A while back, about forty of Colonel Marion's men attacked sixteen of Bloody Tarleton's cavalry soldiers early in the afternoon down by Black Creek in the Cheraws district. The British had been sitting down taking a rest, and were mighty surprised when Marion's men came riding down the wagon trail right at them. All but one of the British got to their horses and rode south toward Charlestown as fast as they could go. But there was one soldier who had gone out into the woods to relieve his constipation, and had just dropped his trousers when he heard all the yelling that Marion's men were coming. As soon as he pulled down his trousers and squatted, a rattlesnake struck hard and bit him smack dab on the right cheek of his rump. He ran, contorting his face in pain, yelling, and trying to pull up his pants at the same time, but by the time he got to where his horse was, he was surrounded by Colonel Marion's troops, and all the other British were gone. The British soldier tripped and his pants fell down. His backside was redder than his coat. When he fell, Colonel Marion's men burst out laughing. Then, when the redcoat told them about the snakebite, they laughed even louder. The Patriot lieutenant saw that the British soldiers had too much of a head start, and decided not to pursue them, so he rode back to see what some of his men were laughing so hard about. He tried to be serious and told one of the privates to tie the Brit's hands and transport him back to the main Patriots' camp for questioning. Then, the lieutenant tried to not even smile, but he could not help it, and broke out laughing, too! The prisoner's rump swelled overnight to about the size of a pumpkin, and he died the next morning."

Solomon's story entertained the soldiers around the campfire and had them laughing, as well. About that time another of Francis Marion's soldiers happened to walk by, and said to Solomon, calling him by his last name, "Hey, Wright, tell them the one about the giant alligator." Jonathan needed to go to another part of camp to get some information from Colonel O'Neal, so he did not stay to see if Solomon told that story.

Several weeks passed after the battle at Shubrick's plantation. During the month of August, General Greene's army was still encamped at the High Hills of Santee. Information was received from a Colonel Harden that a large force of more than four hundred Tories was burning homes of Patriots and generally causing lots of trouble in the area around Parker's Ferry, about thirty miles west of Charlestown. Colonel Harden's forces had been decimated over time, and his remaining force of forty men was powerless to stop the Tories. Because Major Tipton's men all had horses, they were assigned to accompany General Marion and his men to provide aid to Colonel Harden as rapidly as possible. General Marion sent a company of mounted troops to Monck's corner to create a diversion, while Marion himself departed at night toward Parker's Ferry on a route that attempted to hide his movement. Shortly after they departed, Francis Marion told Major Tipton, "Colonel Harden is an old friend of mine. He has fought with me many times during this war. It saddens me to learn that he is down to just forty men. I remember when he could muster about two hundred."

On the fourth day after leaving the main American camp, General Marion's force of two hundred men met up with Colonel Harden, who had only thirty-four men present at the time.

General Marion and Colonel Harden devised an ambush on the road leading to Parker's Ferry. Harden knew that the Tories, about 450 strong, were camped about half a mile south of Parker's Ferry.

On a very warm morning in August, General Marion sent Colonel Harden and a company of forty mounted men down the road toward the Tory camp to lure them into the trap. Major Tipton and his men, with the majority of Marion's party, were hidden in a swampy area along the west side of the road leading to the ferry.

The Tory sentries spotted the approaching riders and shouted the alarm. Inasmuch as it was broad daylight, the Tory commander and all of his men could see the approaching riders. Colonel Harden's Patriots stopped briefly, and then turned around and rode back toward the ferry.

Major Fraser and his Tories believed that the mounted Patriots were simply Colonel Harden's party of mounted militia. Not suspecting that there were any other Patriots in the area, Fraser ordered his entire Tory cavalry force of 240 men to charge the company of Patriots immediately. He ordered his 210 foot soldiers to follow as quickly as possible. Thus, Fraser led the mounted troops directly into the ambush.

Holding their fire anxiously, the Americans waited until Colonel Harden and the mounted decoys passed and the enemy force were fully in front of them on the road, only about 125 feet away. Francis Marion personally shouted "Fire," and the skilled marksmen delivered a hail of shots into the Tory lines, knocking quite a few off their horses.

The startled and now disorganized Tories returned fire. Major Fraser ordered them to turn their line left and attack into the swampy ground. Effective firing continued from the Americans in the swamp, most of which were barely visible to the Tories. The battle was a slaughter from the onset. Some of the Tories wisely dismounted, making themselves less easy to target. Major Fraser was wounded, but bravely continued to lead his men. The Tory major was shortly hit again by Patriot rifle fire. Still able to ride, he then ordered a retreat. The Tories continued to sustain casualties as retreated down the road from whence they came.

The surviving Tory cavalrymen soon reached the safety of their advancing line of infantrymen. The reunited Tory force formed a line across the road, extending off to both sides. A field piece was brought into position in the center of the line.

Inasmuch as the Patriots were low on ammunition and were outnumbered, General Marion wisely ordered a withdrawal. Marion rightfully suspected, however, that the Tories believed the Patriot force that had decimated their cavalry was much larger than it actually was. He knew that the Tories would not pursue him.

The result of the battle at Parker's Ferry in terms of casualties was strongly in favor of the Patriots, who suffered from only three men killed and seven wounded. The bodies of about sixty Tories could be seen, however, lying on and alongside the road. Intermingled with them were forty badly wounded Tories who had been unable to retreat. The Tories must have had at least twenty more wounded, including Major Fraser, who had successfully escaped.

Overall, total Patriot casualties amounted to ten men dead and wounded. Tory casualties were at least 120 dead and wounded. It was another clever, efficient victory by General Francis Marion.

Marion's men, low on ammunition, quickly took possession of the weapons and ammunition of the forty badly wounded Tories. Not wanting to take prisoners, the Patriots simply left the wounded Tories where they were.

The Patriots also captured eleven horses that had been left without their Tory riders in the action. Additionally, although none of the men had intentionally aimed at a horse, at least fifteen horses were dead or injured along the road.

Of necessity, General Marion had to take his men back to their regular operating area. Following the orderly retreat, Colonel Harden and his men were left behind to fend for themselves as best they could in the general vicinity of Parker's Ferry. Francis Marion said to Major Tipton, "The Tories in this area will be wary of a perceived presence of a sizeable Patriot force, even though we won't actually be here. That in itself may take a little pressure off of Colonel Harden. Maybe today's battle will also help the colonel's recruiting. He can't do much with thirty-four men."

Arriving back at a regular location along the Santee River, Jonathan and his men settled into camp with Marion's troops. Several plantations in that general area had remained productive because of the difficulty of the enemy in reaching the area and the threat of extreme harassment by Marion's force if they did attempt to go there to steal or destroy the crops. The plantations continued to raise corn and raised rice in the lowlands near the swamps. Likewise, the locals had been able to maintain possession and reproduction of their cattle and hogs. Thus, the Patriots in that limited area, including Marion's men, remained relatively well fed most of the time.

On the second day in camp, General Marion received a message from General Greene and shared its contents with his officers and men. The British commander in the south, Lord Rawdon, had relinquished command and sailed for England. The British army in the south, based in Charlestown, was now commanded by Lieutenant Colonel Alexander Stewart on a temporary basis. The British anticipated the arrival of Major General Alexander Leslie sometime in the next month to replace Lord Rawdon.

General Marion also provided his men with an update on the overall picture of the war in the south. He advised them that the British were still maneuvering and actively fighting throughout eastern and central South Carolina. The same was true for central and eastern North Carolina, where British forces under Major James H. Craig and Tory forces under Colonel Fanning and Lieutenant Colonel Archibald McDugald still numbered well over one thousand. They were proving very troublesome to Americans in North Carolina under General Richard Caswell and General John Butler. Their activities prevented General Greene from focusing solely on the British and Tories in South Carolina. Compounding the issue was the fact that the British controlled the sea, and might land additional forces at any time at Wilmington, North Carolina; Charlestown, South Carolina; or Savannah, Georgia. The final words of Francis Marion's address to his men stuck with Jonathan. Marion said, "General Washington is holding his own in the north, and we are doing better than holding our own in the south now that General Greene is here. We must win our freedom. I, personally, will win, or die trying."

In camp with Francis Marion's troops near the Santee River, Jonathan Tipton lay restless, unable to sleep. So often had Marion's men camped at this remote campsite that they had built two dozen small, three-sided huts with roofs, so many of the men had shelter. The insects were nearly intolerable at that place, which was the only dry land in an area practically surrounded by swamp. Even on the warm days and nights of August, fires were built in front of each three-sided hut so that the smoke helped to fend off the insects. Jonathan shared a hut with Captain Trimble and Captain Anderson. He wished he could be at home. On this particular night his mind wandered into thinking about how successful General Marion had been against the British and Tories. Jonathan had observed General Marion's behavior when his officers and scouts reported to him. If a report of some scouting mission did not include every detail that Marion expected, the general inquired aggressively and specifically about what other information he needed. He expected every detail of the number of British regulars, Tories, and Indians; the number of wagons; how many men were mounted; the number of packhorses; the number of field pieces, and other relevant information. Over time, his men had become more observant simply because of the general's high expectations. Marion's attention to detail along with his logical thought process had contributed to his success, thought Jonathan. He finally drifted into sleep.

Chapter 10

The Battle of Eutaw Springs

IN EARLY SEPTEMBER of 1781 Major Tipton was still serving under General Marion. In camp one afternoon, Francis Marion advised him, "My messenger told me this morning that General Greene received a dispatch from Colonel Sevier stating that he will arrive before the end of September with about forty additional men. Because your men have done well serving with mine, General Greene plans to assign Colonel Sevier and the rest of his men to my brigade, as well."

"It will be good to see some of the men from home," responded Jonathan.

Jonathan did not relish the idea of the arrival of Colonel Sevier, but he did know that over a period of time a mutual respect had developed between himself and John Sevier. It had, he believed, nearly overcome the animosity that existed between them.

During the first three days of September, General Nathanael Greene received conflicting intelligence reports that the British were going to attack his camp or that they were going to establish a permanent base at Eutaw Springs. The small springs at Eutaw Creek were located about midway between General Greene's camp at the High Hills of Santee and Charlestown. A strong British presence at Eutaw Springs would severely hinder Greene's ability to harass the British around Charlestown. Furthermore, it would enable the British to threaten to invade the backcountry again. General Greene believed that the British must be confronted near the coast, limited to the coastal areas, and eventually defeated and forced out. Regardless, the intelligence was consistent in reporting that a large

British force of more than two thousand men under Colonel Stewart had marched to the place called Eutaw Springs.

General Greene decided that it was imperative to confront Stewart's army and, if possible, drive them back to Charlestown. Accordingly, General Greene led his main army to a plantation a few miles northwest of Eutaw Springs, where he met up with General Marion on September 7. General Greene's army included forces that had joined him under generals Andrew Pickens and Thomas Sumter, both of South Carolina. The American army now numbered 2,400 men. Two hundred of them were assigned to guard the small train of supply wagons to the rear, leaving 2,200 men at Greene's disposal.

General Marion reported, "General Greene, my scouts believe that the British are not aware of the approach of your army. They have spotted our leading cavalry company. The British probably believe that it is only my force, possibly with reinforcements, that they are facing. Colonel Stewart likely believes he is facing not more than four hundred troops, and not the more than two thousand that we truly have. If we strike fast, early tomorrow morning, I think we can surprise them."

General Marion described Colonel Stewart's defensive position as observed by his scouts. The British headquarters was at a brick and stone house near the springs. A deep creek bed, through which Eutaw Creek flowed, covered their right. The creek itself was about three to five feet deep. The Congaree road passed the headquarters house. The logical approach was along the Congaree road. The British front was covered rather thickly with pine trees and scrub oak trees, an excellent area for skirmishing should the British be prepared for an attack. Just inside the outer perimeter of the British position, the land was very lightly forested and favorable for a full attack. Marion's scouts estimated that the enemy numbered 2,300. There were about 2,000 British regulars and several hundred Tories. Thus, the British and American armies were practically equal in size.

The Patriot army marched down the Congaree road on the morning of September 8, 1781, to attack the British. Colonel Henry Lee's cavalrymen were in the lead and came upon a British hunting and foraging party, resulting in a light skirmish, with several of the British killed and some captured. The sound of the skirmish, however, alerted the British sentries closer to the British camp. Still, the British likely believed it was just a small group of Marion's men that had attacked their foragers.

Lee's cavalrymen then met up with another party of British footmen and a heavier skirmish began. The Americans brought up two field pieces and commenced firing. With the British camp less than a mile away, General Greene ordered his lines out of column to form into lines of battle. Meanwhile, the British formed their lines behind the line of outlying skirmishers who were by then busy contending with advancing Patriots.

Major Tipton's men were placed with the South Carolina militia under General Marion. Marion's troops and the North Carolina militia under Colonel Malmedy composed the right of the American front line. Other South Carolina troops under General Pickens formed the left of the front line. On the right side of the front line the American militia was quite different from the less experienced North Carolina militia under Colonel Malmedy. There was no doubt that General Marion's militiamen would attack and maintain the fight once the battle began. General Marion's own men were veterans of many small battles, skirmishes, and raids. Most of the men under Major Tipton who were in General Marion's brigade for this battle had fought at the Battle of King's Mountain, and all of Tipton's men had fought in battles with the Indians.

General Greene's continental troops from Maryland, Virginia, and North Carolina formed the second line, with a small force of less than one hundred Delaware continentals in reserve.

Lieutenant Colonel "Lighthorse Harry" Lee's cavalrymen were on the right flank, and far to the left, Colonel Wade Hampton's cavalrymen held the left flank. Lieutenant Colonel William Washington's cavalry formed the mounted reserve, to be used where General Greene deemed necessary.

The Americans had only four field artillery pieces. Two guns were moved forward in the center of the front line, while two were maintained in the center of the second line.

As the main front line of the Americans caught up with their skirmishers, the British skirmishers retreated hastily to the main line of their army. Then, as the Americans on the right approached the British line, the smoke from the skirmishing thinned, allowing for clear visibility. Jonathan could see through openings in the flat, moderately forested land a line of red and the bristling gleam of bayonets. It appeared to Jonathan that the enemy line was now only a quarter of a mile away. The breadth of the entire American line was almost half a mile wide, as was the British line.

General Marion's marksmen advanced, firing accurately into the British line. Many redcoats fell. Major Tipton looked to his left and to the right. Nowhere did he see a single American fall. Maybe the redcoats had shot high again, he thought. Jonathan then saw some men a few hundred feet to his left fleeing to the rear. He knew they were not Marion's troops. They must have been some of Colonel Malmedy's men. The next time Jonathan looked in that direction he was relieved to see a large number of continental soldiers moving forward, replacing the men who had fled and filling in the hole in the line.

A big surprise came when General Marion's men were only 150 feet from the enemy line. Instead of retreating, the battle-hardened British charged forward in orderly fashion with fixed bayonets. Knowing that his men did not have bayonets, and that many of them had just fired and could not reload quickly enough, General Marion immediately shouted "Retreat, retreat, retreat!" Turning and moving toward the rear, Major Tipton and his men found that the Virginia continentals were immediately behind them with their support. Like the British, the continentals advanced with fixed bayonets. After retreating only fifty feet, Major Tipton and his men gladly made way for the continentals to pass forward through their ranks. Turning again toward the British, Major Tipton and his men were now the second line. The continentals ahead of them were in a fierce bayonet battle with the British.

Jonathan instinctively shouted to his men, "Help the Virginians." Jonathan and his men ran forward, each with a rifle in one hand and a long knife or tomahawk in the other, covering the short distance to the fight in a matter of seconds. Jonathan slashed with his tomahawk, delivering a fatal blow to the side of the head of a redcoat who was engaged in parlaying a bayonet thrust from one of the Virginians. Suddenly, shouts of "Hurrah" broke out among the Americans. The British fled all along the line in a massive retreat. The loud cracks of artillery fire that had come from both sides earlier in the battle were now limited to shots fired by the American side. General Greene had ordered two artillery pieces drawn forward, and their fire on the brick house near the Eutaw Springs had become the audible focal point of the battle.

Although the enemy in front and along the main line retreated, heavy fire continued in the woods to the far left of the American line. After another ten minutes, that fire lessened, as well. General Marion's men, along with the Virginia continentals, reached the site of what had been part of the main British camp. There they found dozens of campfires, most accompanied by large pots of boiled beef and potatoes, ready to eat. The enemy's abandoned breakfast was irresistible to the near-starving Americans, who stopped their pursuit of the British and began to eat. A rush for food ensued among the hungry men, continentals and militia alike. Accepting a finger-sized chunk of boiled beef from the hand of one of his men, Jonathan strode toward General Marion. "General," he said, shifting the partially chewed beef inside his right cheek so he could talk, "some of the British have fortified themselves in the brick house, and the others have not fled far beyond it. You can see solid stretches of red in the woods just beyond the house. This battle may not be over." General Marion and Major Tipton immediately began summoning men who had already obtained at least some morsel to eat to come forward and establish a line. A colonel of the Virginia continentals was making the same attempt, and had gathered about forty of his men into somewhat of an organized line. Major Tipton had gathered ten of his thirty-seven remaining men, and General Marion had formed up fifty other men along the line. These efforts were just in time, as the British suddenly advanced in a massive counterattack.

The British troops advanced quickly in the front, firing, reloading, moving forward, and firing again. Jonathan realized that if the British got much closer, a bayonet charge would be imminent. The Virginians formed up quickly alongside Marion's troops, but the British continued the attack. A fierce battle raged, both sides firing repeatedly and both sides taking heavy casualties in dead and wounded. Finally, running out of ammunition, General Marion had no choice but to retreat, and the Virginia continentals retreated alongside. The entire American line fell back, in good order. Fortunately, the Virginians and other continental units had adequate shot and powder remaining. They levied repeated volleys of fire, slowing the British and facilitating the orderly retreat by the Patriots. As Jonathan retreated he could see that the field was strewn with dead and dying. The retreating Americans retrieved and carried their wounded as best they could. The British regained their original camp, but they were exhausted and had neither the strength in numbers nor the inclination to pursue the feisty Americans any further.

The battle had lasted for more than three hours. The tired Patriots retreated a short distance further, posted double the normal sentries, and set camp. Tending to the wounded and foraging for food became the principal concerns for the afternoon. Additionally, remaining supplies of powder and shot were distributed so that all units had at least several rounds available. Seven kegs of powder that were seized when the British lines had been overrun, along with the powder and shot taken from the hundreds of British prisoners, were critical in this regard.

In mid-afternoon, messengers sent by General Greene's staff approached the officers of every unit, requesting input to General Greene regarding their numbers of killed, wounded, and missing men. Accordingly, General Marion collected information within his brigade and sent it to Greene. Francis Marion promised his officers and men that he would share the overall numbers for the entire battle once he learned that information from General Greene or his staff.

While resting in camp, Jonathan sat down and commented to Captain Trimble, "William, we routed them at the start of the battle. We were slaughtering them."

Captain Trimble replied, "It is unbelievable that after the whipping we put on them they were able to reform and counterattack. I can't believe they held the field at the end of the day."

"The British we fought today are well disciplined and their officers are excellent commanders," Jonathan responded. "Since they drove us from the field, I guess we lost the battle. We sure did put a hurting on them, though."

Late in the afternoon Major General Greene personally visited the camps of each of his several brigades. While Greene was at Brigadier General Marion's camp, Jonathan heard Greene tell Francis Marion, "I have never before witnessed militia perform equally to the best regular line troops of both our side and the British in a major battle. On the right side of our line, your men did just that. I want you to relay to them my personal compliments." Generals Greene and Marion then departed for Greene's headquarters to confer with the other general officers. Jonathan knew that Marion would remember to share with his men the praise that General Greene had given them.

Well after dark, General Marion returned to the encampment of his men. Meeting first with his officers, he shared the results of the battle, as best the estimate could be made. He tasked the officers with imparting the grizzly information to their men. American casualties were terrible, with 205 men killed and 31 more so severely wounded that is was almost certain they would die. Another 260 were wounded seriously enough that they would not be able to fight in the immediate future, and 10 men were simply missing, possibly having been killed or taken prisoner. The total of American killed, wounded, and missing was just over 500 men. Included in the total were 22 officers killed and 35 officers wounded.

Having overrun the British position in the first hours of the battle, the Patriots had captured 420 British prisoners, many of them wounded. Over 230 dead and seriously wounded enemy troops had been counted after the British camp had been overrun. The seriously wounded redcoats that had at one point been captured were left behind when the British counterattacked. The best estimate was there must be at least 200 additional casualties in dead and wounded in the British camp. Patriot leaders were certain that British casualties, including those killed, wounded, and captured, had to total at least 800 and likely even more, compared to about 500 American casualties. Both sides had suffered tremendously.

In the American camp, even the soldiers in continental regiments that had served in battles in the North could not recall having participated in such a bloody and deadly battle. Although the British held the field of battle, the Patriots held 420 British and loyalist prisoners. The enemy, on the other hand, held not more than ten American prisoners. With the total losses in killed, wounded and prisoners obviously so one-sided in the Americans favor, it seemed that the British should not be able to claim victory.

Major Tipton felt fortunate that none of his own men had been killed, and only two wounded. Both wounds were minor, and the two men would be able to fight the next day if necessary.

Late in the evening, Francis Marion walked toward Major Tipton, who was sitting alone at the time. Jonathan stood in a typical gesture of respect. There was no salute, and none was expected. General Marion's camp was much like those back on the frontier. Marion's face reflected the light of a nearby campfire. Unlike the first few hours following the battle, his eyes and mouth did not show signs of stress and concern. He smiled and said, "Jonathan, your men are every bit as good as marksmen as my own, and I thought I would never say this, maybe even better. If times were different, perhaps we would have a shooting competition between our best men." It was the first time that General Marion had called Jonathan by his first name.

"Your kind words are genuinely appreciated," Jonathan responded, "but I could not claim my men to be better. Rather, I can truly state that they are proud to serve with you." With a smile of his own, Jonathan added, "But if we had a competition I would place a friendly wager on my men."

Both men laughed. It was the first laughter either had experienced in at least a couple of days.

Following the brief pleasantries, General Marion told Major Tipton, "General Greene realizes that our army is exhausted and that our losses are serious. He believes as I do that the enemy has been hurt much worse. He expects the British to retreat tomorrow and plans to attack them during their retreat."

Jonathan replied, "Each of my men fired fifteen to twenty shots today. After the battle, most of them had powder and shot to fire only one or two more rounds. After we received some of the powder and shot that was captured from the enemy, we have about five shots per man. Unless we get more ammunition I don't think it would be wise to attack the British tomorrow."

"I agree, but General Greene is in charge. Perhaps he will use the continentals as the main force to pursue the British, and will let us harass them from the side."

On the following morning, British reinforcements arrived from Charlestown, and General Greene abandoned his plan to renew the attack on Stewart's army. Nevertheless, later in the day the British under Colonel Stewart made a rapid retreat toward Charlestown, taking the reinforcements with them. Stewart wanted no more confrontation with General Greene's tenacious army. Additionally, Colonel Stewart had no idea how low the Americans were on ammunition. Instead, he thought that the powder and shot that had been captured from his force had simply increased the Patriots' supply.

On the tenth of September, General Greene began withdrawing toward the High Hills of Santee. Greene directed Major Tipton to detach from Francis Marion's command. Jonathan and his men would return to the main American camp at the High Hills of Santee. Jonathan would then remain with Greene until the arrival of Colonel Sevier. At that time, General Greene would decide if Sevier's troops, including Major Tipton and his men, would be assigned to General Marion's brigade. General Marion, meanwhile, returned to his favorite location in the Santee River swamp.

The Patriot army arrived at the High Hills of Santee on September 12. More than three hundred of the returning men had been wounded at Eutaw Springs. Some of the wounded men were carted on supply wagons; some were able to travel by horseback; and many had to walk, assisted as necessary by healthy comrades. Thirty-one of the wounded men died after the army reached camp. Burials became commonplace for several days.

On the same day that the battered army limped back into camp, Colonel John Sevier and forty men arrived at the High Hills of Santee. Major Tipton and his thirty-seven remaining men were immediately attached to Sevier's small regiment.

"Landon, it's good to see you," said Jonathan, welcoming the young friend from home. "How is your father?"

"Sir, he passed away last month."

"I'm sorry. I had no idea of that." After a moment of awkward silence, Jonathan continued, "Colonel Carter was a great man. With all that has happened, I don't think your father ever got the recognition for everything he did to establish and settle the frontier over the mountains. Now, the new governor and General Greene, and all the other generals and legislators just know that John Sevier is the colonel in Washington County. In the future, Sevier will be recognized, but I think your father will be remembered only by those who were fortunate to know him well. It will be a shame, but it is an honor to be one of the people who knew him. Your father was indeed my best friend."

"Thank you for your kind thoughts, Major. I know they are genuine. My mother said that I should give you her fondest greetings."

"Your poor mother! I will certainly visit her when I return home."

"That would please her very much. I should get back to my men now."

"That you should, Landon," replied Jonathan in a friendly tone of voice. The major and his young friend parted. At least they and the now-expanded group of men from home were together in the same camp.

Inasmuch as meat was rarely available within the army's own supplies, Jonathan directed his captains to send out three hunting parties daily while in camp to provide meat for their men. It was possible to acquire small quantities of game such as deer, rabbits, squirrels, and an occasional turkey at this time of year if hunting at least two miles away from the American camp. However, there was practically nothing in the way of food crops or livestock in the area. Over several years, British foraging parties had widely confiscated not only food crops, but also cattle, pigs, and chickens from the citizens. It was difficult to feed the army consistently. The Americans preferred to use hunting parties and voluntary contributions of food from the local citizens, except that Tory farms were targeted by the American side just as the British plundered all sources of food. Food was the only commodity that was more precious than ammunition.

Even when food was scarce, the Patriot soldiers were discouraged from stealing from the farms of nearby Patriots, because the British had already done so much damage to these people. Often, when able, these fine people would contribute what little food they could in the form of crops or livestock to the army.

One afternoon in camp, Captain William Trimble smelled the pleasant odor of meat roasting. Walking toward the smell, he found a cow roasting on a pole rigged over a campfire. He demanded, "Who stole the cow?" At first there was no response to Captain Trimble's inquiry, so he added, "And from what farm did you steal it?"

Private Stephen Lowell stepped forward from a group of eight men near the campfire. He looked Captain Trimble in the eye and said, "Sir, I found him in the thick brush on the other side of the river. At first I could not see much of the animal and thought it was a deer, so I shot him. Finding a dead cow and not a deer, I came back and got help to clean it and bring it back to camp, and we decided to eat it. Honestly, sir, I don't know what farm it came from."

Captain Trimble smiled and said, "Lowell, you are so honest and you men are all so deserving of a good meal that I will not inquire further about the cow. I will, however, return in a short time to check the taste of the cow." With that, Captain Trimble strode away toward another part of the camp.

On the next morning, Colonel Sevier's regiment left the main American camp and ventured south to join Francis Marion. Because of losses suffered by General Marion at Eutaw Springs and prior engagements, Marion was in dire need of reinforcements. General Nathanael Greene believed that Sevier's frontiersmen would fit the need well.

No time was wasted in putting Sevier's men to work. Francis Marion had learned that the British were reinforcing a plantation about twenty miles northwest of Charlestown. The enemy's intent was to use the plantation as an outpost to protect their area of control around Charlestown. Marion called on Colonel Maham and 120 of his men, along with Colonel Sevier and his seventy-seven men, to attack the outpost. Major Tipton and his men constituted part of Sevier's command. Because of his lengthy experience with Marion, as well as his geographical knowledge of the area, Colonel Maham was in overall command.

The Patriot force of 197 riflemen reached the plantation on September 17. By that time, the British had assembled 450 troops at the plantation. It was too large a force for the Patriots to conquer in an all-out battle. Maham's scouts had observed, however, that one of the outbuildings was being used as a hospital, and a small building next to it was being used for supply storage. These buildings were almost 200 yards from the main plantation house, around which most of the British were camped and posted. Inasmuch as the main British force was far too strong to attack, Colonel Maham devised a plan for a hit and run attack on the hospital and stores buildings. Maham's 120 men would rush in and form a line between the main enemy camp and the hospital, firing at the British and retreating slowly, while Colonel Sevier and his 77 men made a direct attack on the lightly defended hospital and stores buildings. If things went according to plan, all useful supplies and food stores that could be carried would be taken, and the remainder burned. Any prisoners that were taken at the hospital would be released so the mounted riflemen could make a fast escape.

The mounted Patriots avoided the road, surprised the British sentries, and attacked from the woods at a gallop. Moving the wounded quickly outdoors, Major Tipton's men set fire to the hospital. At the same time, the bulk of Colonel Sevier's frontiersmen raided the adjacent stores building, easily overcoming the four guards posted there. Meanwhile, Colonel Maham's men dismounted as planned, and formed a skirmish line between the plantation house and the hospital. Almost immediately, skirmishing broke out between Maham's men and the few enemy soldiers who could react quickly. Then, as the large British force grabbed their muskets and began to form ranks, the firing intensified.

Colonel Sevier's men busied themselves at the stores building, confiscating fifty muskets, twenty bayonets, four small kegs of powder, fifty pounds of shot, and four gallons of rum, all of which they took to carry away on horseback. The stores building and all stores that could not be carried away were set afire.

Jonathan glanced toward the plantation house. He could see literally hundreds of British soldiers advancing toward Colonel Maham's outnumbered troops. As planned, the Patriots retreated, reloaded, fired, and retreated again. Maham's line had retreated to the site of the hospital by the time Jonathan's men set fire to the hospital. The Americans would have to depart immediately or be slaughtered.

Almost simultaneously, colonels Sevier and Maham began shouting at the top of their voices, "Let's go! Let's go!"

The Patriots ran eighty feet to the far side of the hospital, where their horses were being held. Mounting quickly, they made a hasty escape. The force of over four hundred British infantry soldiers could not possibly catch the mounted Americans as they fled. The small British cavalry force of forty men and horses did not dare to chase the force of nearly two hundred mounted Americans.

Just a half mile away, the Patriots slowed their horses to a walk. The normal scouts were posted forward and to the side, and a small rear guard was assigned to trail the column.

After reports were made to Colonel Maham and Colonel Sevier, the summary was that six British soldiers had been reported killed and perhaps as many as a dozen wounded. On the Patriot side, only one had been killed and five wounded. The hit and run attack was a clear American victory. Harassment of the British was important, but perhaps more important was the confiscation of the powder and shot that were desperately needed by General Marion.

On the way back toward General Marion's camp, Major Tipton rode alongside Colonel John Sevier and said, "John, one of the prisoners at the hospital told Smith Ferrell that the British have a new commanding general in Charlestown. When Ferrell told me, I confirmed it with one of the other wounded prisoners, a lieutenant. He said the new commander is Major General Alexander Leslie, and that he arrived not long ago with four ships of the line and several companies of reinforcements. I know that General Marion and General Greene are expecting news of General Leslie's arrival, so if you want to tell them about it, I am sure they will be interested."

"I will tell the general when we arrive at his camp. You should come with me in case he wants to verify the source of this information."

Arriving back at General Marion's camp, Jonathan Tipton stood by as Colonel Sevier told Marion about the arrival of the new British major general. Even though he knew that General Marion was expecting the news, Jonathan realized that this was the first time he had ever known any significant bit of intelligence about the enemy before Francis Marion knew it. His thought was that Marion not only had excellent scouts, but also seemed to have eyes and ears all over the countryside.

After listening to the news of the British general's arrival, Marion reached into his shirt pocket and pulled out a piece of paper. Looking first at Colonel Maham and then toward Colonel Sevier, he said to them and to Major Tipton, "Gentlemen, I have a bit of news, as well. I will read you part of a letter that I received today from General Greene." Unfolding the paper, Francis Marion read aloud, "Dear General Marion, having at last received a limited supply of powder and shot from Virginia, it is my pleasure to advise you that two wagons are in route to you with same. The wagons are traveling separate routes with small escorts, lest either be discovered and captured by the enemy. Absent any mishap, both should arrive at your camp on September 20. Yours sincerely, Nat Greene, Major General."

Chapter 11

Ambush at Hunger
and Hardship Creek

A s promised by General Greene, two wagons of powder and
shot arrived at General Marion's camp. For one of the few times
in 1781, Marion's brigade had both ample food and plenty of
ammunition.

On October 15, General Marion called a meeting of all the officers
in his brigade. Among those present at the meeting were Colonel Ervin,
Colonel Maham, Colonel Horry, Captain Waites, Captain Milton, and
Captain Hammond, all from Marion's regular brigade; and Colonel
Sevier, Major Tipton, Major Robertson, Major Valentine Sevier, Captain
Trimble, Captain Edwards, and Captain Williams, all under John Sevi-
er's command.

Francis Marion opened the meeting by coming straight to the point.
"Gentlemen, I have received a dispatch from General Greene. It seems
important enough to share with all of you, and for you to share with your
men. General Washington's main army has left New York and has gone
to Virginia. He has Cornwallis' whole army trapped and under siege at
Yorktown. The Americans have a French army on our side. Including the
French, the whole of General Washington's army is more than twenty
thousand men. They are surrounding Cornwallis' nine thousand men.
Unfortunately, I do not know any more than that. I would think that
if the British fleet does not bring reinforcements to the enemy, Washington will defeat them. If we destroy or capture such a large British
force, I believe we will have a good chance to win the whole war. I know

that Clinton's British army is still in New York and the British army we are facing is still operating out of Charlestown. Nonetheless, if General Washington defeats Cornwallis in Virginia the advantage will be with our side. You are free to discuss this news among yourselves and with your men. That is all."

Shortly after the officers' meeting disbanded, John Sevier approached Jonathan Tipton. "Jonathan, come with me. General Marion and I have a mission for you." The two men met with Francis Marion under the shade of a large tree.

Sevier initiated the discussion. "Jonathan, we want you to take the men who have been with you all along, along with several of the general's scouts who have ridden with you before on a patrol. General Marion wants to give you some directions about it."

Jonathan listened attentively, but could tell that no response was yet necessary.

Francis Marion chimed in, "You will have forty-two men including yourself. I want you to go down past Eutaw Springs. The British are no longer there, of course. You will go to Monck's Corner, or at least near there. Stop short of Monck's Corner at first, and send two of my scouts to spy on the size of the British garrison there. When the scouts return, ride right down the road toward Monck's Corner and see how close you get before the British or Tories spot you or confront you. Attack any enemy patrol that is smaller than your own, but make a hasty retreat from any large enemy force. Leave the area of Monck's Corner as soon as you encounter any British or Tories, regardless of whether or not you fight them. Again, attack any force that is smaller than your own, but avoid a battle with a superior enemy force. After you approach Monck's Corner, return here. If General Greene has ordered me and Colonel Sevier to take the brigade somewhere else by then, some of my men will be here with my instructions on whether or not you are to join us. Your report may help me determine whether or not to mount an attack on Monck's Corner with the full brigade, so be very observant. Do you understand?"

"Yes, General. I do have two questions. When will I leave, and how many days should the patrol require?"

"At first light tomorrow. Depending on what you encounter, the patrol will take two or three days, not more."

"Yes, sir. We will need extra powder and shot beyond what we have now," said Jonathan.

"See Colonel Ervin, and he will see to it," replied Marion.

Major Tipton's small force of forty-two mounted riflemen departed at daybreak. The first day of the patrol was eventless as they approached within five miles of Monck's Corner. At the end of the day, the small force detoured a few hundred feet off the main road and camped overnight on a small rise adjacent to an old Indian trail.

Just at the first dim light of dawn the next morning, a sentry awoke him. The sentry was Elijah Bates. There was great concern in his voice as he whispered, "There are sounds down on the trail."

Major Tipton stepped quietly a few paces toward the trail. The sounds he heard were those of harnesses and the sound of more than one squeaking wagon wheel. These were white men, not Indians, and there were lots of them.

Unable to see the men yet due to the scant light and the thinly forested area between his men and the trail, Jonathan could hear the sounds clearly. He thought that the number of men on the trail was certainly greater than the number in his small force. Taking a few more steps toward a clearing for a better view, he could now see them. They were British. There were four wagons loaded with supplies, escorted by at least seventy to eighty mounted soldiers.

Jonathan calmly directed action to the sentry. "Bates, go over there and get Captain Trimble. Then both of you go man to man as quickly as you can and roust them all up quietly. Tell every one of them to keep quiet, and that lots of redcoats are on the trail. Have all of them go down to our horses and be prepared to ride."

It was good that their horses were down the opposite side of the small rise, where the other sentry stood watch. That location was out of sight from the British cavalrymen, and hopefully the Patriots' horses were also out of earshot of the British.

Jonathan knew his small force would not likely be successful in an attack on a force so much larger. If, however, he could get to General Marion's main camp quickly enough, he could get reinforcements and arrange to ambush the redcoats. He knew from Marion's scouts that the trail the British were on went generally northwest toward a British outpost at a Tory plantation. It happened to be the closest British outpost to the place where General Marion was presently camped. That outpost, only twenty miles from Marion's camp, was obviously being resupplied. Additionally, the outpost was apparently being reinforced with cavalry, as well, unless the redcoats were simply escorting the resupply effort.

Major Tipton could now see that there were several non-uniformed Tories with the British. The Tories likely knew the area well and would guide the British to the east of where General Marion's men were camped in order to pass safely. Of course, the Tories did not know exactly where General Marion's force was encamped. They just knew that Marion's men were well known to control the general area. Jonathan was glad that he and his men had not been seen nor heard by the larger British force. Private Bates had done an excellent job as a sentry.

Jonathan strode rapidly from his vantage point to join his men where they were gathered with the horses. He addressed the men calmly, and at this time not very loudly: "The British are almost past our position. We will cross the trail behind them and head through Johnson's farm, where we passed yesterday. We are going directly to General Marion's camp to get reinforcements. Their wagons will slow them down, and we can hit them hard around mid-day tomorrow, before they reach their outpost."

Jonathan's company reached General Marion's camp before dark. He could not believe his eyes. Only about fifty men and three camp-fires existed where yesterday there had been over 250 soldiers, along with General Marion and Colonel Sevier.

Jonathan saw the officer who had been left in charge at the camp. "Captain Hammond, where are the rest of the General's men, and where has he gone with them?"

"The General took them east to raid the redcoats near Georgetown, on the coast. He will be gone about five or six days. He knew you would be here with us to protect this area. General Marion ordered me to tell you that you are in command here until he and Colonel Sevier get back."

"Why did he leave so quickly?" Jonathan inquired.

"That's just the way he is, sir. Besides, the redcoats have been burning the homes of our men who are from the area near Georgetown. The Tories told them which homes to burn."

"Captain Hammond, how many men do you have here?"

"Fifty-four healthy men and six that are wounded or sick and cannot ride. But we have only forty-four good horses."

"Get your forty best riders mounted right away. Leave your sergeant and the other healthy men and the other four good horses here to guard this place and protect the sick and wounded men. We have to attack a British supply train tomorrow before they reach the garrison at their outpost. Hurry up!"

Within minutes, Jonathan's force, now numbering eighty-two men, mounted and proceeded to intercept the British force and its four wagons of supplies. Major Tipton had his own soldiers, the few from Marion who had been his guides, and the forty men under Captain Hammond. He thought to himself that his own force was now about equal in number to the British.

Jonathan had one of the guides describe to Captain Hammond exactly when and where the British had been observed earlier that day.

As they rode to intercept the British detachment, Captain Hammond turned his head toward Jonathan and remarked, "Major Tipton, the British will have to pass a place where a small creek runs into the river. The trail has a good ford just north of the creek where it runs into the river. Since the wagons will slow them down, we can get to Hunger and Hardship Creek tomorrow before the redcoats do. We can camp a few miles down this trail tonight."

"Good. We will ambush them in the style of General Marion. We'll give them a hot surprise, indeed. What did you say the name of that creek is?"

"Hunger and Hardship Creek, sir, right where it runs into the river."

The eighty-two mounted Patriots proceeded to the place described by Captain Hammond, and on the following morning they set up the ambush. Six men guarded the hobbled horses in the woods to the rear of the main line of troops. The main line of sixty men took cover in the brush along one side of the road leading to the river. The remaining fifteen men, with Captain Hammond, concealed themselves just across the shallow ford, on the far side of the river.

The wait was short. According to Major Tipton's plan, the Patriots allowed the forward British scouts to cross the river and pass by unmolested while the Patriots succeeded in remaining concealed.

When the lead riders of the British column were just over the ford and the first two wagons were in the water, crossing at the ford, the Americans let loose a furious volley of fire. The fire from Captain Hammond's men on the opposite side of the river downed two of the eight enemy riders who had crossed the river. The remainder, two of them wounded, scrambled back across to the side from which they had approached.

As Jonathan had directed, two of the Patriots shot the lead horses of the wagons that were in the water. The disabled wagons, along with the surprise volley of fire, completely stopped the forward movement of the British column.

The British skillfully and immediately turned the two remaining wagons to their right, off the road and then back on the road, and raced them back in the direction from which they came. Then, about two hundred yards down the small, two-rutted road, they hustled the wagons off the road into a clump of trees on a small hill that was surrounded by a relatively bare landscape. The young officer commanding the retreating British force had managed to find and take a good defensive position.

On foot, Jonathan's men had to rush to their rear to retrieve their horses. By the time they mounted and returned to the road, the British cavalrymen were riding off the road into the clump of trees. The Patriots pursued the enemy at first, but approaching the British position, Major Tipton gave the order to halt. Breaking off the attack, he had the men retreat slowly toward the river. Jonathan did not want to take losses by attacking from open land when the British were in a strong, covered position.

Captain Hammond expressed Jonathan's precise feelings, saying to him, "The British officer in charge of that detachment has learned how to fight in the way of ourselves and the Indians. He has taken cover. It would be suicide to attack them from the open ground around their location."

Jonathan replied simply, "You are correct."

Then, turning toward Captain Trimble, he said, "Captain, stay here, just this side of the river, with most of the men, to dissuade the British from making a counterattack, though I think they would be foolish to do so. Captain Hammond and I will take twenty men and check the cargo of the two wagons that are stranded at the river crossing."

Wading through the shallow water at the ford, the Patriots found the lead wagon laden with British uniforms, a wooden box holding thirty-six wool blankets, and a British flag. The Patriots promptly carried the blankets ashore and tied them in bundles to their horses. They threw the remaining items into the river. An assortment of cooking pots was also in the wagon. Several of the smaller pots were taken, and all of the others were tossed into the water.

Simultaneously unloading the second wagon, the Americans found a cargo of eight sacks of potatoes, four wooden chairs, and three empty clothes chests. The men took the potatoes ashore and lashed them onto their horses for transport. They bashed the chairs against the sides of the wagon, breaking the chair legs, and threw the chairs into the water. The clothes chests were also discarded into the water. Like the chairs, the chests floated slowly downstream. The energetic process of unloading the wagons had taken only six minutes.

Major Tipton shouted to Captain Trimble, "It's time to go." With that, Trimble and the majority of the mounted Patriots crossed the river, joined Major Tipton and the men who had unloaded the wagons, and rode away from the British position.

As they rode at a slow pace, Major Tipton commented to Captain Hammond, who was beside him, "The British managed to save two wagons. I'll bet those wagons had their most valuable cargo, possibly powder, shot, and muskets."

Hammond, who had been on similar raids during his service with Francis Marion, replied, "That is almost a certainty. At least we got blankets and potatoes. Plus, the British will probably turn around and head back toward Charlestown. They will fear that we may ambush them again. I do not believe they will resupply the outpost as they had planned."

"The officer in charge of the supply train was clever. He turned his men around quickly in the face of our ambush and found an excellent defensive position," Jonathan commented. "He was likely a captain, or perhaps a lieutenant. I wish I knew his name."

"Major, we usually gain that kind of information from prisoners, and of course we have no prisoners. Since two of the British cavalrymen who crossed the river were killed, and the others escaped with their main force, we will probably never learn the officer's name."

"It really doesn't matter," Jonathan responded in summation.

About that time, Captain William Trimble rode up alongside Major Tipton and Captain Hammond. "Jonathan," he said, using the typical informality of the militia, "we had only one man wounded, Elijah Bates. He was shot in the shoulder, but he can ride just fine. The best we can tell, we killed two redcoats and wounded three more that we know of."

"Well," Major Tipton replied, "It was a small skirmish, but at least we won and had nobody killed. With winter coming soon we can sure use the blankets, and the potatoes will not go to waste tonight and tomorrow."

The Patriots camped overnight twelve miles down the road toward the British outpost. Jonathan sent scouts back toward the river in the evening, and again on the following morning to observe the movement of the British resupply detachment. The scouts reported by mid-morning the next day that the British had taken their two remaining wagons and headed back toward Charlestown, and were not attempting to resupply the forward outpost. Thus, Major Tipton led his men back to Marion's camp, where General Marion and Colonel Sevier would be expected to return within several days. Jonathan wondered why Francis Marion had not mounted an attack on the British outpost. Perhaps it was the next item on his agenda.

Three days later General Marion, Colonel Sevier, and their men returned to the camp. On that same day Colonel Sevier advised Major

Tipton, "General Greene has requested us to take the Washington County regiment—he calls us the over mountain regiment—back to his main camp at the High Hills of Santee. We will leave General Marion's camp this afternoon."

Several days later, at the main American camp, the shadows of the trees were lengthening in the late afternoon. Jonathan was outside of General Greene's tent, talking casually with Colonel Sevier, Colonel Thomas Taylor and General Nathanael Greene. Colonel William O'Neal of General Greene's staff approached, along with a soldier. Colonel O'Neal looked the general in the eyes and said, "General Greene, sir, a Private Johnson with the mounted militia has requested to speak personally with you. I listened to what he had to say. I talked with Colonel Hampton, who is his superior officer, and decided to bring Private Johnson to you. Colonel Hampton verified what Johnson has to tell you." There was an anxious tone in O'Neal's voice, as he was aware that General Greene tended to have a short temper at times. That is why he approached with Private Johnson at a time when he could hear the general and his party discussing non-essential, casual matters instead of topics of military significance.

Colonel O'Neal had picked his time carefully. He was relieved when General Greene turned toward the soldier instead of responding directly to Colonel O'Neal himself.

The general looked at the soldier, who appeared to be somewhat over twenty years of age. General Greene spoke, "Well, Private, what is your concern?"

"General, sir, I am from an area not too far from Orangeburgh. We just learned that the Tories burned my neighbor's barn last week and stole both of his remaining horses. They would have killed him if he had been at home, and they even beat his twelve-year-old son and threatened to kill his wife. They have been doing things like that for a while. I'm afraid for the safety of my family and everything I own."

General Greene, appearing to feel sincere concern, interjected, "What do you suggest?"

"Sir, I came here and joined your army, bringing my own horse. I have been with Colonel Hampton's cavalry ever since, for more than five months. I know that being here is what my orders are. I will not abandon the army. But, sir, I want to ride with General Marion's men. I've heard they sometimes patrol the area near my home. I mean, I want to be with them permanently, sir. I mean, if it can be arranged."

General Greene was silent for a moment. He immediately admired the youthful man who was speaking his mind so freely, boldly, and yet respectfully. This Private Johnson, he thought, showed intelligence, as well as judgment beyond his years. It passed quickly through Greene's mind that it was men like this that had true loyalty to the Patriot cause and could help win the war.

"What is your name again, Private?"

"Johnson, sir. Joseph Johnson."

"Well, Johnson, it just happens that General Marion will arrive in camp within the next several hours."

Then, turning his head to the left, General Greene addressed Colonel O'Neal. "Speak personally to General Marion on my behalf tonight when he arrives. See that he accepts Private Johnson at my request for whichever of his mounted companies most frequently patrols near the Orangeburgh area."

Then, speaking for the benefit of all who were present, General Greene said, "Tomorrow I shall talk with General Marion myself, and will ensure that the Tories near the Orangeburgh area are pursued with vigor. As always, I will look forward to meeting with General Marion, for he is the eyes and ears of my army."

As soon as Private Johnson had walked away, Greene looked sternly at Colonel O'Neal and ordered him, "Colonel, matters involving transfers of private soldiers do not require my personal attention. You will coordinate such matters with the officers involved. Don't you realize this? Do you understand?"

Colonel O'Neal, who was a large, muscular, and intelligent man, replied sheepishly, "Yes, sir, General." O'Neal almost always exercised good judgment, but realized that in this minor situation he had not done so.

Early in the afternoon of Saturday, October 27, 1781, the American camp was abuzz with rumors. One rumor was that General Washington had captured Cornwallis' whole army. Another was that the British were attempting to escape by sea.

Finally, Colonel John Sevier returned from meeting with General Greene and the other senior commanders. He called the entire Washington County regiment of frontiersmen together.

Sevier spoke loudly, so everyone could hear. "We have received news that General Cornwallis surrendered his army at Yorktown in Virginia to General Washington on the nineteenth of this month. The French fleet was present to block any British reinforcement or escape by sea. It is a grand victory for our cause!"

A loud cheer rose from the frontiersmen.

Sevier raised his hands to quiet the men, and continued, "We have not won the war yet. The British still have General Clinton's large army in New York, and of course they have the army in Charlestown that we have been fighting. General Greene has orders from General Washington to keep the British bottled up in the Charlestown area, and to wipe out Tory resistance in South Carolina, North Carolina, and Georgia. We will remain with General Greene's army for the next couple of months to help win the war. Then we must get home to our families. General Greene has agreed that we can depart by the end of the year."

Another round of cheering came from the men, not quite so loud as the first. On the one hand, the men could see an end in site to their separation from their homes and families. On the other, they knew that two months of fighting against the British and Tories would be an unpleasant and possibly deadly task.

After the men had dispersed, Jonathan Tipton talked privately with John Sevier.

"Colonel Sevier," said Jonathan, addressing John Sevier by his rank instead of by his first name, "I need to discuss something important with you."

"Of course, Jonathan," replied Sevier.

"It's about my men, John. We came here in July, and have been away from home for more than three months already. The rest of your men came with you in the middle of September. If they serve until the end of December, it will be more than three months' service for them, but it would keep the men who came with me away from home for a much longer period of time, far too long. They need to go home now. I am asking you to let me take those men home. We would leave tomorrow."

"I don't know if General Greene will let me release you and your men. I really don't."

"Will you ask him tonight?"

"Jonathan, your request makes sense. I will ask General Greene to let you go. If he will do it, I will have Major Robertson get with Colonel O'Neal to prepare discharge papers for you and the men. But you have to be prepared to stay. He may deny the request."

"I understand," said Jonathan.

John Sevier, a man of his word, walked directly toward the part of camp in which the tent of General Nathanael Greene was located.

Less than thirty minutes later, Colonel Sevier returned and called Major Tipton aside.

"Jonathan, I have good news! General Greene has agreed to release you and your men to return home. The papers will be prepared and signed tomorrow, the twenty-eighth of October, I believe it is. I told the general that we have need of your men at home for defense against Indians, which is true to a good extent. Unfortunately, as the general told me, the real reason he is willing to let your men go home is that he does not have enough powder and shot to support the entire army, so it is better for it to be just a little smaller. He is going to let a few units of South Carolinians go home, too."

"When can we depart?"

"You can leave as soon as the papers are signed. It will be tomorrow."

"Can I tell my men now?"

"Yes, absolutely," replied Colonel Sevier. "By the way, General Greene said he is going to send a regiment of infantry, with some mounted troops, to Orangeburgh to ensure the Tories do not regain control of that area. More important to me, Greene is sending me and the remainder of my men back to General Marion's brigade. Being with General Marion, we are now supposed to get a better part of the army's ammunition so that we can strike the enemy in Marion's typical style in the area between Orangeburgh and Charlestown and raise general havoc among them."

"John, I hope you know that I will pray for the safety of you and all of the men from home. The battles with the British and Tories seem even more dangerous and deadly than battles with the Indians."

"And I will pray for a safe return home for you and the men who are traveling with you."

That night, Jonathan, like his men, was so excited about the impending departure for home that he had a difficult time sleeping. He thought of his children and of Frances in her long skirt, with her dark, shoulder-length hair. He thought of his home. The cabin, with its two rooms, two fireplaces, and his own bed would seem like a palace in heaven, he thought, after having slept on the ground for almost four months.

On the following afternoon, with discharge papers in their possession, Major Jonathan Tipton and his men rode out of camp and left the High Hills of Santee. They would head northwest, then west and back over the mountains to their precious families and homes.

Chapter 12

Home and Liberty

ON A COOL afternoon in early November of 1781, William Tipton's arms were loaded with firewood up to his chin. The lad, nine years of age, walked toward the front door of the cabin. The boy easily handled the large load of wood as he had done so many times before. His mother opened the front door of the cabin to let him in.

As William stepped inside, a movement in the distance caught Frances Tipton's eye. A warm feeling of happiness and relief encompassed her. She recognized the approaching rider. It was Jonathan!

"Children, it is father! He's home!" she exclaimed.

The welcome home that Jonathan received was similar to those he had received before. Hugs, smiles, and expressions of joy ruled the minute. The only difference this time around was that Frances openly wept with joy. Jonathan, the brave soldier and frontiersman, held her tightly, with tears of happiness appearing in the corners of his own eyes.

"Father, mother, why are you smiling and crying at the same time?" asked six-year-old Hannah.

"All I can tell you, dear Hannah," said Jonathan as he hugged her, "is the same thing I've told you before. Home is the best place in the whole world!"

Months ago, on the day in July that Jonathan had departed to join General Greene's army, the men who remained at home were just beginning to build a new church near the Watauga settlement. Arriving home in early November, he found the church complete.

On the second Sunday of November, Jonathan and Frances Tipton, along with Samuel, Mary, Johnny, and Hannah, climbed into the wagon. William rode just ahead on one of the family's horses, as the family headed to church. They would be attending just the fourth service at the brand new church building. For about three years, regular Sunday services had been held, and the old church building had long been outgrown.

Jonathan recalled when, only a few years ago, Reverend Lane and Reverend Doak had not yet arrived in the Watauga area. Back then, Ebeneezer Tarpley, a devoted Christian layman, had led church services on the first Sunday of each month. The services at that time had often lasted less than an hour. Those services had consisted of praying, reading passages from the Holy Bible, and singing two or three of the several hymns that almost everyone in the community knew by heart.

Since Reverend Lane and Reverend Doak had arrived, the weekly services at each of their churches all lasted about two hours each. Inasmuch as the church ministered by Reverend Lane was somewhat closer to home, Jonathan and his family attended it regularly. Even though Jonathan recognized the Sabbath as a holy day, he could not help but think that Reverend Lane's sermons were too long. By the time a family rode all the way to the church, attended the service, and rode home, most of the daylight hours were gone, especially in the winter. Even on Sunday, he thought, there were many chores that had to be done out of necessity.

The family's wagon had always been useful when Jonathan and Frances wanted to take all their children to visit any of the neighbors who lived within several miles of their home. The narrow trail to the Watauga settlement as well as the trails between several of the neighbors' cabins had been clear of large stones and stumps for over two years. The wagon was now useful for taking the family to church, as well. Jonathan and Frances felt somewhat safe leaving their home unoccupied for several hours on Sunday because their neighbors, the Callahan family, always left two of their teenage sons at home when they went to church. Tom and Mary Callahan would rotate among the three sons which one would accompany them to church. The location of the Callahans' cabin offered a clear line of site to the Tipton home. The oldest son of that family, Thomas Callahan, now aged nineteen, had fought alongside his father at King's Mountain, under Jonathan's command. Thomas had also been with Major Tipton in two campaigns against the Indians.

Upon the first church service that Jonathan was able to attend after his return home, it was clear that the weekly gathering at the new church had already become an even more important community event than ever before for sharing news and socializing. Sunday services had not taken on the all-day nature of the days at church that he remembered back in Virginia, though. At those services, everyone brought food and ate together after the service. The children played and the adults talked for several hours. Perhaps that would come, Jonathan thought, although he was not sure it would be a good thing if it did. Jonathan had been away from his home so much that he did not care about being away for a couple of hours longer even one day each week.

During the first eight months of 1782, Jonathan remained at home with his wife and children, working, loving, and living. Jonathan, along with all of the leaders in Washington County, became increasingly concerned when Indian raids resumed and then increased in frequency during the period of May to August of that year. Small bands of Chickamauga Cherokees made numerous raids on the homes of individual settlers. Over a period of three months, six men, six women, and twelve children were killed, and two children were taken away by the Indians. Eight homes and four barns were burned. Chief Dragging Canoe was again trying to send a message to the white settlers that they should not expand their settlement westward.

In September, Colonel John Sevier organized a campaign intended to find and attack the main force of Chickamauga Cherokees and kill or capture Chief Dragging Canoe. John Sevier, Jonathan Tipton, Charles Robertson, and Jesse Walton gathered a militia force of 280 men, all with horses. Just before they departed, Colonel Sevier summarized the theory behind their mission. He stated, "The Chickamauga Indians will not stop killing innocent settlers, burning their homes, and stealing their horses and property unless we kill or capture Chief Dragging Canoe."

The plan was to use several dozen scouts, deployed in many directions, to locate the Indians as the force proceeded generally toward the southwest. The Chickamauga Indians were believed to be located within two or three days by horseback. If further away, they could not be perpetrating so many raids on the settlers. Proceeding deep into Indian lands, the militia force finally caught up with Dragging Canoe at a place called Lookout Mountain. After a brief skirmish, however, Dragging Canoe and his force separated into dozens of small parties and escaped.

Before the skirmish, when the Chickamauga women and children were fleeing the area, a white woman who had been captured by the Indians managed to escape. During the brief battle she hid in thick woods. After the Indian warriors disbanded and fled, Jonathan saw a woman in Indian clothing running directly toward Smith Ferrell. The woman was Mary McCorkle.

Smith Ferrell joined in with several other militiamen in welcoming her. Upon learning her identity, Jonathan shouted orders to Allen McClintock, "Go find Sergeant Bragg's men. Alexander McCorkle is with him. Get McCorkle here fast. Tell him we have found his wife."

Although the Chickamauga warriors had been pushed deep into Indian lands, and they had then dispersed and fled in small groups, the militia campaign had failed. Chief Dragging Canoe had escaped. Casualties were light, the militia having suffered only three men wounded. Eight frontiersmen reported that their shots had downed enemy warriors. Several of the men were almost certain that their shots had been deadly, but the Indians had carried away the fallen warriors and not even one Indian could be confirmed to have been killed. The one saving grace of the campaign was that Mary McCorkle had been freed. She had been held captive by the Indians for almost two years. Now, Mary McCorkle had been given the use of one of the packhorses and she rode alongside her husband back toward the white settlements.

After returning home, Jonathan rose early on a cool morning in early December. He put on his pants and a deerskin shirt, and started the morning fire. He stepped outside and picked up an armload of firewood from under the lean-to that protected the wood from rain. Bringing the wood inside, he said, "Frances, I'm going to walk to the other side of Smoke Hill. I saw some wild turkeys over there last week. A roasted turkey would make a nice dinner this evening."

"It does sound like a good idea," replied Frances.

"I feel like walking today, anyway. I'm going to take Rocky with me." Rocky was their dog. He was a mix of some sort of retriever and other breeds but was a good family dog with an excellent temperament.

"When will you be back?" she asked.

"Around midday."

"OK, get two turkeys if you can," she joked, knowing he would be fortunate to get just one.

Frances and Jonathan communicated effectively, and knew each other's habits well. She knew that if he was not back by the middle of the afternoon at the latest, then something would be wrong. Frances was not a worrier, and she assumed he would return as planned, when planned.

Jonathan set out on foot with his dog and his rifle. As usual, he also carried a pistol and a long-blade knife. After ten minutes he was out of sight of his home. Another fifteen minutes later he had reached the top of Smoke Hill and started down its lightly forested far slope.

The dog sensed it first. Jonathan saw Rocky lift his head, ears erect, obviously sniffing the air. What it was, Jonathan did not yet know. He put his left hand gently on the dog's back for a moment as a signal not to bark.

The wind was from their left rear. Could the dog be sensing something that was behind them? Just as Jonathan turned to look behind, two Indians only fifty feet away rushed directly down the hill at him.

He was barely able to get a shot off with his rifle at the Indian on the left, but missed. Having no time to react otherwise, Jonathan swung his rifle by the barrel, crashing the stock into the jaw of the Indian, just as the Indian was beginning to thrust a knife at Jonathan. The force of the blow with the rifle was so hard that it split the wood stock and caused a spray of blood and teeth to emerge from the Indian's mouth. The Indian fell, stunned, dropping his knife. At the same instant, Rocky lunged forward, trying to bite the other Indian, causing that Indian to trip and fall. This Indian had both a knife in his left hand and a tomahawk in his right. While the Indian was abruptly getting up from his fall, Rocky was now biting his leg. He rose and struck at Rocky first with the tomahawk, hitting the dog's hindquarters, and then made a skillful and fatal thrust with his knife into the dog's throat. At the same moment of that fatal thrust a shot rang out from Jonathan's pistol, the ball crashing into the Indian's lungs.

The delay caused by Rocky had saved Jonathan's life at least for a few seconds. He now had to deal immediately with the first Indian who, although bleeding badly from the mouth, had recovered his knife and had risen to his feet. Jonathan now had no weapon of real use but his knife. Having dropped his discharged rifle, he held the knife and his pistol. It was a one-on-one knife fight, and despite his physical strength and proficiency with firearms, Jonathan was not exceptionally skillful as a knife fighter.

Jonathan did have one advantage. The Indian was badly wounded, with blood streaming from his mouth and nose and the side of his face already appearing to be deformed. This Indian was in terrible pain. He was also tremendously angry and fierce.

Jonathan held his otherwise useless unloaded pistol in his left hand, trying to use it to deflect right-handed knife thrusts by the Indian, but the Indian skillfully made a quick thrust and withdrawal, giving Jonathan no opportunity to counter. The Indian's right foot slipped briefly on a small rock, but he regained his balance. An uninjured person would never have slipped like that. It dawned on Jonathan that if he could make this fight last at least several minutes, time would be on his side, for the Indian was stunned and losing an amazing amount of blood. The Indian made three more thrusts with the knife, withdrawing quickly each time. It was all Jonathan could do to dodge and deflect the thrusts. The wounded foe was a skilled fighter. Jonathan's first counter-thrust with his long knife missed badly. The Indian stabbed at Jonathan again. This time the opponent's knife blade sliced into two of Jonathan's fingers on the hand with which he was holding the pistol to deflect the thrust. Some instinct made Jonathan change hands with his weapons. He put the knife in his left hand and held the pistol by the barrel in his right, just as he had with his left hand, only now his intent was different. The Indian, perhaps not as fast as he was moments before, thrust again. Jonathan managed to deflect the thrust with his own knife blade, and then stepped forward quickly and slightly to the right, delivering a powerful overhead blow with the pistol to the left side of the Indian's head. The Indian staggered slightly. Jonathan struck him again with the pistol, knocking him to his knees, and then fatally stabbed the now-defenseless Indian in the chest.

Jonathan was exhausted. He checked both Indians to be sure they were dead. Then he touched his dog, Rocky, and called his name hoping for a sign of life. There was no movement and no sound. Rocky was dead.

Jonathan's sliced fingers were bleeding steadily, but not profusely. He would be fine. Although very tired, he decided he would bury Rocky right now. Then he would go home. He would come back with neighbors and his oldest son tomorrow to bury the Indians, or what was left of them if animals of the forest got to their bodies overnight. There would be no turkey dinner today, but he would be home on time, as expected.

Arriving at his cabin, Jonathan propped his damaged rifle against the outside wall. He opened the door with his right hand. Then he reached back outside with the same hand and moved the rifle indoors against the wall just inside the door, and entered the cabin.

Frances looked at him and immediately noticed the bleeding from his hand and the blood on his shirt and trousers.

"Jonathan, you are injured! Let me look." As Frances spoke, she reached for a cloth potholder near the fireplace. "Sit down." Frances poured water over the bloody hand, revealing the two slices into his fingers as the bloody water dripped onto the cabin floor. She then wrapped the potholder around both fingers. "Hold this while I get cloth for a bandage," she instructed Jonathan. Frances returned from the back room of the cabin within seconds.

While she bandaged his fingers with strips of cloth, Jonathan told her and the children a quick version of being attacked by two Indians and the death of the family's beloved dog. Upon learning that Rocky was dead, Hannah began to cry. Soon Samuel, Johnny, and Mary were also crying, and even William, the oldest of the children, had tears in his eyes.

Frances finished bandaging Jonathan's fingers and wanted Jonathan to lie down and rest. Although Jonathan was somewhat tired, the last thing on his mind was to lie down. He wanted to send William to their neighbor's home to get Tom and Thomas Callahan. Jonathan intended to lead them to the bodies of the dead Indians right away. He had changed his mind, and thought it would be better to go then than to put it off until the next day. Jonathan pleaded with Francis, "Even the bodies of Indians should not be left to be devoured by the beasts of the forest." On this occasion Frances prevailed. Jonathan remained home. He did not lie down, however. Instead he sat in his favorite wooden chair near the fireplace and read passages from the Holy Bible. Finally, he did doze off in the chair. Frances kissed Jonathan on the forehead as he slept. She was happy, for she felt that Jonathan would have pushed himself to exhaustion had it not been for her persuasiveness. It was the next day when Jonathan, the neighbors, and William buried the two deceased Indians.

After returning from burying the two deceased Chickamauga Indians, Jonathan Tipton sat on a short section of a chopped log outside of his home. He watched young Samuel and Hannah as they played with the two tomahawks that William had retrieved from the place where the Indians had been killed. He felt the cool, gentle breeze and breathed the fresh air. He thought about the battle against the Chickamauga Cherokees at Lookout Mountain in September. He recalled the events of having so recently faced such a large force of Indians. Jonathan perceived their willingness to fight and die to protect their land from being taken by white settlers. The Chickamauga Indians had retreated again, but they always regrouped and later renewed their attacks on the settlers. Jonathan was already concerned about the long-term safety of settlers on the frontier. Now that he had been personally attacked so close to his own home, he wondered if the mountains would ever be safe for his family.

At age thirty-two Jonathan Tipton was still strong and healthy, but was weary of being away from home so much. Even though many of the Indians were peaceful, it was the young chiefs like Dragging Canoe and the deceased Chief Bear Cloud who were almost constantly at war with the settlers. Would they take over completely once all the older, more peaceful chiefs passed away? If so, the sheer numbers of Indians could make life on the frontier difficult for the settlers.

The best hope, he believed, was that the new settlers who were making their homes in the area west of his own would create a new frontier. Eventually there may be enough new settlers to the west, he hoped, to have the effect of moving the frontier westward. Those settlers might provide a buffer between his home and the Indians. Jonathan's pensive moment was broken by the cry of a hawk circling above. Looking up, Jonathan said aloud to himself, "Even the hawks have work to do."

Early one morning, later in the month of December, Jonathan went outside to get some firewood. He was greeted by a gust of cold wind, and was chilled by the time he entered the cabin with the firewood.

"Frances, the ground is covered with ice. It is extremely cold and the weather is poor. I think you and the children should remain home and not attend church today. I believe that I should attend, though."

Frances felt the penetrating cold wind when Jonathan opened the door to bring in the wood.

"Are you sure you want to go?"

"Yes, I really should attend. It's the last service of the year."

"If you want to go, we should all go as a family," said Frances. "We can bundle the children up. They are used to the cold, anyway. They don't want to stay indoors even when it is freezing outside."

Jonathan Tipton, Frances, and the children braved the weather for the cold trip of several miles to the church. Jonathan wanted to attend because of his religious commitment, and he increasingly felt that attendance was essential from a community and social perspective, as well.

Those who braved the weather to attend church on December 29, 1782, were amply rewarded. Colonel John Sevier arrived just minutes prior to the start of the service, and took Reverend Lane aside to speak with him.

After Reverend Lane and John Sevier conferred briefly, Reverend Lane stood at the pulpit. He addressed the smaller than usual congregation, "Colonel Sevier has some important information, and I will let him share it with you before we begin today's service. I have never before placed a layman before you for something other than a message of the Scripture, but I believe that even the good Lord will agree with my decision to do so this time."

John Sevier took the minister's place at the pulpit. "I have exceedingly good news," he said, scarcely able to contain his own excitement. "Last evening I received a dispatch from General Marion. The British have evacuated Charlestown!"

Excited conversation in the congregation interrupted Colonel Sevier.

He waited momentarily and continued, "Just over two weeks ago, on December 14, a great British fleet departed. They took with them all the British troops and over three thousand Tories, including women and children, and headed for England. All of the British and the worst of the Tories are gone!"

At this time, a standing ovation and loud shouts of joy interrupted Sevier again.

Colonel Sevier waited for a few seconds and then raised his both of his arms and said, "Please be seated." Then he continued, "General Marion's letter said there were dozens and dozens of ships. So many ships were moving about that the citizens of Charlestown could not make an accurate count of them. General Greene's forces have entered Charlestown and now control it for the Patriot side."

Another round of exhilarated cheering followed, and was soon quieted by the colonel.

"I now give you back to Reverend Lane for the service that you came to this sacred place to attend. I must leave and try to reach Reverend Doak's service before it is over and give the people there this same good news." John Sevier quickly left the church, receiving a round of cheers and a standing ovation as he walked down the center aisle to exit.

Returning to the pulpit, Reverend Lane proposed, "Let's all bow our heads and begin the service with a prayer." He continued, "Dear Lord, thank You for all You have given us. Thank You for delivering us from the turpitude and vengeance of our enemies, and thank You, Lord, for protecting the men in this congregation who went over the mountains to fight for our freedom. Amen."

Suggested Reading

Angiel, Lucien. Rebels Victorious: *The American Revolution in the South*, 1780–1781. New York: Ballantine Books, 1975.

Axelrod, Alan. *The Complete Idiot's Guide to the American Revolution*. New York: Penguin Group, 2000.

Blanco, Richard L., ed. *The American Revolution*, 1775–1783, two-volume encyclopedia. New York and London: Garland Publishing, 1993.

Carpenter, Hugh. *King's Mountain—An Epic of the Revolution; with Historical and Biographical Sketches and Illustrations*. Knoxville: Prv. Ptd., 1936.

Carter, Landon. "Diary." *William & Mary Quarterly*, XVI (1907), 149-152, 258-264.

Commager, Henry Steele and Morris, Richard B., eds. *The Spirit of Seventy-Six: The Story of the American Revolution as Told by Participants*. Edison, New York: Harper & Row, 1958, 1976.

Draper, Lyman C. *King's Mountain and Its Heroes*. Cincinnati, Ohio: Peter G. Thompson, 1881.

Ferling, John. *Almost a Miracle: The American Victory in the War of Independence*. New York: Oxford University Press, 2007.

Gragg, Rod. *Planters, Pirates and Patriots: Historical Tales from the South Carolina Grand Strand*. Nashville, Tenn.: Rutledge Hill Press, 1994.

Greene, George W. *The Life of Nathanael Greene, Major General in the Army of the Revolution*. 3 volumes. New York: Hurd and Houghton, 1871.

Greene, Nathanael. *The Papers of General Nathanael Greene*. Edited by Richard K. Showman and Dennis M. Conrad. Chapel

Hill: University of North Carolina Press for the Rhode Island
Historical Society, 1976 to Present.

Hilborn, Nat and Sam. *Battleground of Freedom: South Carolina in
the Revolution.* Columbia, SC: Sandpiper Press, 1970.

Historical Section of the Army War College, submitted by Davis,
Dwight L., Secretary of War. "Historical Statements Concerning
The Battle of King's Mountain and The Battle of Cowpens South
Carolina," www.history.army.mil/books/revwar/KM-Cpns/
AWC-KM-fm.htm 70th Congress, 1st Session House Document
No. 328. Washington, DC: United States Government Printing
Office, 1928. (Accessed Nov. 21, 2007)

Hoffer, Edward E. *Operational Art and Insurgency War: Nathanael
Greene's Campaign in the Carolinas.* Fort Leavenworth:
Command and General Staff College, 1988.

James, William Dobein. *A Sketch of the Life of Brig. Gen. Francis
Marion and a History of His Brigade.* Charleston, SC: Gould
and Milet, 1821.

Kelly, C. Brian. *Best Little Stories from the American Revolution.*
Nashville, TN: Cumberland House Publishing, 1999.

Landers, H. L., Lt. Col. *The Battle of Camden South Carolina.*
Historical Section, Army War College. Washington, DC: United
States Government Printing Office, 1929.

Leckie, Robert. *George Washington's War.* New York: HarperCollins,
1992.

Lee, Henry. *The Campaign of 1781 in the Carolinas.* Philadelphia: E.
Littell, 1824.

Lumpkin, Henry. *From Savannah to Yorktown: The American
Revolution in the South.* New York: Paragon House, 1981.

Mackenzie, George C. *King's Mountain National Park Service
Historical Handbook No. 22.* Washington, DC: 1955, Reprinted
1961.

McCrady, Edward. *The History of South Carolina in the Revolution, 1775–1780.* New York: Macmillan Company, 1901.

Messick, Hank. *King's Mountain: The Epic of the Blue Ridge "Mountain Men" in the American Revolution.* New York: Little, Brown, and Co., 1976.

Middlekauff, Robert. *The Glorious Cause: The American Revolution, 1763–1789.* New York: Oxford University Press, 1982, 2005.

Morrill, Dan L. *Southern Campaigns of the American Revolution.* Baltimore, MD: Nautical & Aviation Publishing, 1996.

Moultrie, William. *Memoirs of the American Revolution, So Far as It Related to the States of North and South Carolina, and Georgia.* Compiled from the most authentic materials, the author's personal knowledge of the various events, and including an epistolary correspondence on public affairs, with civil and military officers of that period. 2 vols. New York: David Longworth, 1802.

North Carolina (State). *The State Records of North Carolina.* Published under the Supervision of the Trustees of Public Libraries. By order of the General Assembly. Edited by Walter Clark. XI-XXVI (1776–1790). Winston, NC: M.I. & J.C. Stewart, 1805-1906.

Ramsay, David. *History of the American Revolution.* 2 vols. London: John Stockdale, 1793.

Ramsey, J. G. M. *The Annals of Tennessee History to the End of the Eighteenth Century.* Entered according to Act of Congress in the year 1853. Charleston: Steam Power Press of Walker & James, 1853.

Saunders, William L., ed. *Colonial Records of North Carolina.* 10 vols. Raleigh: P.M. Hale, 1886-1890.

Shaara, Jeff. *The Glorious Cause.* New York: Random House, 2002.

Starr, Emmet. *History of the Cherokee Indians and their Folk Lore.* Muskogee, OK: Hoffman Printing Co., 1984. Reprint of 1921 ed. Indexed.

Stiles, T. J. *Founding Fathers: In Their Own Words.* New York: The Berkley Publishing Group, 1999.

Tarleton, Banastre, Lt. Col. *A History of the Campaigns of 1780 and 1781, in the Southern Provinces of North America.* Dublin: Colles, Exshaw, et al., 1787.

Recommended Historic Sites

Bethel Presbyterian Church. Clover, SC.

Biggin Church Ruins. Berkeley County, SC.

Charleston, SC. Various historic sites in and near Charleston, SC.

Chota and Tanasi Village Sites. U.S. National Register of Historic Places. Vonore, TN.

Colonel John and Landon Carter Mansion. Elizabethton, TN.

Colonial Dorchester State Historic Site. Dorchester, SC.

Cowpens National Battlefield. Chesnee, SC.

Eutaw Springs Battleground. Eutaw Springs, SC.

Fort Moultrie National Monument. Sullivans Island, SC.

Greensboro Historical Museum. Greensboro, NC.

Guilford Courthouse National Military Park. Greensboro, NC.

Hezekiah Alexander Homesite. Charlotte, NC.

Historic Brattonsville—Huck's Defeat. McConnells, SC.

Historic Camden Revolutionary War Site. Camden, SC.

House in the Horseshoe State Historic Site. Sanford, NC.

King's Mountain National Military Park. Blacksburg, SC.

Musgrove Mill State Historic Site. Clinton, SC.

Ninety-Six National Historic Site. Ninety-Six, SC.

Old English Cemetery. Salisbury, NC.

Orange County Visitors' Center. Hillsborough, NC.

Snow Camp Community & Drama Site. Snow Camp, NC.

Sycamore Shoals State Historic Area. Elizabethton, TN.

St. David's Church. Cheraw, SC.

Tomb of Thomas Sumter, and the High Hills of the Santee. Stateburg, SC.

About the Author

LEWIS TERRY RICH is proud to have served as an active duty commissioned officer in the armed forces of the United States of America and to have volunteered for an additional year as a weekend warrior in the reserves. His subsequent management career included working for over seventeen years for a major defense industry contractor serving the United States military. A member of the United Methodist Church, he was born and raised in middle Georgia, and now lives in the metropolitan Jacksonville, Florida, area.

A lifetime student of American military history, he is a graduate of Valdosta State University and also earned a master's degree in human resources management from Webster University.

The author has eight direct-line ancestors who fought on the American side in the Revolutionary War. His wife, Deborah, a member of the Fort San Nicholas Chapter of the Daughters of the American Revolution, is similarly proud to have several Patriot ancestors, one of whom was Major Jonathan Tipton III. There are stories behind all of these patriots and their families. Look for future novels by Lewis Rich about the American struggle for freedom.

To Contact the Author

trich32@comcast.net

A Garland Series

ROMANTIC CONTEXT: POETRY

Significant Minor Poetry
1789-1830

Printed in photo-facsimile
in 128 volumes

selected and arranged by
Donald H. Reiman
The Carl H. Pforzheimer Library

David Booth, *1766-1846.*
and
Elizabeth Hitchener

Eura and Zephyra

The Fire-Side Bagatelle

The Weald of Sussex

with introductions
for the Garland edition by
Donald H. Reiman

Garland Publishing, Inc., New York & London

1978

Bibliographical note:

these facsimiles have been made from
copies in The Newberry Library
Eura and Zephyra (Case 3A 263);
the University of Illinois Library
The Fire-Side Bagatelle (821.H63f);
and the Beinecke Library of Yale University
The Weald of Sussex (Im.H637.822).

The volumes in this series have been printed on
acid-free, 250-year-life paper.

Library of Congress Cataloging in Publication Data

Booth, David, 1766-1846.
    Eura and Zephyra.

    (Romantic context : Poetry)
    Reprint of the 1816 ed. of Eura and Zephyra, by
D. Booth, published by Gale and Fenner, London; of the
1818 ed. of The fire-side Bagatelle, by E. Hitchener,
printed by Barlow & Bishop, London; and of the 1822 ed.
of The weald of Sussex, by E. Hitchener, printed for
Black, Young, and Young by J. Barlow, London.
    1. English poetry—19th century. I. Hitchener,
Elizabeth. The fire-side Bagatelle. 1978.
II. Hitchener, Elizabeth. The weald of Sussex. 1978.
III. Title. IV. Series.
PR1222.B6 1978   821'.7'08   75-31163
ISBN 0-8240-2117-7

 Printed in the United States of America

Introduction

David Booth (1766-1846), a Scot, first appears in literary records in 1799 as an admirer and correspondent of William Godwin (see *Shelley and his Circle*, ed. Kenneth Neill Cameron and Donald H. Reiman, II [1961], 542-544). In 1805 and 1806 he published a Prospectus and an Introduction to *An Analytical Dictionary of the English Language*, which he proposed to issue in parts. In 1808 he visited Godwin in London, perhaps seeking a publisher for his dictionary, but he returned to Scotland, where he operated a brewery in Newburgh, Fifeshire.

In 1809 Booth married Margaret Baxter, eldest of the five daughters and two sons of William Thomas Baxter, a manufacturer of canvas in Dundee, Scotland, to whom he introduced Godwin. Young Mary W. Godwin lived at Dundee with Baxter's family from June until November 1812, and after a visit to London by Mary and the two youngest Baxter daughters, Christina ("Christy") and Isabella, she returned to Dundee from June 1813 to March 1814. The Baxter girls—particularly Isabella—became Mary's closest friends (*Shelley and his Circle*, III [1970], 100-105, 399-400). In 1814, Margaret Baxter Booth died, and Booth—contrary to the marriage taboos of the Glassite sect, to which both he and the Baxters belonged—married Isabella Baxter, the sister (or half sister) of his deceased wife (and a girl almost young enough to have been his granddaughter). For this offense, both Booth and Baxter were "disjoined" from the Glassite church.

In spite of—or, perhaps, consequent upon—their own ostracism, the Booths would not accept Mary Godwin's elopement with Percy Bysshe Shelley in July 1814. Mary's Journal for November 3, 1814, records: "Receive a letter from Mr. Booth; so all my hopes are over there. Ah! Isabel; I did not think you would act thus" (*Mary Shelley's Journal*, ed. F.L. Jones [1947], p. 24).

INTRODUCTION

In 1816 Baxter's business failed in the postwar depression, and Booth decided to sell his brewery. The two, therefore, came to London to seek new fortunes. Because the Godwins had reconciled themselves with Shelley and Mary after they were married in December 1816, Mary Shelley and Isabella Booth (who had remained in Scotland) tried to renew their friendship late in 1817 over the objections of David Booth. Eventually, a combination of Shelley's words and actions and the wounded pride of Booth and Baxter led to a second rupture of relations. The story is thoroughly documented in the letters written by all parties in December 1817-March 1818 that are published and analyzed in *Shelley and his Circle* (V [1973], 332-342, 345-347, 371-392, 505-508). Shelley—much angered by what he regarded as Booth's tyrannical behavior in separating Mary Shelley from her closest friend—developed the emotional kernel of the situation into *Rosalind and Helen* (1819), the least successful long poem of his maturity.

David Booth, who remained friendly with Godwin, aided him in the statistical portions of his *Of Population: An Answer to Mr. Malthus's Essay* (1820) and defended that work in *A Letter to the Reverend T.H. Malthus, being an Answer to His Criticism of Mr. Godwin's Work on Population* (1823). In 1824, as part of his work for the Society for the Diffusion of Useful Knowledge, he published *The Art of Brewing, on Scientific Principles* (London: Knight and Lacey, 1824). In 1822 Booth had finally begun to issue in parts his major work, *An Analytical Dictionary of the English Language, in which the Words are Explained in the Order of their Natural Affinity, Independent of Alphabetical Arrangement . . .* , a work which, I have argued, was a forerunner of both Roget's *Thesaurus* and Fowler's *Modern English Usage* (*Shelley and his Circle*, V [1973], 386). This *Dictionary* was collected and published as a whole in 1835, with a corrected edition following in 1836. Booth, however, failed to achieve recognition and eventually retired to Scotland, leaving manuscripts on grammar and composition unpublished at his

INTRODUCTION

death in 1846. Mary Shelley, who after her return to England in 1823 had renewed her friendship with Isabella Booth, helped support the widow in her later years.

The only disinterested contemporary judgments of Booth that I know are found in Henry Crabb Robinson's diary for February 4, 1818, and July 6, 1819. On the earlier occasion he wrote:

> I called on Godwin, and at his house met with a party of originals. One man struck me by his resemblance to Curran—his name Booth. Godwin called him, on introduction, a master of the English language, and I understood him to be a learned etymologist. His conversation was singular, and even original, so that I relished the short time I stayed.
>
> (Robinson, *Diary, Reminiscenses* . . . , ed. Thomas Sadler, 3rd. ed. [1872], I, 310)

The other reads:

> . . . went to Godwin's by invitation. Charles and Mary Lamb were there, also Mr. Booth, a singular character, not unlike Curran in person. A clever man, says Godwin, and very like in his exterior to the Grub Street poet of the last century.
>
> (*Books and Their Writers, ed.* Edith J. Morley [1938], I, 233)

Shelley's own judgment of Booth's abilities—though given, in a letter to Baxter, partly for rhetorical effect—is also worth quoting:

> Mr. Booth is no doubt a man of great intellectual acuteness, & consummate skill in the exercise of logic. I never met with a man by whom in the short time we

INTRODUCTION

exchanged ideas, I felt myself excited to so much severe
& sustained mental competition; or from whom I
derived so much amusement & instruction.—

(*Shelley and his Circle*, V, 383)

The modern student of Shelley and Godwin will gain some
sense of another aspect of Booth from *Eura and Zephyra*,
which contains (so far as is known) all of his creative writings.
The works themselves reveal that Booth took more interest in
mastering various languages than in the craft of poetry, and
the Advertisement exhibits his hardheaded candor. Booth
owes his place in this series entirely to his dealings with
Godwin and Percy Bysshe and Mary W. Shelley, but once here,
he can be taken as representative of a group of individuals
trained in the values of the Enlightenment who saw scientific
and technological progress as the key to the expansion of
human happiness. These were the individuals who, adopting
the doctrines of Bentham, James Mill, Brougham, and the
Westminster Review, drove England and Scotland to the land
of dark Satanic mills decried presciently by Blake and painted
by Dickens and his contemporaries in *Hard Times* and other
writings. Yet Booth himself, coming out of a rural and humane
environment, aimed only at making the benefits of technology
available to a broader spectrum of the British people. He was,
unlike Blake, Wordsworth, and Shelley, unable to see farther
down the road upon which the course of economic and
technological development—as well as his values and those of
his contemporaries—directed the future of Western civili-
zation.

Donald H. Reiman

EURA

AND

ZEPHYRA, &c.

EDINBURGH:
Printed by James Ballantyne and Co.

E U R A

AND

Z E P H Y R A,

A CLASSICAL TALE:

WITH

POETICAL PIECES.

BY

DAVID BOOTH.

———

LONDON:

PUBLISHED, FOR THE AUTHOR, BY

GALE AND FENNER.

———

1816.

ADVERTISEMENT.

This small *Volume owes its publication to the Tale,*
which is one of a series that will be given to the Public,
provided the present specimen be favourably received.—
The Poems were added in order to swell the work to the
size required by the Bookseller :—A Book must sell at
a certain price before it will bear the expence of adver-
tising.

Of the Poetical Pieces, " Old Age,"—" The Rose,"
and the Verses " To a Mirror," are imitated from the
French ;—" The Complaint" and " The Dream" are,
partly, from the German ; and " The Father to his
Infant Daughter" is from the Danish.

March 4, 1816.

CONTENTS.

————

EURA

AND

ZEPHYRA.

EURA

AND

ZEPHYRA.

———

THE loves of Zephyrus and Flora have been often sung by the poets. Amid orange groves, with underwood of myrtles and roses;—in bowers of jessamine and woodbine, where spring follows in the train of autumn, banishing winter from the blissful clime;—there these happy immortals whispered the tender accents of love.

After some ages had rolled (for ages to the Gods

are but as hours to earthly lovers,) Flora was seen
to languish. Even the tender dalliance of her
husband was less pleasing than formerly. She
sought the solitary shade;—she loathed those re-
pasts which form the delight of the Gods. A
council was called on Olympus, and Flora was
consigned to the care of Lucina, who soon added
Zephyra to the list of female divinities.

Flora was enraptured with her child. Every
night it slept in her bosom, and every morning it
was awakened by the caresses of Zephyr. The
buds of spring were neglected;—the roses lan-
guished on their stalks, and the woodbines lost
their perfume. These were only the children of
Nature, though once the darling objects of Flora's
care, but Zephyra was the daughter of her heart;
—the production of her enraptured soul;—the
pledge of her husband's love. Nature made a com-

plaint at the court of Jupiter. Flora was forced to
resign her child, and Zephyra became the ward of
Minerva.

It was about the same age of the world that
Eurus, whose icy heart had ever been impenetra-
ble to the shafts of Cupid, was driving his sleety
blasts over the dreary desarts of Lapland.   Not a
tree to spread even its leafless arms to check the
fury of the winds.   Only here and there a stinted
shrub, nestled under the western side of a naked
rock, returned a shivering murmur while the blast
howled over the plain.   It was winter;—but to
the shepherd who reclines at ease on the sunny
plains of Arcadia, it were vain to attempt to describe the winters of Lapland.   It was December.
It was dark and dreary, save, now and then, a flash
of lightning which burst through the gloom and
played around the pole.   Even Eurus shuddered

while he rode on the storm, and was fain to rest, when he heard his tempests whistling through the dark recesses of a rocky cave. There a Naiad sat leaning over a frozen urn. Her hair, tangled with ice, seemed like the snakes of Medusa. Her palsied eye was fixed motionless on the skeleton of a bear, who, the strongest of his race, had latest braved the pelting of the storms and the pangs of hunger. Could the superior powers have become subject to mortality, the Naiad, too, had, long ere then, been frozen and insensible as the waters of her urn.

What infernal demon assumed the garb and form of Cupid? Some hell-born fiend, with arrows hissing hot from the flames of Tartarus, must have melted the ice-bound hearts of Eurus and the Naiad. He certainly was not the god of love. Earth quaked under the horrid embrace, and the

Gods themselves were astonished at the birth of Eura. Grim were the demons that saw her spring into existence. No gentle being smoothed the couch of the mother. The furies watched to receive the child; but Juno, in pity, snatched it from their grasp and adopted Eura as her daughter.

Torn by pangs which Nature disowned, and which, before, no immortal ever knew, the Naiad became, in some degree, assimilated to the human race. Her breath became more poisonous than the arrows of mortality. She was doomed to pine for ever on a flinty bed. Pain holds his vultures to her liver, and Megrim fixes his blisters on her head. She is known on earth by the name of Spleen.

If we except Cupid, the Gods have not had to pass through the infant stage of imbecility. He, indeed, like all his votaries, though ages roll over his head, must be still a child. But, though the mind has not, slowly and gradually, to increase its powers, through a period of childhood and adolescence, yet the new-born Divinity is destitute of experience while mature in the faculty of reason. It is in this sense that we may speak of the education of Eura and Zephyra.

The character of each individual of the human race is supposed to have been modified by the primary composition of his nature;—by his education, or by both combined. Neither the character of Eura nor that of Zephyra enables us to decide the general question. Their education corresponded with the circumstances of their birth. Reality tallied with metaphor—body with soul. One was rough, boisterous, cold, and unfeeling; the other was mild, gentle, warm, and benevolent. Whether or not Minerva could have infused tenderness into the hardened heart of Eura, or Juno could have stamped the frown of a termagant on the gentle countenance of Zephyra, it is not for mortals to determine.

The precepts of Minerva have been little attended to by the historian. The still small voice of wisdom has been seldom listened to or regarded by the flatterers of power. History is scarcely any thing but the record of folly or of crime :— We can, therefore, give only a slight account of the education of Zephyra. The Muses were her instructors in harmony and science, and the Graces were chosen for the companions of her gayer hours. Free from factitious wants, she was insensible to the allurements of vanity or ambition. Happy herself, she had leisure to study the happiness of others; ever ready to hear the tale of sympathy, or to attend to the claims of benevolence :—But the description languishes under the pen. The abode of wisdom and happiness is too sequestered to attract the eye of the passenger. He sees not the ivy-covered cottages of peace and contentment, but gazes on the battlements of war and the proud palaces of ambition. It is not the vale of plenty, nor the glassy surface of the lake, that figures on the canvass of the painter. He pourtrays the rugged and tremendous cliff, hanging over the tempestuous ocean, and the sailor clinging to the mast in the storm that dashes his bark upon the rocks.

Education, as far as it relates to the affections of the mind, is, for the most part, if not altogether, the acquisition of habits. Habits are formed from imitation. It is hence that we acquire the opinions and the prejudices—the follies and

the vices, of those who more immediately surround us.   In order, then, to form a more accurate conception of the character of Eura, we must
be daring enough to enter into the secret cham-
bers of Jupiter and Juno.

It is well known that Jupiter, although he wields
the thunderbolts which frighten the inhabitants of
this lower world, is himself afraid of the thunders
of Juno.   The perpetual scolding of the female
tongue is more grating to the ear than the clank-
ing of chains in the cell of the restless maniac.
The amours of her husband were the perpetual
theme, and certainly the god is not to be praised
for the inconstancy of his love.   But we know not
all the motives that were the causes of his conduct.
Some of them, however, are recorded, and others
may be imagined by those who have had the misfortune to be tied to a termagant.

For many ages Jupiter was faithful to his queen. He strove to please her whose ill-humour could never be appeased. He smiled when she frowned, and caressed her when she was peevish—all was unavailing. If he left her, for a moment, to cast his eyes on the affairs of the universe, his ears were assailed with complaints of his inconstancy and unkindness. If he deigned to smile on the goddesses around him, the demon of jealousy sprung to her heart. She watched every motion of his eyes, when present, in order to catch the furtive lightning of love, and, when absent, she searched every grove for seats of assignation. It was in vain that he pleaded his innocence. To her alone belonged every thought of his soul and every motion of his frame. To please her he must cling closer than Hercules with his distaff, and even this would not please. Jupiter saw that his toils were increasing and vain. For one female must the order of the universe be suspended? He broke his chains, and Juno was, occasionally, without her lord. His return was attended with none of those rapturous emotions which are said to be felt, at meeting, by lovers who have been long absent. Clamorous complaints and loud jealous accusations greeted his entrance. Patience herself would have fretted at the incessant din.

At last the god grew weary of his home. His absences became more frequent and protracted; and he began to seek consolation at a distance from the arms of her who once engrossed all the affections of his heart. From this moment, open war was proclaimed. Juno had her spies and informers on his conduct, and it was Jupiter's care to evade or to punish them. Thus a sort of hell was established in the centre of heaven;—the prototype of those which have, since, been so profusely scattered over the surface of the earthly globe.

Under such care, and with such an example before her, the temper of Eura was formed. The mind of youth is a mirror that reflects the feelings of those around; but no gentle passion ever mantled the countenance of her protectress to shoot its electric glance on the mind of Eura. Were the windows of Momus fixed in the breast of man, there are, perhaps, moments in the lives of the purest of human beings, in which pride, fear, or delicacy would induce them to draw the curtain. But the breast of Eura was that of a fiend which was never pure. Pride, jealousy, hatred, and all the other vengeful passions, nestled in her heart. She was even more ruthless than her protectress; for there was once a time in which the soul of Juno was the seat of the tender passions;—that time when her heart, yet uncorrupted with power, expanded, with pleasure, to acts of kindness;— when her eyes beamed only with the shafts of love, and shot forth those glances of endearment which thrilled with delight the breast of the governor of the world. There were moments too, even in her later years, when memory regained its empire;— when the furies lost possession of her eyes, and a fleeting spark of sympathy reminded her partner of what she once had been. At such moments he would press her to his bosom;—for an instant she would forget to be jealous, and he would resolve to be faithful. It was otherwise with Eura. Fostered from her earliest years on the chilly bosom of unkindness, no after recollection of warmer feelings could thaw the ice-bolts that bound her to misery and crime.

Employment is the order of nature. There is

neither deity nor demon who has not some part to perform in the œconomy of the universe. Idleness once attempted to fix her abode on Olympus. The wheels of the world dragged heavily along and must soon have stood still. Jupiter interfered. She was thrown down to earth; and, to punish her temerity, was doomed to be for ever the slave of Ennui,—a demon who curses her days with listlessness and languor, and tortures her nights with frightful dreams. The votaries of Idleness share in her pangs, and find relief only by bending at the shrine of Labour.

Minerva was interested in the happiness of Zephyra, and consulted with Jupiter respecting her future destiny. It was about this period that man was placed upon the earth. Solicitous for his happiness, Jove formed for him a partner to solace his cares. He well knew, however, that the females of the human race must be irregular, fickle, and capricious, and would require the superintendance of a directing hand; without which their best resolves would be fleeting and evanescent:—their loves and hatreds as unstable as the traces on the sand of the sea-shore. To regulate the female heart, and to render it as lovely as the outward form, seemed to be a task worthy of the pupil of Wisdom. Minerva gave her acquiescence, and Zephyra was appointed to be the guardian angel of womankind.

It is difficult to conceive the mode of operation by which the superior powers are enabled to influence the minds of the inhabitants of this lower world. However this may be, the fact is indisputable. Man is a machine in the hands of necessity. His wishes and his wants are formed by the objects around him, and over these objects he

B

has little, if any, controul. If he be dragged along, by the impulses of his nature, to satisfy the cravings of appetite and affection, some power, unseen by him, must have planted those feelings in his breast. It was to direct those feelings in her own sex that Zephyra was sent upon earth.

Sympathy, whether it be that of joy or of sorrow, is the balm of human life; and there is no sympathy so endearing as that which is shewn by the partner of our pains and pleasures. She whom a man has singled from the world as the companion of his heart and the sharer of his happiness, should be best fitted to be the soother of his sorrows. What then must be the misery of him who, buffetted by the storms of adversity, finds himself not only deserted by the world, but also neglected and despised by her who enjoyed the sun-shine of his better days? Neither constancy nor fortitude, however, are the birth-right of woman; and it was, therefore, a charge of peculiar value to inspire these virtues into her soul. Without them she might, indeed, please for a moment by the fleeting charms of beauty; but, like the withering rose, she would soon be overlooked and forsaken, for one more newly from its bud, alluring with a fresher fragrance and a brighter bloom.

Man first rose into existence in the warmer regions of the world. The fruits of the earth grew, spontaneously, under his hand, requiring but little of his culture or his care. Ennui was then unknown, for neither Luxury nor Idleness had as yet infected society. The occupations of man were too light to weary, and too varied to cloy. He gathered the ripened fruit from the loaded bough; or he pressed the juice from the clustered grape. He traced the shining orbits of the stars, as he

rested under the shade of his Banana; or he formed his sequestered bowers of love.

We, whom fate has placed in the cheerless old
age of the world, cannot easily imagine the extent
of connubial delights that existed when time was
young. We, who are accustomed to see the lowering frowns succeed each other on the brow of
beauty, like the shadows of the summer clouds
when they flit over the plain, can but faintly conceive the effect of the bewitching smile which the
lover, in those times, left upon the morning face of
his mistress; and which, when the business of the
day was over, he found still dimpling her cheeks
on his return. The courtly matron, who, invert-
ing the order of nature, after having spent the day
in broken slumbers and feverish dreams, leads her
daughter to the midnight-ball, remembers with a
sigh the days that are past. She envies, and vain-

11

ly strives to imitate by art, the glow of youth that crimsons the cheek of her child ; and sees, with an aching heart, the flutterers of fashion that hover around her. For the mother the novelty of the scene has long been past, and she returns home, with the morning sun, jaded in the search for pleasures which she has long ceased to enjoy. How can she call in the aid of Fancy to form a picture whose similitude she has never seen ? Can she paint the lovely rustic girl arising with Aurora, and bounding over the dewy lawn to cull the fairest flowers to weave a chaplet for her mother ? The gems of India, however much they may dazzle the eye, cannot communicate a pleasure to their possessor equal to that which thrills through the frame of the fond mother, as she receives the simple wreath from the hand of her darling child.

In those happy times mankind formed one large

family, knit together by the bonds of fraternal affection.   Ambition had not yet begun to divide
the world into tribes and kingdoms hostile to one
another; nor had conquerors desolated the earth.
Luxury and Pride had not poisoned the repose of
families.   Equal in condition, no proud palace
frowned contempt on the simple cottage.   The
happy union of the parents was perpetuated in the
children.   No father had his heart torn with anguish at the sight of a profligate son.   No mother
moistened her pillow with tears for the fate of a
beloved daughter,—the prey of seduction.   Thus
happy was the reign of Zephyra.   Poets have celebrated the period under the name of the Golden
Age.

Juno became jealous of the praises that were bestowed upon Zephyra.   Eura was eclipsed by the
pupil of Minerva, and her protectress was deter-

mined on vengeance. Olympus resounded with clamour; and a convocation of the Gods was assembled to hear the fate of Eura. It was unalterably recorded among the decrees of Destiny; and even Jupiter himself trembled when he read the fatal scroll: " EURA SHALL BE THE EVIL GENIUS OF MANKIND. BY HER INFLUENCE OVER THE FEMALE MIND, SHE SHALL PROVE THE TORMENT OF THE HUMAN RACE !" The fiat was irrevocable. Juno gave a shout of exultation, and the rest of the assembly retired in silence. Eura instantly darted down upon the earth; and wherever she approached, happiness fled from her view:—As the lark, when hovering over the nest which holds her young, trills her varied notes of pleasure, but as soon as she descries the descending flight of the vulture, she, abruptly, ceases her song, and shrowds herself under the covert of the brake.

Wherever society exists, there are always some general relations that are connected with the whole rather than with individuals. These general concerns must be managed by a few. These managers are the depositaries of power; and, until society be much corrupted, are generally superior, either in knowledge, or in energy of mind. Weaker minds, however, are capable of envy; and would willingly possess, and have often attained, situations which they were not able properly to fill. This is the history of all societies, and, in miniature, the evil often exists in the bosom of families. It was this love of sway that was nursed by Eura in the female breast; and, unfortunately, it is found to prevail, in every individual, in direct proportion to her ignorance.

Putting out of the question any natural inferiority in the structure of the mind, there is a necessary distinction, in the education and habits of woman, which must for ever keep her behind the other sex in the pursuit of knowledge. With a frame comparatively weak and irregular, she is less fitted for the external duties of society; and, if she be destined to fulfil the end of her creation, she has scarcely escaped from the mimic nursery, when she is doomed to direct the real nursery of life. Here she spends the best part of her existence, surrounded by helpless infancy and clamorous childhood; and it is only when old age approaches that she can find leisure, if she can then find the inclination, to study those sciences which form the glory of the human race. Conversant, then, only with baby-clouts and with dolls, is it for her to obtrude her ignorance, by the assumption of importance and the issue of commands?

The human character assumes a degree of permanence in proportion to the increase of years. Those, therefore, who had become mothers, under the guardianship of Zephyra, were less liable to infection from the poison which Eura so assiduously strove to instil into their hearts. The first generation passed away;—not, indeed, free from the portentous threatenings of a lowering sky, but unassailed by those storms and tempests which have, since, overthrown all the barriers between vice and virtue. Her first success was with the young and inexperienced;—with those giddy girls who had just started into women, still retaining all the folly and petulance of children. Such escape from the controul of their parents like birds from the confinement of the cage:—equally enamoured of their freedom and equally incapable of existing, unassisted, in the world. Vain of the attention of boys, young and thoughtless as themselves, the pulse of youth beats high; and, in their feverish delirium, they dream of nothing but of pleasure and of power.—Such became the easy prey of Eura. She fostered their vanity and stimulated their presumption. Nature, unconsciously, assisted in the delusion. Hymen profaned his sacred torch by lighting it to childhood; and the destinies of families were entrusted to the guidance of ignorance and conceit.

From unions so preposterous it had been vain to expect happiness, although the extraneous stimulus of vanity had never been applied. In this, nevertheless, Eura was incessant:—so as almost effectually to shut out any glimpse of reason, that might otherwise have penetrated and dispelled the clouds of ignorance which speedily involved the human mind. The contagion of folly became general. Cupid, who had hitherto attended through life on the wedded pair, deserted them with the

honey-moon; and the bowers of Venus were pol-
luted by the presence of Mars.   The husband no
longer looked for happiness in the connubial embrace.   He sought the solace of a mistress; while
the wife revenged his infidelity in the arms of her
paramour.   The saplings were similar to the parent tree; and the once gay prattle and innocent
amusements of fraternal affection were exchanged
for the furious brawlings and discordant yells of
imps and fiends.—Thus the reign of Eura commenced.   It still continues.—This is the Iron
Age !

Philosophers vaunt of the omnipotence of Reason; but she is, too often, found powerless when
she enters the lists with Habit and Example. The
passions of the future man are roused in the nursery; and, if they be there ungovernable, though
he wage war through life, he will perhaps find

them strong enough for his philosophy when he is ready to descend into the tomb.

Bred, from infancy, in the midst of strifes and contentions, the nurslings of Eura exhibit, in mature life, the characters of their childhood. In almost every country and under every clime, man is either an oppressor or oppressed,—a tyrant or a slave. Love and Friendship, who formed the union of the human race in the golden age, are now seldom seen; while Rapine and Fraud stalk uncontrouled over the earth. Ceres may yet spread her waving grain over the vallies, and Pomona may ripen her loaded boughs; but Power, with a rod of iron, guards the harvest, and proclaims with tyrant voice, " THE FRUITS OF THE EARTH ARE MINE, AND BEFORE YE TASTE, YE MUST BECOME MY SLAVES !" Prejudice enregisters the claim, and Timidity bows to her authority. " Wherever we go we find a master. War and Superstition have divided the world between them."

Thus, then, the female mind, by its effects on education, has had a most powerful influence over the moral world. It is not that Eura has been superior in talents to the pupil of Minerva, but that she has been assisted by a train of auxiliaries, over which neither Wisdom nor Reason has, hitherto, had any controul. The parents of Eura were no idle spectators in that scene of depravity which has overspread the globe. Their horrid intercourse was not terminated by the birth of Eura. Hysteria, Hypochondria, and Mania, three sister furies, who seize, with unrelenting hearts, the souls of their victims, were, in succession, the offspring of Eurus and the Naiad. Reason and Philosophy may in vain appeal to the precepts of Wisdom :—The shattered frame of the female mind can never be re-built while those harpies sit brooding over its ruins.

The empire of Eura, however, is not universal. Whether it be that the minds of some females are formed in a more generous mould, or, that a happy combination of circumstances has fostered the kinder affections of the heart, there is still a remnant of the wise scattered over the earth, and Zephyra yet retains a portion of her power. Let us indulge the hope that the baleful star of Eura has reached its meridian; and that, at some period of revolving time, its setting rays will disappear before the sunbeams of Reason. But the curtain is now ready to fall, and the writer is no longer the historian of a fancied tale.———

——— Shade of her who gave me being! to thee I dedicate my work! If thou retain any recollection of the past, and be informed of the fate of thy offspring, thou wilt be pleased with this incense of gratitude which I offer to thy memory. Under thy care I passed, with pleasure, the years of my childhood. When scared, or agitated, by the tempests and passions which, at times, arise even in the little world of infancy, thy young ones would fly to thee for protection, and nestle under thy wing. Like the mariner when tossed on the stormy ocean, we gazed on thy countenance. It was our heaven, and our fears were hushed, for we never beheld a lowering sky.—There was one whom, in thy declining years, thou lovedst as thy daughter :—But the name is too dear, and the loss yet too recent, to flow easily from the pen.————

———— Farewell, ye, who were so long the companions of my life and the soothers of my sorrows ! Fondly would I embalm your memory ! Could I indulge the hope that this little work will survive its author, I would paint your virtues to posterity. I would say to the youth who sighs over the scene of ignorance and vanity exhibited by the female world, that I have known some hearts which remained uninfected amidst the general contagion; and that, even in these bitter regions of the north, he may yet hope to find a daughter of Zephyra.

POEMS.

THE

BUD OF APRIL.

Bright in the sun the pearly dew-drop shines,
  Sweet Bud of April, on thy beauteous form;
But, ah! for thee, too swift the day declines;
  Too early dost thou brave the threatening storm.

The nipping frosts of eve are gathering round,
  Oh, bid the glittering dew-drop quick depart,
Ere, to thy breast with icy fetters bound,
  It chill the little spark that warms thy heart.

Oh, speed, ye Zephyrs, and, with gentle wing,
  Fan your soft charge in twilight's dangerous hour;
So shall my Bud escape the damps of spring,
  To bloom, in summer skies, a lovely flower.

Like thee, sweet Bud, my Delia, peerless maid!
   With tears untimely glistening in her eye,
Seeks, in her spring of youth, the evening shade,
   Unmindful of the cold inclement sky.

Ah, wipe that tear! 'twill blight thy beauty's bloom,
   And check that heaving sigh! It sounds to me
As death's chill blast, re-echoing from the tomb
   To burst a heart that fondly beats for thee.

While thus she wanders through the twilight grove,
   Alone, to breathe, unheard, her secret pain;
Pensive I court the magic lyre of love,
   And dream that Delia listens to my strain.

Oh, could I, on some Zephyr's airy car,
   Reach the dear wood where now my Delia strays;
Unseen by all, save Evening's splendid star
   To light my path with love's benignant rays,

I'd clasp the mourner to my throbbing breast,

   Around her angel form my arms should twine,

I'd kiss the falling tear:—beloved and blest,

   Her softer sighs should mingle warm with mine.

Yes,—through the storms of life, my constant care

   Shall guard thy blossom from misfortune's power:

I'll shield from every blast my beauteous Fair,

   And to my bosom press the lovely flower!

WHAT IS LOVE?

———

Sweet trill'd the Blackbird's varied song
  To cheer his mate on birchen spray;
Silent the streamlet stole along,
  While Echo answer'd to the lay:

The lambkin sported near its dam,
  In giddy maze, from flower to flower:
My child, more playful than the lamb,
  Was dancing round the woodbine bower.

Her artless pranks were bliss to me,
  (A mother's breast such bliss can prove!)
The pretty fondling climb'd my knee,
  And, smiling, asked me, ' What is Love ?'

11

Like thee, my child, in early years
   I form'd a tender mother's care;
Who shared my joys and dried my tears,—
   Who call'd me lovely, good, and fair.

How fondly, still, does memory trace
   The soften'd look,—the melting charms,—
The sun-beam smile that chear'd her face,
   As oft she clasp'd me in her arms !

Light was my heart,—no cares I knew,
   No restless passion then could move,
How swift these happy moments flew !
   And sure I thought that this was Love.

How fair the plant of Friendship grows,
   Enchanting o'er life's early stage !
Its flowers illusive round me rose,
   But vanish'd ere the noon of age.

How oft, my Mary, have we sworn
    Eternal Friendship's mutual vow!
These were the dreams of youth's gay morn,
    But where, my Mary, are they now?

Less warm and kind thy hand than when
    We twined our garlands in the grove;
Our minds were form'd for Friendship then,
    And sure we thought that this was Love!

Yet Love has still a stronger chain,
    When ripening years their hopes unfold;
Nor could I wonder nor complain,
    Though Mary's heart for me grew cold.

Dear to the child the filial tie,
    And dear is friendship's sacred shrine;
But, ah, more dear the lover's sigh;—
    More dear the heart that once was mine!

Even dear to me yon church-yard gloom,

    Where oft, at eve, I pensive rove;

Where, bending o'er the silent tomb,

    Remembrance tells me What is Love.

TO HOPE.

FLATTERING Goddess! Queen of guile!
  Gentle soother of our pain!
Fairy pleasures round thee smile,
  Syrens wanton in thy train.

Oft, in youth, I felt thy power,
  Check the tear that sought to flow,
Dear illusions blest the hour,
  Misfortune else had sunk in woe.

Painted prospects gaily rise,—
  Fancy reigns with magic sway;—
Gilded forms in tempting guise
  Float on youth's delusive ray.

Age th' enchanting scene dissolves,—

    All is fled that charm'd the view;

Fortune's giddy wheel revolves,—

    Burst the phantoms we pursue !

SPRING.

═════

The Spring's pleasing verdure adorns every plain,
  And Flora's gay carpet is spread o'er the green,
The sweet sylvan songsters chaunt cheerful the strain,
  And Beauty's endearments enrapture the scene.

In youth's rosy paths, how delighted ! I tread,
  While Hope's fairy phantoms fleet lightly around.
Love's pleasures invite to the grove or the mead,
  And with Delia's soft smiles my blest moments are
    crown'd.

But Winter, the tyrant that blasts the gay year,
  Will nip the fine flowers, tender nurslings of Spring ;
Will shed the fair foliage the woodlands now wear,
  And chill the light warblers that sport on the wing.

The roses of youth, though they flourish, must fade,

When the sage snowy honours of age bring their
claim.

Hope's painted illusions will sink in the shade,

Though the flow'rets of Fancy may flatter with fame.

The blossoms of Beauty, though bright they may
bloom,

As the buds that are blasted, will lose all their
charms ;

And thou, lovely Maid, thou must press the cold tomb

With that form which, so fondly, I fold in my arms.

Then why should we waste the gay morning of
Spring ;—

The spring-tide of youth which will quickly be o'er :

Arrest the gay pleasures that sport on the wing,

For they fly with our years and will soon be no
more !

VICISSITUDE.

How gay the morn ! when Nature smiles,
  How sweet appears the woodland scene !
Fond Fancy then each care beguiles,
  And paints the prospect ever green.
But, hark, the storm ! it howls around;
  The lightnings flash, the thunders roar :—
The echoing rocks return the sound,
  And morning smiles delight no more.

How gay the Spring ! its budding charms,—
  Its tender blossoms scent the air;
While Flora pants in Zephyr's arms;—
  Soft nymph, that claims his fondest care.

But tyrant Winter blasts the year,

   Nor blush the flowers, nor blooms the grove;

No more the woodlands fair appear,

   No more the songsters sing of love.

How gay, when Youth's dear phantoms rise,

   And Hope, sweet flatterer, cheers the hour;

When pleased we view the gilded skies,

   Nor dread the frown of Fortune's power !

But Age will come, and Youth no more

   Shall, rapt, exult in opening bloom:

He sighs while pensive, pondering o'er

   The steep that rolls him to the tomb.

Yet hoary Time, who marks the range

   Of Being's circling, endless chain,

Unchanged will see, while seasons change,

   The bloom of Morn and Spring again:

D

Will see, while Age shall leave the scene,

    Youth's sportive band with garlands crown'd;

And Beauty's train, who once have been,

    Again will tread the giddy round.

Say, Nature, in thy boundless sphere,

    Eternal wrecks shall Pity mourn?

Or, in some distant, viewless year,

    Shall prospects past again return?

Say, shall the same idea rise,

    And thought proceed, as thought has flow'd?

Say, that in these, or other, skies,

    This breast shall glow, as once it glow'd!

OLD AGE,

AN ELEGY.

Ye Loves and Pleasures, whither do ye fly?
  Ye fond companions of my youthful spring!
Like faithless friends, when wintery age is nigh,
  Prepared for flight, ye plume the parting wing.

Ah, stay! the storm that beats my weary head,
  Without your shield, will lay its victim low:
Already, see! autumnal hairs are shed:—
  Those that remain are silver'd o'er with snow.

Return, ye Loves! Ye Pleasures too, return!
  As erst I found you in the nuptial bower;
When life's warm current made my bosom burn
  A willing slave, I own'd your magic power.

Say, when old Wisdom whisper'd in my ear

    To trust you less, did I not faithful prove?

When Reason press'd me, did I stoop to hear,

    Or fly the dear delusions that I love?

In vain I call:—the fleeting Loves depart,

    And, one by one, they fluttering leave my cell:

Awhile the Pleasures linger at my heart;—

    Feel its weak throb, and take a last farewell.

Sweet Muse of Song, restrain their vagrant flight,

    (For sure the Muse can Pleasure's flight restrain!)

Thy loved Anacreon found, in age, delight;

    Toy'd with his nymph,—drank nectar with his
    swain.

Parnassian flowers conceal his wrinkled brow,

    In wreaths unfading round his temples spread;

With warmer tints his darling roses grow,

    And melt the snow that hovers o'er his head.

Around their favourite, Youth's gay train advance,

 Pleasure, with loosen'd zone, attunes the lyre;

The Bard with Beauty treads the mazy dance,

 And burns, in age, with Love's consuming fire.

Such was Anacreon :—and, ye Powers of Song,

 Till life's last ebbing wave, be his my doom;

Let Loves and Pleasures constant glide along,

 To smooth my path and deck with flowers my

  tomb !

THE

MELANCHOLY LOVER.

———

DEAR was the Maid I once possess'd,
Whose heart estranged I now resign,
I fondly clasp'd her to my breast,
And, raptured, fondly call'd her mine.

At morn we climb'd the mountain's brow,
At eve we sought the shelter'd grove,
And oft, where murmuring streamlets flow,
We tuned our rustic reeds to love.

And this the song : ' We'll never part,'
Echo, thou didst the notes resound !
' We'll live to love, long as the heart
Impels life's crimson current round !'

Ye lovers, in the woodland shade,
   Oh, do not blame my wandering fair !
She was the truest, tenderest maid
   That ever sooth'd a lover's care.

And oft has Care, my brow to bind,
   Arranged his demons round my bed :
I saw them weave, with nettles twined,
   A thorny chaplet for my head.

Dear Boy of Love ! this is the hour
   When Delia seeks the hawthorn tree ;
Or, in her fragrant woodbine bower,
   Perhaps even now, she thinks on me.

O, lead her to yon crystal spring,
   That, dimpling, strays her woods among ;—
To each loved haunt my Delia bring,
   Loved haunts when pleased she heard my song !

'Twas there we told how much we loved,
  While time, unheeded, pass'd us by;
Careless of minutes as they moved,
  We mused how future years might fly.

Dear God of Love! you gave her charms
  Might lure the hermit from his cell;—
I lost the world in Delia's arms:—
  She bound me with a magic spell.

Nor beauty's charms alone I prize,
  Else these might other nymphs bestow;
For other nymphs have sparkling eyes,
  And rosy cheeks and breasts of snow.

The eye with brighter lustre beams
  When constant as the tender dove:
Though fair the breast, it fairer seems
  When heaving to the hand of Love.

As softer colours tinge the rose
  When dew-drops gem the gentle flower,
A lovelier bloom the cheeks disclose
  When moist with pity's pearly shower.

But hold! my Delia waves her hand:
  'Twas all a dream! she still is kind!
Love lights the scene, with fairy wand,
  And leaves the world and care behind!

With pensive thoughts no more oppress'd,
  My heart to pleasure I resign:
Again I'll clasp her to my breast;—
  Again I'll fondly call her mine.

Ha! see he comes, with solemn mien,
  And stalks, regardless of my joy;
He shrouds in shade each passing scene,
  Pleased only pleasures to destroy.

I know him well ! his looks severe

    Blight every bud of bliss that springs :

His words unkind I must not hear,

    Else mute my lyre or sad its strings.

Pass then, harsh Monitor ! nor say

    ' That years shall chill my head with snow ;

' That, prostrate on my parent clay,

    ' Time's ruthless scythe shall lay me low !'

I know that Nature's stern decree,

    Remorseless, spares not beauty's bloom ;

Then why avert that hand from me

    Which digs, unseen, my Delia's tomb ?

But pass, rude Sage ! nor press to view,

    With dark design, th' insidious truth :—

Far hence, ye pensive, baleful crew,

    That damp, with saws, the joys of youth !

Yes, circling years shall see us blest,

   On life's enchanting busy stage :—

The fire that warms my youthful breast

   Shall melt the mountain frosts of age.

No, Delia, no rude hand shall trace

   The marks of life's departed prime,

Till, raptured in our last embrace,

   We sink amidst the waves of time !

THE

HEBREW CAPTIVES.

WHERE silver streams, with soothing murmurs, flow,

   And gently wave on Babel's fertile plains

Where blooming flowers, with grateful fragrance,

     blow,

   And music tunes the harp to syren strains,

Our pensive thoughts in sadness paint the scene,

   While fond remembrance shews our former years :

In vain the lawns are dress'd in pleasing green,

   While captive sorrow pours the gushing tears.

Our trembling hands unstring the useless lyre ;—

   No more the notes of rapture rend the skies,—

No more our altars blaze with sacred fire,

   Nor hymns of praise from thankful bosoms rise.

While crush'd beneath Oppression's iron hand,

    What pleasing accents can our voices raise?

Yet now our tyrants songs of mirth demand!

    Even now our harps must strike to joyful lays!

Shall solemn sounds, with grateful ardour, swell

    The pomp of praise? alas! the thought were vain.

In vain the music floats along the gale,

    While mirth deriding mocks the pious strain.

Ye dear Judean plains, where oft I've stray'd,

    (In fancy's view I see the landscape rise!)

Often, in youth, I trode the silent shade,

    Near yonder sacred dome which ruin'd lies.

If e'er the prospect fly this faithful heart,

    Be mute my tongue, nor more my skill employ

The living lyre, whose rapturous sounds impart

    A calm delight and mark the hours to joy.

When sacred Salem felt the conqueror's rage,
   Then Edom's sons could no soft pity share;
No plaintive cries their harden'd hearts assuage,
   Nor shrieks of woe, nor groans of deep despair.

Though righteous heaven correct with servile chains,
   The hour may come, relenting at our moan,
Will pour the tide of fury o'er these plains,
   And, raging, pay, with justice, groan for groan.

Ye soft Assyrian nymphs, who careless roam,
   Or lie reclined beneath th' embowering tree,
The hour may come, far distant from your home,
   You'll feel the pangs that sorrow gives to me.

The tender child, unconscious of its foes,
   Some ruthless hand its youthful blood may stain:
The murdering fiend may laugh to hear your woes;
   To him, relentless, ye may weep in vain!

THE

MUSE OF FREEDOM.

The Muse, unwilling, leaves the sacred shore
   Where erst she loved to prompt the patriot strain;
Hangs, with regret, on scenes so dear before,
   The last sad wanderer from the pensive plain.

She views where once the sons of Freedom stray'd,
   Whose hard misfortunes claim the sigh sincere;
She saw fair Genius fly his native shade,
   And dropp'd the parting tribute of a tear.

Yet why, sweet maid, so fondly dost thou cling
   To rugged rocks where no soft verdure grows,
While climes more grateful court the tuneful string,
   And spread their vales of pleasure and repose?

Haply thou lov'st to blunt the deadly dart,

   Hurl'd at the breast which power has doom'd to

      mourn,

To gild the gloom around the victim's heart,

   Or bend, with Pity, o'er the Patriot's urn.

Or, haply, where, beneath the iron hand

   Of stern Oppression, Youth's fair flow'rets fade,

Kindly, with Sympathy's endearing band

   And bright-eyed Hope, thou chear'st the dun-

      geon's shade.

For him who, warm'd by Freedom's genial fire,

   With soul unfetter'd, drags the despot's chain,

Perhaps thy hand attunes the living lyre

   To soothe his woes by Music's magic strain.

And thou, gay Fancy, bless his languid hours:

   Each flattering phantom let thy care bestow,

11

To strew his lonely path with fairy flowers,
   And pluck the noxious nettles as they grow!

But, ah! too light the visions Fancy forms;
   They shrink dismay'd where ruthless demons dwell:
Their flow'rets, blasted, die beneath the storms
   Which hell-born furies raise around his cell.

See, baneful Envy whets her venom'd sting,
   And, see, the shaft already wing'd to fly:—
Malice, assisting, draws the stretching string,
   While scared Timidity stands trembling by.

And, 'mongst those horrid fiends that round him rise,
   To tear his tortured soul with anguish wild,
See haggard Famine pictures to his eyes
   The ghastly features of his starving child!

E

Haste, Muse of Freedom! sound the clarion shrill,

   And leave to Peace thy lute's melodious strain:

Let War's rough echoes strike from hill to hill

   To call th' embattled legions to the plain.

Yes, though I hate to view the blood-stain'd field,

   Be the last standard of the globe unfurl'd,

Till Tyranny her sceptre cease to wield,

   And Liberty console a bleeding world!

THE ROSE.

SWEET Bud, caress'd by zephyrs mild,—
   Fairest that in my garden grows,—
Thou queen of flowers,—Aurora's child,
   Hasten to bloom, my darling Rose!

But stay! ah, yet a moment stay,
   Nor rashly now expand thy bloom:
The hour that spreads thy blossoms gay,
   Will veil their glory in the tomb.

My Delia is a lovely flower,
   Whose fortune in thy fate I see:
Like thee, she shines her destined hour,
   And then, alas! must fade like thee.

Come, from thy verdant thorny throne,

    With crimson wreath adorn her breast :

As thou the fairest flower hast shone,

    So, more than others, art thou blest.

Go,—on her lovely bosom lie,

    And there thy throne and tomb combine

Envious, I wish like thee to die,—

    To share a bliss and death like thine.

But lest some hand, unhallow'd there,

    Should soil thy bloom,—thy beauties scorn,—

With thee my sharpest vengeance bear,

    And, for my rivals, point thy thorn.

MARIA TO HER HARP.

How sweet, my Harp, at evening hour,
  When wandering pensive and alone,
To spread around thy magic power,—
  The music of thy melting tone !

How sweet ! to wake thy sounding strings
  Accordant to my secret song ;
To bear my love on airy wings,
  While rocks and woods the strain prolong.

When I have sung my thoughts to thee,
  Sole listener to my simple tale,
A kindly echo wilt thou be
  To waft them on the evening gale.

But mild, my Harp,—and soft thy strain,

Nor far from hence my accents bear :

Low,—when you hear my voice complain,

Nor waft the notes to Henry's ear !

TO A MIRROR.

=====

Mirror, whose magic pencil paints my form,
  Thou bear'st my image whatsoe'er I be:—
It moves, it breathes, it seems as nature warm,
  And, had it voice, were every way like me.

In thee, the movements of my soul I trace;
  From youth to age each varied change I view:
Hope lights the eye,—Despair deforms the face;
  Yet still I find th' enchanted portrait true.

The artist's hand, improved by labour'd years,
  May catch the fleeting likeness of the hour:
That hour is past:—another form appears,
  Derides the art and mocks the painter's power;

But thou canst trace the features as they rise,

    And mark the motions of my changeful frame :

Thy work, still varying, strikes the wondering eyes,

    Is always like, yet never is the same.

Painter of Nature ! all thy art to prove,

    Take for thy task young Beauty's melting charms,

Draw me the picture of the maid I love,

    And paint her blushing,—sinking in my arms.

THE PORTRAIT.

THE sister arts have features strong
   That speak their varied reign:
The Painter's scene, the Poet's song,
   And Music's melting strain.

The pencil's magic traits supply
   The charms that grace the fair;
They mark the lustre of the eye,
   The face, the form, the air:

But when the eye with rapture beams,
   What tints its power can prove?
Or say why bright its radiance streams—
   For Friendship—or for Love?

The Bard alone, with deathless lay,
   Can trace the sparkling fires
That gently flame in Friendship's ray,
   Or light the warm desires :—

Yet who can paint the words that glow
   When thrill'd with wild alarms,
The voice of Love that murmurs low,
   And brightens Beauty's charms?

Quick ! string the lyre to rapture's bounds
   As fits my passion'd strain !
Then let its softest silver sounds
   Give Delia's voice again !

TO A BROOK.

Flow, gentle Brook !—I saw thee flow
   When Childhood's visions round me rose ;
Then did thy banks with flow'rets blow,
   And flow'd thy stream as now it flows.

With stretching hand I cropt thy flowers,
   Or sought thy stream my limbs to lave :
To memory dear the fleeting hours
   I pass'd beside thy placid wave.

Oft did I stray thy banks along,
   Before the morning's rising ray,
To hear the sky-lark's warbling song
   Announce from far the dawning day ;

And oft, when evening's dusky veil
   Involved the earth, and main, and sky,
I loved to hear the nightingale,
   Or list the lone owl's moaning cry.

Still rolls thy stream as then it roll'd,
   Still on thy margin flowers appear;
Through summer's heat and winter's cold,
   Still rolls the changing circling year.

And still the lark, to hail the morn,
   Trills, in the air, her joyous strain :—
Yon ruin grey and aged thorn,
   Still hear the birds of eve complain.

Again the Maypole's jocund ring,
   Led by the rustic minstrel's sound,
With annual tributes, seek thy spring
   To thrid the dance on daisied ground.

As green thy banks,—as pure thy stream,—
  As calm and cool thy willow shade,
As when, in Love's delusive dream,
  I fondly clasp'd my darling maid.

Then, why, when thus unchanged the scene,
  Do Hope's gay phantoms cease to shine?
Thy waves, thy banks, thy village green,
  Look bright in every eye but mine.

Illusions all ! the scene is fled
  That charm'd in Youth's enchanted clime,
And every kindred pulse is dead
  That throbbing mark'd the flight of Time.

Another lark, with joyful strain,
  Hastens to hail the rising morn;
And other birds, at eve, complain
  From ruin grey and aged thorn:

And even thy stream, with ample range,

    Sweeps onward to the whelming sea :—

New waters flow with ceaseless change,

    Yet still thy stream is dear to me.

Emblem of thought's unceasing flow,

    Wave after wave resistless press'd !

When ruffling billows cloud thy brow,

    'Tis Memory's fiends that tear thy breast.

When sad thy stream,—its hollow moans,

    (As when the widow'd wood-dove mourns,)

Bear to my harp accordant tones

    Which each responsive string returns.

SONG.

———

THE sun had sunk in clouds of flame
   To gild the western wave,
When here unseen my Anna came
   To meet the vows I gave.
How blest the hours till morning light
   Beneath the hawthorn tree !
Can I forget the happy night
   She own'd her love to me ?

The hazel copse's friendly shade
   Conceal'd from every eye;—
No sound save what the streamlet made,
   As soft it gurgled by.

How blest the hours till morning light
    Beneath the hawthorn tree !
Can I forget the happy night
    She own'd her love to me ?

The moon rode round on silver car
    The guardian of the grove,
And veil'd each little twinkling star
    Might peep upon our love.
Then blest the hours till morning light
    Beneath the hawthorn tree :
I pass'd with her the happy night
    She own'd her love to me.

Thrice has gay summer's fairy wand
    Outspread the blushing flowers ;
And thrice has winter's ruthless hand
    Unleaf'd the woodbine bowers,

11

Since first reclined till morning light
  Beneath the hawthorn tree,
I pass'd with her the happy night
  She own'd her love to me.

Ye little Loves, that watch the Fair,
  And light young Beauty's eye,
Play through the ringlets of her hair,
  And flutter on her sigh.
How gay ye tript till morning light
  Around the hawthorn tree,
Your gladsome vigils cheer'd the night
  She own'd her love to me.

Ah, whither fled, ye tiny train?
  Ye've left my Anna now;
Say where ye lurk?—I search in vain,
  The frowns that shade her brow.

F

Has she forgot the blushing light
   That tinged the hawthorn tree?
Must I regret the happy night
   She own'd her love to me?

From Hymen's shrine, with haggard mien,
   A demon scours the groves,
With hurried steps,—with eyes of green,—
   He frights the little Loves!
Now clouds obscure the morning light,
   And shade the hawthorn tree:
May I forget the happy night
   She own'd her love to me!

A FATHER

TO

HIS INFANT DAUGHTER.

———

Soft be thy sleep, my darling Child,

Thy mother's eye no longer beams;

Yet, hovering round, her spirit mild

Inspires thy blissful fairy dreams.

Thy smiles (as if my cheeks were dry)

Unconscious seem to mock my pain:

I'll wipe the tear-drop from my eye

Lest thou shouldst wake and smile again.

Image of her who once was dear,

While on thy infant face I gaze,

Memory's enchanting scenes appear

As when they charm'd in happier days:

11

I see the witching smile arise

   That mantled when I call'd her mine;

And even the lustre of her eyes

   Already faintly beams in thine.

As pure as hers now beats thy heart,

   But who shall guard from passion's sway?

What watchful eye to thee impart

   Where hidden snares shall cross thy way?

In youth we tread on fairy land,

   Bewildering meteors round us glow:

Deluded then, some guilty hand

   May seek for pleasure in thy woe.

Soft be thy sleep, my darling Child!

   Be thine to soothe thy Father's care:—

Be his, through youth's enchanted wild,

   To mark, for thee, each hidden snare.

But ah ! if, like the fading Rose,

   Which fostering showers bedew in vain,

Thy moisten'd, pallid cheeks disclose——

   Oh, sleep, and never wake again !

———

In the following Poem allusions are made to customs still preva-
lent in Germany:—Among all ranks, a garland of myrtle is the
only ornament worn on the wedding-day; and, among the vil-
lagers, wreaths of flowers are hung over the graves of young
virgins. "Thirty years ago, when sentimentality was the fashion, the sight of these wreaths suffused many a bright eye;
but now, that polished apathy has usurped the place of sensibility, the ladies of the *ton* discover, instead of the dewy eye of
feeling, the contemptuous sneer or the sarcastic grin. If we
must have affectation, let it be the affectation of sensibility.—
This only made girls silly,—the present fashion makes them
absolutely vicious."

———

THE DREAM.

LAST midnight, witching hour ! I dream'd
  That Edwin came to me:
So like in shape and air he seem'd,
  I scarce can doubt 'twas he.

My bridal ring, from off my hand,
  He broke, nor would he stay;
And, for my ring, a pearl-band
  He threw, and fled away.——

Sadly I sought the secret bower,
  Which late we fondly wove,
Where ready bloom'd the myrtle-flower
  To wreathe our wedded love.

Then burst my pearl-band in twain,
  And spread upon the ground :—
I sought the scatter'd pearls in vain,
  They nowhere could be found.

Methought, had I those pearls arranged,
  The Band of Love were made :—
When, lo ! the Myrtle bower was changed
  And form'd a Cypress shade !

Ah ! word for word, the Dream foretels
  What now my fate must be :
I need not seek the Spaeman's spells,
  For all is clear to me.

The Ring's my heart ;—the Pearls he gave
  Are tears for falsehood shed :
Where Myrtles bloom'd, see Cypress wave
  To mark me with the dead.

Edwin, if thy enchanted bowers
    E'er lure another love,
Oh! let her pluck my Myrtle flowers,
    But shun my Cypress grove.

Haply, when years shall lay thee low,
    Thou'lt share this spot with me;
And surely o'er our grave may grow
    My once-loved Myrtle tree.

Then bring not here another maid
    Thy broken faith to mourn;—
Be mine alone this gloomy shade,
    And mine this wreathless urn.

Her injured ghost might raving come,
    And pierce my clay-cold ear,
By shrieking round my silent tomb,
    A name that once was dear.

THE COMPLAINT.

LOUD, howling through the leafless glade,
  The winds tempestuous roar,
While, sadly, sits the love-lorn maid
  Beside the sea-beat shore.

Cold is the night, and dark the sky,
  And, dashing, bursts the wave;
She sighs to storms that mock her sigh,
  She weeps while billows rave:—

" Closed in the tomb are all thy joys,—
  Thy hopes are fled from me;
No more, false World, I raise my voice
  To ask a boon from thee.

Father of Nature !—here exiled,—
  All earthly bliss I've proved ;
Take back to heaven thy care-worn child,
  For I have lived and loved."

Alas ! thy tears are vainly shed,
  'Tis fruitless to complain;
Thy voice can ne'er awake the dead
  To life and love again :

For louder roars th' unfeeling blast,
  Regardless of thy doom:—
As ruthless, when thy hour is past,
  'Twill rage around thy tomb.

THE PROPHECY.

Thou fear'st for poverty;—I fear for pride:—
    Between these rocks direct thy careful way:
Steep are the shores and rough the swelling tide,
    And frail thy bark and sunk the solar ray.

Heed not those shining orbs that wandering roll,
    Deceitful guides! to lead thy course afar;
They whirl like Fortune's wheel: but mark the Pole,
    It stands unmoved,—'tis Wisdom's favourite star.

There Pallas keeps, through time, her splendid fane,
    Midway in Heaven's wide vault, nor low nor high,
No bending parasite in Phæbus' train,
    Nor changeful as her sisters of the sky.

Hark ! 'tis her voice ! she claims my rustic lyre
    To strike with bolder notes its sounding strings :
I yield the shell ; I hear a muse of fire
    Tell to the world the changing tide of things :

" Pride raised those towers, and Pride shall lay them
        low ;
    And, though that rock rears high its pointed form,
The bolt of Jove shall rend its cloud-clad brow
    Like yon proud pine that braved the ruthless storm.

" To grow,—to fade—alike are Nature's care,
    Then fear success and hope in misery's hour :
See Winter's chilling nakedness prepare
    The lovely vestment of the vernal flower.

" Stretch'd on his straw, within his wind-torn shed,
    Sleeps the poor Slave till morn renew his toil ;
His wife,—his babes,—Want hovers o'er their head,
    While yonder Lordling claims the fruitful soil.

" Nor deem that Lordling happier than the hind,

 Power kneels to power,—the wise are blest alone:

View him to-morrow's sun, we then shall find

 A reptile sprawling 'neath a blood-stain'd throne.

" See Superstition's smoking altars rise,

 Wide o'er the globe her thick'ning clouds are spread

The Sorceress rears her phantoms in the skies,

 And bids her Furies hover o'er the dead.

" Ye Nations hear !" The Goddess then foretold

 Events of which the Muse forbears to say :—

When Power has terrors to appal the bold,

 Ah ! what avails the Minstrel's feeble lay ?

TO ECHO.

Nymph of the rocks! who oft hast heard my strain,
   Once more attune to mine thy rustic shell :
Nymph of the rocks! I court thy aid again
   To bid these hills and groves a long farewell!

Charm'd by thy song, no more the Dryad waves
   Her rustling branch, nor shakes her whispering
       spray;
The fairy elves that haunt the mountain caves
   Catch at the chorus and prolong the lay.

To every friend I gave a last adieu,
   To all who dropt a parting tear for me :
Still, like the lover to his fair one true,
   I linger here to bid adieu to thee.

Soon, when the angry Demon of the storm
  Howls through the shrouds and bends the crack-
          ling mast,
Fancy will paint my Echo's gentle form
  Shrinking in silence from the roaring blast.

And, when, on jungled marsh or burning sand,
  Scared by the serpent's hiss or lion's roar,
I list the Echoes of a distant land,
  My native wild-notes shall return no more;

For, ah! no gentle spirit hovers nigh
  To mountain, grove, or mead, or mazy stream;
Mute are the tenants of yon sultry sky,
  Save where the vampires groan, or vultures scream.

Farewell, sweet Echo! through each circling year,
  While notes of joy re-vibrate in thy grove,
Memory shall call thy beauteous landskip near,
  And fondly trace the scenes of early love.

When ruddy morning gilds the distant spires,

   Or crowns with saffron flowers the mountain's brow;

When curling blue smoke marks the village fires,

   And mist-form'd seas wave o'er the vale below;

Then the light breeze that ushers in the morn;

   The soaring lark that trills her warbling song;

The soft-toned linnet from her favourite thorn;

   The plough-boy whistling as he winds along:

These sounds, upborne upon the scented gales,

   Shall touch thy viewless harp's responsive strings;

Then, sweeter far! thy voice shall charm the vales,

   And soften'd strains return on airy wings.

When May's mild twilights linger in the west,

   And Love's fond votaries see their star decline;

When morn's tired songsters seek their dewy nest,

   And, bright as now, yon moon's full orb shall shine,

G

The blackbird piping from the blossom'd geen;

    The stockdove cooing from the pine-clad hill;

The noisy pastimes of the village green;

    The ceaseless dashing of the mountain rill;

The bark of shepherd's dog that pens his flocks;

    The bleating ewes that call their wandering young:

When these, soft-mingling, from thy cavern'd rocks,

    Wide o'er the lawns with mimic tones are flung;

When, in some future year, I seek this shade;

    When all I love have ceased to think of me;—

Wilt thou, sweet Echo! like a faithless maid,

    Forget the strains I sung to love and thee?

THE END.

Introduction

Elizabeth Hitchener (1782 or 1783-1822) was the daughter of
Thomas York, a wine and liquor smuggler who had changed
his name to Hitchener when he settled down to pursue a less
taxing vocation as keeper of a public house in Brighton,
Sussex; Miss Hitchener, inspired by her own teacher Miss
Adams, kept a school for girls at Hurstpierpont, Sussex,
attended by a daughter of Captain John Pilfold (brother of
Shelley's mother).

In May 1811, while staying with Captain Pilfold in nearby
Cuckfield, Sussex, Shelley was introduced to Miss Hitchener.
They almost immediately began an intellectual correspondence
that ran to at least forty-seven long letters by Shelley and
probably an equal number by Hitchener (of which twelve
survive) between June 5, 1811, and June 18, 1812, in which
they exchanged views on religion, politics, literature, and more
personal concerns. Shelley continually urged her, the "sister of
his soul," to give up her school and join him, his new wife,
Harriet, and Harriet's sister Eliza Westbrook in their quixotic
attempts to advance the cause of truth and justice in Ireland
and Wales. Elizabeth Hitchener (who chose the classical name
"Portia" under which to write) resisted these entreaties, partly
because she feared—from the solid evidence of slanders that
had already reached her ears—that she would lose her
reputation by joining the radical ménage. But in July 1812,
after Shelley's repeated urgings and invitations (and, probably,
at the end of her contracted school year), Hitchener joined the
Shelley household at Lynmouth, Devon, and—now called
Bessy—shared their fortunes for a few months.

Open hostility between her and Harriet Shelley and Eliza
Westbrook, as well as Shelley's disillusionment with her
intellectual and moral pretensions, led to her leaving the
Shelleys soon after they returned to London early in

INTRODUCTION

November 1812. Thomas Jefferson Hogg, who has given us a vivid (if distantly recalled) picture of the day of Hitchener's departure, thus sums up his impressions of her on this, his only encounter with her: "She appeared to me a fair average specimen of a schoolmistress, and well adapted in every respect for the employment, which she had long exercised, and might doubtless long continue to exercise with advantage" (*Life of Percy Bysshe Shelley*, ed. Edward Dowden [London, 1906], p. 477; Chapter XXIV, first paragraph).

After her departure from the Shelley household (apparently on Shelley's promise that he would pay her £100 per year to indemnify her loss of her school income), Elizabeth Hitchener's career is sketchily documented. Gibbons Merle (who had once carried messages from Shelley to Hitchener) reported a visit with her at her father's home in Sussex, "sitting alone and in melancholy mood, with one of Shelley's works before her. Her fine black eye lighted up, her well-formed Roman countenance was full of animation when I spoke of Shelley. But she did not allude to her elopement, nor did I touch upon a theme which might have been painful" (*Fraser's Magazine*, XXIII [June 1841], 709-710). According to Merle, Miss Hitchener attempted to set up another school in Sussex, but could not attract any pupils in her first efforts. Edward Dowden learned, however, that "in later days she and her sister conducted a girls' school at Edmonton [Middlesex] with credit and success. 'The school-days I passed at Edmonton,' writes a former pupil, under the kind and judicious teaching of Miss Hitchener, were some of the happiest in my life. . . . I consider her to have been a high-principled, clever woman, with a remarkable capacity for teaching. I think all her pupils loved her'" (Dowden, *Life of Percy Bysshe Shelley* [1886], I, 315).

The fullest (but by no means reliable) account of Hitchener's last years was given to T. J. Wise by Henry James Slack, who for a time possessed Shelley's letters to her and some of her replies. As Roger Ingpen retells Slack's story (via T. J. Wise), Hitchener "became governess to the children of a gentleman who held some official position, probably in the diplomatic service, and she accompanied his family to the Continent. Before she left England, however, she deposited with Mr. Slack, Shelley's letters to her, together with transcripts of some of hers to Shelley, and that these pages were never reclaimed. While abroad Miss Hitchener made the acquaintance, and afterward married, an officer in the Austrian service, but she parted from him soon after, and, returning to England, assumed her maiden name. She then appears to have gone to Edmonton, where, with the aid of her sisters, she kept a school . . ." (Roger Ingpen, *Shelley in England* [London, 1917], pp. 555-556). This account has never been challenged, but it seems clear to me that the story about Miss Hitchener going abroad was a fabrication by Mr. Slack to explain how he came into possession of Shelley's letters to Hitchener.

The key evidence appears in *Rossetti Papers, 1862 to 1870*, compiled by William Michael Rossetti (London, 1903), pp. 404-405, in which W. M. Rossetti, meeting Slack in 1869, learned from him that the letters in his possession were really the property of a Mrs. Buxton and that Slack did not want them to receive undue publicity, lest Mrs. Buxton should claim them. Slack, who died on June 16, 1896, was described as barrister-at-law (Ingpen, *Shelley in England*, p. 556). He was undoubtedly born far too late to have been Elizabeth Hitchener's confidant or to have been entrusted with any letters if she did go to the Continent sometime between 1813 and 1818 (the year she published the *Fire-side Bagatelle*). Slack, as a solicitor, may have been associated with H. Holste of 22 Bush Lane, London, who was the executor of Miss Hitchener's estate in 1822, in whose possession Shelley's letters were at that date. (He mentioned to Rossetti in 1869 that "a Mrs. Holst" had owned the letters before he did.) It seems likely, then, that Slack in his old age (ca. 1890 when T. J. Wise was publishing Shelley's letters to Hitchener) invented the story of Elizabeth Hitchener's trip to the Continent and

INTRODUCTION

marriage to justify his possession of letters that, he knew, rightfully belonged to someone else. (His wife made up for any qualms of conscience the couple may have had by arranging for the letters to be donated to the British Museum; they are now in the British Library.)

Having cleared away the probable fabrication of Elizabeth Hitchener's continental travels and marriage, we are left, as solid evidence of her life after she left Shelley, with Merle's late recollections, the reminiscence in her former Edmonton pupil's letter to Dowden, the letter from Holste, her executor, to Sir Timothy Shelley, the Letters of Administration of her estate (£450) dated March 8, 1822, which were found in Somerset House (Ingpen, *Shelley in England*, p. 556), and the two volumes here reprinted. According to Thomas Medwin, Shelley in Italy used to regale him with an account of Elizabeth Hitchener's feminist poem, which began, "All, all are men— *women* and all!" Nothing in her published poetry sinks (or rises, if one reads the line as containing a subtle substitution) to this level. Dowden, perhaps, has best characterized *The Weald of Sussex* as proving "that its author, though not a poet, was a woman of some culture and vigour of mind." Elizabeth Hitchener would never occupy a place in literary history or in this series had she not been so closely connected with one of the great poets of the age. But since she is here, let her poetry stand as an example of the work of an intelligent, decently educated, and well-read female school teacher of the day.

Donald H. Reiman

THE

FIRE-SIDE BAGATELLE:

CONTAINING

ENIGMAS

ON THE

CHIEF TOWNS OF ENGLAND AND WALES.

BY

ELIZABETH HITCHENER.

LONDON:

Printed by Barlow & Bishop, 60, Cannon-Street, City.

SOLD BY J. WALLIS, 42, SKINNER-STREET, SNOW-HILL;
HARRIS, CORNER OF ST. PAUL'S CHURCH-YARD;
AND DARTON AND HARVEY, GRACECHURCH-STREET.

1818.

PREFACE.

THE Writer of this little work is induced to offer it to the Public, from the hope that it may be found useful: considering every thing, however insignificant in itself, yet acceptable, if in the slightest degree calculated to excite in young minds, a spirit of inquiry, and a taste for Literature.

In the Orthography, any departure from Johnson is only when in more strict conformity to Derivation.—In the measure of the verse, agreeable to modern poetry, no elision is made in the dactyl.

December 14, 1818.

DEDICATORY ODE,

AFFECTIONATELY ADDRESSED

TO SOME

AMIABLE YOUNG FRIENDS.

———

WHAT tho', dear Girls, my Muse is rude;
    Yet oft it you delights:
Even tho' the matter's strange and crude,
    It cheers our winter nights.

Then, when you to your home depart,
    Take with you, ere you go,
This little tribute of our art:
    For what it hides, you know.

Perchance it may some hours amuse
    Of sisters, brothers dear:
Some slight instruction may infuse,
    And fire-side evenings cheer.

May such to cheer be your delight,
    Thro' life's advancing day,
Your labor amply 'twill requite,
    Most gratefully repay.

Domestic pleasures will insure
    Contentment, health, and ease:
They all of earthly bliss, secure,
    And never fail to please.

For Home's—the empire of the Heart;
    Its circle, Nature's trace!
Then, faithful to her wish, impart
    Affection's winning grace.

More fascinating is its power
    Than fashion, beauty, gold:
Confined not to life's youthful hour,
    But triumphs when we're old.

It soothes, refines, it softens man,

  And solaces his care!

In Paradise its source began,

  And followed, leads us there!

Then let us still its course pursue,

Agreeable to Nature true.

ENIGMAS

ON

THE CHIEF TOWNS

OF

ENGLAND AND WALES.

ENIGMAS.

―――

1.

MY *first* is holy, happy, good, and true;

    From blemish free, pollution, spot, or stain!

Beyond my *next*, the just will never go,

    But prudently within its bounds remain:

These joined together will a town unrol,

In county famed for marble and for coal.

2.

In opposition to decay and age,

    My *first* appears, with charms before unknown:

My *next*, the dwelling of knight, squire, and page,

    When British chiefs made feudal power their own

A town these form, Monk-Chester called of old;

But since, from Robert's building named, we're told.

3.

My *first*, with vowel changed, will show us where

    The weary and luxurious seek repose:

There's naught on earth, can with my *next* compare;

    But, as my first, so equal change it owes:

My *whole* within that county, where, of old,

From Saxon arms, fled Britons firm and bold.

4.

My *first*, among conjunctions you may find :

My *next*, a salt-house : these together joined

Will show my *whole*, a town in county famed,

And which Iceni's ancient kingdom claimed: *(b)*

The memory of whose virtuous queen is dear;

For Romans learned from her—no slaves were here.

5.

Upon the banks of that meandring stream,

From which a town and county take their name,

My *first* protects the richest works of fame,

A fair display, beyond even artists' dream!

My first discovered, brings my *whole* to mind,

Which Henry Eighth to his possessions joined.

6.

Imagination formed for gods, my *first*,

    To which then add a soft and liquid sound:

My *next*'s of those which are o'er seas dispersed,

    And Ocean clasps them like a zone around:

A town in county these will bring to mind,

Where Eden, tho' not Paradise, we find.

———

7.

Omit a letter, and my *first* is seen

    With splendid knight for tournament prepared:

Then to my *next* a letter add, I ween

    You'll see with what the son of Jesse dared

To lay the champion of Philistia low:

These joined, my *whole* 'mong England's tin-mines show

8.

To Capraæ's fair isle, with secret news,

    What time Tiberius Cæsar there reposed,

    My *first* was seen, with letter changed, transposed:

My *next*, the haggard child of Error shews,

But then a letter claims: these rightly place,

The abode will show of Iceni's brave race.

9.

My *first* was formed for Gallia's idiot king:

    My *next* a pronoun, nominative case:

My *third*, reversed, to mind will quickly bring

    A palfrey spruce, with little ambling pace:

My *whole*, in that rich land of Demetæ *(c)*

Given to Cunedda's son, the brave and free. *(d)*

10.

A juice from plant of isles West Ind. distilled,

 Then add a sign of the pluperfect tense,

Transpose and blend them; when you've this fulfilled,

 An ancient town you'll find they evidence:

Its name from Saxon language, a compound

Of hill, and islet by a river bound.[*]

11.

If, for my *first*, that Persian king you take,

 Who wept as he reviewed his bands, we're told,

Reflecting on the havoc Death would make

 Ere Time another century had enrolled:

Then its two letters change, my *whole* to show,

On that fair stream from which its name doth flow.

[*] Of the latter, the present termination is a corruption.

12.

My *first,* with particle prefixed, you'll find
Receives that juice which enervates mankind:
My *next*'s the last sad office we receive
From fellow hands, who then take final leave:
My *whole*'s in that brave county which withstood
The conqueror's arms, and seemed a moving wood.

13.

Change in my *first* a letter, it will tell
Who at the base of Pompey's statue fell!
My *next* an adverb, not of place, but time;
These shew my *whole*, tho' gingled into rhyme—
Once chief of Cambria South, Marid'num* named,
And for the birth of its sage Prophet, famed. *(e)*

* Maridunum.

B

14.

When Paris on Mount Ida took his stand,

    Aud beauty's prize to Lemnius' bride assigned,

He gave my *first*, the boast of Britain's land!

    My *next* a preposition, you will find:

Together placed, a town my *whole* appears,

In beauteous land, famed for its lovely meres.

15.

'Mong architecture's orders five, there's one

    Pourtrays my *first*, tho' three-fifths it affirm:

My *next* a camp, Castrum in Latian tongue,

    From which derived is now its Saxon term:

Together these, a town in county show

Where hapless Edward met Elfrida's blow.

16.

Part of a river you my *first* will find:

My *next*, its pass: when these you have combined

My *whole* is seen, and, from my first, has name

In land the Trinobantes once could claim: *(f)*

Whose prince, false Mandubratius, authors write,

Went o'er to Gaul, great Cæsar to invite.

17.

My *first*, in British, we a fortress find :

My *next* reversed, a movement quick you'll see :

My *third*, with letter changed, implies to bind

A power even o'er ourselves, no longer free :

These joined together will my *whole* declare,

Where Cambria's Prince was born, and England's Heir.

18.

When England's realm owned the Usurper's sway,

My *first*, in crimson hue exalted high,

Compelled the unsubmissive to obey !

Tho' vanished now, with other days gone by :

Thus see my first, with history's page combined :

My *whole* a town, which in my first we find.

19.

On Venus de Medicis' lovely face,

My *first*, with its last letter changed, we trace :

My *next*, in Ahasuerus' Court was seen,

Preferred by Media's Monarch for its Queen !

These joined, my *whole* within that county show,

Where, in this Isle, first twanged the Norman bow.

20.

My *first* is seen when, wearied with his toil,

Exhausted man lays down this mortal coil:

My *next*, by Inguar's forces basely slain,

And still, the name and mausoleum remain

Combined within my *whole*, in county fair,—

Whose rustic bard has made it classic air.

21.

My *first*, from Gallia's tongue we make our own:

My *next* receives sweet Aries, tho' we find

Of its five parts, three only need be known:

My *third* will show a neuter verb declined,

Tense pres., mode indic.: and my *whole* is found

In lovely Mona, by the ocean bound.

22.

When for two centuries factious houses bled,
  Contending cruelly for England's crown!
My *first*, tho' pale, majestic reared its head,
  Till bowed, at last, by power rebellious down:
My *whole* a town, which in my first we trace,
Where mighty Emperor's chose their court to place.

23.

My *first* forms part of a mechanic power:
  My *next*, a neuter verb, in land of Gaul,
Tense pres., mode indic.: and my *last*, the dower
  Which Eve, alas! bequeathed her children all;
But then two parts suffice: my *whole* is near
Where Tyrrel's dart took royalty for deer.

24.

Apollo and the Muses found my *first*,

When from Castalia's lovely shores they fled :

Nor wandered on Permessus banks as erst :

My *second* raises o'er my first its head ;

But for my first, my second ne'er had been :

My *whole*, where Prasutagus reigned, is seen.

25.

With letter changed, my *first's* a Cornish game :*

A letter added to my *next*, will name

That fated hour, when, o'er South Britain's land,

The curfew bell proclaimed the king's command :

United, these will bring my *whole* to sight,

Where Cambria's mountains and sweet lakes delight.

* The primitive rather of this game, from which are named some curious
stones in the parish of St. Cleer, in Cornwall.

26.

My *first*, with its last letter changed, connects :

And to my *second* we the same change give,

It then pourtrays of time the' advanced effects,

Which all experience if long they live :

Together these will bring my *whole* to mind,

Where of the conqueror's castles, one we find.

27.

My *first*, with letter changed, will show a law,

Excluding females from the Gallic throne :

Before my *next*, arrives that hour of awe,

Which opes our entrance to a world unknown :

These joined will form a town, near that strange pile

Which Cæsar notes, 'mong wonders of our Isle.

28.

To find my *first*, a letter you must change

    In that fine creature, pride of sylvan scenes,

Which seems with conscious gracefulness to range:

    My *next* to cross the river's current, means:

These show my *whole*, in county where they tell,

That he, who made Kings at his pleasure, fell.

29.

Where Runic numbers the wild muse inspires,

    My *first* appears, three-sevenths of that brave land,

Whence emigrated to this Isle our sires!

    My *next*, with letter changed, doth towering stand:

United these, my *whole* you then may see,

Where ranged the Ordovices, bold and free. *(g)*

30

Among the nine earths you my *first* will find,

　　And is that substance which does most abound:

Discovered it will bring my *whole* to mind,

　　Near where Winfreda's holy well is found:

Here first the White Rose yielded to the Red!

Nor distant far, the noble Car'doc * bled. *(h)*

———

31.

My *first*, an adverb, is of grateful sound,

　　And cheering import to the drooping mind,

　　Owned by that pious Shunammite resigned,

In her reply to Carmel's Seer renowned:

A letter add to this, my *whole* to show,

In county fair, where healing waters flow.

* Caradoc.

32.

My *first's* that style and title of address,

Which those of Baron, Viscount, Earl, possess:

My *next* is seen at full meridian hour:

These blended show the seat of wealth, and power:

Its origin, a colony from Rome,

Tho' seventy thousand found a fiery tomb.

33.

From Marchell's son my *first* derives its name, *(i)*

    When he, as Regulus, the district swayed:

To us descended has its sound the same;

    Tho' having change of letters three obeyed:

My *whole,* where Honddu and the Usk unite,

Nor yields all Cambria South more pleasing sight.

34.

My *first's* the' abode of those ill fated men,

  Whose trade was murder, and whose glory blood!

The Romans Castrum deemed the savage den;

  But since, in Saxon language understood:

My *whole* is thus pourtrayed, in county found,

Where fossil, sea, and fountain salt abound.

35.

My *first* was seen in that ill-fated hour,

  When Papal right prevailed, and England's heir

Obtained the crown; then, with vindictive power,

  To death condemned, affection's matchless pair!

My first discovered brings my *whole* to mind,

Which we in kingdom of the Regni find. *(j)*

36.

My *first*'s the sport of savage men, and bold:

A sport for which was mighty, we are told,

Assyria's founder: then for pompous pride

My *next* proverbial is, and doth reside

With formal state, in sweet Iberia's land:

These joined together will my *whole* command.

37.

My *first*, if we its derivation trace,

    Had letter more, a fortress to pourtray:

    My *next*, transposed, a province will display,

Tho' letter changed, that has in Scotia place:

My *whole* in land where Silure chief had home, *(k)*

Ere sent by Publius Scapulæ to Rome.

38.

My *first*, with letter added, forms an art
    Which female hands most skilfully intwinc :
My *second* oft a pleasure does impart,
    Tho' Asia's sons durst not to such incline :
My *whole* these show, short distance from a wood,
Where fearless ranged the famous Robin Hood.

39.

My *first*'s the source of exquisite delight,
    Improves, refines, and elevates mankind !
Brings men and ages past, before our sight,
    Gives liberality, and strength to mind !
My first pourtrays my *whole*, near that retreat
Where the Third Edward fixed his rural seat.

40.

My *first* we seek in sickness and in health,

And in the hour of poverty or wealth,

Needful alike to tyrant and to slave:

My *next* implies a passage thro' the wave:

These show my *whole,* to his descendants nigh,

Who gave up life for—Truth and Liberty.

41.

My *first* is seen in Switz's and Savoy's lands,

    With whitening summit towering to the sky:

My *next* transposed and letter changed, commands

    What present brings even objects long gone by:

These show my *whole,* derived from Roger's name,

And Henry Eighth gave to the shire the same.

42.

Would you the character's trace of my *first*,
A lovely color you will find reversed:
My *next*, before a noun or pronoun stands,
And case accusative it then commands:
My *whole* within a county these make known,
Whose waters change whate'er they touch to stone.

43.

My *first* an English article we find:
My *next*, with letter changed, will bring to mind
That hapless admiral at Portsmouth shot,
Pretence, that orders he obeyed not:
My *third* resides in Spain's romantic land:
These, joined together, will my *whole* command.

44.

My *first* adorns famed Britain's lovely isle,

    And oft triumphant o'er the ocean rides:

My *next* the hungry welcome with a smile;

    Tho' Jew, nor Ali's sons, durst touch its sides:

Both these together will my *whole* complete,

In county fair, where **Manners** has a seat.

45.

Two letters change and then my *first* transpose,

    Female to show, benevolent and kind!

    Whom we from Lydda a short distance find,

And who from death, at Peter's mandate, rose:

My *whole* in land where Cambria's freedom fell,

As brave Llewellyn's bedd and dingle tell. *(l)*

C

46.

Man trains my *first* for labor, and for food:

My *next* implies a passage thro' the waves:

These join, my *whole* will then be understood,

Where in the Thame, her stream fair Isis laves.

Here Britain's youth receive that precious store,

Bequeathed in Latian and in Grecian lore.

47.

A point from the' Equinox ninety degrees:

Then add three parts of that bold Patriot's name

Whom the' English much revere: and join to these,

A term which first from Saxony hither came:

United all, they bring my *whole* to mind,

In that same shire where we saltpetre find.

48.

Possessive pronoun, nominative case,

    In Gallia's language, you my *first* will find :

My *next* is seen in every human face :

    These form a town, when they're together joined :

The birth place of a King, by fame renowned,

The first who was of France and England crowned.

49.

My *first* was seen in those ill-fated days,

    When York and Lancaster for England's crown,

Continual factions in the land did raise;

    Till Richmond triumphed, and my first bowed down :

My *whole* is thus pourtrayed in that fair land,

Where poor Caernarvon met the murderer's brand.

50.

Save but for man, delighted roams my *first ;*

　　But fears my *next,* transposed, the work of men:

My *last* creates too oft unpleasant thirst,

　　Forbade by him, who left us precepts ten:

These show, if you should them correctly place,

My *whole,* in county famous for its lace.

———

51.

My *first* was seen in Second Richard's days,

　　For tournament prepared with tilted lance,

'Gainst Mowbray, Norfolk's Duke, who sought for praise;

　　But banished by the King, they fled to France:

My first pourtrays my *whole,* in county found,

For juice of the Hesperides' fruit renowned.

52.

My *first*, when you've a letter changed, is bad ;

Tho' not so bad as of the last degree :

And when my *second* equal change has had,

A movement then you'll very quickly see :

These form a town can show such English ware,

As will with Dresden, or with Sève, compare.

53.

My *first*'s an article among the Franks,

With gender masculine, nominative case :

My *next*'s congealed, with elements it ranks :*

My *third* in Heaven's blue concave hath a place,

But first a letter change : these all combined,

Near Bosworth's famous field my *whole* you'll find.

* Rather it was formerly so ranked ; but chymical analysis proves it is not an element.

54.

Great termagants indeed you'll find my *first*,

    Most wittily by Avon's Poet drawn !

My *next* consigns man to his native dust,

    To wait till his eternal day shall dawn :

Together these an ancient town will show,

Where the fine waters of Sabrina flow.

―――

55.

My *first*'s a crime that's stained with human gore,

    And stamps mankind 'mong animals of prey :

When sinks that orb which Persia's sons adore,

    My *next* appears in lurid splendor gay :

These shew my *whole*, to that famed Castle nigh,

Where Leicester gave such cheer to Royalty.

ADDENDA.

A LIST OF THE TOWNS

CONTAINED IN THE PRECEDING ENIGMAS.

No Key is given lest it should defeat the Writer's design; but Notes are added.

Abingdon

Appleby

Beaumaris

Bedford

Bodmin

Brecon

Buckingham

Bury St. Edmund's

Caermarthen

Caernarvon

Cambridge

Canterbury

Cardiff

Cardigan

Carlisle

Chelmsford

Chester

Chichester

Denbigh

Derby

Dorchester

Durham

Exeter

Flint

Gloucester

Guildford

Harleigh

Hereford

Hertford

Huntingdon

Ipswich

Lancaster

Launceston

Leicester

Lincoln

London

Monmouth

Montgomery

Newcastle

Northampton

Norwich

Nottingham

Oakham

Oxford

Pembroke

Radnor

Reading

Salisbury

Shrewsbury

Stafford

Warwick

Wells

Winchester

Worcester

York

NOTES.

(*a*)—Robert, Duke of Normandy, the second son of William the Conqueror, built a castle at this place.

(*b*)—Iceni, an ancient district of this country, named according to some, after the river Ichen, for so the Britons are reported to have called the Ouse; or from I-cen-i—" the head ones."

(*c*)—Demetæ, an ancient division of this Island, supposed to have been Latanized by the Romans, from the British word Dyfed, or Deheufod, " the Southern Country."

(*d*)—Caredig, a chieftain of North Wales, who distinguished himself by his services in expelling the Irish, about the middle of the fifth century, and received this province, then called Tyno Coch, or the Red Valley, as his reward.

(e)—Merlin, a celebrated magician and prophet, who flourished about
the middle of the fifth century, and is ranked with Merddin
Wylt, or Merlin the Wild, and Taliesin, as one of the three
principal Bards of Britain.—His poetical celebrity, probably
gained for him the reputation of prophetical inspiration; while
his fame as a magician may reasonably be attributed to his at-
tainments in mathematical knowledge, and the superiority of
his learning in a dark and ignorant age. Nennius, the earliest
writer who mentions him, calls him Ambrosius, and states that
the account he gave of himself, when brought before Vortigern,
was, that his mother was a nun, and his father a Roman officer,
by whom she had been seduced.

(f)—Trinobantes, or Trinovantes, an ancient district of this country
deriving its name from the British word Tranovantwyr, " inhabitants beyond the stream."

(g)—Ordovices, an ancient division of this Island, named from the
British Oar Devi, " on the Devi ;"—or from the tribe Vicii,
thence, Ardvices, " the Northern or upper vices."—or from
Arddyfeich, " inhabitants north of the river Dyfi," Dovey.

(h)—Caradoc, a leader of the Britons, against the Saxons, under Offa,
King of Mercia : in a dreadful battle which they fought in the
year 795, on a marsh called Morfa Rhyddlan, the Britons
were defeated, and Caradoc was slain.

(*i*)—Brychan, a prince or regulus, who held this territory under his dominion, about the beginning of the fifth century; inheriting it in right of his mother, Marchell, or Marcella, the only daughter of Twdrig, or Tudor, and as his heiress, possessing the government of Garth Madarin.—It is said Brychan had twenty-four sons, and twenty-five daughters.

(*j*)—Regni, or Renci, so named by Ptolemy, probably from the Celtic verb reign, to divide; these people having separated to another district, from the original colony who settled in this Island from Belgium.

(*k*)—Silure, Siluria, an ancient district of this Island, Latinized by the Romans from the British word, Syllwg, or Essyllwg, " beautiful region."

(*l*)—Llewelyn ap Gryffth, the last native prince of Wales who wore the ensigns of royalty : in his struggle with the English, he was attacked unarmed by one Adam Francton, who thrust a spear through him, in a small dell about two hundred yards below the scene of action, thence called Cwm Llewelyn, or Llewelyn's Dingle : the body was afterwards dragged to a little distance, and buried in a place still known by the name of cefn y bedd, or cefn-bedd Llewelyn, " the ridge of Llewelyn's grave," near the banks of the Irvon.

GLOSSARY.

BRITISH.

Ard .... High.

Bedd .... A Grave.

Caer .... A Roman Fortress.

SAXON.

Dur .... A Hill.

Ceaster, now Chester .. A Camp.

Holme .... A River Island.

Printed by BARLOW & BISHOP, 60, Cannon-Street, City.

THE

WEALD OF SUSSEX,

A POEM;

BY

MISS E. HITCHENER.

LONDON:

PRINTED FOR BLACK, YOUNG, AND YOUNG,

TAVISTOCK-STREET, COVENT-GARDEN.

———

MDCCCXXII.

LONDON:
PRINTED BY J. BARLOW,
60, Cannon-Street, City.

PREFACE.

THE very few books affording historical knowledge of Sussex, and the Author's being unacquainted with those who are best informed of the topography of the County, will, it is trusted, plead an apology for the imperfect description conveyed in delineating that extensive and beautiful valley, known by the name of the Weald, comprising the greater part of the counties of Sussex, Surry, Hampshire, and Kent.

Imperfect as is the description, should it lead the subject to a pen capable of doing it justice, it would give sincere pleasure to the Author, who has been prompted to introduce it, from that attachment of the heart which unites us to the scenes of our childhood.

August 9th, 1821.

APOLOGETIC STANZAS.

Yes, little volume, yes, unshielded go,
    Without the sanction of patrician name,
O'er thy defects a splendid veil to throw,
    Or gain the meed of cheaply purchased fame.

No link of bondage binds thee to a clan,
    For thou wert reared in freedom's holy bower,
Thy only ties, the kindred ties of Man,
    And heaven-born liberty, thy brightest dower!

Stranger alike to fashion's winding maze,
    Where tread the great, the beauteous, and the gay,
Or where rich science her bright path displays,
    In all the splendor of meridian day.

Yet, armed in panoply of high intent,
   Strong in the purpose of courageous soul,
Which nobly dares, on loftiest being bent,
   To think, and freely every thought unrol.

No cultured graces gave thy form to light,
   No scenes sublime from Nature's awful face,
No flame enthusiast charmed thee into sight,
   And stamped the lineaments of Genius' race.

Not thine the glowing tint, associate mind
   Weaves in the woof for those of happier birth;
Thy parent's solitary loom intwined
   Nought but the sombre hue, of lonely hearth.

No kindred friendship soothed thine infant years,
   No brilliant converse to elicit truth,
When leaps the soul, as sweet response it hears,
   And wisdom mingles with the fire of youth.

Yet once,—a vision waked thy slumbering lyre,
   Which fancy whispered wise, and great, and fair.
One which could loftiest, noblest strains inspire,
   And to sweet cadence, tune thy wildest air.

No learned porch, nor academic grove,
   Unlocked to thee the treasures of their store !
Bade thee with Greek and Latian sages rove,
   To cull the beauties of their hidden lore.

Tho' rude alike thy language and thy form,
   Thy step untrained to learning's measured pace;
If nature stamp thy feelings pure and warm,
   Hers is, I ween, the element of grace.

Yes, tho' no splendid robes thy frame adorn,
   Yet go, and seek the sufferance of mankind ;
May this slight vesture shield thee from their scorn;
   And win excuse for each defect they find.

But, should they ask, " why wander from your home,
  With all these disadvantages of birth?
Why venture 'mong the sons of men to roam,
  Whence spring your views? what your pretence to
    worth?"

Say, you have soothed your parent's lonely hours,
  (A source of pleasure sacred, fond, and dear;)
Relieved the mind from burden which o'er-powers,
  The gathered thoughts of many a silent year.

That to indulge this selfishness of soul,
  And justify the love which cherished thee,
A useful aim has been thy hope, thy goal,
  This aspiration reared thine infancy,
And should thy wish, so fond, so ardent fail,
Virtue the deed for its intent will hail.

PART I.

There's a bower of roses by Bendemeer's stream,
 And the nightingale sings round it all the day long;
In the time of my childhood 'twas like a sweet dream,
 To sit in the roses and hear the bird's song.
That bower and its music I never forget,
 But oft when alone in the bloom of the year,
I think—is the nightingale singing there yet?
 Are the roses still bright by the calm Bendemeer?

MOORE.

Straight mine eye hath caught new pleasures,
Whilst the landscape round it measures,
Russet lawns, and fallows grey,
Where the nibbling flocks do stray,
Meadows trim with daisies pied,
Shallow brooks, and rivers wide.

MILTON.

        I beheld those islanders renown'd,—
So tutor'd from their birth to meet in war
Each bold invader, and in peace to guard
That living flame of rev'rence for their laws,
Which not the storms of Fortune, nor the flood
Of foreign wealth diffused o'er all the land,
Could quench or slacken.

AKENSIDE.

THE

WEALD OF SUSSEX.

PART I.

MY native downs, with wearied step, I climb, (*a*)

Eager to gaze on the loved scenes below ;

And on the towering Beacon's * height repose, (*b*)

Where the wild thyme its fragrance scatters round.

(Pre-eminently rises this grand point,

Amid the verdant chain of Sussex' Hills ;)

---

* Ditchling Beacon, the highest point in the county of Sussex, being eight hundred and fifty eight feet above the level of the sea.   It is about four miles from Brighton.

And, having gained the' ascent, the' enraptured sight

Delighted views, and ranges o'er the weald : (c)

Assemblage sweet, varied and gay appears,

Emits the Halo of intelligence,

By culture animated and adorned,

As mind irradiates the face of Man.

    Enchanted by the pleasing sight, wrapt thought

The' effect of human labor contemplates,

Which, in this scene, has wrought such wondrous change

Since that among the Roman Cæsars, he,

Their mighty founder, Caius Julius named, (d)

Prompted by ardent thirst of towering fame,

Or led in search of knowledge, high pursuit,

Oft deemed ambition, and with which, in sooth,

Ambition, base and vile, is mingled oft,

The' ignoble passion of a noble mind,

(Yet who the supposition can dispute,

That it was this, not avarice, nor revenge,

That actuated noble Cæsar's mind,)

Invading smiling Britain's sea-girt shore,

To Rome's unwieldy empire joined her isle !

Years fifty-four, ere in the East was seen

That brilliant, wonderful, and unknown star,

Which led the magi into Juda's land,

To worship him, that time in Bethlem born.

   For when those Belgians, Regni termed of old, (*e*)

Had first, as Cæsar from the Rhemi learned,

Crossed o'er the Rhine, they entered Gallia's land ;

Borne o'er the billows thence to Britain's shore,

They gained possession of this lovely scene,

O'er which the eye now wanders with delight ;

But then a forest drear, Coid Andred called,

Extending, so our ancient records say,

From Ringwood, amid Hampshire's woody vales,

To distant Newenden in fertile Kent;

And, South to North, it covered thirty miles.

Then, 'mid its shades, no goodly dwelling rose,

No shelter rude could lonely wanderer find,

But deep morass, and dark impervious wood.

A frowning gloomy wilderness it seemed,

The' abode of such wild animals alone,

As are indigenous to this our isle.

Here in those days, 'tis said, might ravenous wolves (f)

Be frequent found.

              In this, its savage state,

The Roman warriors landed on our shores.

But when, within a century's rapid lapse,

All Britain, South the Tweed, confessed their sway,

What time the' imperial purple Claudius wore,

Who, to dispel its native ignorance, placed

Teachers of legal knowledge in the land,

Then was this wild no more Coid Andred termed,

But designated Lucus Andates;

Thro' which, their military roads they made, (g)

That naught the marches of their legions, swift

And daring, might impede; and by these ways,

Erected Baths, Mutations, Mansions, Inns,

Nor these alone, for here, they often raised

The Graves and Monuments of their great men;

That passers by, with tombs of Heroes struck,

And noble deeds, might of their virtues catch

The' exalted spirit, and emulate their lives.

For, Phœnix like, the greatly good ne'er die! (h)

What, tho' their bones may moulder into dust?

Yet still their deeds emit immortal fires,

At which the ardor of their generous souls,

Successive Heroes light.

                        Should some, secure

In selfish apathy, regardless pass,

Where rest such sacred ashes, yet—the Grave

Speaks even to these, and tells them—they must die!

   Thus sought the Romans to instruct mankind,

" And heedless rambling impulse taught to think."

But when declined their wide extended power,

And Rome, inadequate support to yield

Those Provinces remote, and distant Isles,

Which had too long sapped her internal strength,

As cumbrous branches of an o'er-grown tree;

Had ordered home, compelled, in century fifth

Of Christian time, her widely stationed troops,

Then softened Britain their departure—wept.

For 'mong her sons, in sacred bonds they dwelt,

Their mutual struggles long had ceased to rage;

And Britains, 'neath their powerful conqueror's rule,

Instructing friends, and fostering brothers found !

   Oh, may they still inform us as of old !

And soldiers,—if men must be such,—may they

Rome's warriors imitate, and learn from them,

Not wantonly to war 'gainst man as man,

But 'gainst his ignorance !

                  And yet, not even

A savage race to culture and improve,

Can sanction conquest ; for,—whate'er the plea

Which avarice vile and vain ambition urge,

With specious veil, their motives to disguise,

(A plea that justice never will admit,)

Conquest with slaughter still must pave its path,

Nor can refinement's highest boast be deemed,

For independence an equivalent.

A truth which hapless Britain proved too soon.

  For, when by those deserted, upon whom

They had so many years their trust reposed,

Their state, a mass inert and weak became;

Devoid of power, to guard the hapless land

Against the' encroachments and the' inroads fierce,

Of its invasive neighbours of the north,

By later Britons named, the Pict and Scot, (i)

But Cäel termed, by those of elder time.

Who first retreated from the Belgic arms;

Then, from the Roman power, for refuge strong,

To vales and mountains of North Britain fled,

Which, was from Cäel, Caledonia named.

But now, assailed by these marauders oft,

The Britons to the Saxons sent for aid. (*j*)

   A wily and a warlike tribe were these,

Who from Germania's northern border came,

Their ancestors, the Saci, a stern race,

Bred in the Scythian or Sarmatian wilds.

Nor was to them the prayer of Britain vain ;

They bade their sails unfurl, and gained her shores,

In the fifth age of Christian chronicle,

Commanded by two leaders, fierce and bold,

Hengist and Horsa, enterprising chiefs,

Both brothers, from immortal Odin sprung.

   O'er Pict and Scot they triumphed ; cleared the land

Of all free-booters,—save themselves:—the Isle

Of Britain, lovely was, too lovely far,

Once seen, to' escape the victor's eager grasp:

And soon these base allies formed treacherous league,

With those whom they were summoned to resist.

To aid their faithless cause, auxiliar troops

From every German tribe unnumbered poured ;

Among the foremost, Ella and his sons ;

Then other bands arrayed in martial pride

Came daily flocking o'er ; more Saxons, Jutes, (*k*)

And Angles, cruel, superstitious all ; (*l*)

Offering as sacrifice, each captive tenth,

To their vindictive Gods.

               Such were the rites

Which they to Woden paid, their God of War,

From whom we Wednesday name ; as from their god

Of potent thunder, Thor, is Thursday called ;
Freya, the blessed divinity of peace,
Her name of soothing sound to Friday gave ;
To Seator Saturday was consecrate;
Tuesday Tuisco owned its guardian god ;
Sunday and Monday, from those heavenly orbs,
That cheer with influence sweet the hours of man,
Their lasting and impressive names derived.
Such was their adoration, such their rites.
Who, when the impulse of their savage minds
Obeying, deeds of blood they ruthless wrought,
Assumed a merit, as have others since,
For duty and obedience, to the will
Of gods they loved; to them the glory gave.

   The bloodiest deeds that stain the page of man,
To superstition may be traced, foul fiend !

The child of ignorance, and nurse of crime,

> " Whose chain of adamant, can bind
>
> That little world, the human mind,

And sink its noblest powers to impotence." *

Nor was stern Woden's patriarchal code,

More kind to man, than his ensanguined creed.

For Liberty, that birth-right nature gives,

That best inheritance of man from Heaven,

The only—just hereditary claim,

Which stamps on man, the character of—*man*,

And elevates his rank above the brute,

Expanding every feeling of his heart,

---

* Justice to its author, withholds me from enriching this little volume with one of the brightest jewels in the Crown of Poesy, Mr. Rogers', " Ode on Superstition :" a poem calculated to preserve to latest posterity the language in which it is written.

Enlarges, cherishes, matures his mind,

Subdues his harshness, and refines his soul,

And leads him forth to dwell among his kind,

In peace, benevolence, and genuine love!

That bright, that equal boon, on—all bestowed,

That universal sympathy of man,

Absorbed, degraded, was in slavery lost.

Nor life nor limb had feudal power left free;

Those captives, whom fell superstition spared,

As bondmen, lived a life unworthy man!

But some for freedom to fair Cambria fled,

And there, in safety, dwelt 'mid her wild glens;

Her soft romantic vallies, jagged rocks,

And towering mountains, Nature's Fortresses,

Which stand impregnable, against all force,

Save hers; those giant masses, she alone

Can back to realms of shapeless chaos hurl,

Who drew them thence, when heavenly order forth

Was called, and beamed to man a smiling world.

   The heights of Idra such, such Snowdon's towers, (*m*)

Which Aber-glassllyn as a moat defends ;

Whose peering mounds exclude the azure light,

But for those ambient clouds that sail below

These bold and rocky heights ; here Gellert's grave, (*n*)

Poor faithful hound ! recalls his hapless fate,

And tells us where the brave Llewellyns dwelt.

Within these fastnesses and rocky dells,

The harassed Britons peace and shelter found.

   What, tho' in after times of England's kings,

He who its standard to the red-cross joined,

And over Palastine his banners waved,

Where sunk the poisoned weapon in his arm,

Tho' Ellen's faithful and devoted love

The venom drank, and quelled its power malign,

Still, as its deadly force had reached the soul,

He seemed to stand, like Java's fabled tree, (o)

And spread his baneful influence around,

A withering spell, where heaven-born freedom reigned,

Destroying Liberty and Nature's rights.

This witnessed Scotia's sons, and Falkirk's field;

Her Wallace see, her noble Bruce behold!

Could not such virtue stay the tyrant's hand?

Must " Julius' Towers" be drunk with sacred blood?

Proud Pile, beware! such blood thy base will sap,

And bow thy lofty structure to the dust.

Nor fell on Scotia's sons alone the blast

Of that pestiferous despot's impious ire;

He came, with tyger's grasp, and giant stride,

To sink the " iron deep" in Cambria's " soul,"

And sweep the sons of Liberty from earth.

But vain his efforts, fruitless the attempt,

Serving but as a Beacon, to display

How impotent and imbecile that power,

Which would immortal freedom's spirit crush !

   What tho' still Conwy's waves reflect those towers, (*p*)

Which stand memorial of the tyrant's aim ?

Not Conwy's towers the virtuous soul could awe,

And this experience, even to Edward taught.

Who then, with coward wile, could abject treat

With those, whom to exterminate he came.

And who, despite his power, remained, to show

To many generations then unborn,

What this brave race, the early Britons, were.

   For 'mid the captive tribes to bondmen sunk,

Of Britain's first inhabitants, were few ;

But chiefly colonists from other climes,

Strangers to Albion's every green recess,

To those sequestered dells and dingles wild,

Where fled her native sons, asylum sweet !

As if, till then, had never human form

An entrance found, nor human voice been heard.

Strangers to these recesses of the Isle,

The colonists, their character subdued,

Served but as passive slaves to till the ground,

For their oppressors, artful and unjust,

Who stretched their iron sceptre o'er the land,

And humbled Britain crouched beneath their sway.

But, when the Saxons' firmly 'stablished power,

Had to a Heptarchy reduced the Isle,

Sussex, now bowed to conquering Ella's arms,

Was thence the kingdom of South-Saxons termed.

And tho' the Regni stubborn contest held,

Yet, when compelled Anderida to yield,

Anderida, the city of their strength,

They in their spacious forest refuge sought;

Now Lucus Andates no longer termed,

But Andradswald, whence named, the Weald or Wild.

PART II.

⸻

They made themselves a fearful monument!
The wreck of old opinions ——
   Mankind have felt their strength and made it felt.
They might have used it better, but, allured
By their new vigour, sternly have they dealt
On one another, pity ceased to melt
With her once natural charities. But they
Who in oppression's darkness caved had dwelt,
They were not eagles nourished with the day;
What marvel then, at times, if they mistook their prey?
And good with ill o'erthrew.   BYRON.

⸻

Nor think 'tis only the gross spirits, warmed
With duskier fire and for earth's medium formed,
That run their course; — Beings, the most divine
Thus deign thro' dark mortality to shine.   MOORE.

⸻

  Truth smiles! and where is now the cloud
  That blackened o'er thy baleful reign?
  Grim darkness hurls his leaden shroud
  Shrinking from her glance in vain.
Her touch unlocks the day-spring from above
And lo! it visits man with beams of light and love. ROGERS.

PART II.

AMID the various Names the Weald has borne,

Whether Coid Andred in the British tongue,

Or Lucus Andates, to Romans known,

Or Andradswald by Saxon victors styled,

Their common meaning still remained unchanged,

Anderida's Wood, Goddess of Victory :

Successively by its possessors clad,

In language, such as owned their native land ;—

Its names were all but variations slight ;

But much indeed had its appearance changed.

Can man, weak man, the creature of a day,

Thus change, in twice nine centuries, Nature's face ?

How wonderful the powers on him bestowed,

How passing wonder *He* who formed them all. *

With what conviction must a scene like this,

On the reflecting mind deep impress make

Of industry's effects, and mental power ;

Enabling man such wonders to achieve.

These bade fair Culture wave her magic wand,

With kindly influence, o'er the dreary waste ;

Transformed the desert rude, to scene most fair,

Till Sussex, smiling, owned her sway benign.

    ' How passing wonder he who made him such.   YOUNG.

And can we, witnessing such blessed effects,

Culpably blind, the' omnipotence deny

Of *mind—*o'er *matter?*

     View its Villages,

Its numerous Marts, and sacred Fanes behold,

Its stately Mansions, and its Dwellings snug,

Where many yeomen live in splendid wealth,

Each luxury theirs, that Britain's Isle affords,

Not the rich produce of her lands alone,

But that which grateful Commerce wafts, from shores

Of either Ind.

    A race of men are these,

Such as to our fore-fathers was unknown ;

Can they from feudal villanage be sprung ? (*q*)

Tho' changed by time, alas, they still retain

Traces too numerous of their origin.

But let us Fancy's telescopic glance,

Turn to the prospect of a future age ;

When, in this Weald, shall their descendants rise,

By Letters tempered, softened, and improved,

See Literature advance to´ enlarge their minds,

To polish and refine them ; to bestow

Those liberal sentiments and just ideas,

Which man,—as social,—claims from fellow-man.

    Yet deem ye not the Sussex Yeomen void

Of sterling worth ; their greatest failing seems

A sort of—clan-ship, and a jealous dread

Of those, who 'mong them they—" *new-comers*" term.

Forgetful that mankind are Brethren all ;

Let this corrected be, there would be men

Reflecting lustre on their Country's name,

The boast of England ! *

                    If acquired wealth

Own not ameliorating culture's power,

It wears an aspect proud, forbidding roughness :

The mind still holds its dark and groveling course,

How full so-e'er the coffers may be crammed.

   But when, thro' ancestorial line, it comes,

Its face is softened, changed, bears other stamp,

And purified descends ! for chivalry, (r)

The fascinating child of other days !

Has given it grace, and raised it to a spirit

Of dignity and height beyond itself.

   * Tho' this is the general character, yet it is but justice to add,
that there are many exceptions : the author is happy in the acquaintance of some, whose benevolent hearts and liberal minds, are an
honor to human-nature.

This is the lustre of nobility,

Who, if they came with William bandits fierce,

Yet have they passed thro' the refining Court

Of our third Edward ;—and a court more pure,

Ne'er yet the mighty steps of Monarch trod,

Each virtue in its lovely circle beamed,

And brightly there personified was seen.

Not fabled gods of Greece, by fancy drawn,

Pourtray the graces of this royal band ;

For not even fancy's image is her own,

Her bright conceptions, be they ne'er so just,

May yet be traced to some existing source,

And from the living many, One be formed.

How then could Grecian Bards such virtues draw,

As shed their rays round the black Edward's brow,

Or stamped their features on Philippa's face,

And in one band the noble brothers joined.

Since group like this fair Greece had never seen

When fashioning her forms of deity ;

For then, not her Leonidas had been,

Miltiades, and Aristides just,

And all those virtuous patriots of her land,

Who, of the noblest energies of soul,

A living image stamped on mortal sight,

And showed their kind the—stature of the man !

   Yet, the mild gentle virtues of the heart,

And the soft influence of female worth,

No picture brings more ably to our minds,

Save her's whose hapless fate we all deplore,

For who the virtuous Charlotte e'er surpassed ?

Britannia's loveliest rose, her pride and hope,

No brighter Star has royalty e'er seen ;

Forgive, blest shade, the selfish vain regret *,

Which would have kept thee 'mong the sons of earth,

So thy example, lovely, just, and fair,

Not only had to Courts a pattern been,

But dignified thy Sex, pourtrayed their powers,

Raised from opprobrium a degraded race,

The force of female excellence displayed,

And virtue's purest lessons taught to all ;

Thy worth, thy greatness, centered in thyself,

Contingent, not on sceptres nor on crowns.

Candor and truth adorned thy lovely brow,

And graced thine every act;—nor boast the Sex,

A virtue masculine, that was not thine.—

Firm in thyself, in every virtue bold,

* See Epitaph, Brading Church Yard, Isle of Wight. (s)

Above the glittering tinsel of thy state ;

All mean and narrow policy above,

And every littleness of soul ;—serene,

By wisdom led, thy views were simple, free,

Open to all ;—no creeping subtlety,

Marred thy plain acting ;—wiles and stratagems

Of Machiavelian school, thy mind disdained.

   What tho' there be, who vilely dare pollute

Thy noble life, by making thee Compeer

With shrewd Elizabeth ? to thee compared,

She was a child of feeble, timid soul ;

Winding herself, with cruel subtlety,

Thro' all the crafty policies of Courts,

And labyrinthine folds of human hearts ;

On power she raised her pinnacle of fame,

Scorned the soft ties that kindred minds unite,

Renounced the' endearing privilege of sex,

And prized the' unmeaning homage of the Queen,

Beyond that magic sympathy of soul,

Which more than present being blends in one ;

The past unites, anticipates the future,

The Alpha and Omega of the heart.

She never tasted of that full-fraught bliss,

Which life domestic knows ;—her idol power,

Absorbed her every faculty of soul,

And in herself worshipped its mighty image ;

Cheerless she lived, and unlamented died.

How unlike—her—a potent nation's tears,

A virtuous Consort's deeply woe-fraught soul,

Can better speak ;—beyond the Muses power,

These tell of Charlotte's high and matchless worth.

In the simplicity of Nature wise,

She sought no power beyond affection's smile,

In her dear Leopold's and England's love.

To thee, blessed Saint, is this weak tribute due,

When we of royalty relate the worth.

Thee, with Philippa, justly we may join,

And place thy picture in her Edward's Court,

Where all of female excellence combined ;

And o'er its nobles its high lustre spread.

Tho' now too many of their sons forget

That spotless honor, disinterestment pure,

Are all that constitute—the truly noble ;

Yet these the graces are,—that captivate—

Preserve and charm.

Oh cherish these, as bloom

Of fairest fruit !—when time, unfolding mind,

Shall, at a brighter period of the world,

Remove the shade that screened its infant years,

And bid it gaze, undazzled with the light,

On full meridian day ;—truth's brilliant orb,

The shadows framed by fancy shall dissolve,

And Error's every mist shall fade away ;

But, till the' invigorating warmth mature,

Tear not in haste, the veil of dewy dawn,

Lest the world's youth exposed to withering blight,

In bloom decay, and manhood ne'er attain.

   Then let us not imagination spurn,

Nor roughly rend the flowery bands she weaves ;

But ken with deeper search the heart of man.

Since Nature wastes no time in idle work,

Nor e'er made aught in vain ;—but use designed

For all that springs from her creating hand.

That use, appropriated rightly, forms

What Man calls Wisdom, virtue's leading star.—

The light of truth ;—that with its piercing glance,

Keen as the eagle turns, at noon-tide hour,

To heaven's effulgent orb, the' undazzled eye,

Thro' all things quickly darts, and thus perceives

Their moral fitness, adaptation true ;

Creation's laws, and all the just design !

Surely this light instructs that Nature framed

Imaginations prompt and magic power,

The cause of virtue proudly to sustain,

For whilst society remains, as now,

Too weak to own stern Truth's severer sway !

Not few the minds which thence derive support,

And justly our sweet Moralist has sung,

" Honor's a sacred tie,**********

D

That aids and strengthens virtue, when it meets her,

And imitates her actions, where she is not;

It ought not to be sported with."

                Then pause,

Great reason's advocates! tho' sound and just

Your disquisitions, your inquiries free,

Yet for a moment pause, ere from mankind

The bands you tear, which bind their harmony,

And confidence 'twixt Man and Man inspire;

What tho' a nobler Theory you have framed,

Conducive more to happiness and peace,

Than that whose influence now your species sways,

A doubtful question still remains to solve.—

Say, are the mass the many, all prepared

With pure intent, your Theory to' adopt?

Remember what superior minds conceive,

Is imperceptible to vulgar souls.

And thus, how good and beautiful so-e'er

Your plans, the result of reflection deep,

Impracticable they would still be found,

For—general use. (*t*)

              Ere you of order's law

One line destroy, think well can you restore ?

For may not anarchy, with discord fierce,

Again to savage life reduce mankind,

And, in one common sea of ruin, wreck

All, all the lovely charities of life,

Its social compacts, civil policies,

Abstruse researches, various sciences,

Inventions wonderful, ingenious, vast,

Stupendous works, and arts mechanical,

That make man gaze, astonished at the sight,

And at his race, till, questioning, he seems

To doubt, if what he sees can be produced,

By creatures, as ephemeral as himself?

  If these should e'er annihilated be,

And this fair cultured scene, this lovely Weald,

Rudely defaced by wild and lawless hands,

And barbarism once more obscure our Isle,

Who then shall re-illumine it? what land

Shall send another Julius to its shores?

  Delightful Isle! when once thy splendor sets,

It sets in murky gloom, no more to rise,

Among the nations of the peopled Earth.

Tho' now they dread, and tremble at thy frown,

Then will thy power, that power which wide extends,

To earth's remotest verge, and o'er each sea,

Where vessels dauntless cleave the yielding wave,

Be vanished all ; thy name obscurely known,

Thy fame obliterated ; even thy place

Almost forgotten ; and some future page,

In after times, may of thy empire doubt,

As of old Troy, if e'er existent,—save

In Poet's brain, which—" gives, to airy nothing,

A local habitation, and a name !"

   But should bright History's lasting page enrol,

And to posterity transmit thy fame,

With that of polished Greece and mighty Rome,

Like them for an immortal memory,

Thou wilt indebted to thy sages be,

Who spread a lustre o'er their native land.

Not learned Porch, nor Academic Groves,

Which bounteous Cimon to his Athens gave,

Could boast more precious lore than Albion's Isle.

Her Newtons, Miltons, Lockes, a chaplet weave,
And grace, with wreath of Amaranths, her brow.

 The greatly good tread with immortal step,
And their impression on their Country stamp,
The muse delighted would preserve their name,
For dear are such to every Child of Song.

 Then say not, idle is the Poet's life ;—
By fame commissioned, he the record keeps,
With which she decks the archives of her throne ;
To Ages down insures his Country's name ;
What, tho' in penury his life be past,
Yet he shall live, when who for wealth have toiled,
In luxury revelled, or in pleasure laved,
Shall not, in dying, merely cease to be,
But the' ends of being proving not they 've been,*

  * Proved by the ends of being to have been. Pope.

They shall be blotted and effaced from earth;

Which, like too many of her Children, vain,

Preserves, in pleased remembrance, those alone,

In whom she finds a source of conscious pride.

(Whilst fame repays the debt to Office due,)

And, 'mid her Annals, stamps the Poet's name.

How many, clad in purple and in gold,

Unheeding past, or with contempt and scorn,

The venerable sages of their land.

See the great Bard of Greece grope thro' a throng,

Oppressed by blindness, more obscure than that

Which he, in loss of visual ray, sustained :—

For what with mental darkness can compare?

Nor was the meed of Genius scorn alone,

Malice and hate too oft repaid her sons;

See Socrates, fair Wisdom's favorite Chief,

And pure Pythagoras, Virtue's chosen Son,

With HIM, whose soul, beneficient and kind,

Its essence all benevolence and love,

Approached, and traced the source from which it sprang.

Ah ! little the near-sighted mass fore-saw,

That Greece would, save for these and such as these,

In after Ages no remembrance bear.

  Sure letters have celestial origin,

Are emanation from a source divine,

Even by their power, proclaiming whence they sprang.

Bear they not in them evidence of soul,

Possessing more than needs this transient earth,

And sympathies beyond a nether state ?

  If then there be, for all created, use,

Shall Mind, creation's matchless master piece,

Be lavished for no end ?—say, why is Man,

If creature of mere sense, so oft disposed

Those pleasures to forego, which thence arise ?

Or why so oft does he reject the means,

Afforded equally to all mankind,

To give whate'er the craving senses need ?

See yonder vale ;—there Otway had his birth, (*u*)

There wooed in infancy his sorrowing muse,

And felt the influence of her power divine.

Ah ! had he not a powerful impulse known,

And vast desires beyond this stage of life,

Beyond earth's utmost stores, to gratify,

He had provided for those grosser wants,

Which, at the last, demand imperious made,

And, with vindictive ire, destroyed his frame.

Otway ! while thus I gaze upon the spot,

Made sacred by the footsteps of thy youth,

Its beauty rises o'er the neighbouring vales;

Fancy beholds thy spirit 'mid its shades;

With Belvidera and Monimia there,

Sweet forms of thy creation, loves to stray,

And mingles with them Sympathy's soft tear.

Yet thy fate, harder still, from feeling claims,

A deeper grief, than what thy verse inspires;—

Ah, melancholy Bard, pale Sorrow's child!

So faithful ever to thy parent proved,

Her every feature thou so well couldst paint;

She grateful claimed thee, as her darling son,

And bade thy natural element be tears.

In teaching us to weep, thy life was spent,

And such thy death, as gave us ample cause,

Both with and for thee, ever blending grief.

Even now my soul in homage bends to thine,

With pensive sadness, pity, and regret.

  Couldst thou, blest shade, re-visit yonder vale,

There tell the feelings of thy early youth,

The impulse deep, awakened 'mid its scenes,

Those thick embowering shades, where nature lists

To all the aspirations of the soul ;

Methinks, thy gentle spirit, would unfold

The energy inducing thee, to bear

Keen poverty with its attendant ills,

Even to starvation's horrid form of death ;

(Choaked, as 'tis said, too eager in the' attempt,

The long untasted morsel to devour.)

And what such death, the crimes of hunger tell,

Temptation beyond Nature's power to bear,

As towns besieged, and ship-wrecked crews attest.*

    * See the ship-wreck of the Medusa. (v)

See the starved wretch on more than carrion feed,

Insatiate glut on more than fellow flesh,

The living pulse from his own life-blood tear,

And, whilst yet throbbing, greedily devour.

Behold the cravings of the softer sex,

The mother, *once* the tender gentle mother,

Whose tear responded to her infant's plaint,

Now on her own babe feed.   Forbear to say,

" I never so would act;" Man at the best,

But little knows himself, and least in this.

All other passions, Nature has designed

To work her own effects, her end to' obtain ;

Starvation has no aim, sinless its crimes,

It is beyond the pale of Nature's laws,

Bound by no ties, and owns no cognizance.

Bear this in mind, be cautious how you judge,

Ye who have never such temptation known ;

Ye who make wanton waste of human food,

Or who in speculating schemes for wealth

Shut out from man the daily stay of life,

Bethink how great your crime; think at your hands

That power retributive, which governs all,

Will justice for starvation's crimes demand.

   England, my Country ! why neglected live.

Thy Bards, yet almost deified when dead ?

Give them the meed of honorable aim,

Nor let starvation's frightful form obtrude

On the perspective of the Poet's life.

They little need of wealth, whose minds are stored

From Fancy's rich and unexhausted looms ;

But, 'mid the changes and the chance of life,

Let just security at least be theirs,

That safe Asylum from all nature's wants,

Awaits them in those later days of life,

When age enfeebles all the powers of Man,

Increasing his dependance on his kind ;

Shall he considered as a pauper be,

Who would not grossly libel human kind,

By deeming, that the being who supplies

The body's meaner wants ; would find reward

Richer than his who stores the craving mind.

    Otway ! if still thy spirit hover near

The land, which could desert thee in thy need,

Yet call thee her's, and boast thee for her son,

Pity, and spare the darkness of the age.

(Like crime, oh Chatterton, sad Shade, forgive) ! (*w*)

Ah ne'er again such stain may England know.

But whence the spirit, which could so sustain ?

This energy from more than mortal source,

From purer richer fountain sprang,—tho' twined,

In union intimate with matter, free,

Self-centered, unsubduable it stood.

Such, hapless, yet immortal Sons of verse,

Your nobler souls, admitting no restraint,

From that which they despised, corporeal power;

But ardently would their own pleasures seek,

In letters found them, in their joys indulged ;

Proved them a cordial in life's tearful vale,

A light, that all but cheered the saddest form

Of death's dark hour.—

           Say, ye Philosophers,

Ye learned and deep-thinkers, is not then

The mind immortal, bearing striking proof,

Within itself, of immortality ?

Reject ideas, principles innate?

But is there not *within* a something still,

Perceptions of the senses to receive?

The senses, but as windows to the soul;

Say, what is that resolves, combines, retains?

   Forgive ye pious, that my mind inquires,

Appeals to reason, for what you would say,

Religion shows, and Holy-writ contains.

   All lovely as religion pure, appears,

When sweetest influence o'er the mind it holds,

And every feeling of the heart attunes

To Truth and Love, a harmony divine;

Yet it forbids not, rather it commands,

To' exert those talents upon Man bestowed.

   Shall we then reason smother or reject?

Oh, that Mankind should quibble about words!

'What's grace, but reason? come not both from HIM,

'Who human powers to his wise ends adapts?

What, more than reason *wills*, does Man believe?

What more than reason *willing*, say, is grace,

And grace, than feeling, which to every mind

Is reason, its own reason, and its guide?

  (Yet let me guard against construction false,

Nor be one moment wrongly understood;

My meaning would be ill indeed conveyed,

Iu tolerating au opposing sense,

To this plain rule,—respect the rights of others,

And feel for the infirmities of all.

This bind as a phylactery on the brow,

Or that unerring law, "Whate'er ye would

That men to you should do, that do to them.") (*x*)

  Yet, what is reason, but result of feeling,

E

Of feeling analyzed ?   In sooth, I deem,

That reason, feeling, grace, resolve in ONE.

How sounding words confound, perplex, mislead,

Dis-joined by men, who then dis-join themselves ;

For whilst each does what he considers best,

What but his reason leads and governs him ?

    Then be indulgence meet allowed me too,

If thus my reason dictate to my thought,

That either ignorance, the womb of ERROR,

Conceiving all that is deformed on earth,

Timidity, the monster's cradling nurse,

Or prejudice, its guardian, and its friend,

Bids us inquiry to avoid and dread.

    The more we search for truth, of wisdom born,

Its lustre more resplendent will appear,

Inquiry's test it loves, and well can stand,

And, tho' the maze, the labyrinthine wilds,

Which man's all various paths have traced around,

Seem at first view inquirers to perplex,

Till they exclaim, they know not what *is* truth;

Yet let them in their virtuous path hold on,

(For virtuous *is* the effort to be right,)

Examine every beaten road with care,

Nay those with impress slight of novel step,

Let them but deeply *human-nature* ken,

Their search will not be vain.

                    The minds of men

So variously are formed, Identity

Itself may show to each with different hue.

Reflected shadows, tho' the substance, ONE,

In self-the same.

                    Say is not light, still light?
                         E 2

Tho' all the Iris' colors it contains,

Which, though so various and so opposite,

Yet, when agreeably united, form

A pure, a spotless white.

            And is not Truth,

The Sun of light to this, the moral world,

Tho' vivifying, darting diverse rays?

  Ah thus would Man, in happy union, blend

Its numerous colors, and so constitute

A full, an universal harmony,

Then, how-soever various their ideas,

If in this one great principle agreed,

What numbers in sweet peace and love would dwell,

Who now in fierce hostility exist,

With rancorous persecution's bitter hate,

Pursue, and oft destroy their fellow-man,

For such faint shades of difference, that, when zeal
And bigotry, to aid the mental sight
Their magnifying optics lend, even then
Scarce is the slight distinction visible.

  Is there aught excellent, 'mong sons of earth,
In which religion, reason, virtue, truth,
Are not alike all equally combined ?
And teach not they a just humility,
A liberal conduct, and forbearance mild ?
Such virtues these, as social Man requires,
And such should practise with his fellow-man,
Till these be learned, he is but savage still,
Nor fitted 'mong society to live.

  Of all the ills from ignorance that spring,
Fell persecution is Man's direst foe :
Even now life's current freezes in my veins,

Whilst, by too busy memory, conjured up,

The painful scenes of former times I trace;

Tho' fire and faggot long have ceased to blaze,

Yet still my soul with apprehension trembles,

Lest the almost extinguished flame revive,

And christian sects, with blind and brutal rage,

Again oppose, again destroy each other.

Oh pause, my Countrymen, pause, and reflect,

Whether of primal Papal Creed, or ye

Who 'gainst a portion of that Creed protest,

Whate'er may be your forms, whate'er your faith,

Forget not ye are MEN, and that your God,

The Christian's God, the Father, Son, and Spirit,

Bids you to live in love, among each other,

" For if ye love not Man whom ye have seen,

How can ye love God whom ye have not seen?"

Such that Redeemer's law, whose mercy shone

Conspicuous, in the actions of his life,

And on whose mercy is your only stay;

Of all your parties, the sole cherished hope,

To Him you all lay claim, in Him unite,

His followers all presume to call yourselves;

And Him avow, your Master and your Guide.

His holy name, then, dare not to blaspheme,

Nor e'er with impious hands destroy your race,

That race which *He* in mercy died to save.

His followers be indeed, and prove your faith,

By that pure love you to each other bear,

Transcribe his life in yours;—model more pure,.

Ne'er yet has Fancy in her happiest hours

Conceived; her bright ideas of the just

And free, wear not that winning gentleness,

That mien attractive, which appeared above

Or manly majesty or female grace;

What pencil ne'er can paint nor language tell.

Here Art and Science fail, tho' Milton write,

And glowing West design;—*action* alone,

Of life benevolent and ardent love,

Can best delineate HIM; the happiest those

Who faithfully the copy trace, and love

Even the Samaritan.

                         Examine too

The lives of his disciples,—varying much;

For, tho' religion tempers, softens Man,

It changes not the mould in which he's cast;

Since Christ then chose Men of such different shades,

With a variety so strongly marked,

This surely should a striking lesson teach.

What wisdom infinite so well ordains,

Shall we presumptuous change? tho' some as guide,

Adopt the liberal, temperate, reasoning James.

Others the eloquent and active Paul.

Some the affectionate and placid John.

And others Peter, ardent, rash, sincere.

What tho', as suits his CAST Man follows these,

" They are but *parts*, of one stupendous WHOLE,

Their body *Nature* is, but *God* their soul."

   Oh thou, all-just, all-powerful Deity!

Whose shining, glorious attribute, is MERCY,

Thy essence, just benevolence and love,

How has thy heavenly eye endured the sights,

The horrid sights, this earth so oft displays?

And, worst of all, that rank, that foul offence,

Doubtless to Thee, most heinous, most offensive,

That which, with sophistry so plausible,

Blasphemously, in *thy* name, for *thy* sake,

(Oh, impious lie!) would seek to injure MAN!

   If christianity breathed not of peace;

Of love, good-will, and mercy to mankind,

Who is there, that with rapture would behold

Its sacred fanes adorn yon lovely Weald?

But now, whilst gazing here, faucy reverts

To times long past, when contemplating thus,

We might, amid Coid Andred's gloomy shades,

Have seen fierce superstition's direful flames,

With baneful blaze, and smoke impure ascend,

Defiling Nature's purest atmosphere.

In yonder groves, where stately oaks for ages,

Dominion undivided have possessed,

Even there perhaps, the trembling victim bled,

Beneath the Druids' knife; since, o'er this Isle,

(The seat of Science in a later day,)

Their cunning and Man's weakness to them gave

An undisputed sway.   But, if gone by

Be now the mystic rites of Druid old,

And MIND improved, as is this cultured scene,

Let us the hope indulge, that more is wrought

Than merely change of soil, or altered name.

Ne'er may such *spirit*,—under any form,

Again revive.

    But onward may we press,

With vigorous step,—" light after light attaining,"

No more, with stern and sacrilegious feuds,

Retard our happy progress; swift as time,

In his recording annals rolls our years,

May each, the' impression of advancement bear.

That our descendants, when like us reflecting

On those, who trod the path of life before,

May trace our steps which cleared the rugged road,

And smoothed for them, the rough unbeaten way.

But gradual this advance, as that of time,

Whom sound improvement for its parent owns :

No hurried movements execute its work,

For violence and haste retard its steps.

And 'tis to *gradual progress*, Sussex owes

That rich display, which graces all her Weald !

PART III.

Far to the south a mountain-vale retires,
Rich in its groves, and glens, and village-spires;
Its upland lawns, and cliffs with foliage hung,
Its wizard-stream, nor nameless nor unsung:
And thro' the various year, the various day,
 What scenes of glory burst, and melt away!   ROGERS.

               In these behold the tools,
The broken tools, that tyrants cast away
By myriads.   BYRON.

We'll twine the roses, red and white, together,
And both from one kind stalk shall flourish.

               Are not these woods
More free from peril than the envious court?
Here feel we but the penalty of *Adam*,
The season's difference.   SHAKSPEARE.

PART III.

WHEN Rome its powerful legions had withdrawn,

And Danes and Saxons bloody contest ceased,

Then Andradswald its rude appearance changed,

No longer one vast wood, but 'mid its wilds,

Arose at intervals the Atheling's Dome, (y)

With frowning towers, abrupt and angular;

For such the heavy taste of lofty Thane.

Near to these gloomy Structures of the Great,

The lowly Hamlet lay, where meekly dwelt,

Plying the force of his mechanic skill,

The humble Artizan; here shelter found

Those, who, by feudal law, were Villains termed,

And who, slaves of the soil, were bought and sold,

As if but cattle, with the lands they tilled.

   Where the Lord's Aula proudly towering stood,

Annexed was found a verdant Park's demesnes,

Richly o'er-shadowed with majestic oaks,

Those early nurslings of Britannia's strength,

In the meridian of her day of power.

Among these shades, arose the humble roof

Of the stern Keeper of the graceful Herd.

And tho' the mighty Owner and his Dome,

With all their power, are to the dust gone down,

This low abode has 'scaped the grasp of Time,

Here we may trace the Antler's wide domains,

Which every ancient village still preserves,

As the *park-farm* in Sussex' lovely Weald.

Tho' first the Romans to Britannia's Isle,

Had brought the Christian faith, yet Saxon Creed,

With rites impure again defiled the land;

But Rome's stern Pontiff to her rocky shores,

His Missionaries sent, to spread, so veiled,

That mighty power which once triumphant reigned.

What, tho' its sword no longer awed mankind,

Its Crosier was but Standard in disguise:

Still Rome, with artful wile, ruled o'er the world.'

England, once more, was tribute to its power;

For Anglo-Saxon owned the Romish faith,

And in this Weald its lofty Spires arose.

But Norman-William came, with conquering sword;

F

And to the warlike chieftains of his band,

The Land allotted at his sovereign will.

Then in De-Warren Lewes saw her Lord,

With part of Sussex for his rich domain.

The Conqueror's daughter blest him with her charms,

For royal Gundred owned De-Warren's name.

   To them indebted is thy stream, fair Ouse,

They graced thy banks with all the arts they knew,

And on thy shore the lofty Turret raised.

With pious hearts on pilgrimage to Rome

They reached the Garonne's side ; but thence returned,

To rear thy holy-walls, to cherish there,

Those Monks austere who Berno's order bore,

And who at their request from Clugni came.

   Thy Priory raised St. Pancras' name* retained,

And tho' in ruins now upon thy banks,

---

   * It was erected on the site of an old wooden church, long dedicated to St. Pancras ;—a Phrygian nobleman who suffered martyrdom at Rome, under the Emperor Diocletian.

By Henry's avarice, humbled to the dust,

Its mouldering vestiges remain, to show

The cloistered pile magnificent arose,

Gracing thy beauteous, thy romantic town :

And Town more pleasing boasts not Albion's Isle ;

Tho' raised without design to please the eye,

Design could not more sweet effect produce ;

The lofty hill, rich valley, softest shades,

And the meandering of thy fertile course ;

The distant Ocean's breeze, the castled tower,

The interesting ruin ivy-wreathed,

An emblem as of Liberty's green flag,

Which seems, o'er tyranny and gothic strength,

Triumphantly its standard thus to rear.

These all are thine, fair Lewes, these are thine !

Nor, 'mid thy walls, has revelry its home,

Nor dissipated throng o'er thee presides

But Beauty, Grace, and Science, are thine own,

Thee all the Graces, all the Muses love.

   Methinks, even now, as in my early years,

I view enraptured all thy classic haunts,

And see another Tempé in thy vales.

   If dear to us the scenes of childhood's hours,

More justly dear is every sacred spot,

Where Science first unlocked her pearly stores,

And oped her treasures to the infant mind;

Or History drew us, with her winning grace,

To study, in her page, the heart of Man,

And Poesy beckoned to its land of flowers.

   Thus seeks my Muse its own excuse to plead,

For having long on lovely Lewes dwelt,

When it of Warren should and Gundred speak,

And their descendants; who, in after years,

Of Sussex and of Surry Earls became,

And Lords of Lewes and of Arundel.

In the third Edward's reign, this lovely scene,

Far as the eye's insatiate glance can view,

To them belonged, thro' many a circling year,

Till only females of their line remained.

Tho' not Eurynome's fair daughters these,

Yet were they Sisters three, nor wanting grace,

I ween, nor splendor, mirth nor mantling joy.

These, as co-heiresses, their rightful claim,

Soon of the whole equal division made ;

What time the English Standard was unfurled,

And waved triumphant over Gallia's land,

Till France acknowledged our fifth Henry, Heir

To her imbecile Charles, and for his Bride,

The lovely Catherine to the Hero gave;

And made him Regent over all the land.

　　From the fair Sisters of De-Warren's line,

The noble House of England's Norfolk sprang; (*aa*)

Such Aberga'ny's and such Lenthal's source,

But Lenthal soon extinct, reversion made

To the remaining branches of the race,

Tho', in a later age, great Norfolk's part,

Division shared, and classic Dorset 'rose. (*bb*)

　　And still to these much of the Weald belongs;

As would the whole, but for that monarch sage,

Who kenned, with Wisdom's eye, the ills around,

Saw feudal power unequalize mankind,

Degrade, enslave, and brutalize the race.

This power with certain influence to destroy,

He to the nobles of the land proposed,

That at their pleasure they should cut entail.

And quickly then arose around him men,

Free, independent, virtuous, brave, and bold,

No longer *Villains*, but *Freeholders* termed.

　To aid the wise design, his fostering hand

Called forth that art, whose power unites Mankind,

And barters wide the produce of their lands ;

Which, if by selfish policy, untouched,

Would make the world one lovely garden seem,

Where each might gather what his taste directs,

And Man be like one family on earth,

Whose only aim were universal good.

So Henry deemed, and beckoned Commerce hither,

A scale of equability to raise,

That of the realms' three states, each might alike,

A just and equal balance thus possess.

Ah, Tudor, much Britannia owes to thee!

A second Alfred rising o'er her land,

By wisest means, healing her civil feuds.

No longer York with the Lancastarian strove;

Their roses Hymenæus mingling, wreathed

With the amaracus; in sweetest bands,

Thy fate intwining, with that royal Maid,

Who Sister, Niece, and Daughter of a king,

To thee united, Wife of one became.

Endiademed descended all her race,

Her Son a King, and such his Children see,

The offspring of her Daughters too beheld,

In Suffolk's Jane, and Scotland's beauteous Queen

Thus fair Elizabeth and Henry quelled

That long disgraceful warfare of their sires,

Which for two centuries had drunk England's blood.

Not all the clamor of a people fierce,

Long used to faction, and to furious strife,

Could e'er make Tudor yield to their desires,

And plunge in war with all its evils dire,

Nor work a Nation's ill, to gain its smiles.

Superior he to popular applause,

That puerile vanity of little souls,

Nor could the bubble glory e'er mislead

A mind like his; whose quick perception saw,

Thro' all of splendid victories dazzling lure,

And barren conquests, which too oft had been,

The glory of this Isle, purchased, alas,

By loss of British happiness and lives,

Of wealth and virtue.

    What, like WAR, corrupts

And undermines the morals of Mankind?

Accustomed long to idleness of life,

Or worse to that of plunder, rapine, blood,

Until familiar grown with crimes like these,

The *Soldier* oft forgets the social tie,

Forgets the powerful duties of the MAN ;

The very best, an isolated race,

Who seem to stand aloof from all their kind,

And to themselves, as to their kindred, lost,

Their place in life, neglected and disowned,

Foresworne the link, uniting *Man* to *Man* :

Their birth-right sold for less than Esau's cost ;

Their will, their power, their conscience, not their own ;

Another's sense of right must govern theirs ;

They dare no power of heart or mind assert,

But sink, despised, to mere machines or tools,

In others hands, to murder at their will.

A Soldier's very limbs are not his own,

But they must move to please another's eye ;

The stiff, the tortured gait, the starting ear,

Distorted visage, by the' unnatural force

Of hair in thong,* and neck in hardened case,

Pourtray the *cast* of European slaves ;

And slaves more vile, not Helotes of old Greece,

Nor poorest Villains of the feudal age.

   The veriest wretch, who dusts another's shoes,

Or sweeps the path-way of the busy mart,

Is nobler far ; for he is still himself,

A Being free, his will and power his own :

Nor to the ennobling duties of the MAN,

  * It is but justice to add, that the present Commander in Chief of the British Forces, his R. H. the D. of York, has, with humane con-sideration abolished this practice, proving himself in this, as in every other instance, the Soldier's friend.

Durst one deny his right, his equal claim,

Or bend to sense of duty, not his own.

　　Nor end the Soldier's ills with active life;

Suppose him to have 'scaped the murdering ball,

The blade, deep-tinged in dye of human gore,

The gloomy dungeon of vindictive foe,

The typhus, horrid offspring of fatigue,

That neither the forced march thro' various climes,

Of polar snow, nor full meridian rays,

The sandy desert, nor the swampy bed,

The trampling horse's hoof, nor city's blaze,

Have e'er that form impaired, which nature stamped

With all the perfect features of the MAN.

　　Yet see him in the vale of life descend;

When Memory, as the brilliant Orb of Day,

Declining in the vast Atlantic wave,

Reflected rays emits on Evening's scene,

So cheers the Evening of Man's setting day,

If bright like that, his path has ever shone,

And lights his footsteps, even to the tomb.

But not that age, whose youth was spent in arms,

And life, matured upon the hostile plain,

No, not to such, brings Memory sweet delight,

Whose Mind reviews no images of bliss ;

Nor Fancy, wrapt in shadows of the past,

Still gives a lively pulse and ardent glow.

No city's comforts, nor embowering woods,

Canals, nor roads, quick intercourse to speed,

And level distance, even to Man's desires,

No cultivated farm nor garden sweet,

That brings another Eden to our view,

No lovely cottage, nor mechanic skill,

No wise invention matter to subdue,
And subject earth to every use of Man,
Thus saving life from waste and labor's toil,
And leisure giving to mature the mind ;
No art improved, nor sciences enriched,
No sweet designs of a benevolent thought,
To better life, and leave the human race,
A loved remembrance of his virtuous path.

Not thus on useful life can he reflect,
Nor Memory sooth him, as he views the past ;
Since nought exists to prove he e'er has been,
But Misery's scourge, inflicted on his kind.
The din of battle, and the clash of arms,
The field of carnage, and the reeking plain,
Of slaughtered thousands, rise before his sight,
And mar the province, memory should adorn.

Nor knows the Soldier's life earth's sweetest bliss,

The fire-side pleasures of a little home,

And all that treasured happiness of heart,

Which he enjoys in peace and tranquil scenes,

Who feels nor agitation, nor alarm,

Lest the dear Partner of his happy hours,

Be ravished from him, and his children slain,

Resting secure, that nought will him attend,

But natural ills, that wait on all Mankind

Ask the poor Soldier, if his life be such : —

But, no, forbear, lest it should mockery seem,

Since blood and terror ever trace his way,

And cross the path, even of his happiest hours.

Not all the wonders of a distant clime,

Nor proudest trophies of the laureled field,

Can sooth his mind, if conscience but awake,

Whose arm has been imbrued in life's fair stream.

    Say, ye, whose medals tell of warlike plains,

And stamp the Heroes of the rustic group,

Say, as ye wander in this lovely spot,

Whose modest fields recall nor strife, nor blood,

But refuge now, as in the days of yore,

Where all the gentle virtues love to dwell,

And bliss domestic from the world withdrawn ;—

Nor breathes in Europe atmosphere more pure,

Even from her northern cape, to classic haunts

Upon her southern shore :—this lovely spot

Has ne'er pollution known from heaps interred

Warm from the reeking sword; no trumpet shrill,

Nor other clarion save the Hunter's horn,

Has e'er the voice of Nature, 'mid these dells

Awaked, with Echo's magic sympathy. (o4)

Oh say, while wandering 'mong your native scenes,

With mangled limbs, and scars that silent speak

Telling the tale that hastens to the grave.

Had ye not happier closed your day of life,

If tracing here the fields your hands had tilled,

The flocks you oft had tended, and the feats

Of honourable and of honest labor,

That blest your Kind, and made your children own

With pride, their Sires ?—oh ! may the Peasants glory,

Ne'er know again dire war's polluting stain,

But long descend, unsullied, to a free,

And virtuous race.

     When war to war succeeds,

What can we e'er, save civil discord fierce

Expect ?—who have in camps been born and bred,

Will they e'er useful citizens become ?

G

Yet over Men thus turbulent and fierce,

Thou wert, oh Tudor, called to sovereign sway.

But how superior rising 'mong thy Kind,

Most meet indeed to be a nation's Chief!

Ah! that crowns ever circled heads like thine!

Not their most brilliant jewels could compare,

With the high lustre of thy intellect,

Thee with a diadem had nature crowned,

Beyond the costly purchase of a prince,

Or far more splendid crown, a people's gift.

Wisdom upon thy brow triumphant sat,

As all thine acts bear strongest evidence,

Each emanating from a mighty mind,

Perceiving what was for thy people's good,

Joined to such pure disinterested soul,

As, with determined force, pursued that good,

Regardless both of censure and applause.

　Thy predecessors but like children seem,

Compared to thee, what was annexing France,

Or mighty Europe with its numerous states,

Nay what was universal rule itself,

Like to conferring on one little spot,

Upon one nation, howsoever small,

The heavenly blessings of good-will and peace,

Tranquillity and love; such to procure,

For thy loved realm, for favored Albion's Isle,

(Since not to England was thy love confined)

See Margaret from great Augusta's Court,

And fairest scenes that grace thy lovely Sheen,

From their delights, at thy command, depart,

And bear the Olive into Scotia's land,

Securing peace to all Britannia's realm.

Such was the study of thy virtuous life,

Britain in thee a parent's hand can trace,

A father's anxious care, a father's love,

Who for his children providently plans,

Nor for that offspring more immediate his,

But for his race, to every distant age.

Thro' the long vista of remotest time,

The good and ill in the perspective 'rose,

Before thy searching eye; thy piercing glance,

Darted on error, tho' by distance veiled,

And thy enlightened mind devised such means

As gradually should chase not that alone,

But the gross ignorance of thy murky times.

Nor didst thou only weed the' uncultured soil,

But planted too; as those rich fruits evince,

We gather now; and our more pleasant path,

Which owes its flowery verdure much to thee.

   Oh, when will all as Henry thus grow wise,

When glory rate but as an empty sound,

Too often as a tawdry covering used,

A Nation's wretched nakedness to hide?

   But hallowed freedom, should a foe invade,

Dastards are those who abjectly submit;

And justly Man forfeits that noble name,

Fit only to become a crouching slave,

When yielding quietly his equal rights,

In individual or collective sense;

These to defend, or strive, if lost, to gain,

Is the imperious duty of the Man.

Thus to contend and guard, is not to war,

But to secure to those who after come,

That patrimony which to them is due.

This is the deed of virtue, this is glory.

Oh, may my Countrymen preserve it long,

And their remote descendants grateful bless,

With Memory's lasting tongue, the present age.

Then will my native Weald yet more increase

Its beauties rich, Culture's progressive power,

Adorn it more and more ; its habitants,

Like those residing now amid its shades,

With gratitude their ancestors adore;

Tho' not for individual Acres left,

But for those *rich bequests*, that give to each

The BIRTH-RIGHT of a MAN, and grace to walk,

Erect and free, 'mong nations of the Earth.

NOTES.

NOTES.

" *My native Downs.*"

THE sea-coast of Sussex has very high green hills, called the Downs, supposed by some to have been originally coral rocks : as they now consist of chalk ; and marine fossils are frequently found in them.   This supposition is strengthened by the opinion, that Britain was formerly united to the Continent, by an Isthmus which extended from Dover to Calais; for on both these shores the coast projects considerably.

Camden says, " Between Kent and Calais in France, *the land* runs so far out into the sea, and the channel is so contracted, that some are of opinion that a breach was there made to receive the sea, which till that time had been excluded : and to confirm it, they bring *Virgil's* authority,"

> " *Et penitus toto divisos orbe Britannos.*"
> " And *Britain* quite from all the world disjoyn'd."

" *Because,* says *Servius Honoratus, Britain was anciently joyned to to the Continent.*"   And that of *Claudian* they urge, in imitation of Virgil,

> " *Nostro diducta Britannia mundo.*
> And *Britain* sever'd from our world.'"

See Gibson's Translation of Camden's Britannia, page 2, also, page 206.

" The coast of Kent is parted from the Continent of Europe by a narrow sea, where some are of opinion that it wrought itself a passage throw.

" Strabo, inferring what's to come from what's past, concludes that *Isthmus's* or necks of land, both have been wrought throw and and will be again."

Seneca says, " You see that whole countries are torn from their places; and what lay hard by, is now beyond sea. You see a separation of Cities and Nations, so often as part of Nature either moves of itself, or the winds drive some vast sea or other; the force whereof as drawn from the whole is wonderful.   For though it rage but in some part, yet it is of the universal power that it so rages. Thus has the sea rent Spain from the Continent of Africa.   And by that inundation so much talked of by the best Poets, Sicily was cut off from Italy."

    " Whence that of Virgil :

          Hæc loca vi quondam, et vastà convulsa ruinà
          (Tantum ævi longinqua valet mutare vetustas)
          Dissiluisse ferunt, cùm protinus untraque tellus
          Una foret, venit medio vi pontus et undis,
          Hesperium Siculo latus abreidit, arvaque et urbes
          Littore diductas, angusto interluit æstu."

          " These shores long since, as old traditions speak,
          (Such strange disorders powerful time can make)   }
          With violent fury did asunder break.
          When battering waves collecting all their force,
          Thro' solid land urg'd their impetuous course,
          While towns and fields on either side gave way,
          And left free passage for a narrow sea."

" Pliny too has taught us, that *Cyprus* was broken off from Syria, *Eubœa* from Bœotia, *Besbicus* from Bythinia ; which before were parts of the Continent."

" But that Britain was so rent from the Continent, no one of the Ancients has told us ; only those verses of Virgil and Claudian (which I have quoted) along with Servius's conjecture, seem to hint so much."

" Notwithstanding, there are that think so, as *Dominicus Marius Niger, John Twine* a very learned man, (" several English and Foreign Authors,") and whoever he was that wrested these verses concerning Sicily, to Britain :"

————————————————" Britannia quondam
Gallorum pars una fuit, sed pontus et æstus
Mutavere situm, rupit confinia Nereus
Victor : et abscissos interluit æquore montes."
" Once did the British touch the Gallic shore,
Till furious waves the cliffs in sunder tore ;
Thus broke they yielded to the conqu'ring main,
And Neptune still in triumph rides between."

This idea is so elegantly expressed in a Poem which is an honor to our age, (the Giant's Causway, by Dr. DRUMMOND) that it cannot fail of being acceptable to the reader.

Thus, if aright, the philosophic sage
Read the dark records of creation's page,
From Gallia's strand did ocean's rushing tide
The chalky cliffs of Albion erst divide ;
Thus earthquake's fury from Ansonia tore
The sounding caverns of Trinacria's shore :
And Europe saw where great Alcides' hand
Fix'd the proud limits of Hesperian land,
Th' Atlantic floods their feeble barriers cleave,
And o'er the plain a whelming deluge heave,

> Where now the midland billows court the gales,
> And Afric's sands disjoin from Europe's vales.

Camden then observes, that as the authority of writers, has left us no positive information, attention should be paid to the following questions.

Whether the nature of the soil be the same upon both shores? And how broad, and how deep such straits might be?

He then says, that " where the sea is narrowest, both coasts rise with high rocks almost of the same matter and colour. That the Straits are not much broader than those of Gibralter and Sicily, viz. 24 miles : and as that of Sicily does not exceed 80 paces in depth, so this of ours is scarce 25 fathom ; and yet the sea on both sides of it, is much deeper." See these and other curious remarks, page 207.

When the sea forced itself a passage, would not the depth of water by having a current decrease from the Shores? To this day does it not continue to decline on the Southern Coast of Sussex? Camden's observations on Shoreham, Brember, and Portus Adurni, (now Aldrington,) strengthen this opinion ; he says page 173.

" Shoreham, anciently Scone-ham, which by little and little has dwindled into a poor village, now called Old Shoreham ; (having given rise to another town of the same name) the greatest part being ruined and underwater, and the commodiousness of it's Port, by reason of the banks of sand cast up at the mouth of the river, wholly taken away: whereas in former ages, it was wont to carry ships under sail as high as Brember* ;" some suppose from it's name and situation as far as Shiplay.

---

* Brember,' a castle formerly of the Breoses ; supposed to have been built in the reign of Edward the Confessor K. William I. gave it to William de Breose, from whom the Breoses, Lords of Gower and Brecknock are descended, from whom also the Knightly Families

That ancient port called also Portus Adurni, as it seems is scarce three miles off the mouth of the river, where, when the Saxons first infested our seas, the band of *Exploratores* under the Roman Emperors had their station ; but it is now choaked up with heaps of sand driven together.

" Both the name remaining entire, and some near adjacent cottages named *Portslade,* that is, the way to the Port, do in a manner persuade that this was Ederington," now called Aldrington, a *ruin,* the whole of the parish contains neither house nor inhabitant.

Note *b,* Page 1st, L. 3.

" And on the towering Beacon's height."

DITCHLING Beacon, the highest point in the county of Sussex, and where a beacon-light was formerly placed.

These Beacons are a kind of watch-tower, Camden says " they have been in use in England for several ages ; they are sometimes made of a high pile of wood, sometimes of little barrels filled with

---

of the Shirleys" (*now Earl Ferrers*) in this County and Leicestershire.

" Instead of a castle there is now nothing but a heap of ruins ; beneath which lies Steyning, which in Alfred's will, if I mistake not, is called Steyningham.   In latter times, it had a cell of Black Monks, wherein was enshrined St. Cudman, an obscure Saint, and visited by Pilgrims with oblations."   See Camden, page 173.

pitch set on the top of a large pole :" and according to Stephenson's History, from which I find an extract in the notes to the " *Lay of the Last Minstrel* :" sometimes, " of a long and strong tree set up, with a long iron pole across the head of it, and an iron brander fixed on a stalk in the middle of it, for holding a tar-barrel."

" They are placed on the highest eminences, whence they can command a view of the adjacent country ; and thus by being set on fire, give notice of the approach of an enemy ; hence they derive their name from the old word Beacnian, i. e. to beckon."

" In the reign of Henry VIII., the 19th of July, 1545, the French landed a squadron, at Aldrington, with an intention to burn Brighthelmstone and Shoreham ; but the Beacons having been fired in time to alarm the country, a force was soon collected on the Downs, sufficient to intimidate the invaders ; who departed without having done any material injury, Camden says, " they suddenly set one or two cottages on fire at Brighthelmsted."

" Certain Hundreds and Boroughs were obliged, under pain of forfeiture or other penalty, to keep the Beacons in proper condition, and to fire them at the approach of an enemy, in order to alarm and assemble the inhabitants of the Weald."

" These formed the *Night-Watch*, there was also the *Ward*, which consisted of men at arms and horsemen called *Hobilers*, these were settled in several places to signify the approach of the enemy by day ; and seem to have been bound to perform this service by the nature of their tenure. They were a sort of light cavalry, dressed in jackets called *Hobils*, and mounted on fleet horses." These watch and ward keepers, were divided into districts, and entrusted to the care of some Baron or Religious House, by certain Commissioners called, Rectores Comitatus." See the History of Lewes, pages 463–4.

No longer ago, than the year 1803 when there was some expectation of an invasion by the French, several Beacons were placed on the Downs : one by the Telegraph near Brighton, as a signal for the others : and Men stationed to watch, and light them in case of danger, the Men have been lately discharged ; but the Beacons still remain.

Note c, Page 2nd, L. 2.

" Delighted views, and ranges o'er the Weald.."

The fine tract of Country, known by the name of the Weald, ("Weilde") or Wild, comprises the whole of that part which lies between the South Downs and the Surry Hills, being from South to North in many places thirty miles, and from East to West, one hundred and twenty, extending into Kent and Hampshire.

Though it now forms a most beautiful and picturesque appearance, being in a high state of cultivation, and containing a number of towns, villages, churches and gentlemen's seats, as well as many of the best farm-houses, and neatest cottages in Great Britain, and some of the most excellent roads in the island, which have, of late years, been wonderfully improved, through the exertions of some public spirited gentlemen, and the ability, industry, and integrity of Mr. John Heath, of Horsham, under whose very able management, many of them have been placed;* yet this vast tract of land, was formerly one continued wood, unpeopled, and Camden says " unpassable!"

Lambard and Somner, two Kentish Antiquaries, affirm that, " for a great while, the whole Weald was scarcely any thing else, besides a desert and vast wilderness ; not planted with towns, or peopled

---

* Their gold we see the wealthy give Mankind,
  And leisure's envied sons their time bestow ;
 Yet these without the mighty aid of Mind,
 We but a vain incumbrance ever find,
  To Mind alone, we all improvement owe.

with men, but stuffed with herds of deer, and droves of hogs only."—
See Gibson's Translation of Camden's Britannia, page 179, and also,
in his own remarks:—he says, " That no part of the Weald appears
by the several Grants, to have been let out by the King, (the only
Lord and proprietor of it) in *Manours*, but in so many *Dens*, which
implied only a woody place, yielding covert and feeding for cattle;
and that there is no other use of them expressed, but only *Pannage
for hogs.*"

This immense Wood must have long formed a place of retreat and
defence, serving, in a rude State, as a fortified City: and to this, it
appears, fled the Aborigines from the Belgic Adventurer; this was
also the place of retreat from the Romans, and long afforded shelter
against the Saxons. Its first inhabitants were probably Swine-Herds:
mention is made of a Swine-Herd, who here stabbed Sigebert, King
of the West Saxons, after he was deposed, at a place called Pryfetes
Flodan.

Its highest lands appear to have been first cultivated and inhabited:
not only the Churches, but the villages, we may observe stand on
rising ground.

In the reign of Elizabeth, according to Camden, the glass-trade
was carried on here; but, when Gibson translated Camden's Work,
A. D. 1695, there was not a glass-house remaining. In Camden's
time, there were also iron-mines and furnaces for casting it: and
speaking of these also, Gibson says, " it is most famous for the iron-
works, which are in several places of this County; some whereof
have both a furnace and a forge, others a forge only, and some only
a furnace."

They have now however, for about half a century, generally
ceased to work: not from any deficiency of the Ore, but from want
of fuel. The Iron made here has been esteemed superior to that o
any other country. " The rails of that magnificent balustrade
around St. Paul's Church-Yard, London, were cast at Lamberhurst
Furnace, in the Weald of Kent: these rails, which are five feet six
inches high, with seven iron-gates of beautiful workmanship, weighed

two hundred tons, eighty one pounds, and cost sixpence per pound, which with other charges, amounted to £11202. 0s. 6d."

Many of the Cannon on the fortifications of Gibraltar, were cast at Darvel Furnace, near Robertsbridge, in the Weald of Sussex.

Here are also various quarries of grey turbinated Marble: which bears a good polish, and is very hard and durable, if dug up in its perpendicular state; but if horizontally, it usually peels off in flakes.

This Marble was formerly in great esteem in Sussex, for decorating religious buildings. The whole Weald was anciently called Coid Andred, then Lucus Andates, and after that Andradswald: deriving these names, from the adjoining City of Anderida or Caer Andred, latinized by the Roman Settlers in Britain, and called by the Saxons Andred-Ceaster; supposed to have been built in grateful commemoration of a decisive victory, gained there by the Regni over it's former inhabitants. Camden places it as far Eastward as Newenden in Kent: Lambard and Somner, near Hastings and Pevensey; but Dr. Tabor has with more certainty, fixed its site near Eastbourne, where many Roman ruins have been discovered.—See Phil. Transact. and the History of Lewes, page 6.

This City and that of Regnum, which the Saxons named Ringwood, i. e. *the Wood of the Regni*, formed the two chief towns of the Regnian Kingdom.

All that now remains of the once famous Wood of Anderida, as *forest land* in Sussex, are the forests of Arundel, St. Leonard, Word or Worth, Ashdown, Waterdown, and Dallington: and these belong to the six hundreds into which Sussex is divided: namely, Chichester, Arundel, Brember, Lewes, Pevensey, and Hastings, these hundreds have each a river and a castle.

NOTE *d*, PAGE 2nd, L 2.

" Their mighty founder Caius Julius."

CAIUS Julius Cæsar invaded Britain fifty-four years before the
birth of Christ, provoked to do so, some say at the supplies, sent
thence into Gaul; others because the British had received the
Bellovaci; but Suetonius says that he was excited by the hope of
British Pearls, the weight and size of which he would often poise and
and try in his hand; though, that the love of glory actuated him is
the received opinion, and to this surely we may add his desire of
knowledge and his disposition to inquiry: so hateful is the love of
conquest, that we are apt to condemn those who have pursued it, as
instigated only by avarice, revenge, or ambition; yet both Cæsar
and Alexander seem to have had extended and comprehensive views:
though they were doubtless possessed of ambition.

" The' ignoble passion of the noble mind," yet utility, might have
been their first motive.

Cæsar made two expeditions into Britain, and both times landed at
Deal in Kent: he may be said rather to have discovered the Island to the
Romans, than to have conquered it; for, though the Britons agreed to
pay three thousand pounds annually as tribute to Rome, yet this they
soon neglected.

Seneca says, " Claudius might first glory in conquering the Britons,
for Julius Cæsar did no more than shew them to the Romans."

Nor till the reign of the Emperor Claudius, in the 50th Year of
the Christian Æra, could Britain be considered as subject to Rome,
and then only the southern part; but, in the reign of Vespasian,
Agricola was sent into Britain, and as far as it ever was conquered,
(for the Highlands never appear to have been completely subdued,)
it was conquered by him. He also ascertained it to be an Island;

though it was first discovered to be such, by a Cohort of Usipians, who had been raised in Germany and sent over into Britain: these men having killed their Captain, and the Soldiers who were dispersed among them, to teach them military exercise, fled, and embarked in three vessels: after being tossed about on the British Seas, and reduced to great extremities for want of provisions, they at last fed on each other, beginning at the weakest: thus they floated round Britain; and were at last taken as pirates and sold to some merchants; but this adventure first discovered it to be an Island !!

Agricola sent out his admiral to sail round it, who coasting along the nearest side, arrived in safety at the Haven of Trutulensis, from which he had set out: thus he proved it to be an Island and also discovered the Orkney Isles.

NOTE *e*, PAGE 3rd, L. 10.

" For when those Belgians."

Belgic settlers in Surry and Sussex. Cæsar saith, " the innermost parts of Britain, are inhabited by those, who, according to tradition, are believed to be Aborigines: the sea coasts by such as came out of Belgium in Gaul on purpose to make new conquests, and these people are generally called by the names of the Cities whence they came "

" The Belgæ, Cæsar learned of the Rhemi, were descended from the Germans, and passing over the Rhine, were induced by the fruitfulness of the place, after they had expelled the Gauls, to settle there; whence they came over into Britain; but at what time it does not precisely appear: unless possibly when Divitiacus, King of the Suessiones who flourished before Cæsar, had the government of a great part of Gaul, and also of Britain."

H 2

Though these Adventurers were generally named after the Cities from which they came ; yet those who possessed themselves of Sussex and Surry, were called the Regni or Renci, probably from the Celtic verb, reign, to divide: being separated from the other Colonists by the forest of Coid Andred.

Thus we learn from Camden that—

Danmonii included · · · · · · · · · · · · · · · ·	Cornwall, Devonshire.
Durotriges ·	Dorsetshire.
Belgæ ·	Somersetshire, Wiltshire, Hampshire, Isle of Wight.
Atrebates ·	Berkshire.
Regni ·	Surrey, Sussex.
Cantium ·	Kent.
Dobuni ·	Gloucestershire, Oxfordshire.
Cattieuchlani · · · · · · · · · · · · · · · · · · ·	Buckinghamshire, Bedfordshire, Hertfordshire.
Trinobantes ·	Middlesex, Essex.
Iceni ·	Suffolk, Norfolk, Cambridgeshire, Huntingdonshire.
Coritanii ·	Northamptonshire, Leicestershire, Rutlandshire, Lincolnshire, Nottinghamshire, Derbyshire.

Cornavii ······················	{	Warwickshire, Worcestershire, Staffordshire, Shropshire, Cheshire.
Silures ······················	{	Herefordshire, Radnorshire, Brecknockshire, Monmouthshire, Glamorganshire.
Dimetæ ······················	{	Carmarthenshire, Pembrokeshire, Radnorshire.
Ordevices ····················	{	Montgomeryshire, Merionethshire, Carnarvonshire, Anglesea, Denbighshire, Flintshire.
Brigantes·····················	{	Yorkshire, Durham, Lancashire, Westmoreland, Cumberland.
Ottadini ·····················		Northumberland.

Note *f*, Page 4th, L. 11·

" *Here in those days, 'tis said, might ravenous wolves.*"

THAT Wolves have existed in this Country some Writers affirm and others doubt.—PETER HEYLYN in his Cosmography written in 1648, says,

" That the Deer might graze with pleasure, and the Sheep with safety, great care was taken by our Progenitors for the destruction of Wolves. I know it hath been a tradition of old Writers, that England never had any Wolves at all, and that they would not live here, brought from other places; but it is not so: here being store of them, till Edgar King of England commuted the 20lb. of Gold, 500lb. of Silver, and 300 head of Cattle imposed as an yearly tribute by King Athelstane upon Idwallo Prince of Wales, for the like yearly tribute of 300 Wolves: by which means they were quite rooted out in time, the Welch protesting at the last they could find no more."

———

Note g, Page 5th, L. 7.

" Thro' which, their military roads."

"These were called by the Romans, *Viæ Consulares, Regiæ, Prætoriæ, Militares, Publicæ, Cursus Publici,* and *Actus,* as we find by Ulpian and Julius Frontinus. Ammianus Marcellinus, calls them *Aggeres Itinerarii,* and *Publici:* Sidonius Apollinaris, *Aggeres* and *tellures inaggeratæ:* Bede and modern Authors Stratæ."

These High-Ways were made by the Romans, and went from sea to sea, they consisted of four principal ones, viz.

> Watling-streat,
> Ikenild-streat,
> Erming-streat,
> And the Fosse."

" Near upon these roads, were the Cities built, as also inns or mansions for the accommodation of travellers with all necessaries and mutations (for so those places were then called) where travellers could change their post-horses, draught-beasts, or waggons."

"At the end of every mile along these roads, there were erected Pillars by the Emperors, with figures cut in them to signify the number of miles."

"By the sides of them were also the graves and monuments of famous men."

"For the repairing of these ways, there were standing laws, as we may see in the Theodosian Code, under the title *De Itinere muniendo.*"

"There were also overseers appointed for them. And in our ancient laws, there is mention made *De pace quatuor Cheminorum,* that is, of the peace of the four principal roads." See Camden, page 66.

According to some Antiquaries, it appears that Ermin-streat began at Newhaven, in Sussex; went through Rodmil and Lewes, and then by the Surrey Stane-streat, at Croyden and Streatham, and to have crossed the Thames at the ferry called Stangate, by Lambeth. A branch of Ermin-streat was accidentally discovered on St. John's Common in 1779, and some years after a Roman Bath was found between Clayton Church and the Rectory: and as Baths were placed by those ways, this was most probably a continuation of the same branch. Many of these ways may be traced in the Weald, Camden says, "The famous High-way Stane-streat causeway, which is in some places ten yeards broad, but in most seven, comes to Arundel out of Surrey by Billingshurst.* It is a yard and a half deep in stones (which they discover by passages to let in water,) and runs in a streight line. It is made of flints and pebbles, though no flints are found within seven miles of it." See page 171.

---

* No longer since than the year 1811, a Roman Bath was discovered at Bignor, between Billingshurst and Arundel.

NOTE *h*, PAGE 5th, L. 16.

" For, Phœnix like."

ROLLIN, in speaking of the city of Heliopolis in Egypt, gives the following account of this most extraordinary Bird.

" Of this kind of birds, if we may believe the ancients, there is never but one at a time in the world. He is brought forth in Arabia, lives five or six hundred years, and is of the size of an eagle. His head is adorned with a shining and most beautiful crest; the feathers of his neck are of a gold colour, and the rest of a purple, his tail is white, intermixed with red, and his eyes sparkling like stars. When he is old, and finds his end approaching, he builds a nest with wood and aromatic spices, and then dies. Of his bones and marrow, a worm is produced, out of which another Phœnix is formed. His first care is to solemnize his parent's obsequies, for which purpose he makes up a ball in the shape of an egg, with abundance of perfumes of myrrh, as heavy as he can carry, which he often essays beforehand ; then he makes a hole in it, where he deposits his parent's body, and closes it carefully with myrrh and other perfumes. After this he takes up the precious load on his shoulders, and flying to the alter of the sun, in the city of Heliopolis , he there burns it."

" Herodotus and Tacitus dispute the truth of some of the circumstances of this account, but seem to suppose it true in general. Pliny, on the contrary, in the very beginning of his account of it, insinuates plainly enough, that he looks upon the whole as fabulous ; and this is the opinion of all modern authors."

" This ancient tradition, though grounded on an evident falsehood, hath yet introduced into almost all languages, the custom of giving the name of Phœnix to whatever is singular and uncommon in its kind."

Tacitus in his Annals Book vi. says

"In the consulship of Paulus Fabius and Lucius Vitellius,* after a long vicissitude of ages, the Phœnix arrived in Egypt, and furnished the most learned of the natives and Greeks, with matter of large and various observations concerning that miraculous bird. The circumstances in which they agree, with many others, that however disputed, deserve to be known, claim a recital here. That it is a creature sacred to the sun, and, in the fashion of its head, and diversity of feathers, distinct from other birds, all who have described its figure, are agreed; about the length of its life; relations vary. It is by the vulgar tradition fixed at five hundred years: but there are those who extend it to one thousand four hundred and sixty-one, and assert that the three former Phœnixes appeared in reigns greatly distant; the first under Sesostris, the next under Amasis; and that one was seen under Ptolemy the third king of Egypt of the Macedonian race, and flew to the city of Heliopolis, accompanied by a vast host of other birds gazing upon the wonderful stranger. But these are, in truth, the obscure accounts of antiquity: between Ptolemy and Tiberius the interval was shorter, not two hundred and fifty years; hence some have believed that the present was a spurious Phœnix, and derived not its origin from the territories of Arabia, since it observed nothing of the instinct which ancient tradition attributes to the genuine; for that the latter, having completed his course of years, just before his death builds a nest in his native land, and upon it sheds generative power, from whence arises a young one, whose first care, when he is grown, is to bury his father; neither does he undertake it unadvisedly, but by collecting and fetching loads of myrrh, tries his strength in great journies; and as soon as he finds himself equal to the burden, and fit for the long flight, he rears upon his back his father's body, carries it quite to the altar of the sun, and then flies away. These are uncertain tales, and

---

* Consuls in the reign of Tiberius, in the 34th year of the Christian Æra.

their uncertainty heightened by fables; but that this bird has been sometimes seen in Egypt, is not questioned."

In the notes to Lalla Rookh is the following extract from Richardson.

" In the East, they suppose the Phœnix to have fifty orifices in his bill, which are continued to his tail; and that after living one thousand years, he builds himself a funeral pile, sings a melodius air of different harmonies through his fifty organ pipes, flaps his wings with a velocity which sets fire to the wood, and consumes himself."

═══

Note i, Page 8th, L. 14.

" By later Britons named, the Pict and Scot."

THAT these were originally one people with the inhabitants of South Britain, most Antiquaries allow as to the Picts; but many are of opinion that the Scots are descended from the Irish; the following quotation however, " From a Dissertation concerning the Poems of Ossian," appears so clear, as probably to end further disputes, and almost past doubt, to prove them to have been one people.

" When South Britain yielded to the power of the Romans, the unconquered nations to the North of the province were distinguished by the name of *Caledonians.* From this very name, it appears, that they were of those *Gauls,* who possessed themselves originally of Britain. It is compounded of two Celtic words, *Caël* signifying *Celts,* or *Gauls,* and *Dun* or *Don, a hill*; so that *Cael-don* or Caledonians, is as much as to say, the *Celts of the hill country.* The Highlanders, to this day, call themselves Caël, their language *Caëlic,* or *Galic,* and their country Caëldock, which the Romans softened into Caledonia. This of itself, is sufficient to demonstrate that they are the genuine descendants of the ancient Caledonians, and not a pretended colony of Scots, who settled first in the north, in the third or fourth century."

"Towards the latter end of the third and the beginning of the fourth century, we meet with the *Scots* in the north. Porphyrius *
makes the first mention of them about that time. As the *Scots* were not heard of before that period, most writers supposed them to have been a colony, newly come to Britain, and that the *Picts* were the only genuine descendants of the ancient Caledonians. This mistake is easily removed. The Caledonians, in process of time, became naturally divided into two distinct nations, as possessing parts of the country, intirely different in their nature and soil. The western coast of Scotland is hilly and barren; towards the East the country is plain, and fit for tillage. The inhabitants of the mountains, a roving and uncontrouled race of men, lived by feeding of cattle, and by what they killed in hunting. Their employment did not fix them to one place. They removed from one heath to another, as suited best with their convenience and inclination. They were not, therefore, improperly called by their neighbours, *Scuite,* or *the wandering nation,* which is evidently the origin of the Roman name of *Scoti.*"

" On the other hand, the Caledonians, who possessed the eastern coast of Scotland, as the division of the country was plain and fertile, applied themselves to agriculture, and the raising of corn. It was from this, that the Gaelic name of the *Picts* proceeded; for they are called, in that language, *Cruithnick,* i. e. *the wheat or corn eaters.* As the Picts lived in a country, so different in its nature from that possessed by the Scots, so their national character suffered a material change. Unobstructed by mountains, or lakes, their communication with one another was free and frequent. Society, therefore, became sooner established among them, than among the Scots, and, conse- quently, they were much sooner governed by civil magistrates and

* St. Hierom and Ctesiphon.

laws. This at last produced so great a difference in the manners of the two nations, that they began to forget their common origin, and almost continual quarrels and animosities subsisted between them. These animosities, after some ages, ended in the subversion of the Pictish Kingdom, but not in the total extirpation of the nation, according to most of the Scots writers, who seemed to think it more for the honour of their countrymen to annihilate a rival people, than to reduce them under obedience."

" It is certain, however, that the very name of the Picts was lost; and those that remained were so completely incorporated with their conquerors, that they soon lost all memory of their own origin."

" The end of the Pictish government is placed so near that period, to which authentic annals reach, that it is matter of wonder, that we have no monuments of their language or history remaining. This favours the system I have laid down. Had they originally been of a different race from the Scots, their language of course would be different. The contrary is the case. The names of places in the Pictish dominions, and the very names of their kings, which are handed down to us, are of Gaelic original, which is a convincing proof that the two nations were, of old, one and the same, and only divided into two governments, by the effect which their situation had upon the genius of the people."

―――

Note *j*, Page 9th, L 5.

" *The Britons to the Saxons.*"

" MANY are of opinion, that the Saxons are descended from the Saci, the most powerful people of Asia, and from them called Sacasones, that is the Sons of the Sacæ: that they came by little and little into Europe, out of Sythia or Sarmatia Asiatica, along with the Getes, the Swevi, and the Daci."

"When they first began to have a name in the world, they lived in Cimbrica Chersonesus, which we now call Denmark ; where they are placed by Ptolemy, who is the first that makes mention of them."

"Afterwards passing the river Albis,* part of them, by degrees broke in upon the Suevian Territories, at this day the Dukedom of Saxony, and part took possession of Frisia and Batavia, which the Franks had quitted. From which time, all the inhabitants, of that sea-coast of Germany who lived by piracy, have gone under the name of the Saxons, as before they were called Franks."

"The Saxon Nation, as is observed by Fabius Quæstor Ethelwerd, who was of the royal line of the Saxons, included all the sea-coast between the river Rhine and the city Donia, now called Dane-marc."

From this coast it was, that the Saxons, encouraged by the many slaughters of the Romans, frequently broke into their Provinces, and for a long time annoyed this Island; even to such a degree, that the Romans were obliged to guard the coasts, by stationing troops and a fleet, under the command of an officer called *Comes Littares Saxonici.* See Camden, page 125.

When the Roman Garrisons abandoned Britain in the year A. D. 422, and in the reign of Valentinian the younger, the Roman Empire in this Island fully expired, it being the 476th Year from Cæsar's coming in. The Britons, thus left to form their own government, and choose their own rulers, nothing but dissensions and contests for superiority arose: the Picts and Scots taking advantage of their situation, poured down among them in great numbers; till at last Vortigern, whom the Britons had constituted their General or who had usurped that title, in order to secure his own government and to recover the sinking state, sent for assistance to the Saxons.

He was, says Ninnius, " apprehensive of danger from the Picts and Scots, from the Roman power, and from Aurelius Ambrosius," the rightful claimant of the Crown.

---

* Elbe.

Note *k*, Page 10, L. 10.

" *Jutes.*"

So called according to Camden, " from the Gutes, Getes, or Goths, and inhabited the upper part of Cimbrica Chersonesus, which the Danes to this day call Juitland, (*now Jutland.*) It is possible they may have descended from the Gutti, whom Ptolemy places in Scandia, and whose present seat is Gothland. But not the country of those Goths, who conquered and over-run Europe: since the most ancient, the best and most approved writers have told us, that they lived beyond the Ister, near the Euxine Sea, and were formerly called Getes."

Note *l*, Page 10, L 11.

" *Angles.*"

Camden says " between Juitland and Holsatia (the ancient seat of the Saxons,) there is a small province in the kingdom of Denmark, and under the City of Flemsberg, called at this day Angel, which Lindebergius, in his Epistles, terms *Little England*; Camden quotes that ancient Author Ethelwerd; who writes thus; " Old *Anglia* is situated between the Saxons and Giots, the capital town whereof is called in Saxon *Sleswick*, but by the Danes Slaithby. In the very same place Ptolemy seems to seat the Saxons."

" These Angles, marching into the inner quarters of Germany, and mixing themselves with the *Longobards* and *Suevians*, broke into Italy, and are generally supposed to have left behind them some relics of their name; such are Engelheim, (the native country of

Charles the Great) Ingolstad, Engleburg, Englerute in Germany, and
Engleria in Italy."

The Frisians it appears came also with the Angles into Britain:
Camden has an extract from Procopius, whose work was not extant
when he wrote: but which was sent to him from a copy in the King's
Library at Paris, and transcribed for him by Fransciscus Pithæus,
which says " The Island Britain is inhabited by three most populous
nations, each whereof has their several Kings.—The names of the
people are the Angles, the Frisones, and those of the same name with
the island of the Britons."

According to Tacitus the Frisians inhabited along the sea-coast,
between the Rhine and the Amisia, *(now Embs.)*

These are the several people of Germany who seated themselves in
Britain. That they were but one nation, and called by one general
name, sometimes Saxons, sometimes Angles, or (to distinguish them
from those left behind in Germany) Anglo-Saxons; is pretty plain
from Gildas, Boniface, Bede, Paulus Diaconus, and others.

The exact time when they were invited into Britain, is a dispute
among Writers, according to some in 428, others say 448.

NOTE *m*, PAGE 14, L. 4.

" *The heights of Idra such, such Snowdon's Towers* "

Snowden, the highest Mountain in Wales, 3456 feet above the
level of the sea.—Mr. PENNANT observes, " that, from the top, it
seems propped by four vast buttresses; between which are four deep
cwms, or hollows: each, excepting one, has one or more lakes,
lodged in its distant bottom. The nearest Flynnon Las, or the
Green Well, the waters of which from this height, appear black and
unfathomable, and the edges quite green. From thence is a succession

of bottoms, surrounded by lofty and rugged hills, the greatest part of whose sides are perfectly mural, and form the most magnificent amphitheatre in nature. The Wyddfa is on one side; Crib-y-distill, with its serrated tops, on another; Crib Goch, a ridge of fiery redness, appears beneath the preceeding; and opposite to it is the boundary called Lliwedd. Another very singular support to this mountain is Y Clawdd Goch, rising into a sharp ridge, so narrow as not to afford breadth even for a path." He also observes that the view from this exalted situation is unbounded, that he saw from it the county of Chester, the high hills of Yorkshire, part of the north of England, Scotland, and Ireland: a plain view of the Isle of Man; and that of Anglesey, with every rill visible. Mr. Pennant's account of ascending Snowden, is too interesting to be omitted.

"I took much pains to see this prospect to advantage: sat up at a farm on the west, till about twelve, and walked up the whole way. The night was remarkably fine and starry: towards morn, the stars faded away, and left a short interval of darkness, which was soon dispersed by the dawn of day. The body of the sun appeared more distinct, while the rotundity of the moon before it, rose high enough to render its beams too brilliant for our sight. The sea which bounded the western part was gilt by its rays, first in slender streaks, at length glowing with redness. The prospect was disclosed like the gradual drawing up of a curtain in a theatre. We saw more and more, till the heat became so powerful, as to attract the mists from the various lakes, which, in a slight degree, obscured the prospect. The shadow of the mountain was flung many miles, and shewed its decapitated form; the Wyddfa making one, the Crib-y-distill the other head. I counted this time between twenty and thirty lakes, either in this county, or Meirioneddshire. The day proved so excessively hot, that my journey cost me the skin of the lower part of my face, before I reached the resting-place, after the fatigue of the morning."

In North Wales, there are two mountain ranges, the summit of Snowdon forms the most elevated point of the more northern, and

Cader Idris that of the other. The Snowdon chain is constituted of the whole mountainous tracts of Caernarvonshire. The mountain chain of which Cader Idris forms the most elevated part, is in Merionethshire, and consists of many lofty peaks, among which, are the Arrans, and Arennags."

"Cader Idris, is in height next to Snowden, 2914 feet above the sea and rises on its shore, close upon the northern side of the estuary of the small river Disynwy. It is very steep and craggy on every side; but the southern descent, especially to the border of Talyllyn lake, is the most precipitous, being nearly perpendicular. Its breadth bears but small proportion to its length; a line passing along its base, and intersecting the summit, would scarcely equal four miles and a half; and, in the other parts, it is a mere ridge, whose base hardly ever exceeds one mile in breadth. It is much loftier, and more craggy, than the slates and secondary mountains which surround it."

The lakes in the midst of this Alpine scenery add much to its beauty, and present a most striking contrast; being in Merioneth, placid, and smooth as glass or polished steel, nearly surrounded by gently rising hills, and hanging woods, where wave the larch, pine, and mountain ash, which, descending even to the shores of the lakes, fringe with graceful foliage their banks; amid which rise the habitations of taste or sequestered greatness;—whilst, around those of Caernarvon, neither leaf nor shrub is to be seen, but bounded by craggy rocks and mountains, which, though containing slate and lead mines, are entirely barren on their surface, and of an immense and almost perpendicular height: these lakes appear deep, black, and gloomy, awfully sublime, imposingly wild and majestic, offering no place for the dwelling of Man, but receiving bold and rushing torrents, which forbid, in foaming thunder, the human voice to be heard, or human footsteps to approach; as if indeed formed by nature, for the residence of her Bards, ere Edward's cruel policy destroyed their race, who might oft have felt less isolated here, than in the city's tumult, amid the stupifying hum of Men.

H

Such are the mountains and lakes of Wales; but language is inadequate to convey a just idea of their beauty: they must be seen to be known and felt, for they are capable of making us feel, and of exciting that exquisite pleasure, which all lovers of nature, who have been among mountain scenery, can comprehend, but which no words can describe, to those,

> Who ne'er with her, in happiest sympathy,
> Sweet converse hold.

────

Note n, Page 14th, L. 8.

"*Here Gelert's grave.*"

BEDDGELERT, a village near Snowdon and not far from the conflux of the Colwyn and the Glasllyn, of which a traditionary account is recorded by the bards, stating " that their prince Llewelyn [*] had a hunting seat at this place, and, during the absence of the family, a wolf entered the house, and Llewelyn returning first, was met at the door by his favorite greyhound Gelert,[†] whose mouth was covered with blood. The prince, alarmed at the circumstance, hastened in, and found the cradle overturned, and the ground wet with gore. In his momentary alarm for the fate of his infant son, supposing that it had been killed by the dog, he drew his sword, and stabbed the animal, while it was in the act of caressing its master. But what was the consternation of the latter, when, on turning up the cradle, he found his son alive, and sleeping by the side of the wolf; which had

---

[*] Llewelyn ap Jorwerth, who began his reign in 1194.

[†] This dog was a present to him from his father-in-law King John.

been slain by the faithful and vigilant Gelert. The circumstance appears to have had such an effect on the prince's mind, that he erected a tomb over the dog's grave, on the spot, where subsequently a conventual church was built, which was from this incident, denominated Bedd Gelert, or the grave of Gelert."

" Llewelyn also founded a monastry here for the good of his soul, and as a grateful offering to divine Providence, for the preservation of his child."—No part of this building now remains, but it is probable the present very pretty church has at times, been repaired out of the ruins.

> Devoted Gelert! in thy hapless fate,
>   As in a mirror, numbers view their own:
>   Ah! have not many false construction known,
> And even affection's faithfulness,—too late?
> Yes! when the cradled covering is removed,
>   And stains, as on that watchful dog, are seen
>   In their true colors;—then regret most keen,
> Like poor Llewelyn's, o'er the tomb beloved,
> Is theirs alas! who hastily condemned;
>   And, ere inquiry taught them to be just,
>   Could to fierce passion's sudden impulse trust,
> And plunge a death-wound, in such faithful friend:
> Who, still confiding, foresaw this regret!
> And from the silent tomb, would say, *forget*.

The course of the Aber-Glasllyn, which, for some miles, divides the counties of Merioneth and Caernarvon, presents some of the most striking scenery in Wales; winding itself through a deep ravine of the mountains, which rise immediately on its banks, to a most tremendous and almost perpendicular height. Giraldus says, " that, if the shepherds conversing together from their summits, should agree to meet, they could scarcely effect their purpose in the course of the whole day."—No appearance of vegetable or animal life is to be

seen, save here and there a solitary goat, hanging on the rocky sides
of the mountains.—The entrance to this extraordinary pass, is by a
narrow road, on the edge of the river, from which it is separated,
by a low narrow wall, of loose stones: this entrance soon becomes
imperceptible to the eye, the road continuing on the side of the
Glasllyn, its circuitous windings render invisible the opposite
opening, and the traveller appears suddenly immured in this
astonishing chasm.

The road which leads through such wonderful scenes of Nature,
conducts to what is equally astonishing in Art; the embankment from
the sea of six thousand acres of land, formerly an entire bed of sand,
denominated the Traeth Mawr; but now presenting to the eye, land
in a high state of cultivation, on a part of which stands the interesting
little town of Tre-Madoc.—This embankment also opens an advantageous communication, between Merioneth and Caernarvonshire:
for this great and beneficent undertaking, the nation is indebted to
William Alexander Madox, Esq. Tre-Madoc is seven miles west of
Bedd-gelert.

> See Ocean, with despotic power, advance,
> To grasp from Cambria her native shores;
> Or spread his wily sands, to lure their steps,
> Who, wearied with the mountains' stony heights,
> Seek their path homeward o'er the smooth Traeth-Mawr.
>
> Alas! what numbers weep these treacherous sands!
> Here, deep imbedded, a fond mother sinks,
> Who ne'er again shall clasp her little race,
> Nor cheer her husband with affection's smile.
> Nor is this grief a solitary woe,
> On the same eve, a father and his son,
> Save a few steps had reached the mountain's side,
> When, deep ingulphed, they sank; leaving a tribe
> Of hapless females, to deplore their loss!
> Three generations felt the bitter pang.

The aged mother clasps her widowed child,
Whilst, round their knees, the weeping daughters cling,
And on their sire and brother call in vain.
　Dreadful such eve! but ah, more dreadful far,
Ere that the earth had traced her annual course,
Many such eves must Cambria have wept,
O'er her lost sons, deep in these sands interred
By Ocean's billowy and impetuous tide.
No funeral chaunt, no sacred rites were theirs,
But Snowdon, with a pitying eye beheld,
And o'er them howled a melancholy dirge.
　These direful sands, which Earth and Ocean claimed,
Seemed as by Nature for her senate formed;
Hither oft came the spirit of the storm,
And oft the spirit of the northern blast,
The mountain, river, cataract, the rocks,
The floods, all hither frequent came, to meet
The spirit of the deep and distant seas,
And here their elemental council hold.
Successive ages found this spot unchanged.
The briny surge still rolled triumphant o'er,
Horror and devastation, scattering round :
Nor yet had intellect, nor feeling strong,
The means discovered to remove the ill.
　But, 'mong the generous sons of Cambria, rose
One, who, by Ancestorial right, was hers,
And well became the lineage of his sires.
He, with deep thought, and philosophic mind,
His heart alive to others weal and woe,
And all the patriot glowing in his soul,
Devised a project, mighty as his mind.
He checked the' impetuous billows in their course,
And limits to the swelling Ocean gave.

118 NOTES.

Then, wide around, the waving corn-fields smiled,
The meadows rich, the gardens' bounteous store,
Flowers, fruits, and herbage, crowned the watery waste,
And the Traeth-Mawr a second Eden bloomed!
Nor such alone, the dwellings of Mankind,
From the low roof, to all that taste can give,
Adorn this lovely scene;—nor is forgot
The holy temple of Britannia's land,
Where Man in social sympathy unites,
And, with one voice, an equal Parent owns.
Here too consideration just and wise,
Kindly erected a more humble fane,
The liberty of conscience to allow.

　Behold this work, ye triflers of a day!
See what a Madox in few years has done,
And own, *important is the life of Man!*

Note o, Page 15, L. 4.

" He seemed to stand, like Java's fabled Tree."

The Upas or Poison Tree in the island of Java is thus described by N. P. Foersch, a surgeon belonging to the Dutch East India Company who was stationed at Batavia, in the year 1774.

"The Bohon Upas is situated in the island of Java, about 27 leagues from Batavia. It is surrounded on all sides by a circle of high hills and mountains; and the country round it, to the distance of ten or twelve miles from the tree, is entirely barren. Not a tree nor a shrub, nor even the least plant or grass, is to be seen. To this tree the criminals are sent for the poison, into which all warlike instruments are dipped."

"The poison is a gum, that issues out like Camphor from between the bark and the tree itself. Malefactors, condemned to death, are

the only persons employed to fetch this poison, which is the only
chance they have of saving their lives. They are provided with a
silver or tortoise-shell box, and are properly instructed how to proceed while they are upon their dangerous expedition, viz. they are
told to go to the tree before the wind ; so that the effluvia from the
tree may be blown from them, and they are told to use the utmost
despatch. They are then sent to the old priest, who lives on the con-
fines of the desert, who prepares them for their future fate, by prayers
and admonitions. When about to depart, he gives them a long
leathern cap with two glasses before their eyes, which comes down
as far as their breast ; and also provides them with a pair of leather
gloves. They are then conducted by the priest and their relations about
two miles on their journey. Here the priest repeats his instructions,
and tells them where they are to look for the tree : he shows them a
hill which they are to ascend, and on the other side they will find a
rivulet, which they are to follow, and which will conduct them
directly to the Upas-tree. They now take leave of each other, and,
amidst prayers for their success, the delinquents hasten away. The
old priest assured me, that during his residence there, of 30 years, he
had dismissed upwards of seven hundred criminals ; and that scarcely
two out of twenty ever returned ! all I could learn from one who
returned was, that it stood on the borders of a rivulet, that it was of
a middling size, that five or six young trees grew round it, but that
no other plant, shrub, or atom of vegetation, was to be seen within
miles of it ; and that numerous skeletons were in every direction
scattered round it.''

That this account is partly fabulous there cannot be much doubt,
the Author's Brother who was a short time at Batavia could not hear
of such a tree ; though there appear to be Upas *trees,* since a French
traveller relates that a friend of his assured him, he had frequently
stood under their shade without receiving the smallest injury : and in
that elegant and truly interesting little work, the Oriental Voyager
by J. JOHNSON, Esq. R. N.—he says, " the whole of Mr. FOERSCH's

account, may be set down as an ingenious fiction; though there is no doubt that they are possessed of a most dreadful poison, wherever they may procure it, with which they occasionally poison their arrows and other weapons.—Speaking of the Malays, he says,—

"It is well known how dangerous those people are with their poinards, called kreeses, or kresses, especially when they take opium, and run the *muck*, stabbing every one they meet. It is said these weapons are poisoned with the celebrated juice of the *Upas* tree, but I believe very few of them have this property. I was once bargaining with a Malay for one of those kresses, which he said was deadly poisoned, and in drawing it out of the scabbard, cut myself between the fore-finger and thumb, at which I was not a little alarmed; an old man, however, who was standing by, opening a leaf of betel, took out a piece of *chunam* and applied it to the part: whether this had any effect or not I cannot tell, but I felt no more of the cut."

"It is probable that the greater number of their *kresses* are poisoned, merely by heating them red hot, and then plunging them into *lime juice:* the rust thus produced on the surface, and in the grooves of these weapons, leaves a most dangerous wound: not, however, so dreadfully fatal as the gum of the celebrated Upas-tree is said to be."

The pen of Dr. DARWIN has in immortal substance this "airy nothing" clad.

> "Where seas of glass with gay reflection smile,
> Round the green coast of Java's palmy isle,
> A spacious plain extends its upland scene,
> Rocks rise on rocks, and fountains gush between:
> Soft zephyrs blow, eternal summers reign,
> And showers prolific bless the soil,—in vain!
> No spicy nutmeg scents the vernal gales,
> Nor tow'ring plantain shades the mid-day vales;
> No *step retreating*, on the sand impress'd,
> Invites the visit of a *second guest!*

Fierce, in dread silence, on the blasted heath
Fell *Upas* sits, the *hydra tree* of death.
Lo! from one root, th' envenom'd soil below,
A thousand vegetative serpents grow :
In shining rays the scaly monster spreads,
O'er ten square leagues, his far diverging heads,
Steep'd in fell poison, as his sharp teeth part,
A thousand tongues in quick vibrations dart ;
Snatch the proud eagle tow'ring o'er the *heath*,
Or pounce the lion, as he stalks beneath :
Or strew, as marshall'd hosts contend in vain,
With human skeletons the whiten'd plain.''

NOTE *p*, PAGE 16th, L. 7.

" *What tho' still Conwy's waves reflect those towers.*"

Conwy Castle, on the river Conwy in Caernarvonshire, built in
1284, by the command of Edward the first, as a security against, and
to over-awe the Welch ;—" Not long after its erection, Edward was
besieged in it, and by famine reduced almost to an unconditional surrender ; but he was extricated by the arrival of a fleet, with provisions
and reinforcements.''

" It appears to have remained uninjured, though surrendered to
the parliamentary forces, when they took the town of Conwy by storm,
in 1646 ; till the restoration of Charles, when, by a grant from him,
it came into the possession of the Earl of Conwy and Kilulta ; who
ordered an Agent to remove the timber, iron, lead, and other valuable materials, and transported them to Ireland, under a pretence that
he did so for His Majesty's service ; and this noble pile was rendered
roofless and floorless, and the whole nearly reduced to its present

condition; though, by being thus exposed, it has suffered material injuries from winds and weather."

" As in the pride and grandeur of its strength, a more beautiful fortress never arose in the precincts of Britain;—so as a ruin it is now no where surpassed.—This majestic building stands on a super-eminent rock, the base of which is washed by a noble tide river ; and it is said, no fortified building, viewed as a whole, or with its com-ponent parts examined in detail, can exceed this structure in grandeur and relative proportions."

Here Edward and his consort Eleanor, accompanied by the chief English nobility and gentry, spent a Christmas;—and that hall, whose ruinous arches and broken walls are now clad with darksome ivy in the most fantastic forms and luxuriant profusion, echoed to all the festive sounds of feudal times ;—hence also issued many of the severe edicts against the Welch.

> As thus we see the Despot's Hold decay
>   Freedom bright hopes amid the ruin finds,
> Which whisper that tyrannic grasp gives way,
>   As Time on every mouldering turret binds
> The happy omen of a milder day.

NOTE *q*, PAGE 23rd, L 14.

" *Can they from feudal villanage.*"

" THE origin of the feudal establishments is attributed by the generality of the best writers principally to the northern nations, (which in the fourth and fifth centuries over-ran the western part of the Roman Empire,) and at length out of its ruins formed the principal of the various states and governments, into which we now see Europe divided."   HARGRAVE.

" The feudal law was established by those nations who overturned the Roman Empire. The first of these were the Vandals, the Suevi, and the Alani. They inhabited the countries bordering on the Baltic. About the year 406, they made an irruption into Gaul; from Gaul, they advanced into Spain; about the year 415, they were driven from Spain by the Visigoths, and invaded Africa, where they formed a kingdom. About the year 431, the Franks, the Allemmanni, and the Burgundians penetrated into Gaul. Of these nations the Franks became the most powerful; and having either subdued or expelled the others, made themselves masters of the whole of those extensive provinces, which from them received the name of France. Pannonia and Illyricum, were conquered by the Huns: Rhætia, Noricum and Vindelicia, by the Ostrogoths: and these were, sometime after, conquered by the Franks. In 449, the Saxons invaded Great Britain. The Herulians marched into Italy, under the command of their king Odoacre, and in 476, overturned the Empire of the West. From Italy, in 493, they were expelled by the Ostrogoths. About the year 568, the Lombards issuing from the Mark of Brandenburgh, invaded the higher Italy, and founded an empire, called the kingdom of the Lombards. After this, little remained in Europe of the Roman empire, besides the middle and inferior Italy. These, on the final division of that empire, between the sons of Theodosius, in 395, had fallen to the share of the emperor of the East, who governed them by an officer called the exarch, whose residence was fixed at Ravenna, and by some subordinate officers, called dukes. In 743, the exarchate of Ravenna, and all the remaining possessions of the emperor in Italy, were conquered by the Lombards. This, as it was the final extinction of the Roman empire in Europe, was the completion, in that quarter of the globe, of those conquests which established the law of the feud."

Blackstone says, " Folk-land, or estates held in Villenage, was a species of tenure neither strictly Feodal, Norman, or Saxon; but mixed and compounded of them all, and which also, on account of

the heriots that usually attend it, may seem to have somewhat Danish
in its composition.   Under the Saxon government there were, as Sir
William Temple speaks, a sort of people in a condition of downright
servitude, used and employed in the most servile works, and belonging,
both they, their children, and effects; to the lord of the soil, like the
rest of the cattle or stock upon it.   These seem to have been those
who held what was called the folk-land, from which they were re-
moveable at the lord's pleasure.   On the arrival of the Normans here,
it seems not improbable, that they, who were strangers to any other
than a feodal state, might give some sparks of enfranchisement to such
wretched persons as fell to their share, by admitting them, as well as
others, to the oath of fealty; which conferred a right of protection,
and raised the tenant to a kind of estate superior to downright slavery,
but inferior to every other condition.   This they called villenage,
and the tenants villeins, either from the word vilis, or else as Sir
Edward Coke tells us, a villa; because they lived chiefly in villages,
and were employed in rustic works of the most sordid kind."

 "These villeins, belonging principally to lords of manors, were either
villeins regardant, that is, annexed to the manor or land : or else they
were in gross, or at large, that is, annexed to the person of the lord,
and transferrable by deed from one owner to another.   They could
not leave their lord without his permission; but, if they ran away, or
were purloined from him, might be claimed and recovered by action,
like beasts or other chattles.   They held indeed small portions of
land by way of sustaining themselves and families; but it was at the
mere will of the lord, who might dispossess them whenever he
pleased; and it was upon villein services, that is, to carry out dung,
to hedge and ditch the lord's demesnes, and any other the meanest
offices : and their services were not only base, but uncertain both as
to their time and quantity."

 "A villein could acquire no property either in lands or goods :
but, if he purchased either, the lord might enter upon them, oust the
villein, and seise them to his own use, unless he contrived to dispose

of them again before the lord had seized them, for the lord had then
lost his opportunity."

"In many places also a fine was payable to the lord, if the villein
presumed to marry his daughter to any one without leave from the
lord: and, by the common law, the lord might also bring an action
against the husband for damages in thus purloining his property. For
the children of villeins were also in the same state of bondage with
their parents."

"From the tenure of pure villenage have sprung our present copy-
hold tenures, or tenures by copy of court roll at the will of the lord."

———

Note r, Page 25th, L. 10·

"And purified descends! for chivalry."

"The first, most universal, and esteemed the most honourable
species of tenure, was that by knight-service, called in Latin *servitium
militare*, and in law-French *chivalry*, or *service de chivaler*. This
differed in very few points, from a pure and proper feud, being
entirely military, and the genuine effect of the feodal establishment in
England. To make a tenure by knight-service, a determinate
quantity of land was necessary, which was called a knight's fee
feodum militare.—The heir to a knight's fee when he came of full age,
received the order of knighthood, he was compelled to take it upon
him, or else pay a fine to the king. For, in those heroical times, no
person was qualified for deeds of arms and chivalry who had not
received this order, which was conferred with much preparation and
solemnity. If the Knight died without heirs of his blood, or if his
blood was corrupted and stained by commission of treason or felony;
whereby every inheritable quality was entirely blotted out and
abolished, in such cases the land escheated, or fell back, to the

lord of the fee; that is, the tenure was determined by breach of the original condition, expressed or implied in the feodal donation."

BLACKSTONE.

That chivalry comprised a high sense of honor is evident from its court. Blackstone says " the court military, or court of chivalry hath cognizance of contracts and other matters touching deeds of arms and war, as well out of the realm as within it. And from its sentences an appeal lies immediately to the king in person. This court was in great reputation in the times of pure chivalry, and afterwards during our connexions with the continent, by the territories which our princes held in France: but is now grown almost entirely out of use, on account of the feebleness of its jurisdiction, and want of power to enforce its judgments; as it can neither fine nor imprison, not being a court of record.—Whenever the common law can give redress, this court hath no jurisdiction, its claim was to give relief to such of the nobility and gentry as think themselves aggrieved in matters of honour; and to keep up the distinction of degrees and quality. Whence it follows, that the civil jurisdiction of this court of chivalry is principally in two points; the redressing injuries of honour, and correcting encroachments in matters of coat-armour, precedency, and other distinctions of families."

" As a court of honour, it is to give satisfaction to all such as are aggrieved in that point; a point of nature so nice and delicate, that its wrongs and injuries escape the notice of the common law, and yet are fit to be redressed somewhere. Such, for instance, as calling a man coward, or giving him the lye; for which, as they are pro-ductive of no immediate damage to his person or property, no acti n will lie in the courts at Westminster: and yet they are such injuries as will prompt every man of spirit to demand some honourable amends, which by the ancient law of the land was appointed to be given in the court of chivalry. But modern resolutions have determi ed, that how much soever such a jurisdiction may be expedient, yet no action for words will lie therein. And it hath always been most clearly·

holden, that as this court cannot meddle with any thing determinable by the common law, it therefore can give no pecuniary satisfaction or damages; inasmuch as the quantity and determination thereof is ever of common law cognizance. And therefore this court of chivalry can at most only order reparation in point of honour: as, to compel the defendant *mendacium sibi ipsi imponere*, or to take the lie that he has given upon himself, or to make such other submission as the laws of honour may require. Neither can this court, as to the point of reparation in honour, hold plea of any such word, or thing, wherein the party is relievable by the courts of common law. As if a man gives another a blow, or calls him thief or murderer; for in both these cases the common law has pointed out his proper remedy by action."

" As to the other point of its civil jurisdiction, the redressing of incroachments and usurpations in matters of heraldry and coat-armour : it is the business of this court, according to Sir Matthew Hale, to adjust the right and armorial ensigns, bearings, crests, supporters, pennons, &c.; and also rights of place or precedence, where the king's patent or act of parliament (which cannot be overruled by this court) have not already determined it."

" The proceedings in this court are by petition, in a summary way; and the trial not by a jury of twelve men, but by witnesses, or by combat. But as it cannot imprison, not being a court of record, and as by the resolutions of the superior courts it is now confined to so narrow and restrained a jurisdiction, it has fallen into contempt and disuse. The marshalling of coat-armour, which was formerly the pride and study of all the best families in the kingdom, is now greatly disregarded; and has fallen into the hands of certain officers and attendants upon this court, called heralds, who consider it only as a matter of lucre and not of justice."—

Hume very justly remarks that " the feudal institutions, by raising the military tenants to a kind of sovereign dignity, by rendering personal strength and valour requisite, and by making every knight and

baron his own protector and avenger, begat that martial pride and
sense of honour, which, being cultivated and embellished by the poets
and romance writers of the age, ended in chivalry. The virtuous knight
fought not only in his own quarrel, but in that of the innocent, of the
helpless, and, above all, of the fair, whom he supposed to be for ever
under the guardianship of his valiant arm.   The uncourteous knight
who, from his castle, exercised robbery on travellers, and committed
violence on virgins, was the object of his perpetual indignation; and
he put him to death, without scruple, or trial, or appeal, wherever
he met with him.   The great independance of men made personal
honour and fidelity the chief tie among them; and rendered it the
capital virtue of every true knight, or genuine professor of chivalry.
The solemnities of single combat, as established by law, banished
every thing unfair or unequal in rencounters; and maintained an
appearance of courtesy between the combatants, till the moment of
their engagement.   The credulity of the age grafted on this stock the
notion of giants, enchanters, dragons, spells, and a thousand wonders,
which still multiplied during the times of the Crusades; when men
returning from so great a distance, used the liberty of imposing every
fiction on their believing audience.   These ideas of chivalry infected
the writings, conversations, and behaviour of men, during some ages;
and even after they were, in a great measure, banished by the revival
of learning, they left modern *gallantry* and the *point of honour*, which
still maintain their influence, and are the genuine offspring of those
ancient affectations.''

Note s, Page 28th, Note.

" See Epitaph."

In Brading Church Yard, Isle of Wight, on the grave-stone of Mrs. Ann Berry, is the following epitaph, which has been beautifully set to Music by Dr. Calcott, as a glee—for three voices.

> " Forgive blest shade, the tributary tear
>   That mourns thy exit from a world like this ;
> Forgive the wish that would have kept thee here,
>   And stay'd thy progress to the seats of bliss."

> " No more confin'd to groveling scenes of night,
>   No more a tenant pent in mortal clay ;
> Now should we rather hail thy glorious flight,
>   And trace thy journey to the realms of day."

Note t, Page 35th, L. 5.

" For general use."

" Mon cher condisciple, je ne puis trop me plaindre de ce que vous êtes atteint de cette folie épidémique, que fait consister la vraie philososophie, à déclamer sans cesse contre les moeurs, les usages, la religion, les lois de votre nation, et de tous les peuples policés. Vous avez cru qu'il n'y a point d'autre gloire, que la bruyante et funeste réputation, d'avoir secoué le joug des préjugés, ou plutôt de toute bienséance et modération; vous avez dit en vous même, *philoso-*

I

phons, et vous avez pris un vain fantome pour la philosophie ; vous
vous êtes plaint de ce que votre façon de penser effarouchait les
esprits des ecclésiastiques et des magistrats, et ils ne se sont effarouchés
que du fantome que vous avez embrassé pour la vérité ; vous n'avez
point considéré qu'en criant contre l'intolérance, vous deveniez into-
lérant vous même ; qu'en pestant contre la tyrannie des lois, vous
frondiez ouvertement ce que fait votre sureté, et votre appui ; qu'en
vous rodissant contre les préjugés, les usages, vous embrassiez un
systéme qui entraine après lui plus d'abus, et plus de maux que toutes
ces choses dont vous vous plaignez si haut.—Ignorez vous encore,
qu'il est de la nature des choses d'ici bas, d'être imparfaites, ou de
nous paraitre telles ? Que diriez vous d'un homme qui s'emporterait
contre le debordement des riviéres, et qui voudrait s'opposer à l'in-
temperie des saisons?—Vous avez dit que la véritable force d'esprit
consiste dans la liberté de penser ; je le crois avec vous, mais c'est
à cette seule liberté qu'il faut se borner. Si l'on veut gouter cette
paix de l'âme, cette tranquillité d'esprit qui font le bonheur de la
vie, l'on doit supporter les defauts de ses semblables, les plaindre
s'ils ont des ridicules, les éclairer s'il est possible: l'on doit éviter
la satyre, l'aigreur, les reproches, les emportemens, la raillerie, qui
sont la source de la haine, et de la dissention, et qui ne peuvent que
remplir nos jours de douleur et d'amertume. La religion, les lois
de chaque pays sont ce qu'elles sont ; si elles apportent quelque
désordre réel ou apparent, elles causent d'ailleurs tant de bien, qu'
elles seront toujours un objet respectable aux yeux d'un honnête
homme. Nous ne sommes point dans ce monde ci pour clabauder,
piailler, ou controller ; nous sommes venus pour agir."

Le Compère Mathieu.

" Il y a certains maux dans la république, qui y sont soufferts,
parcequ'ils previennent ou empêchent de plus grands maux. Il y
a d'autres maux, qui sont tels seulment par leur établissement, et
qui étant dans leur origine un abus ou mauvais usage, sont moins.

perñicieux dans leurs suites, et dans la pratique, qu' une loi plus juste, ou une coutume plus raisonable. L'on voit une espèce de maux que l'on ne peut corriger que par le changement ou par la nouveauté, qui est un mal fort dangereux. Il y en a d'autres cachés et enfoncés comme des ordures dans une caque, je veux dire, ensevelis sous la honte, sous le secret, et dans l'obscurité ; on ne peut les fouiller et les remuer qu'ils n'exhalent le poison et l'infamie. Les plus sages doutent quelquefois s'il est mieux de connaître ces maux que de les ignorer. L'on tolère quelquefois dans un état un assez grand mal, mais qui détourne un million de petits maux, ou d'incon-véniens qui tous seraient inévitables et irrémédiables. Il se trouve des maux dont chaque particulier gémit, et qui deviennent néanmoins un bien public, quoique le public ne soit autre chose que tous parti-culiers. Il y a des maux personnels, qui concourent au bien et à l'avantage de chaque famille. Il y en a qui affligent, ruinent ou deshonorent les familles, mais qui tendent au bien et à la conser-vation de l'Etat."
                                                                     LA BRUYERE.

Note u, PAGE 41st, L. 6.

" See yonder vale ;—there Otway had his birth."

THOMAS OTWAY, the celebrated Tragic Poet, was born, March 3rd. 1651, at Trotton, a village near Midhurst in the Weald of Sussex :—he was the son of Mr. Humphry Otway, rector of Wool-beding, another village in that neighbourhood.

Time has long proved the merits of Otway ; his tragedies of the Orphan and Venice Preserved, the one exhibited in 1680, and the other in 1685, still keep their place on the stage, among our most admired pieces.—Whatever may be the vain opinion of criticism, that must be true to the feelings of human nature, which can hold sympathy with it through almost a century and a half.—Among his works, we find, " Alcibiades ;"—" Don Carlos ;"—" The History and Fall of Caius Marius ;"—" The comedies of Friendship in Fashion," and, " The Soldier's Fortune ;"—and the Poem of, " The " Poet's complaint of his Muse ;"—He translated from the French, " Titus and Berenice ;"—" The Cheats of Scapin ;"—and, " The History of the Triumvirate."

When we consider the number of the above works, it must be allowed that his industry was great; his first work, the tragedy of Alcibiades, was produced in his twenty-fifth year, and he died in his thirty-fourth, April the 14th, 1685.

The Earl of Plymouth once procured for him a cornet's commission ; but a military life not being congenial to Otway, he soon abandoned it.

Of his death, Johnson says, " having been compelled by his necessities to contract debts, and hunted, as is supposed, by the terriers of the law, he retired to a public-house on Tower-Hill, where he is said to have died of want ; or, as it is related by one of his biographers, by swallowing, after a long fast, a piece of bread which charity had supplied. He went out, almost naked, in the rage of hunger, and finding a gentleman in a neighbouring Coffee-House, asked him for a shilling. The gentleman gave him a guinea; and Otway, going away, bought a roll, and was choaked with the first mouthful. Pope, relates, in Spence's memorials, that he died of a fever caught by violent pursuit of a thief, that had robbed one of his friends. But that indigence, and its concomitants, sorrow and despondency, pressed hard upon him, has never been denied, whatever immediate cause might bring him to the grave."

NOTE v, PAGE 43rd, Note.

"See the shipwreck of the Medusa."

In the narrative which Messrs. Correard and Savigny have given of the shipwreck of the Medusa, in a voyage to Senegal, in 1816, they relate the following account of one hundred and fifty of the crew, who endeavoured to save themselves on a raft, which they had constructed from the masts, &c. of the vessel.

"We had all left the frigate without taking any food: hunger began to be severely felt; we mixed our biscuit-paste (which had fallen into the sea) with a little wine, and we distributed it thus prepared: such was our first meal, and the best we had the whole time we were on the raft.—An order, according to numbers, was fixed for the distribution of our miserable provisions. The ration of wine was fixed at three-quarters* a day: we shall say no more of the biscuit: the first distribution consumed it entirely.—The day passed over pretty quietly."

The night was a night of death! many lost their lives from a tremendous sea washing them off the raft; but far the greater number from a dreadful mutiny, which was followed by nights and days of elemental horror and destruction, till their numbers were awfully reduced: it appears that only between sixty and seventy were remaining, destitute of food many of these became highly delirious; some even went mad.—According to the narrative, "Those whom death had spared, fell upon the dead bodies, with which the raft was covered, and cut off pieces, which some instantly devoured. Seeing that this horrid nourishment had given strength to those who had made use of it, it was proposed to dry it, in order to render it a

---

* *Trois quarts*· it is not said of what measure; probably a pint.

little less disgusting. We tried to eat sword-belts, and cartouch-boxes. We succeeded in swallowing some little morsels. Some ate linen. Others pieces of leather from the hats, on which there was a little grease, or rather dirt.—The fourth morning's sun, shewed us ten or twelve of our companions, extended lifeless on the raft. We gave their bodies to the sea for a grave; reserving only one, destined to feed those who, the day before, had clasped his trembling hands, vowing him an eternal friendship."

The horrors they experienced, and a second mutiny, again reduced their numbers: continuing the narrative,

" We were now only twenty-seven remaining; of this number, but fifteen seemed likely to live some days: all the rest, covered with large wounds, had almost entirely lost their reason; yet they had a share in the distribution of provisions; and might, before their death, consume thirty or forty bottles of wine, which were of inestimable value to us. We deliberated thus: to put the sick on half allowance would have been killing them by inches. So, after a debate, at which the most dreadful despair presided, it was resolved to throw them into the sea."

Next they were consumed by a raging thirst, and they eagerly moistened their parched lips with any liquid they could obtain, however foul its nature; some found pieces of pewter, which being put into the mouth produced a kind of coolness. To such a state of misery had this extreme thirst reduced them, that despising life, many of them did not fear to bathe in sight of the sharks, which surrounded their raft; others placed themselves naked on that part of it which was submerged, and by these means diminished a little their burning thirst.

NOTE ω, PAGE 46th, L. 14.

" Like crime; oh Chatterton."

The celebrated Poet Thomas Chatterton was born at Bristol, November the 20th, 1752. He was the son of Thomas Chatterton, the master of a free-school in that city; it appears the father died two months preceding the birth of his unfortunate son.

· It is curious to learn, that young Chatterton was dismissed from his first school, as a dull boy and incapable of improvement; but the error of the pedagogue was corrected by the judicious management of the mother, whose superior sense soon taught her to initiate her son into the first rudiments of learning.—" When about eight years of age, he was admitted to Colston's charity-school in Bristol ·—his first years passed unnoticed; but in his tenth, he acquired a taste for reading, and before his twelfth year, he wrote a catalogue of the books he had read, amounting to seventy:—before he left school he had attained some knowledge of music and drawing, and had made some considerable progress in arithmetic.—His mind was always of a pensive and melancholy cast, and from the time he began to learn his disposition appeared gloomy; but it was observed that he became more cheerful after he began to write poetry."

" In his fifteenth year he was bound apprentice to an attorney, to learn the art of a scrivener: he continued this course of life for upwards of a year, when he first attracted the notice of the literary world, by a letter which appeared in the Bristol journal, giving a description of " *The Fryars first passing over the old bridge,*"—and which he said was taken from an ancient manuscript: on being pressed on this subject, he informed the inquirers, that he had come into possession of the paper in question, together with many other manuscripts, through his father, who had found them in a large chest, in the upper room over the chapel, on the north side of the church of St. Mary Redcliff, Bristol;—of which Parish the family of Chatterton had, for above a century and a half, held the office of sexton: —these manuscripts were written on parchment much discoloured, and consisted of poetical and other compositions by Mr. Canynge, and a friend of his Thomas Rowley:—such at least appears to be the account which Chatterton thought proper to give, and which he wished to be believed."

" His thirst for literary fame now rapidly increased, and he began to supply periodical papers, not only with extracts from Rowley's manuscripts, but with a variety of pieces of his own, both in prose and verse.—The evidence of his master is in favor of his having conducted himself with the greatest regularity during the time of his apprenticeship, from which however he was dismissed before the expiration of three years, on suspicion that he entertained the idea of committing suicide."—Soon after this, in his eighteenth year, April, 1770, he bade adieu, a *final* adieu, to his native city:—tempted by poverty, and allured by his imagination and his desire of fame, he entered London,—as have too many of the sons of genius,—a literary adventurer!

His reception from the booksellers and printers, with whom he had corresponded was favourable to his wishes;—but alas! delusive were his hopes,—short was his career!—in a few months he found the necessities of nature press hard upon him, frequently not having it in his power, to procure even the simplest sustenance: and for three days previous to his death it appears, he had not tasted food!

" On the 24th of August, 1770, he terminated a life of disappointment and disgust, by swallowing arsenic in water: he was buried in a shell, in the burying ground of Shoe-lane Work-house."

He had not attained his eighteenth year!!—It was a favorite maxim with him, " that man was equal to any thing, and that every thing, might be achieved by diligence and abstinence."

If any uncommon character was mentioned in his hearing, his sister, (Mrs. Newton) says, " he would only observe, that the person in question merited praise ; but that God had sent his creatures into the world with arms long enough to reach any thing, if they would be at the trouble of extending them."

Chatterton appears to have been one of those extraordinary characters, which elude all calculation, and evince that there is in human nature, a subtilty, beyond human-power to define.—It has been well observed by one of his Biographers, that, " his genius will be most completely estimated from his writings."

It is unnecessary here to enter into the dispute of the manuscripts ; for whether we consider Chatterton as the author, or transcriber, it must be allowed, that acute research, indefatigable industry, and powerful genius, were at least his own ;—and most feelingly can we say with Knox,

" Unfortunate boy !—short and evil were thy days, but thy fame shall be immortal."

In reviewing genius it is painful to find, that penury and distress are almost always its inseparable concomitants !—Thus " Bacon lived a life of meanness and distress ;—Sir Walter Raleigh died on the scaffold ;—Spencer, the charming Spencer, died forsaken and in want ;—the death of Collins came through neglect, first causing mental derangement ;—Milton sold his copyright of Paradise Lost for fifteen pounds at three payments, and finished his life in obscurity ; —Dryden lived in poverty, and died in distress ;—Lee died in the streets ;—Steele lived a life of perfect warfare with bailiffs ;—Goldsmith's " Vicar of Wakefield" sold for a trifle, to save him from the gripe of the law ;—Fielding lies in the burying-ground of the English Factory at Lisbon, without a stone to mark the spot ;—Savage died

in prison at Bristol, where he was confined for a debt of eight pounds;
—Butler lived in penury, and died poor;—and Dean Swift died in
a lunatic hospital, which he had himself erected."

Nor is this melancholy fate of genius confined to any particular age
or country, "Homer was a begger;—Plautus turned a mill;—Terence
was a slave;—Bœthius died in gaol;—Paul Borghese had eighty-
four different trades, and yet starved with them all;—Tasso was
often distressed for five shillings;—Bentevoglio was refused admit-
tance into an hospital he had himself erected;—Cervantes died of
hunger;—Camoens the celebrated writer of "the Lusiad" ended his
days in an alms-house;—and Vaugelas left his body to the surgeons
to pay his debt as far as it would go."

———

Note x, Page 49, and Note y, Page 63,

Are omitted, the Author not being able to obtain the information
designed for them.

———

Note z, Page 66th, L. 3.

"Him Lord of Lewes."

Lewes an ancient town in Sussex, the second in the county for
extent and population: it stands on a beautiful declivity of the South
Downs, which as an amphitheatre seem to surround it, being only
intersected by the course of the river Ouse.—It is a borough by pre-
scription having returned two members to Parliament ever since the

23rd of Edward I. The right of election is vested in the inhabitants paying scot and lot, in number about 390.—Its population is supposed to consist of between seven and eight thousand.

The numerous relics discovered in the town and neighbourhood sufficiently attest its being a place of high antiquity. Some think in all probability it was the site of the Roman station known by the Mutuantonis or Mantantonis. It cannot be doubted that it was of considerable repute before the Norman Conquest. Mention is made of Athelstan directing two mints to be established here, whilst Chichester the capital of the County had but one. And in the Norman survey we learn that in the time of Edward the Confessor, Lewes paid £6. 4s. for tax and toll to the king; who had here a hundred and twenty-seven burgesses. It is supposed to have derived its name from Laquis, in ancient times the valley to the South and North being one complete Lake: hence also the names of the town and of the river, both of which are but corruptions of the equivalent French word Eaux.—Lewes was the only communication between the east and west divisions of the Regni.

When William the Conqueror had seated himself on the English throne, he gave this town and lordship to his son-in-law, William de Warren, Earl of Surrey, who built a *Castle*, or, as some conjecture, repaired a fortress already erected here, and made it the principal seat of his Barony. This he afterwards divided into sixty-two knight's-fees, many of which he bestowed on his Norman friends and followers, reserving for himself the town and castle. In his family they continued for several generations, till, in the reign of Henry III. John, Earl of Warren, having forfeited his estates, this manor, with some other lordships, was given to the queen's uncle, Peter de Savoy; but again restored to the successor of the former owner, as a reward for his adherence to the royal cause. On his death, without issue, his sister, Alice, became his heir; and, by marriage to Edmund Fitz-Alan, Earl of Arundel, carried the estate into that family. The great gateway, or entrance, which was somewhat advanced before the walls of the castle on the south side, is yet entire. At the longest diameter of the area of the castle, which runs nearly northeast and south-west, are two circular artificial mounts for keeps. Of the eastern keep a small fragment only remains; and the western is fast yielding to the ravages of time. The latter which was quadrangular, with a hexagonal tower at each corner, diminishing upwards, commands a wide and highly diversified prospect. From this building extend immense earth-works, with two ditches, on the inner bank of which are some ruined walls. These works, at their northwest corner, embrace a small camp, of a long oval figure, whose north and west sides they fortify. The double keep, termed in old writings Braymounts, is a feature peculiar to this castle. The property is divided between the Earl of Abergavenny and the Dukes of Norfolk and Dorset, one half belonging to the former, and a quarter to each of the latter. In 1774, the site and ruins were leased for ninety-nine years to Mr. Thomas Friend, who, at his death, bequeathed his interest in them to his nephew, Mr. Thomas Kempe.

In 1078 a *Priory*, the first and chief house of the Cluniac order in England, was founded here by the first Earl of Warren, and his wife Gundreda, the fifth daughter of William the Conqueror. In the chapter-house of this priory were interred many persons of distinction. The munificent founder, who died in the year 1089, was here buried, as was Gundred, his countess, and many of their descendants, among whom were the second, fourth, fifth, and sixth Earls of Warren.

Some idea may be formed of the extensive scale of this establishment, from the circumstance that its walls embraced an area of near forty acres; and, from the description of the church destroyed in the reign of Henry VIII. we may reasonably conclude that the buildings were not less remarkable for magnificence than for extent.

We have the following account of this church, " length of it 150 foot, height 63; the circumference about it 1558 foot; the wall of the fore-front thick 10 foot. The thickness of the vaults 4 foot.

There be in the church 32 pillars standing equally from the walls—an high roof made for the bells—8 pillars very high; thick, 13 foot; about, 45 foot. The other 24 are for the most part 10 foot thick and 25 about. The height of the greater sort is 42 foot. Of the other 18 foot. The height of the roof before the high alter is 93 foot. The height of the steeple at the front is 90 foot."——" A vault on the right side of the high alter, that was borne with four pillars, having about it five chapels, which be compassed in the walls, 70 stepys of length, that is, feet 210; an higher vaulte, borne up by 4 thick and gross pillars, 14 foot from side to side, about in circumference 45 feet."

" At the surrender of this abbey, in 1537, its revenues were valued, as Dugdale informs us, at £920. 4s. 6d.; but, according to Speed, at £1091. 9s. 6d. The buildings, it is presumed, were not wholly demolished at the dissolution, for the priory was sometime inhabited by the Earls of Dorset, and thence received the appellation of the *Lord's Place*. It was at length destroyed by fire, but the precise time of this accident is not ascertained. The priory estates came into possession of the Thanet family by the marriage of John Tufton, Earl of Thanet, with Margaret, the daughter and heir of Richard Sackville, Earl of Dorset. In 1709 the site of the priory was sold, together with the manor, borough, or lordship of Southover, to Nathaniel Trayton, Esq. of Lewes, whose son bequeathed it to Samuel Durrant Esq."

Lewes was once strongly fortified ; and the vestiges of intrenchments are yet visible, particularly on the north and south sides of the town.

Before the Reformation, this town, including the suburbs of Southover and the Cliffe, comprehended twelve parish churches, which have since been reduced to half the number.

The most remarkable of these is the church of *St. John sub Castro*, situated in the middle of the small oval camp already mentioned in description of the castle. The south portal is formed by a very ancient Saxon arch, but obscured by a mean modern porch. This church, as it is believed, was originally constructed in the shape of a cross, with the tower in the centre. Some vestiges of the chancel may still be traced; and the marks of the former roof, which was higher than the present, are visible on the tower. Camden describes this edifice as ruinous, and over-grown with brambles. It was afterwards contracted and repaired probably in 1635, as a small stone tablet, with that date, is fixed near the porch in the south wall.

On a hill about a mile from the town is the *Race-course*, accounted one of the best in England. This hill was the scene of an obstinate battle fought on the 14th of May, 1264, between Henry III. and the army of the barons under Simon de Montfort, Earl of Leicester. In memory of this event, an eminence near the Race-course, now used as a beacon, has ever since retained the name of *Mount Harry.* Most of the slain were interred near the spot in barrows, vestiges of which are still sufficiently obvious.

———

NOTE *a a*, PAGE 76*th*, L. 4.

" *The noble House of England's Norfolk sprang.*"

" John de Warren, eighth Lord of Lewes, and Earl of Surrey and Sussex, dying without legitimate issue, was succeeded by his nephew, Richard Fitz-Alan, only son of his sister Alice, and Edmund Fitz-Alan, Earl of Arundel."

" Richard Fitz-Alan, ninth Lord of Lewes, and Earl of Sussex, Surrey, and Arundel, was at his death, succeeded by his son, Richard Fitz-Alan."

" Richard Fitz-Alan, tenth Lord of Lewes, and Earl of Sussex, Surrey, and Arundel, having been attainted and beheaded, his son was despoiled of his rights, which were bestowed, by the King Richard II. on Thomas Mowbray,[*] Earl of Nottingham, who created him at the same time Duke of Norfolk. This Earl was married to Elizabeth, eldest daughter of Richard Fitz-Alan.—In the Reign of Henry IV., the attainder of the late Earl was reversed, in favor of his son, Thomas Fitz-Alan, who was restored to his lawful rights: he dying without issue, his possessions, inherited from the de-Warren line, were divided between his three surviving sisters,

Elizabeth, Dutchess of Norfolk,

Joanna, Lady Abergavenny,

Margaret, Lady of Sir Rowland Lenthal."

" Edmund Lenthal, only son of Sir Rowland, dying without issue, his share fell to

John Mowbray, Duke of Norfolk; and

Sir George Neville, Lord Abergavenny,

who thus came into an equal moiety of the de-Warren possessions."

" Anne Mowbray, only child and heiress to John Mowbray, third Duke of Norfolk, being affianced to Richard Duke of York, brother of Edward V. she survived her young consort little more than a month; and her moiety became divided between

Sir John Howard, Lord Howard, son of Lady Margaret Mowbray; and

William Berkley, Earl of Nottingham, son of Lady Isabel Mowbray;

both the daughters of Elizabeth, Dutchess of Norfolk, and sister to Thomas Fitz-Alan, the last Earl of Arundel and Surrey."

See DUNVAN's History of Lewes.

---

[*] " There is a monument in the church of Horsham, of William Lord Bruce, whose portraiture is fairly cut in stone according to the habit of those times, from whom the Mowbrays are descended."

NOTE *b b*, PAGE 70th, L 9.

" Division shared, and classic Dorset rose."

That portion of the de-Warren possessions, which had devolved on William Berkley, Earl of Nottingham, in right of his Mother, Lady. Isabel Mowbray, was, he not having issue, devised by him to King Henry VII, who conferred it on his mother; and it remained in the Stanley family, till the year 1576, when it was conveyed into that of Thomas Sackville, Lord Buckhurst, who was, by James I., created Earl of Dorset.

See DUNVAN's History of Lewes.

" The House of Sackville, latterly dignified with the Earldom and Dukedom of Dorset, is one of those noble exotics, transplanted from the continent into Britain, by the violent hand of conquest. It had its name, from Sacville, or Sècheville, in Normandy; and its origin in this island, from Herbrand, Lord of Sacville, who was one of William the Conqueror's principal commanders, in his successful conflict with the English forces near Hastings."

See DUNVAN's History of Lewes.

NOTE *c c*, PAGE 80th, L 15.

" Awaked, with Echo's magic sympathy."

No battle ever appears to have taken place in the Weald; that spoken of by Camden, in which Sigebert, King of the West Saxons was deposed, most probably was contested on the neighbouring

Downs: mention is made that Sigebert fled into the Weald for shelter. It does not seem possible that a place merely serving as pannage for hogs could ever have been the scene of contest:—even as late as Henry III., the memorable battle of Lewes took place on the Downs, though Prince Edward pursued, for four miles into the Weald, the Londoners, who had composed the left wing of the army of the brave and patriotic Simon de Montfort, Earl of Leicester.*

Among the innumerable contests which have taken place in this island, not only from its various invaders, but between—the Crown and the Barons;—the Houses of York and Lancaster;—the republican;—and again those of the Pretender;—that among these a valley so extensive as the Weald should never have been the scene of battle, is an idea, so agreeable to philanthropy and poetry, and stamps it a spot, as it were, so hallowed among mankind, that we should grieve to find it erroneous;—yet the Author begs it may be considered as a subject of inquiry, rather than of assertion.

NOTE OMITTED, PAGE 9th, L. 15.

" Both Brothers from immortal Odin sprung.

The origin of Woden, or Odin, is to be traced to a root, existing in the Anglo-Saxon; it signifies " the wild or furious one."

---

* " De-Montfort, immediately after the battle of Lewes, devised a mode of national representation, such as at that time was hardly thought of in Europe.—The previous national councils, consisted only of a turbulent aristocracy, and the obsequious tenantry of the Crown, De-Montfort's institution gave every freeman a mediate influence in legislation."

K

" Woden is known in Brunswick, as the Hunter Hackelburg, a
knight who renounced his share of the joys of Heaven, on condition
that he might be allowed to hunt, until the day of doom.   They shew
his sepulchre in a forest near Usslar."

See " Popular Mythology of the middle Ages."

" It is supposed by some, that Odin was the chief of a tribe of
barbarians, which dwelt on the banks of the lake Mæotis, till the fall of
Mithridates, and the arms of Pompey, menaced the north with servitude.
That Odin, yielding with indignant fury, to a power which he was unable
to resist, conducted his tribe from the frontiers of the Asiatic Sarmatia,
into Sweden, with the great design of forming, in that inaccessible
retreat of freedom, a religion and a people, which, in some remote
age, might be subservient to his immortal revenge; when his invincible Goths, armed with martial fanaticism, should issue, in
numerous swarms, from the neighbourhood of the Polar circle, to
chastise the oppressors of mankind."   See Gibbon's History of the
decline and fall of the Roman Empire, though he remarks that " the
above account cannot be received as authentic history."

" We can easily distinguish two persons, confounded under the
name of Odin ; the God of War, and the great legislator of Scandi-
navia.   The latter, the Mahomet of the North, instituted a religion
adapted to the climate and to the people.   Numerous tribes, on
either side of the Baltic, were subdued by the invincible valour of
Odin, by his persuasive eloquence, and by the fame, which he
acquired of a most skilful magician.   The faith that he had propagated,
during a long and prosperous life, he confirmed by a voluntary death.
Apprehensive of the ignominious approach of disease and infirmity,
he resolved to expire as became a warrior.   In a solemn assembly of
the Swedes and Goths, he wounded himself in nine mortal places,
hastening away (as he asserted with his dying voice) to prepare the
feast of heroes, in the palace of the God of War."

" Till the end of the eleventh century, a celebrated temple subsisted at Upsal, the most considerable town of the Swedes and Goths.

It was enriched with the gold, which the Scandinavians had acquired
in their piratical adventures, and sanctified by the uncouth represen-
tations of the three principal deities, the God of War, the goddess of
generation, and the God of thunder.   In the general festival, that was
solemnized every ninth year, nine animals of every species (without
excepting the human) were sacrificed, and their bleeding bodies suspended in the sacred grove, adjacent to the temple.   The only traces
that now subsist of this barbaric superstition, are contained in the
Edda, a system of mythology, compiled in Iceland about the
thirteenth century, and studied by the learned of Denmark and
Sweden, as the most valuable remains of their ancient traditions."

See Gibbon's History of the decline and fall of the Roman Empire.

" The temple of Upsal was destroyed by Ingo, King of Sweden,
who began his reign in the year 1075, and about fourscore years
afterwards a christian cathedral was erected on its ruins."

See Bibliothèque Raisonnée.

Continuation of the Note on Military Ways.   Page 103.

" The public highways, issuing from the Forum of Rome, traversed
Italy, pervaded the provinces, and were terminated only by the
frontiers of the Empire.   If we carefully trace the distance from the
wall of Antoninus to Rome and from thence to Jerusalem, it will be
found, that the great chain of communication, from the north-west to
the south-east point of the empire, was drawn out to the length of
four thousand and eighty Roman miles.   The public roads were
accurately divided by mile-stones, and ran in a direct line, from one
city to another, with very little respect for the obstacles, either of
nature or private property.   Mountains were perforated, and bold

arches thrown over the broadest and most rapid streams. The middle part of the road was raised into a terrace, which commanded the adjacent country, consisting of several strata of sand, gravel, and cement, and was paved with large stones, or in some places near the capital, with granite. Such was the solid construction of the Roman highways, whose firmness has not entirely yielded to the effort of fifteen centuries. They united the subjects of the most distant provinces, by an easy and familar intercourse; but their primary object had been to facilitate the marches of the legions; nor was any country considered as completely subdued, till it had been rendered, in all its parts pervious to the arms and authority of the conqueror. The advantage of receiving the earliest intelligence, and of conveying their orders with celerity, induced the Emperors to establish, throughout their extensive dominions, the regular institution of posts. Houses were every where erected at the distance only of five or six miles; each of them was constantly provided with forty horses, and by the help of these relays, it was easy to travel an hundred miles in a day along the Roman roads. The use of the posts was allowed to those who claimed it, by an Imperial mandate; but, though originally intended for the public service, it was sometimes indulged to the business or conveniency of private citizens."

GIBBON.

" The following Itenary may serve to convey some idea of the direction of the road, and of the distance between the principal towns."

" From the Wall of Antoninus   Roman Miles.

To York ·······························	222
London·································	227
Rhutupia or Sandwich ··················	67
The navigation to Boulogne ·············	45
Rheims ·····························	174
Lyons ·····························	330
Milan ·····························	324
Rome ·····························	426
Brundusium ·························	360
The navigation to Dyrrachium ···········	40
Byzantium ·····················	711
Ancyra ·····························	283
Tarsus ·····························	310
Antioch·····························	141
Tyre ·····························	252
Jerusalem ·························	168

4,080

or

English Miles 3,740 "

See the Itineraries published by Wasseling, his Annotations;— Gale and Stukeley for Britain, and M. d'Anville for Gaul and Italy.

FINIS.

ERRATA.

———